ELDER OF STORMS

A NOVEL OF THE DECADIN EMPIRE SAGA

BLUEGUARD TRILOGY
BOOK ONE

D.J. JACOBSON

Published in Canada by Dragon Down Publishing

ISBN: 978-1-7781390-2-4

Cover art © 2022 by Ivan Zanchetta & Bookcoversart.com

To Claire,

Who once told a high-school kid,

"You should be a writer."

FOUR WORD

Thank you for reading.

"And anger in the sky..."
  – A. E. Housman, *In Midnights of November*

1

The *Pride of the Empress* cut the waves, her sails snapping and booming in the wind. Sunlight flashed off the forecastle rail—which Early Wills had just finished polishing—and where Early now rested his elbows as he watched the prow of the ship rise and fall. He listened to the crash of waves breaking on the hull and, though his eyes watered from the sun and the wind, he was in the only place in the world he wanted to be. Despite growing up on his parents' fishing boats, no amount of paddling about the Imperial Reserve could have prepared him for the open ocean: the fierce and ever-changing character of the salt waves and the rolling infinity of water meeting the horizon at the edge of the world.

When Early was just a boy he had stood eyes-closed in the prow of his mother's boat, and imagined he was riding on the back of a dragon; not the tiny dracolings wealthy merchants in the High City of Petara kept as pets, but a gargantuan beast from the ancient legends of the world's creation. With his eyes closed, the gentle waves of the Reserve made it easy for young Early to imagine the vast drumbeat of wings holding him and his terrible steed high in the air.

When the sun glared off the wave crests, his imagination transformed them into the peaks of mountains, and the vari-colored scales of a dragon's armored head. When it was time for the imagined beast to unleash its fire-wreathed roar, young Early howled at the top of his lungs, and whatever adult was nearby would shake their head or shout a curt rebuke.

On the cusp of adulthood himself now, Early did not dare shout, though every time the sea sprayed drops across his tanned face or the salty wind blew a lock of dark curly hair in his eyes, he felt a cry of joy swell in his chest and clamped his mouth shut with a smile. Whenever Early caught himself in such a daydream, he would glance slyly back over his shoulder for the flash of a blue officer's cap in the sun, and if he saw one he grabbed up his mop from the rail and returned to the task assigned him hours ago: swabbing the forecastle deck.

Pride of the Empress was an Imperial greatship, the largest sort of ship in the Blueguard navy, and it was a genuine monster. The forward hull beneath Early's feet towered out of the water, and the topcastle—the platform near the top of the mainmast for lookouts and crossbows—must have been a full thirty yards above the waves. The first time Deckmaster Matta ordered Early to stock the topcastle with darts and arrows for use in combat, his climb up the rigging seemed to take hours. At the top the wind howled like a choir of ghosts, and Early remembered his boyhood dragonflight fantasies with real terror. Breathless, he'd clung to the creaking ropes and tried to will himself past the paralysis that trapped other deckhands yards above the planks, the Blueguard officers screaming at them to master themselves and finish the job.

At the thought of the deckmaster's red face under his blue cap, Early took his foot from the rail, grasped his mop, and looked round. He was just in time, as Matta was at that moment

climbing the ladder to the forecastle, brows already drawn up in annoyance over his fierce black eyes.

"Swab! Why isn't this deck ashine?" Matta's voice was ever gravelly from a life spent shouting at young sea dogs like Early, but it carried over the strongest gale.

A week at sea had taught Early better than to answer. He ducked his head and danced his mop over the planks in the proper figure-eight as though he'd been at it all along, tracing the foot of the railing where the boots of the Blueguard cross-bows—the officers specialized in archery—had impressed the most grime. He didn't dare another longing glance out over the rail, where the sun dancing on the waves beckoned him to promised adventure, until Matta had grumbled away and Early heard him harrowing another deckhand elsewhere on the ship.

As the morning wore on, bright and hot, Early lost himself in rumination. The monotonous task of swabbing the deck left plenty of time to drift back into fantasies of what he and the crew of the *Pride* might discover on their expedition. The creak of the forecastle ladder startled Early, and he whirled around, hands tightening on the mop handle. A head of unkempt, sandy hair topped the ladder as an impressively tall and bulky young man climbed up to join him at the bow.

"Morning watch and all is well, Guard," Olan said, tossing Early a mock salute. "How goes it with you?"

"Morning watch and all is well," Early said, smiling. He couldn't quite bring himself to refer to Olan as *Guard*, a member of the Empress's elite who made up the officer class of her navy. Neither of them actually belonged to the Blueguard, but Olan in particular loved to ape the officious manner and elaborate speech that seemed as natural to those men and women as sailing.

Early glanced down the deck in case the deckmaster was storming back in their direction. The deck was mostly clear, and he breathed more easily; at this hour, the officer class was mostly still breaking fast, and the topdeck belonged to the deckhands, who did as little as they could get away with. Early leaned against his mop. "Was that you Matta gave an earful to just now? Surely he wasn't ordering you to help me swab the fo'c'sle?"

"It was, and he wasn't," Olan found the least-wet patch of deck he could and sat, leaning against the railing. He took a long black root and a folding knife from his trouser pocket, and with a deft motion sliced a hunk of the dry, twisted amma root, popped it in his mouth, and commenced to chew. He held up the root to Early and raised his eyebrows.

"Thanks," Early said, catching the second cutting Olan tossed him and putting it in his mouth. The root had a sharp taste not unlike ginger, and it helped sailors new to the water overcome seasickness, along with clearing the sinuses. Even though both Olan and Early had spent their young lives on the water before joining the expedition, chewing amma root had become a habit.

"I was meant to be tallying the crossbows and quarrels, reckoned I could get away with a bit of air up here, first. And maybe you can tell me, Master Wills, what exactly is the use of counting the ammunition every day when we've not loosed a quarrel since leaving port? Busywork!"

"I reckon Matta would say something about discipline, right?"

"Discipline!" Olan chewed and spat. "Ah, sorry. You've just polished that deck, eh? I'll spit overboard."

Early rolled his eyes.

Olan continued, "Blast these Blueguard and their eternal discipline! Who'd dare challenge a greatship of the Decadin Empire, even out on the open sea?"

Early gave Olan a sly look. "Now I suppose Matta would say,

'You never know what dangers might come, and that's why we remain ever ready. That's what makes the Blueguard the Blueguard.' Right?"

Olan scoffed again. "You've certainly done a straight job learning his lessons, Master Wills."

Early was staring back over the deck, past the length of the greatship, imagining the *Pride* in battle. It was a veritable castle at sea, and he was high up on the castle walls, invulnerable as they rode the wind itself to exploration and glory. The thought set a lightness in Early's boots that crept up into his heart until he felt like he was soaring. He paid no attention to Olan's cynical tone.

"One of these days," Early said, the faraway look still in his eye, "I'll be wearing that blue-and-white, just like Deckmaster Matta."

"And then it'll be you ordering me to swab the cursed decks all day? Hah!" Olan spat amma juice again, this time deliberately soiling the planks. "Can't say I look forward to that."

Early looked at him. "Oh, now... you know that's not what I meant, mate. I just... it would be amazing to be that capable, don't you think? Chosen by the Empress herself for your skill and bravery at sea... makes the life of a fisher seem a might tedious."

Early had always been fascinated by the Imperial Guard whenever he'd caught glimpses of them amongst the crowds of the High City. While he and his parents had pushed through the market throngs to sell the day's catch, the Guard had no need to push. Each division wore its signature color in wide patches on the chests and arms of their tunics: blue for the navy, green for the rangers, gold for the city guard, and red for the Empress's personal bodyguards. The squares and stripes of color on their uniforms were contrasted with shining white, so they stood out like proud birds; the common people gave them a wide berth.

Olan sighed and gave his idealistic friend a long-suffering look. "Is this what you think about all day, whilst polishing the decks? Joining the proud ranks of our betters? The dreams of a deckhand should really focus on shore leave, you know... and the landward charms of Darby Crow and their friends."

Early laughed nervously at the mention of Petara's most notorious bar-cum-brothel, and couldn't help a blush coming to his face. He turned back to the waves. But then his look turned sly. "And how often have you been a patron of Darby? You'd need to spend your stips from this whole expedition for a night on their upper floors."

"You're not wrong about that," Olan laughed. "The greatest treasures of the Empire are reserved for the wealthy few."

Early sidled closer to Olan and spoke conspiratorially, though they were the only hands on the forecastle deck. "And who better to join those wealthy few than an officer of the Imperial Guard?"

Olan pondered this for a moment, then rose to his feet with a booming laugh. He clapped Early on the shoulder.

"Very clever, Master Wills. If the Guard recruited as aggressively as Her Majesty's Regulars, you'd do a straight job getting the likes of me to sign up."

Olan looked out across the length of the *Pride*, where there was movement on the high quarterdeck. "Looks like that same blue-and-white you're so impressed by is finished breaking their fast and must now amuse themselves tormenting us honest hands. I'll be counting bloody quarrels all day, and if I finish with the quarrels, I'm sure Matta will find me something else to tally.

"Look," now it was Olan's turn to lean in close and conspire with his friend. "Meet me near the brig at late watch. I bought us a surprise before we left port."

"A surprise?" Early's eyes widened eagerly, but Olan shook his head with a smile.

"Sailors can't live on amma root alone, you know."

As he left, Olan pointed to the spot on the deck where he'd spat. "What are you lollygagging for, deckhand?" He did his best imitation of the deckmaster. "How do you expect to join the Blueguard if you can't even keep this bloody deck clean?!"

Early chased his friend away with the gentle language of sailors, and took up his mop once more.

⚓

The divisions of the Imperial Guard were famously cliquish at the best of times. The women and men of the Guard went about their duties aboard ship with cool professionalism. Nonetheless, it was the skill of any good deckhand worth their salt to see or hear everything that took place behind the scenes; the rations of watery rum and coin given each sailor for their stips were one thing, but the true currency of the deckhands was gossip, real or invented.

In only the first few days of the expedition, Olan had eagerly shared a tidbit picked up from one of the cook's assistants. The Blueguard Captain Mestrum, commander of the ship, had supposedly been heard grumbling about the Redguards' Captain Antmar, chief protector of the Empress's cousin who led the expedition. Captain Mestrum felt the Redguard was undermining her. The rumor gave Early mixed feelings. He looked up to them both: he dreamed of someday being a ship's captain himself, and Antmar was a legendary swordsman. Enmity between two people he admired troubled him.

Today's gossip was less dire. The Greenguard rangers mostly kept to themselves aboard the *Pride*; their work would begin if and when the greatship sighted land. Early overheard a group of the usually taciturn rangers complaining to each other about the relentless sameness of the open sea. They waxed lyrical about the ever-changing sights of the deep forests, and exalted the sun rising behind a black ridge of mountains, seen suddenly from the edge of cliffs above some valley of mist-shaded secrets.

But Early, in love with the water, knew it had its own beauties. His favorite was how, twice a day, water and sun came together to create a perfect golden heaven at the edge of the world, an effect which long ago gave the Sunfire Sea its name. It was the second of these now, when the sun met the water again after its day-long journey overhead. The hint of shadow was far off in the east, and the dazzle of the waves lured him from his duties on the deck, enchanted by their gilded crests.

This evening, his swabbing complete for the moment, he had stolen into the rigging of the foremast while Deckmaster Matta was called to conference with the Captain and her Mate. The Imperial expedition was ten days from port, having set out on the Empress's birthday by old seafaring custom. Looking back over the stern of the *Pride* as he dangled from the lines, Early imagined night falling over the towers and domes of the High City of Petara, in whose environs Early had spent all his days.

Though his parents were fishers and he'd spent his time sailing the inland rivers where Petara's fish were gathered, this was his first chance at the open sea. That chance alone was enticing enough, but there were two other things that drove Early to be among the first hands to volunteer for this voyage: he would get to join the crew of a greatship, and serve alongside his beloved Imperial Guard. The other reason was even more awe-inspiring. The *Pride of the Empress* was following in the footsteps of another, greater expedition... an expedition that was never heard from again. The *Pride* would discover the truth of its fate.

Rumor held that it was not the hidden domain of the sun awaiting them in the east, but a new land no Imperial soul had ever seen. It was five years ago that the first great Imperial expedition set sail, and those six ships with their hundreds of crew and colonists had never returned, nor sent word of their fate.

It was the mission of the *Pride's* elite crew, commissioned in the most solemn terms by the Empress herself, to learn the truth of that expedition's success or failure. Her own cousin, Lord Cyrus Mardigan, was onboard as Her Majesty's representative.

"Deckhand!" Matta barked up at Early from the deck below. "What are you doing up there? Back to your duties!" Early dared a quick smile to himself, having known it was only a matter of time before his slacking caught up to him. He scrambled carefully down the rigging—he was getting better at scaling the thick cables, though he still envied the monkeylike ease with which the seasoned sailors navigated the rigging—and steeled himself before straightening on deck before the Deckmaster and saluting. Matta's eyes narrowed at the perfunctory gesture, searching Early's face for any hint of irony. Early figured he had some leeway, since the master had called him by his profession and not merely "Swab!", his preferred shout when especially angry or impatient.

"Sorry, sir. I was just… keeping a lookout. There's no one else on the forward deck at this hour."

"Let the lookouts keep lookout, and you mind the decks, *deckhand*. This ship is the envy of the fleet, and I'll not let Deckmaster Habard on the *Victorious* claim her swabs keep cleaner decks. See to it!"

"Of course, Deckmaster! At once." Unlike Olan, Early found

no sport in arguing with the blustery man. He climbed the stairs to the forecastle and retrieved his mop and the pail that was ever gummy with tar to keep it watertight.

With a last longing glance at the sunset, Early set himself to his task. He knew it wouldn't be long before the watches changed, and he'd have the chance for a little adventure, meeting Olan for whatever surprise his friend had planned. The life of a deckhand circled endlessly between doing their duties, flouting those duties, being reprimanded, and walking the line just long enough to get away with shirking again. As much as Early admired the masterful discipline of the Blueguard officers, he was no officer, and he knew Olan was right: he was unlikely to ever rise above his low station. With a self-deprecating smile, Early mopped the deck and reminded himself to take his little pleasures where he could find them.

Subdued by Matta's latest tirade, Early spent the rest of the evening with the other deckhands, getting things in order ahead of the night watch beginning their shift. Early enjoyed watching the Blueguard ceremonially hand off their positions to one another, but Olan grabbed him as the shift was changing —a good time to move about the ship without being questioned—and hustled him through the forward hatch, down the ladders past their own quarters.

They snuck into the brig below the forecastle. Since the expedition, of course, had no prisoners, the narrow rectangular room was empty—on both sides of the bars. The cell took up fully one half of the room, which was perhaps only a dozen strides across. The narrow space below the crew's quarters was divided lengthwise into two equally spartan sections: one with a long wooden bench fashioned into the wall where prisoners could sit or lie, and the other with a small but well-made table and two chairs, in deference to the tedium of a long shift watching prisoners that had no reasonable means of escape, and nowhere to go but leagues of deep water.

The chairs were manned now by the two deckhands, a flickering oil lamp between them. Once Early was settled, Olan produced two pewter flagons from the sideboard at one end of the room, and then, with a flourish, brought out his real prize: a small canvas wineskin he'd concealed under his loose-fitting sailor's shirt.

"How'd you smuggle wine aboard?" Early smiled broadly, excited at the prospect of side-stepping the rules with the older deckhand. The deckmaster rationed the crew's alcohol consumption as ruthlessly as he demanded a spotless deck.

"'Smuggling' is such an ugly word," Olan said with a sly wink, uncorking the skin and filling first Early's tankard and then his own with an oily, blackish liquid. The stuff glistened in the lamplight and filled Early's nostrils with a heady, dangerous smell. "And anyway, it isn't wine; this is real black rum, the stuff a proper sailor drinks."

Early considered the contents of his mug, swishing the rum around and carefully inhaling its bouquet. It had a sort of honey-sweet aroma cut with a threatening undercurrent of hard alcohol. He'd tasted mead before, but never rum, and he was simultaneously anxious and eager for the first draught. He watched Olan pick up his mug, swish it around once for good measure, and then hold it up for a toast. He mirrored the motion, they clanked the thick pewter mugs together, and they both put the metal to their lips and tilted back. Olan kept one eye fixed on Early, and the corner wrinkled in humor as he saw his mate do the predictable thing.

Early gulped and gagged almost immediately. To his credit, he got his tankard back on the table without sloshing any over the rim, and he sputtered but managed not to stain his white shirt with a telltale blotch. "Dead gods!"

"So," Olan asked, with put-on nonchalance, "do you like it?"

"This was a carefully engineered plot to poison me!" Early complained, glowering at his friend. Then, with a defiant stare, he lifted his mug to his lips again and took a carefully measured sip. He let the liquid roll around on his tongue. It didn't feel quite like anything he'd drunk before, thicker than water and thinner than ale, with both a dark sweetness and a burning strength. It left wood smoke along the back of his throat when he swallowed. He slowly lowered his mug to the table, never breaking eye contact with Olan, who was grinning with delight.

"That's... a hell of a thing," Early concluded.

Satisfied with his friend's performance, Olan took a swig from his own mug and wiped his lips on the back of his hand. "In truth, the plot was for you to spit the bloody stuff all over yourself, and then watch you try to explain that to Matta next time he darkened our door."

"You're a true mate, Master Mender. You'd get me thrown straight overboard!"

"Don't be so dramatic—he'd merely have you remove the soiled garment and polish the deck with it. Stem to stern, on your hands and knees."

Early grimaced and took another drink. "He would, too. I've heard of such treatment; my friend Regan was a deckhand under him on another fleet ship. A bloody terror, that man is."

"If he *is* a man," Olan said, and gestured dramatically with his mug. "And not a dragon of old, awakened as a plague on deckhands in every generation."

They toasted each other again, in mutual detraction of their tormentor. "May some questions never be answered," Early said.

They'd refilled their mugs twice, and Early had risen to check the door more than once, finding the passage empty to his satisfaction. Olan, grown more expansive than usual by this point, slapped the tabletop. The noise made Early wince as he returned to his seat.

"Siddown, siddown!" Olan said, louder than necessary. Early shushed him, though he giggled despite himself—the rum was powerful stuff, and his head was swimming pleasantly.

"I'm here, I'm here. What??"

Olan smacked the table again, softer this time. "I been meaning to tell you this story."

"About Matta? Being a dragon awakened? You... you already told that one."

"No! Storms take the fiend! This, this one's about a real dragon. Well, anyway... they say it's real."

"Who says?"

"Nevermind who says, let me tell you the story. It's about... ever heard of the Elder of Storms?"

The cabin was quiet a moment, the lamplight throwing weird shadows on the friends' faces. The wind moaned in the passage beyond the sturdy door at Early's back, and he felt the hair stand up on the back of his neck. Olan's sudden hushed tone and the lurid name sent Early's imagination whirling down avenues of dark possibility.

"The Elder of Storms. No, mate. What's that?"

"Well, come here. Listen." Olan motioned for Early to come closer, as though to hear a secret. They leaned in towards each other, despite their solitude and the size of the table.

"You're being well dramatic, Olan! Just tell the story."

"Ssssh! I am telling you! Look, the Elder of Storms, see... it's a dragon, in truth. And... they say it *is* awake."

Early laughed mid-sip and had to cup a quick hand to his chin to deny Olan the satisfaction of seeing his shirt stained.

"Is it bedtime already? You're telling fairy-stories?"

"Mate! It's no fairy-story. Every sailor who works the

Sunfire Sea fears the Elder. It's one of the true dragons, the great ones that went to sleep, or died, or whatever happened to them, after the Lost Gods created the world."

Despite himself, Early was drawn in by the quiet awe in Olan's voice. "But... all the legends I've heard say the true dragons—if they ever existed—have been gone since the world was made. Does it sleep at the bottom of the sea, this Elder?"

"No, that's just it: the Elder never went to sleep, never died. It lives up there, in the clouds that brood before a storm." Olan pointed to the roof over their heads, and both their eyes scanned the dimly lit planks, as though the monster might be overhead that very moment. This was the first Early ever heard about a real dragon, awake and haunting the skies. Olan must have heard it from sailors returning from mercantile ventures down the coast of the Sunfire, because the fishers of the Imperial Reserve told no such tales.

"I've always heard the dragons were so big, the mountains were made from their bones. How could one be flying around without everyone in the world knowing it?" Early was determined to play the cool skeptic, even though the late hour and the rum had his mind's eye swimming with visions of winged monsters circling high above the mainmast.

"They say it rides along in the stormclouds," Olan said quietly. His eyes were wide, and Early saw a flicker of fear in them, beneath the glaze of drink. "They say it *makes* the storms when it's angry. It can churn up smashing waves and smite ships with lightning. I heard of a merchant fleet from the Free Cities a few years back that was late coming in to port, and when the Blueguard went out to look for them, they... they found nothing but splinters floating on the water. A fleet of ships—just gone."

"But... ships founder in storms all the time," Early protested. "You don't need a dragon for that."

"Ah, but these ships, Early, these ships... they'd *burned*. You see?"

Early was silent for a while. He was very aware of the ship rocking around and underneath him, the endless dark water churning below the keel. Maybe it was the rum, but Olan's tale, and his apparent belief in it, played on Early's mind in a way he didn't like.

"Look, who told you all this?"

Olan sat up straight, a cool expression on his face. He clearly didn't appreciate Early's skepticism when he was trying to share a haunting yarn. "It was the same as gave me this rum, here: a mate on the galley *Seven Sons*. He's been on the sea twenty years."

Early sipped his drink thoughtfully. The creak of the ship's beams and the ever-present lapping of waves against the hull had begun to feel oppressive. The rum was going to Early's head, and he felt dizzy, not sure his legs would hold him up if he rose. Even firm in his seat, he found himself gripping the table for support. At last, trying to make a show of courage, he hoisted his cup in a mock toast. "Well, to the Elder of Storms!"

To Early's dismay, Olan's face turned pale. Eyes wide, he blustered, louder than he needed to, "You're a foolish boy, Master Wills! Every sailor knows it's bad luck to toast the Elder of Storms." With that pronouncement, Olan returned to his cup, using its sturdy bulk to conceal how much Early's careless words had shaken him.

For Early's part, the excitement of their illicit drinking session had drained away, and he was starting to wish very badly that he'd gone straight to his bunk after his shift on deck. He didn't relish the thought of lying there now, the ship's incessant rocking reminding him of his bellyful of rum, trying to stop thinking about Olan's Elder of Storms long enough to fall asleep.

2

There was something wrong with the sky. Early ran the length of the ship, and the sky was the same no matter where he looked. Perfectly dark, no clouds, no stars. And yet, Early could see the gentle waves on which the *Pride of the Empress* bobbed: they were lit with a strange, sickly phosphorescence, like he had seen on certain strange nights in secret coves and estuaries where mysterious things were said to live. He and his friends, all children of fisherfolk, used to paddle the wicker boats their parents gave them up the rivers to find the hidden coves, and dare each other to reach out and touch the water where it glowed. Early had always hung back while his friends leaned dangerously out of their little boats. He was so sure something bad would happen when their hands touched the water; a cold, clammy hand with webbed fingers and black fingernails would yank them over the side. Or the glowing water would run up their arms, changing them as it went...

But all that really happened was a momentary glow as the water, and whatever mystery substance produced the faint light, sloughed off of their hands. "It didn't feel like anything," they'd say, with an unmistakable note of disappointment. "Just... water."

Early did not always succeed in hiding his relief.

Tonight it was as though the entire sea were one of those hidden places, emitting a sickly glow that lit the deck of the *Pride*. The glow was vaporous, as though a fog covered the ship, an unnatural fog that illuminated what it should have concealed. Early kept scouring the sky, hoping for a glimpse of the moon, a star, or something that would indicate clouds too dark and heavy to be pierced by their light. In the vault above there was simply nothing and staring into it made Early dizzy. He sagged against the stern railing, clutching the damp wood, afraid of tumbling over the side into the weird, glowing water. Like he had been in his little wicker boat in the hidden cove so long ago, he was sure there was something waiting to grasp him and pull him down, far down to an alien city made of coral-speckled stone.

He imagined weird towers, with windows or doors puckering like black empty mouths. Long, shimmering bodies, obscenely like the shape of human beings, slithered in and out of them. The fable he and his friends had taunted each other with all those years ago brought a name to Early's lips, and he whispered, *"tyrr,"* their word for the horrible, mythical dwellers in the deep.

On this fearful night, he felt sure they were not a myth at all, but real—and waiting for him below.

Early knew he must warn the captain about the missing sky, but the greatship's decks were empty, and the small-paned windows of Captain Mestrum's cabin in the sterncastle were dark. He looked up the long webs of the rigging, up the mainmast to the topcastle, but no deckhand was crawling there, and he knew he'd find nothing at the top except a vertiginous drop into the glowing, lurking sea. Then there was a noise far out on the water, and Early turned back to the rail, straining to see out over the dark expanse. The luminescent fog had begun to swirl around a point far away, whence the noise had come.

The need to run and seek help swelled in his chest, but Early was unable to move. He watched the sea as, at a point hundreds of yards from the ship, it began to funnel down into nothingness, as though being emptied through an enormous drain. The greatship began to move as the current twisted into a glowing whirlpool, and a terrible roar grew as the water rushed, faster and faster, into the abyss somehow draining the entire Sunfire Sea. Early clutched the rail as the ship tilted sickeningly in the direction he was facing, bringing him almost face-first into the water. He saw movement beneath the surface, and somehow he knew what had caused the whirlpool, what whispered horrors hungered for the ship and her crew, and were even now drawing them down into a shadowy submarine world.

As the ship swirled around and around, tilted on its side as the whirlpool swallowed it, Early could only remain frozen to the spray-slick rail and pray. He took a final breath that he knew couldn't possibly be deep enough, last long enough, and then the icy water closed over his head. The current sucked him from the railing, the *Pride* swirling away into darkness, lost to him, his one lifeline back to the surface. He reached out, fingers spread wide, and his reach was answered by long gray fingers, black-taloned, pale webbing stretched between the knuckles.

The hand clamped around his wrist, and Early was pulled around to look into the horror's face. The dead black eyes of a shark glared at him out of a mockery of human features: a strangely flattened snout, a mouth far too small for the red jaws that it stretched wider, and wider, lips distending to reveal misshapen dagger teeth.

Early screamed, and swallowed water, praying to drown before the monster could bite...

And he sat up so fast his head banged against the bunk above. As his five bunkmates shuffled and groaned in protest, Early realized that, while the *tyrr* had been a nightmare, his scream had been real. He rubbed his now-throbbing brow and lay back on the thin pillow. He couldn't remember ever having a nightmare so vivid. He was glad to awaken... only to have his head and his stomach remind him of Olan's secret cache of rum and the awful price of enjoying it.

It wasn't merely banging his head on the bunk that caused it to ache, and Early groaned, pulling the rough blanket up to his eyes. He hoped his bunkmates would forgive the disturbance and let him slip back into sleep untormented; he was suffering enough already. But sailors forced out of their well-earned sleep by another's nightmare were not known for their mercy, and, as the first pillow struck Early, he knew that was not to be.

❧

It wouldn't do, Early thought grimly, to miss roll call right after his covert drinking spree with Olan. He hated to imagine Matta's round red face scowling at him as the first image when he got out of bed, but such was the price to be paid for breaking the rules, even if no one found out but his conscience.

There was another price to be paid, of course, and he realized it as he staggered down from his bunk and pulled on his shirt, his bunkmates doing the same with yawns and muffled jibes at one another. Early wondered if any of their heads, like his, felt a size too small. He pulled on his loose trousers and his boots, and for once was glad he had no blue-and-white uniform to make smooth and spotless before going on deck.

He clambered after his bunkmates up the long narrow ladder to the hatch in the forecastle that brought him out of the crew quarters and into the painful daylight. Across the long wide deck of the *Pride*, gleaming under the sunrise, Early could see a couple of officers emerging from their own quarters in the stern, smart blue uniform jackets and caps brushed and perfect. His head throbbed, and the usual stab of jealousy at seeing the Blueguard was replaced by envy of those not hungover.

Though the sunrise was beautiful, his head hurt too much to admire it. Besides, any accusations of laziness this morning would risk revealing his sins of the night before. Instead, Early sought whatever rope there was in need of coiling, then helped another deckhand adapt the forward sails to the morning breeze. The fellow was younger than Early, though half a head taller, and obnoxiously bright-eyed.

"Another glorious sunrise, eh?" the boy said. "I never get tired of seeing the sun coming off the waves like that, like we're on a sea of great mirrors."

Early sighed and looked out over the water. He couldn't disagree, but this morning the much-beloved sight made him woozy. He blinked heavily, as dark specks swam for a moment in his vision, and he turned away from the sunshine to focus on the knot he was tying. He tried to rub his pounding forehead in a way the other deckhand wouldn't notice, willing his vision to clear.

But when he looked out at the water again, the black specks were still there. Early shaded his eyes and stared, despite the glare of the sun, until his counterpart noticed.

"What's wrong?" the boy asked.

Early had no time to answer. From high above, the morning watch cried down for all the deck to hear: "Black sails!"

Startled, Early gaped up at the topcastle high above. He

could see the tiny face of the watch's mate, white against the brightening sky, the woman's mouth an oval and her eyes wide as she called again, "Black sails!"

The call was echoed from somewhere else on deck, and the quiet of the dawn was shattered by the stomping of boots. Early and his companion took up the cry, and soon the whole crew was boiling out of the forecastle hatches like ants from a hill, while the Blueguard with their crossbows and Greenguard rangers with their short, powerful recurve bows ran from the sterncastle to take up combat positions.

"Pirates!" the boy next to Early cried in mixed amazement, excitement, and terror. Early could only nod; he felt the same way. The symptoms of his hangover had not vanished, but were joined by a cold, squirmy feeling in the pit of his stomach, and it took everything he had not to run to the railing and be sick. If he weren't now surrounded by his fellow crew, he surely would have given in. Instead, he tried to remember how to be useful. Deckmaster Matta came to the rescue, appearing from amid a flock of deckhands, barking orders.

Early joined a group of hands in hauling heavy, interlocking planks into slots on the forecastle rail. The Blueguard crossbows they shielded paid them no heed, too busy with bolt and windlass, preparing for the violence to come. It was a relief to pitch in while others made the decisions; it helped take Early's mind off that same violence. Battle! It had always been a vague possibility when he'd come aboard; expeditionary or not, the *Pride* was a warship, the finest in the fleet. Still, while Early knew of pirates and the deckhands certainly whispered their share of questionable tales, he'd never expected to really encounter any. For that matter, pirates willing to attack one of Her Majesty's greatships, with its high castles and hundred fighting crew... Early's stomach turned again. They must be terrible marauders or utterly mad. He dared a look out to sea where the black specks had appeared. They'd grown into ships, three fast galleons, and their sails, outspread to catch the morning wind and drive them towards the *Pride* with deadly speed, were dyed pitch black as a warning to their victims.

The clear voice of Captain Mestrum boomed over the deck, and Early saw her and two of her blue-coated officers hurry to the rail. One handed her a spyglass, and she inspected the approaching ships, her expression grim. She returned the glass to her mate and loosened the gold-pommeled cutlass that hung at her hip. Whistling to catch the attention of the deckmaster, the captain made a hand signal Early recognized as "To arms!" Sure enough, Matta hollered the same, and the fighters of the Imperial Guard began arranging themselves on deck according to their division: the Blueguard officers huddled with their crossbows behind the shielding planks on the foredeck, or manned the ship's fixed weapons—the arbalests and huge ballistas that could punch a hole in an enemy's hull at fifty yards.

While the elite of the navy took up battle stations, the rangers of the Greenguard found their own places at the railing. Their bows were lighter but no less deadly, and Early envied the speed with which they'd found their sea legs. In the thrill of preparation, he looked about for the bright crimson tunics of the Redguard, four of whom were on the ship as escort for the Empress's cousin, head of the expedition. But the near-legendary sword fighters didn't seem to be on deck; they must have been secure in the stern cabins, safeguarding the expedition's few members of the Imperial Court.

Early only wished he was as brave or skilled a fighter as any of them. Or had his own bodyguards for what was to come.

A voice spoke at his elbow. "But why would pirates, even

three boats of 'em, come at *our* ship? We're no fat merchant blundering through the Strait of Blood!" The hand who'd spoken was Myria, a lanky girl normally assigned to the ship's galley. Early envied her bravery, coming up on deck in response to the alarm when she could probably have remained unnoticed below. All his instincts wanted him to run back through the hatch and hide in a stewpot.

Myria jostled him. "What's wrong, deckhand? Pirate got your tongue?"

But before Early could reply, Olan had appeared at their side. "I bet they're Gold's Marauders," he said, with the easy confidence of a sailor well-informed by tavern gossip. "Their captain's the daughter of Lord Galliat, disgraced and exiled. She'd love to spit in the face of Her Majesty, and burning us up would make quite the statement!"

Myria snorted at the big deckhand's apparent political acumen, but Olan continued, slapping Early on the back, "Or maybe the pirates are just mad on black rum!" The nearby hands chuckled, and Early wished he could appreciate Olan's humor, meant as it was for him. But his stomach only got worse at the thought of the pirates.

The three galleys had split from each other, one to each side of the *Pride* as the central galley came straight on. The greatship now bristled with readied bows along port and starboard both, and the Imperial Guard waited, silent and tense, for the pirates to sail into firing range.

The enlisted crew, less disciplined, hurried about the decks, getting the ship ready for battle. Fierce shouts from the pirate ships could be heard over the froth and spray as the vessels came dangerously close to each other. Around him, Early's crewmates were tying their final knots and hurrying to the armory lockers spaced about the deck to take up arms. Unlike the Guard, deckhands didn't go about the ship with blade or bow at the ready, so Early fell in line behind Olan at a locker. He was eager, if only out of self-preservation, to get his hands on a blade. Deckmaster Matta cursed at the young hands to stop shoving before they stabbed one another.

"The pirates will be here soon enough to do that for you!" he hollered.

Olan, with his big body and long reach, grabbed a weapon first. It was a short-bladed cutlass, and he handed it to Early before taking another for himself. Though he'd trained with a blade, the cutlass still felt terribly heavy, and Early wondered if he had the strength—or the courage—to wield it. Though fear and excitement had mostly doused his hangover, he felt drained and out of breath, as though he'd already done a long day's work instead of a hard hour or so. Early slid the blade into his belt to keep his hands free. It was one thing to calm his inner turmoil, and quite another to brace himself on deck with a sword in his hand.

Then the top watch hollered, "Impact!" just before the pirates' flagship heaved alongside, slamming with reckless abandon against their hull.

The sound the two ships made as the pirates forced their galley alongside the *Pride* was like the wail of a huge, angry beast and Early would never forget it. The deck canted under his feet and he clung to the rigging while all around him crew and officers alike did the same. A chorus of shouts sounded from beyond the rail, and grappling hooks whistled up over the side as the pirates prepared to board.

As the ship righted itself from the collision, the Blueguard crossbows tromped across the deck in four orderly rows, firing as soon as they reached the railing, heedless of the grappling hooks and arrows hissing up from the pirates below. Two pairs of Guards took command of the arbalests on either side of the forecastle rail, cranking massive iron bolts into locked firing position and tracking the other two pirate galleys that circled the *Pride* like predatory birds, seeking their opening. Early knew they mustn't let all three pirate ships get close enough to board them...

Early couldn't take his hands from the rigging, though he was holding the lines so tightly they burned his palms. He was in awe of the Guards and their fearless attention to duty; he couldn't imagine approaching the railing himself, no matter how badly he wanted a look at the pirates. Indeed, he shivered with the realization that, if the Guards didn't repel them now, he'd see the pirates soon enough when they boarded the ship. A dreadful paralysis had settled in his limbs, and he hoped with a hot flush of shame that no one would notice him. Not that it was clear to Early how a mere deckhand mattered when the Imperial Guard was in battle. He held the short, curved cutlass he'd retrieved from the arms locker, but until a threat appeared on the deck, the blade had little to do but make his palm slick with sweat.

The dozen crossbows of the Blueguard sounded their deadly snap high and clear in the air at the same moment, and instantly the Guards ducked behind the forecastle shields to reload the weapons. Return fire was coming up from the pirates now, as a handful of arrows arced high over the rails and clattered onto the deck. The pirates shot at a great disadvantage, with the *Pride's* towering castles a dozen yards above their heads, while the Imperial bows could fire almost directly downward. To Early's left, an arbalest loosed its giant bolt with a barking metallic twang, and from below rose a chorus of outrage as the projectile smashed a hole in the pirates' deck.

With an ominous creak, the ropes tied to the pirates' grapnels pulled tight and the barbed black hooks bit deeply into the rail. With a shout, a green-cloaked Guard called her fellow rangers over, wrestling with the hook for only a few moments before giving up; with the rope pulled from below by the pirates, digging the hook in deep, she stood no chance of dislodging it. Her curved hunting knife flashed from beneath her cloak, and she sawed the rope high up near the sturdy knot. Seven other Greenguard took up positions at her sides and, while two of them joined in severing the grappling ropes, the rest took aim with their deadly bows, their pull and release as perfectly synchronized as the Blueguard crossbows in the forecastle.

Seeing the rangers in action, their movements fluidly coordinated without needing to speak a word to one another, a thrilling feeling spread like a wave through Early's chest. The terror seizing his limbs receded. Gripping his cutlass, he ran to the port railing alongside the rangers, and dared to look down. An arrow thudded into the wood not six inches from his hand. Startled, Early cried out and stumbled back a step. He'd locked eyes with the pirate who'd made the shot, and even at this distance he could see the hatred and determination on the man's face. The ranger on Early's left turned to him and yelled, "Get back from the rail, deckhand! Unless you can find something to throw!"

It was not merely a dismissal. Looking down the rail, Early saw other crewmates hefting large iron darts and the clay pots of lime stowed near the sterncastle, grunting with the effort as they tossed the heavy projectiles over and let gravity make them deadly. At the sound of a scream, Early dared a look back over the rail to see the pirate who'd shot at him writhing in a mist of the blinding powder, only to take a Greenguard arrow to the chest a moment later and collapse to the deck.

Early's head felt light, but the thrill surging through his

body had taken over. Heart hammering in his ears, he sheathed his sword and ran to the stern to take up a dart of his own. His mind was strangely calm as he hurled one, and then two, and then three iron bolts down at the pirate ship, arrows and shouts piercing the air all around him. He hadn't even noticed Olan standing at his side until his friend cried, "Give it to those bastards!" Caught up in the excitement of battle, Early saw his friend as a mighty warrior, sandy hair in a halo around his head, face red with fierce exultation. Olan lifted a lime pot high in the air and threw it down like he was the legendary Elder of Storms itself, smiting his enemies from on high. But the pot plunked into the water, and a rain of pirate arrows forced them back from the rail.

The crew's work had given the Blueguard an opening, though. At the deckmaster's command, they threw their own grappling hooks down and pulled them tight. Once the enemy ship was hauled close enough, the *Pride's* sailors rushed forward in groups of four, each hauling a long cleated gangplank which they pushed over the rail with practiced care, attaching the long curved hooks at the end of the planks to the pirates' rail. No sooner were these in place then Captain Mestrum herself appeared, her cutlass flashing, and stepped nimbly onto the nearest plank. With Greenguard archers providing covering fire, she lead a horde of armed officers in blue and white down the creaking, tilting gangplanks to the deck of the pirate ship, where that ship's captain and the best of her crew waited to meet them.

Given time to think, Early might have wondered why the defenders were leaving the high ground of their mighty ship to fight the pirates on the deck of their own galley. But just watching the Blueguard tramp down the gangplanks was making him queasy. The long planks had no railings, and shuddered under the officers' boots, but the Guards had far sturdier sea legs than he. While he could only imagine toppling off the plank into the narrow gap between the two ships, there to be crushed between the towering hulls, not one of the Blueguard fell... not until they reached the end of the plank and plunged down on the first of the pirates in a clash of steel.

Fascination overcoming his fear, Early clung to the rail and watched his brave captain go on the attack. The pirate captain was there to meet her, and she was not what Early had expected: she was tall and lithe, with a mane of golden hair flying out behind her peaked black hat, and Early had the absurd notion she looked like a noblewoman from the court of the Empress. Noble or not, she waved a saber high in the air and charged to meet the Blueguard with a cry that belied her delicate appearance. She cursed as colorfully as the rest of her vicious crew as they collided with Captain Mestrum and her Guards. The deck of the galley became a writhing mess of uniformed bodies wrestling with pirates, sword against dirk against axe against knife, the air crackling above the creak of the ships and boom of the waves with a thunder of shouts, screams, and curses.

As blood began to spill on the galley, Early ducked behind the rail near one of the gangplanks, his legs trembling. He couldn't bear to keep watching. He told himself he was guarding the plank, and should any pirate escape the melee and attempt to board the *Pride*, he would personally force the interloper into the froth below... but he wasn't at all sure his body would obey if he tried to leave his hiding spot.

Where was Olan? His big friend had run off to gather the other deckhands to defend the greatship while the officers and rangers boarded the pirate galley, but at this moment the deck around Early was empty. The silence was eerie, as though the ship was holding its breath, awaiting the outcome of the battle. Two other hands watched from high in the rigging, and Early knew there were archers in the topcastle, their bows silent now that the Guards were entwined with their foes, but he still felt frightened and alone. The nearest sounds were the creak of the *Pride*'s rigging and the snap of the sails, the complaints of rope and wood as the ship strained against the grapnels that held it fast to the enemy galley. The sound of battle taking place only a dozen yards away was strangely muted, and Early found himself listening to his breathing instead.

Daring another look over the rail, he saw the pirate captain had lost her hat, and her hair flew in the wind as she held back two Guards at once with sword and dagger. The dance of their swordplay was graceful and strangely beautiful, and Early found himself traitorously hoping she wouldn't be killed. Around her, men and women lay on the deck, a few in Imperial blue-and-white, but most in the motley dress of the pirates. Early couldn't see Captain Mestrum, but pairs and trios of Guards were roaming the deck freely, chasing down the pirates; it seemed the battle would soon be over.

Then there was a shout close at hand. A pirate was scrambling up the gangway toward him with a knife in his teeth, another following close behind. What they hoped to gain by boarding with only two when their ship was being lost behind them, Early didn't know, but he stood and kicked at the pirate as the man reached the railing. He managed to smash the pirate's fingers under his boot and the man reeled, trying to balance with his feet on the steep gangplank and take the knife from between his lips before he dropped it in the sea. Early kicked again before the pirate could manage a stab, and the pirate lost his balance, fell backwards, and crashed against his companion. The second pirate cursed and clung to the gangway for dear life. The man Early kicked scrabbled to get a hold on his companion, or grasp the plank, but caught neither and dropped to the water with a splash. Early didn't hear; he was too focused on whether the second pirate would fall, retreat, or climb onward.

After a moment of hesitation, the remaining pirate looked up, eyes blazing, and began to climb towards Early. The young deckhand's heart raced, and a bad taste filled his mouth, but he drew his sword.

The pirate slowly got to his feet on the gangway, steadied himself, and drew a long dirk from his belt. With a roar, he charged, and Early took a reflexive step back, swinging his blade hard through air. The pirate jumped over the rail and landed just in time to be cut across the chin—Early watched the thin red line swell below the pirate's open mouth. But the man came on, and Early backpedaled, praying not to trip.

Heavy feet scampered across the deck behind him, and Olan appeared at his side with the galley hand, Myria. The pirate turned in time to block Olan's sword, and Early slashed at his left arm. Unused to battle as the deckhands were, the pirate was no match for all three of them, and he stumbled back towards the gangway. But Early and his mates pressed the attack, and while the pirate turned to block Myria's cutlass, Early slid his blade into the man's belly. The pirate's scream as he hit the deck made Early's skin crawl. Olan kicked the pirate's dirk overboard, and the three hands backed away, stunned. The pirate was clutching his torn stomach and writhing on the deck.

"What do we do?" Myria asked, breathless.

Early felt the urgent need to escape, which had vanished as he'd fought the pirate, return like a blow. His knees felt weak and the urge to relieve himself was suddenly overwhelming. The victorious deckhands turned as one and ran for the safety of the sterncastle, leaving their victim to writhe and bleed out on the deck.

It couldn't be said that Early and his friends had turned the tide, but the battle was over not long after. A few more pirates tried their luck boarding the *Pride*, but there were enough sailors and Greenguard rangers to dispatch them quickly. Early looked on with disbelief as one fearsome-looking pirate menaced a deckhand in the forecastle with a huge hammer, only to have a Greenguard pierce his neck with an arrow from the top of the sterncastle, thirty yards away. When the ranger, a darkly bearded and grizzled man of middle age, saw Early gaping at him, he gave the overwhelmed deckhand a wink before running lightly across the deck, seeking a new target.

Early lowered himself down unsteadily between the crates where his friends had found sanctuary. Myria was holding up her sword, which was now dark with pirate blood, just like his. She and Olan were watching the red stuff ooze down the face of the blade. Both hands had the glaze of shock in their eyes, and Early knew he must look much the same.

Lost in thought, Early didn't stir until a great victory cry went up from the pirate galley below. Then he and the others crawled to the rail to see the deck of the pirate ship strewn with bodies, not all of them the bodies of the pirates. But the Blueguard had prevailed, and formed up around the pirate captain and what remained of her crew. Captain Mestrum looked on, grim but triumphant, as the pirates were bound and forced up the gangplanks to face Imperial justice.

As Early's head cleared from the thrill and terror of battle, he remembered the other two pirate galleys, and for a moment his throat tightened in fear. But the other pirate ships, seeing how quickly and ruthlessly the Imperial Guard defeated their captain, abandoned her to her fate. Now Early understood why the desperate pirates had fled up the gangplanks into the arms of their foes, instead of diving into the sea: their comrades weren't waiting around to rescue them. Off the starboard bow, Early saw their black sails billowing in retreat, already small against the blue of sky and sea.

When the captives were marched aboard, the deckhands jostled with one another to see. There were six of them: a motley quartet in ersatz garb, a huge, broad-shouldered man with olive skin and shaven head, his uniform a black-and-red mockery of Blueguard livery, declaring him First Mate, and... her. The captain. Early wrestled with Olan, who was more than a head taller, for a clear sightline. She was the most striking woman he'd ever seen. She might have been only a few years his senior, weathered by many more days and nights at sea, but her eyes were clear and shockingly bright, brows delicately arched above them as she stared fearlessly ahead, unwilling to bow her face before her captors. Her captain's hat was gone, and her long blonde hair was a mess of curls and ringlets that the wind blew back over her shoulders like the Empress's golden cape.

Olan noticed Early's gaping mouth and wide eyes and stuck a big elbow into his side, making him wince. "Keep 'em in your head, swabby, or she might pluck 'em right out if she gets the chance!" Early jabbed him right back, and began a witty rejoinder that died on his lips as Deckmaster Matta materialized beside them. He glared at Early, his ruddy face deepening in shade. He hissed at them to be quiet, as Captain Mestrum prepared to formally charge the pirates and deliver justice.

The six captives had been ordered to stand in a line along the port-side rail, where less than an hour before the Greenguard rangers had been firing volleys of arrows to prevent their incursion. Two of the pirates muttered to each other, and one of them cursed and spat, but the huge First Mate turned a baleful eye on them and they grew quiet, glowering at the deck. Like his captain, the mate evidently intended to meet his fate with quiet dignity.

Captain Mestrum stood with her officers at the top of the quarterdeck, watching as the prisoners were arranged. Next to her was Lord Mardigan, the Empress's cousin and representative, flanked as always by his four Redguard. As often as he'd seen them, Early couldn't help but be impressed. Mardigan was a stout man of middle age and friendly face, wearing rich, fur-lined robes against the chill of the sea. With the tall, lithe warrior-fanatics surrounding him, the lord made Early think of a castle keep squatting among its turrets.

Though Lord Mardigan was officially the leader of the expedition, aboard ship Captain Mestrum ruled. She strode down the steps to the main deck now, with a Blueguard officer at each side, their swords drawn. Her gloved hand rested on the hilt of her saber. She walked, unhurried, along the line of the captives, her polished boots tapping a measured beat upon the planks. When she reached the pirate captain, she swiveled to face her, and the two captains stared each other down for a long minute. Neither seemed willing to give up eye contact first, but stood with their shoulders squared, tall and confident in their individual authority. So it was with captains of ships, Early supposed. Though she had her back to the deckhands, Early had no trouble hearing Mestrum's ringing, commanding voice.

"I am Guard-Captain Jessina Mestrum of Her Imperial Majesty's Blueguard, in command of Her greatship *Pride of the Empress*, and it is my duty, in the Empress's name, to pass judgment on the Empire's enemies. Who will hear the charges against you?"

The pirates looked at each other and growled, hostile and unfamiliar with the formal language of a naval court martial. Their captain, however, met Captain Mestrum's gaze with cold silence, and for a long moment did not deign to answer. When she did, it was with a high, clear voice that matched the Guard-Captain's in poise and intensity.

She snapped at her own crew first. "Be silent!"

The pirates shut their mouths and even drew to a kind of lazy attention, anticipating their captain's defiance.

"I am Captain Marie Gold, of the free ship *Black Spirit*, and though I care nothing for your charges, I will hear them." Her words and tone seemed a careful mockery of her captor's, and Early could see the tension in Mestrum's shoulders as she swallowed her anger. The Guards at her sides shifted slightly, hands tightening on their sword hilts, and the rest of the Imperial crew murmured uneasily until Captain Mestrum spoke.

"Very well. If you claim to be captain of this crew, you will hear our charges and pay the penalty. First, the charge of piracy, for assailing Her Majesty's ships. Second, the charge of assault, for seeking to harm Her Majesty's subjects and the Imperial Guard sworn to protect them. Third, the charge of murder. For the deaths of Her Majesty's Imperial Guard at your own hands and those of your crew.

"For these charges, and, no doubt, other crimes unheralded, you—Captain Marie Gold of the free ship *Black Spirit*—will hang from the mainmast at sunrise two days hence.

"Your crew who accompanies you," she added, sweeping her cold glare across the captive pirates, "will be given to the sea."

Now the pirates began to jeer and curse in earnest, and the dour first mate with them. Steel flashed as the Blueguard officers grew restless.

"And your ship," Captain Mestrum concluded, ignoring the unrest, "will be put to the torch. This is the will of the Empress. Do you have any response to these charges?"

The pirates were struggling against the ropes that bound them, and the Blueguard at the captain's side were visibly restraining themselves from violence. Early's throat tightened at the thought of a fresh melee breaking out—though the bound pirates, for all their enmity, would quickly be slaughtered. But Marie Gold shouted once more for her crew to be silent. She stared at Captain Mestrum and took a deep breath. Then she pursed her lips and spat on the captain's boots.

A wave of palpable outrage rippled through the Imperial Guard and the crew behind them. The deckhands started to jostle around as though they'd attack the pirate captain themselves, despite the wall of Blueguard officers already crowding around her. Someone shoved Early against Olan, Olan pushed back, and soon everyone was jolting and shouting, even as Matta bellowed terrible threats at them. The Guards at the captain's side, meanwhile, moved to strike the pirate down where she stood. It looked like the deck would descend into mayhem, no less deadly than the battle they had just survived. Captain Mestrum did not move, did not look away from her counterpart's defiant stare, but took her hand from the hilt of her saber and held it up next to her head.

"CEASE!"

The Guards stumbled to stop from running the pirates through with sheer momentum. The dangerous wave of sound and movement in the crowd behind her dissipated as quickly as it had begun. There would be no mob action on the deck of Guard-Captain Mestrum's ship. She considered the spittle dripping off her boot with cool indifference.

"Take this pirate into custody," she said, once order was restored. "Put her in the brig in irons. She will hang at dawn, two days hence."

The Guards beside her moved to obey. Marie Gold did not struggle, but, proud and defiant to the last, fixed her piercing blue gaze on the captain as she was pulled away. Her crew, however, would not idly accept their sentence. Even as Captain Mestrum ordered the rest of the Guard to put the prisoners overboard, the huge first mate moved. With his hands tied behind his back, he gathered what momentum a few steps could afford and headbutted the nearest Guard. The man tumbled to the deck, and his partner moved in with her cutlass, but the mate had already turned and tried to bull her up over the railing.

The rest of the Blueguard closed in around the pirates, swords in hand. One of the prisoners, apparently preferring water to steel, uttered a curse and flung himself over the rail before he could be caught. Another tried to kick the nearest Guard and got a cutlass through their chest. Despite their oaths and the fiercest resistance the pirates could muster, twice the number of Guards pressed in and forced them back against the rail. One by one, the captives were heaved overboard. The First Mate, finally checked by the tips of two blades pressed to his neck, was last to go. He snarled wordlessly as three Guards hoisted him over to his doom.

The hateful look in the man's eyes stayed with Early, even as the gathered crew dispersed and the deckmaster wrangled the hands back to work. As he swabbed the deck, filthy with boot prints and blood, Early couldn't help seeing the first mate thrown overboard again and again, refusing to scream and only fixing his executioners with that terrible stare. Early couldn't help imagining what it would feel like—the vertigo of toppling overboard, the long fall that couldn't be nearly long enough, the shock of cold water, and then the fruitless struggle. Though the pirate ship was adrift nearby, the captives' hands were tied; they couldn't hope to rescue themselves. Early imagined them paddling with their feet till they lost the strength to keep their heads above water, and then... he held his breath as he imagined that last fateful breath that invited in the sea.

He was sure the captain had given the pirates what they deserved, and yet... he couldn't imagine a worse way to die. Early shivered as he worked his mop, and not from the chilly breeze.

§⚓

The *Pride*'s brig, where Olan had shared with Early his rum and his tale of the Elder of Storms, was a narrow strip of room below the forward crew quarters. It was made even narrower by the bars that bisected it lengthwise, turning half of the room into a cell whose rear wall, below the forecastle, curved outwards along the line of the hull. The long bench which served prisoners as both seat and bed had at one end a round hole covered by a wooden hatch so prisoners could relieve themselves. Early had heard stories of prisoners trying to escape that way, only to be sucked into the ship's wake and quickly drowned. It was a desperate person indeed who would prefer the cold doom of the waves and what lay beneath them to imprisonment, and the cell's current occupant was not desperate, despite her death sentence. She sat at ease on the bench, well away from the hatch.

The night after Marie Gold's capture, Early was in the brig because the Blueguard sentry whose shift it was had asked a favor. Early had wondered what important errand called the Guard away from his post, and heard the man's voice whispering with another from among the lashed-together barrels stowed near the forecastle. But Early took the Blueguard at his word, dutifully set aside his mop, and climbed down to the brig. Punished with a double shift of deck-swabbing for his rowdiness during Marie's sentencing, he was glad for the reprieve.

Seeing the pirate captain sitting patiently in the cell, Early felt like he should introduce himself and explain what was going on, but had to remind himself Marie was a prisoner, not entitled to any explanations. Indeed, proper duty demanded he not acknowledge her at all unless there was some urgent need.

Nonetheless, when she saw him enter and take up a position against the wall beside the door, arms behind his back in his best attempt to mimic a Blueguard's posture, she rose and came to the bars, leaning her forehead against them. Despite carefully ignoring the prisoner, Early couldn't help but notice from the corner of his eye the way her hair curled down around the bars. Golden strands twinkled in the low lamplight that illuminated the room. She simply stood there and watched him, while Early tried to imagine the sea beyond the rear wall of the brig, staring at the planks so intensely he imagined them scorching and peeling back to create a window to the night beyond. Soon he could feel sweat standing out on his forehead.

"Has the shift changed that quickly, then?" she asked.

Early jerked out of his reverie.

"What?"

"I thought the last guard had just arrived, and now he's been replaced. Isn't that strange?" She smiled indulgently at Early. He knew her eyes were blue, but they glittered darkly in the low light that made her fair features enticingly mysterious. Early knew he wasn't to engage her in conversation—and he had no idea how to answer, anyway—so after a moment of gaping at her, he looked back at the wall, sweating more freely.

After what seemed a long few minutes, Marie spoke again. "The other guard sat down, you know." She nodded towards the little table with its two chairs where Olan and Early had shared a drink and Olan told the fearsome legend that still haunted Early's dreams.

"Oh?" Early tried to sound indifferent. He supposed he should have ignored her, but it was difficult—pretending she didn't exist seemed intolerably rude, for one thing.

This must be where the Imperial Guard's famous discipline comes in, he thought, and wondered what was required to learn it.

"So, I reckon you can take a load off. I'm not about to slip out on you." The way she used the word "reckon" broke the illusion of Marie as a high-born lady and reminded Early he was speaking to a pirate. The contrast was strangely endearing. His gaze slipped over to the chair.

"I think I'll remain standing, if it's all the same to you." Early tried to be casual, but when the words came out, it sounded to him as though he were asking permission—hardly the attitude of a guard towards a prisoner. He found himself hoping the Blueguard would return soon. But also hoping he wouldn't.

Marie shrugged and turned away from the bars. Her movements were slow and deliberate, and the combination of delicacy and coarseness in her manner was terribly intriguing. She took up a seat on the edge of the bench, leaning slightly forward, her hair in her face.

"It's no difference to me, deckhand." She smiled warmly—condescendingly?—and it bothered Early that she so easily identified his actual rank. It reminded him of their relative positions: prisoner or no, she was still a ship's captain, and, dead or not, a crew had answered to her command. Early, on the other hand, was merely a washer of planks and a runner of errands. It irked him; she didn't seem that much older than he was. Where had he gone wrong, if a woman her age could be a captain and he could not?

"Sorry," she said, seeing him glower, and her voice grew penitent. "I wasn't trying to give offense. The brashness of a captain is hard to let go."

Marie leaned back against the wall and sighed. "I suppose that's what I'll have to do, though. Do you know, will they truly execute me two days' hence, here on the open sea? Or will your captain have mercy enough to let me live until you reach your destination?" Now it was her turn to stare into space, and Early cringed at the future she must be imagining. Her eyes were shining slightly in the dark, as though she held back tears.

"I'm sorry, I... don't know," Early said. "There's no telling when we might reach our destination, anyway." Marie's keen eyes fixed on Early's face. He blushed. "I mean... that is, the captain... I'm sure she'll keep her word. I'm sorry."

Marie nodded gravely, considering this. "I understand. Thank you, deckhand."

She leaned forward again. "May I... confide something in you?"

Early found himself leaning forward, for her voice had grown quiet. He slid into the chair, eyes wide and attentive. "Well... yes. Yes, of course."

"I've faced death many times since taking command of the *Black Spirit*. At first, the thought of dying frightened me terribly. But as we fought and won, the fear receded until I laughed in its face. When your captain looked me in the eye and sentenced my crew over the rail..." She paused, and put her hands to her face. "I saw it. I saw death in her eyes. And I've been as afraid as ever in my life since then."

Early clasped his hands between his knees and swallowed hard. He didn't know what to say to comfort her—all the words that came to mind seemed vapid. But he felt if there were anywhere he could admit his own fears, it would be here.

"When I made the crew for this expedition," he said, "it was the most exciting day of my life. But that battle, when we... uh, when your ships attacked, when we did all that... I've never felt more scared. And if we find the place we're looking for, well, I don't know *what* will happen then. I've been imagining it as a great adventure. But I never knew what adventure really meant."

Early's words tumbled to a stop. He felt foolish revealing himself this way before a prisoner. But he could not overcome his desire to help the beguiling woman behind the bars.

"You were brave to join, then, and with such eagerness," she said, her gaze so intense on his face he found it hard to meet her eyes. "An Imperial greatship like this, off on a special mission... And special it must be, to have as auspicious an overseer as Her Majesty's cousin!"

Early could only gape and crinkle his brow in confusion. Forgetting himself and his current position as mute sentinel, he sputtered, "How did you know that?"

"Don't be foolish, deckhand," Marie replied, her tone teasing. "I've been a citizen of the Empire longer than you, by the looks of it. And, pirate or not, I once called the Imperial Court my home. Though I was just a little girl, I still recognize the Empress's closest confidants. No mere fishing trip would bring Lord Cyrus Mardigan out on the open sea—he's no sailor, like you or I—and on a ship like the *Pride of the Empress*? No, it must be a momentous errand indeed!"

Early literally bit his tongue, albeit gently, running it along his teeth to keep himself from blurting out the questions bubbling up inside him. Marie must indeed be a noblewoman if she had grown up in the Imperial Court. How, then, had she come to piracy? Her story must be an even stranger one than he'd thought! She had guessed much about the importance, if not the true nature, of their quest. He felt a dangerous temptation to confirm her suspicions, but his better judgment prevailed and he kept silent. His gaze flickered to the portal and back, wishing the Blueguard watchman would return and relieve him.

Marie came forward again, and lowered herself to her knees, clasping the bars. Her voice, when she spoke, was broken, pitiful. "Will you... would you do something for me, deckhand? Though I know it is not my place to ask..."

His heart went out to her. She was fierce, and brave, and he could only imagine the terrible fear of the gallows that could so reduce her. "If I can help... I will do whatever is in the bounds of my duty," he said.

She nodded, her face grave. "I ask nothing beyond those bounds. Only... when you arrive at this new land you seek... will you say my name there? Will you merely remember me? So at least I'll know someone will, and a part of me will have gone on this great journey with you."

Early felt a wetness in his eyes, and he remained very still lest it try to escape. He didn't trust his voice, so only dared reply, "Yes, I will. On my word."

Marie rose with effortless grace, the noblewoman once more. She laid down on the bench, one arm behind her head. She seemed calmer now, and Early supposed—hoped—he'd helped her come to terms with her fate. Only later would it occur to him he'd never mentioned what the expedition sought, and her air had been one of satisfaction at having confirmed her suspicions.

"Thank you, deckhand," she murmured, and smiled to herself.

§

Dawn over the Sunfire Sea. The sun loomed red on the horizon, and the waves were still, murmuring only quietly against the hull of the *Pride*. Six Blueguard officers had marched Marie Gold up from the brig, on to the deck, and up the forecastle steps. Now, with her hands bound behind her and the sea breeze fluttering her golden hair across her face, she stood facing the rising sun.

Captain Mestrum stood before Marie, silhouetted by the red dawn, with her Blueguard arranged along the rail. Lord Mardigan, surrounded by his four Redguard protectors, stood to one side with Lia Dracis, the Imperial Cartographer. The noblewoman had her tablet with her as always, recording the proceedings with quick strokes of her charcoal. The Redguard had their swords drawn, as though the pirate captain might slip her bonds, incapacitate her own guards, and throttle the members of the Imperial Court at any moment.

The execution of a ship's captain at sea was a ceremonial thing. Early had heard tales and seen illustrations in storybooks, but never thought to be present at one. He stood down on the main deck, amongst the rest of the hands and enlisted crew, and pressed and pushed his way front and center for the best hope of seeing what would happen. The pirate captain held a strange fascination for him, especially after their talk in the brig, and he couldn't resist hoping he might see something other than her death this morning.

"Marie Gold," the first officer intoned, squinting to read a script he held up to catch the rising run. "You are the captain of that ship, are you not?"

The first officer turned and pointed off the bow, and Captain Mestrum and the others in the forecastle turned to look. A hundred yards ahead, and just far enough to port for Early to see its bulk, *Black Spirit* drifted where its captors had moored it. The pirate ship's sails had been furled, and the only movement on its deck came from eight Blueguard ship-breakers, preparing to descend a rope ladder into their waiting launch.

Marie drank in the last sight of her ship for a long time before answering. Nobility evident in her bearing, she inclined her head and, looking at her ship and not the first officer, replied, "I am its captain."

The Blueguard continued reading, "You admit to being captain of this pirate vessel, whose crew engaged in an unlawful attack on Her Imperial Majesty's ship. Your crew has been put to death, and the time has come to carry out your sentence, as well. First, to show that no pirate shall profit from their evil labor: watch closely, Marie Gold."

The first officer nodded to another Blueguard, who raised a signal flag. From the deck of *Black Spirit* came an acknowledging whistle, and the distant figures of the Guard did something on deck. There was an audible pop, and a puff of smoke that quickly turned to spreading flames—the ship-breakers had laid bundles of dry reeds soaked in flammable pitch along the deck and in the hold. Now that the fuel was kindled, they hurried to their launch, rowing back towards the *Pride* with all haste.

The crew around Early were murmuring to each other; while they could see the pirate captain and her executioners, the high forecastle kept many of them from seeing the burning ship, and so word was passing through the crowd from others with a better view: a few of the hands had furtively climbed the rigging, hoping their officers wouldn't notice.

Early felt a pang, imagining how Marie must be feeling, watching her ship put to the torch.

Up on the bow, the pirate captain watched with an unreadable expression as fire climbed the pitch-smeared masts of her ship, until the first officer asked if she had any final words. Fixing Captain Mestrum with a careful eye, the pirate said, "I can guess well enough at your mission, Guard-Captain. And I will only say, may the Gods' Luck be with you. In my furthest travels on the Sunfire, I've only ever glimpsed the strange land you seek. But I never did touch its shore... or look to find the lost expedition you must hope awaits you there."

Captain Mestrum stiffened, and sounds of surprise rose from the officers and crew.

"How does she know—?" Lord Mardigan protested, but the captain held up her hand to him politely, eyes narrow with suspicion.

"You say you've seen a land undiscovered by the Empire?" Captain Mestrum demanded of the pirate. "Say more of it."

"You'll know it by the strange and twisted pillars of rock that guard the shore like protective walls," Marie explained, to the mumbled disbelief of both the officers on the forecastle and the hands below. Could this pirate really have guessed at their mission and just happen to know how to find the far-flung land in search of which the Empire's last expedition had vanished years before? It beggared belief, as was plain to see on Captain Mestrum's face. Yet, if there was any assistance to be had in their search, must she not at least consider it?

"Pillars of rock?" the captain asked, skepticism plain in her voice and expression. "You have truly seen this?"

"With my own eyes," Marie said. "We gave them a wide berth. I've seen few other landings so treacherous. If your predecessors attempted to put in there..." she let the peril of such an attempt go unsaid.

"Let's come to it!" Mestrum snapped, clearly growing impatient. "If you've seen the land we seek, you could help our navigators find it, and for this reason we should spare your life. That is what you wish me to believe, yes?"

Marie nodded slowly, her steady, fearless gaze never leaving the captain's.

Captain Mestrum turned and looked out over her crew, then off the bow, where the burning hulk of *Black Spirit* was beginning its fatal roll into the waves. And she looked beyond, where untold leagues of water and unknown dangers awaited them. It had always been on a sail and a prayer that they sought the first expedition; since the ships had disappeared without a trace, they had only the expedition's planned route to follow. No one knew whether it would lead them to a thriving Imperial colony, to a graveyard of ships, to the end of the world... or to so many blank miles of waves they were forced to turn back.

No one aboard the *Pride of the Empress* knew. Except, perhaps, the pirate Marie Gold.

The demands of Imperial justice were clear, but Captain Mestrum, of Her Majesty's Blueguard, served the Empress alone... would the Empress have her put the pirate to death, or put her alleged knowledge to use? It was strange to see the self-assured captain so torn with indecision while she gazed out to sea, squeezing the hilt of her saber as though drawing her resolve from the solid metal.

At last, she turned back and spoke to her first officer. "Return the prisoner to the brig." Turning to the deckmaster, she indicated the rope hanging from the yardarm nearby. "Have that noose taken down."

Both men looked surprised, but Marie, who should have been most surprised of all, glanced at the faces of her captors with the tiniest smile of satisfaction. Early, watching from the crowd, felt the tension all around him break into confusion: there were angry mutterings from all sides, and the crew began to jostle each other until the officers barked warnings. To Early's relief, the captain's voice boomed over their heads, calling for order. "This pirate has bought her life, for now. Our mission must prevail. Justice will be delivered on her at its end, whatever end that be."

The captain's orders given, nothing more was left to be said. The Blueguard formed their protective circle around the prisoner—as much, or perhaps more, for her safety than out of fear that she was a danger—and the crew was propelled back to their various duties by the deckmaster and the other officers. Two hands were sent up into the rigging to take down the noose that Marie Gold's neck had escaped for now, and Early made his way to retrieve his mop and bucket.

A short time later, he swabbed the forecastle in a daze. If Marie could really guide them to an alien shore, the implications for their quest were incredible. Could her story be true? Or had she duped him into revealing just enough of their mission for her to trick Captain Mestrum? Early watched the burning, sinking wreck of the pirate ship and felt his heart sinking as well. Things had been so much simpler when he had nothing to worry about but Olan's Elder of Storms!

3

A week after she'd burned the *Black Spirit*, Guard-Captain Mestrum stood in the forecastle, one hand on the rail and the other holding her hat in place as the *Pride* bucked in a growing wind. Early stood nearby—as close as the Blueguard flanking the captain would let him get, anyway. He could just imagine Deckmaster Matta's eyes boring hatefully into his back, but he didn't care. Despite the sails howling behind them, the view was spectacular, and, this close to the captain, he couldn't help but imagine what it must be like to command a greatship, to make the hard choice: would they try to avoid the building storm, or sail into its very teeth?

The course they'd followed for the past week was a compromise between what they knew of the first expedition's route and the hints Marie dropped when the Guard-Captain visited her cell. Mestrum and her staff remained skeptical of the pirate's word, but were unwilling to dismiss it, knowing Marie's recollection could be the difference between the success and failure of their quest. And so they'd sailed east and slightly south, far from the furthest trade route of the Decadin Empire.

Early looked to both port and starboard, and then back at

the growing mountain of thunderheads blackening the late afternoon sky dead ahead. He wondered if they could find shelter, but they'd not had sight of land in three days, since they'd passed a barren isle far to port. The lookout high in the topcastle had hollered a negative when asked if there were any landing to be had there; the rock was little more than a lone finger thrust up out of the water. Now there was nothing but open sea in every direction.

A hand fell heavily on Early's shoulder. He turned, trying not to wince, expecting the deckmaster... but it was the captain herself, looking him in the eye. She wasn't quite as tall as Early, but her bearing made him feel as though he were looking up at her. She must have seen his misgivings in his eyes, for she gave him a reassuring smile. He couldn't recall ever seeing her smile before.

"What do you make of it, Deckhand Wills?" she asked. In the moment, between the gathering storm and the unexpected conversation, Early forgot to be impressed that she knew his name.

"It l-looks like a bad one, Captain." Early fought down the urge to salute, but stiffened nonetheless. Her laugh, like her every other gesture, was slight and controlled.

"At ease, deckhand. It does, indeed. Have you weathered a storm at sea before?"

Early shook his head slowly, remembering his worst times in rough weather on his parents' boats. Those had been little boats on little water, and he was sure they hadn't prepared him for the wrath of the mighty Sunfire. He'd heard more than his fill of sailor stories, and his imagination churned with waves as high as the greatship, vivid enough to turn his stomach.

He swallowed hard, then realized the captain hadn't seen him shake his head. She was looking back at the gathering clouds, pondering their distance and speed.

"No, Captain," he said at last, his voice quiet. "Not at sea."

But her mind seemed to have wandered, and, instead of acknowledging his reply, Captain Mestrum said, "I'd almost believe that pirate cooked this storm up herself, and pointed us into its teeth." Seeing Early gape at her with alarm, she winked at him.

The mention of Marie Gold brought unanswered questions to mind, and since the captain seemed in an expansive mood, Early dared to ask one.

"Guard-Captain, if it please you, I'd been wondering... why did you burn the pirate's ship?"

"A good question," she nodded, and raised her voice as the rising wind caused the sails to snap above their heads.

"A fine galley like that seems a sin to burn, doesn't it? Normally, we'd bring a captured ship back to the High City as a prize. But Captain Gold is no mere outlaw. She betrayed the Empress, deckhand, and we can show no quarter to traitors." The captain's grim determination chilled Early more than the gale. Then she offered him a thin smile. "More practically, we lack the crew to bring a second ship along with us. As you can see, *Pride* needs all hands on the rigging!"

Early had more he wanted to ask—like why she and her officers had abandoned the high ground to fight Marie on the pirate's own ship—but a vicious gust of wind forced the captain to clamp her hat to her head with an undignified oath, and Early clung to the rail for dear life as the greatship lurched.

"Go astern and find the deckmaster!" Captain Mestrum hollered over the wind. "Tell him to make the ship ready for the storm."

"At once, Captain!" Early couldn't help trying to flash a smart salute as he'd seen the Blueguard do, even though it wasn't his station. He turned and hurried down the forecastle stair, his face burning. Partly he was eager to carry out his duty.

Partly he was eager to give the irascible deckmaster an order for a change, even indirectly. Partly he fled from embarrassment, despite realizing he hadn't waited to be dismissed. A Blueguard, of course, would wait to be dismissed. But he was no Blueguard, and he couldn't bear to turn back and see the condescending look he imagined on the captain's face.

He was passing the mainmast, dodging and side-stepping the other crew coming and going in the narrow middle deck when a truly enormous wave struck the ship. Reflexively, Early grabbed the rigging before he was tossed off his feet. Another hand nearby wasn't so lucky and cursed as they tumbled over a coil of rope. The captain's message for Deckmaster Matta to make ready for the storm seemed redundant now, Early thought; the sea was telling them that by itself.

A half-hour later, the sky was *boiling*. Early stared at the churning clouds, his jaw hanging open. The sky had gone from black to an unnatural shade of violet that was brighter than dusk, but nothing like daylight. All along the deck, Early could hear the crew yelling and boots stomping the planks as they ran back and forth, frantically trying to prepare before the storm engulfed them. Early had his own job to do, helping five other hands batten down everything loose on the stern deck, but he was struck still by the clouds above. They seemed to move like a living thing, and Olan's fearsome tale of the Elder of Storms played over and over in his mind. Someone was calling his name, and Early realized that the deckmaster had been shouting at him for some time. The stout officer clung to the rigging of the mizzenmast, whose huge timbers creaked in protest of the wind.

"Strike sail! Strike sail!" Matta shouted to his hands, hoarse from yelling over the rising scream of the wind.

Early, despite the freezing feeling in his limbs—so familiar from the battle with the pirates—snapped out of his trance and glanced around the deck. The crew crowded around each of the *Pride's* three tall masts, bringing down the sails lest a sudden gust snap the timbers... or heel the whole mighty ship over on its side. As Early hurried to help fasten the ropes, a terrible roar smashed the air, reverberating off the ship and making the very planks of the deck seem to vibrate. Early and the other hands stared in wonder at the roiling clouds, and his imagination formed from them an undulating shadow, a monstrous shape that slithered in the murk overhead, fanning the stormclouds into a veritable cyclone.

One of the hands next to Early screamed, and let go of the rope he held. As Early grasped for it, unable to look away from the sky, he saw strange purple lightning flicker along the underside of the clouds. For just a moment it seemed a dark shape resolved into gaping serpentine jaws, above which burned a cluster of demonic eyes.

With a terrific crash of thunder the whole sky lit up and, blinking the blindness out of their eyes, Early and the others turned to see the top of the *Pride's* tall mainmast shatter, the sturdy wood of the Allevalen tree blackening as it burst into flame. Through his shock, Early realized lightning must have struck the ship directly, and over the rage of the wind he heard the screams and shouts of alarm from his crewmates. Early's ears were ringing. One of the hands next to him had fallen to the deck and was rolling back and forth on the planks, muttering gibberish. Olan kneeled at the other man's side, trying to bring him back to his senses. Early watched the two of them, feeling strangely disconnected from what was going on. Even the deck beneath him felt unreal, as though he were floating. He felt he should surely be doing something, helping in some way, or even just taking refuge from the storm, but he could not move. A deadly paralysis, all too familiar, had settled over his body and clouded his thoughts. *What's wrong with me?* Early wondered. *Is this cowardice?*

Down on the main deck, officers were screaming commands, their blue-and-white uniforms illuminated by the lightning that now flashed every few seconds between sky and waves. Early felt far away, as though he was imagining a story being told to him while he was safe in bed, or while he reclined on the deck of a ship gliding peacefully over calm seas.

Then the deck tilted, throwing Early off balance. He clutched the rigging automatically, but the man lying on the deck began to slide towards the starboard rail. Olan cried out, reaching for his senseless mate, and Early leaped to his aid. They stumbled along the deck as its angle grew steeper, the fallen man sliding faster ahead of them, and Early screamed, "Grab hold of the rail!"

Though the fallen deckhand seemed not to hear, Early found himself taking his own advice as he slammed into the rail hard enough to drive the breath from his lungs. The ship reached the crest of the wave and Early's stomach turned in his belly. He felt the man clutching at his leg; at least the shock of almost falling overboard had brought the deckhand to his senses. Early and Olan saw the terror in his eyes as he scrabbled for purchase on the deck. As much to himself as to his crewmate, Early yelled, "Hold on!"

The *Pride* crested the wave and there was a moment of utter vertigo as the prow dropped through thin air, crashing back into the water. Early and Olan dared let go of the rail long enough to help the other deckhand fully back on board. Only then did Early release the breath he didn't realize he'd been holding. His hands ached from grasping rigging, rail, and his crewmate. The three of them could do nothing but gawk at each other, silently thanking the gods they hadn't all gone overboard.

High above them, the heavens screamed. Though there was a flash of lightning, the sound was worse than mere thunder—as loud, yet more piercing. It touched a current of instinctive fear in Early's soul, and he shivered helplessly. The others slumped on the deck with him did the same, and one of them whimpered, "No..." Early looked up, and immediately regretted it. The roiling clouds were lit with a purple glow, and from within glow, *something* emerged. It was a shadow first, with outstretched wings, and then the clouds pulled back and Early looked upon the Elder of Storms.

The feeling that he was dreaming intensified. The ship, the wind, the spray of the waves, all faded away. Early prayed he was indeed lost in a nightmare. The monster was larger than he could have imagined when Olan had told the story. It seemed to fill the sky, its wings so broad all the sails on the *Pride of the Empress* laid out side by side might not match their span.

Those wings moved almost lazily, clouds eddying from their tips as though they stoked the storm into fury instead of riding it. The monster hovered in the seething air like no bird or flying thing in the world. Its presence seemed to mock all the laws of nature Early knew, and though the sight set his heart pounding in stark animal terror, it was impossible to look away.

Violet energy snarled and sparked along the Elder's length, and its claws, black and the size of longships, flexed and contracted with each burst. The beast seemed barely to contain the evil lightning, ready to burst in rage. Unholy rage. Unnatural rage.

Worst of all was its mouth. It was like a great long beak, but it opened wide in three jaws rather than two, revealing a darkness like a rift in the sky. Deep in this chasm a purple glow pulsed, illuminating rows of stalactite teeth. When it stretched its triple jaws wide and roared, Early's vision swam and his mind blanked in terror. Stars exploded before his eyes and he didn't know if he was seeing things or if lightning poured down on him along with sound, the Elder venting its hatred of the gods that had abandoned it eons ago.

The deck was shaking. Early couldn't tell where he was, for it seemed the ship had begun to take flight around him. His head struck the deck and, in a moment of madness, he begged the dark of oblivion to close down around him... but it didn't. A pillar of flame towered into the sky where the mainmast had been, and, above it, the Elder of Storms tossed and turned in its wrath. Early shook his head weakly, denying what his eyes showed him, but then the monster *looked down at him*, and all he could see were eyes, crystalline and faceted like the eyes of insects. Its gaze drowned out even the sight of its monstrous body, drowned out the whole sky, and Early felt as though he were being pulled into the air, though the boards of the deck were still hard at his back. His reality was dissolving into the monster's eyes, diamondine portals that held only fire, and, behind the fire, nothing. Early saw the end of the world in those eyes and prayed recklessly that it would arrive and end his torment. Then the Elder shrieked one last time, spat lightning —blue, white, violet, blinding—and at last, for a few blissful moments, Early knew no more.

Early opened his eyes at what he assumed was the end of the world. All around him, dark water vanished into the swallowing night. A dreadful howl accompanied a blast of heat and light: the main deck of the *Pride of the Empress* was burning, its giant mainmast a pillar of fire. The stern of the ship was mostly intact, but it was listing badly on its port side, and the bow of the ship... had disappeared beneath the waves. Thoughts sluggish with shock, Early wondered how much of the ship would burn up before it had the chance to sink, and, more personally: did he wish to die by fire, or water? Was it worse to be burned, or drowned?

Movement on the deck wakened him from the grim reverie. Figures danced in fire, and with dreamy detachment Early realized his crewmates were burning, screaming until the air was stolen from their lungs or the part that could scream burned away. He wondered if Olan, or Captain Mestrum, or even Deckmaster Matta were among the burning. Or if they were already lost in the water. He hoped they lived, but hope itself seemed pointless. He couldn't bring himself to move to see who was still dancing, limned in fire, or try to help them were there any way to help; Early wasn't sure he could even move. He felt like a sea-ghost, lingering over the wreck of his ship.

With an ominous groan the huge yard of the mainmast bent ponderously towards the port side, and in a splintering of wood fell like a burning spear, a comet of sparks in its wake as it crashed to the deck. When the burst of fire died down, there was a great hole where a large part of the port-side rail and main deck had been. The sinking ship rocked underneath Early like a disturbed sleeper rolling in bed. *It may be water does me in yet*, he thought.

He looked out to sea. The rolling black waves reared their frothy crests high in the air, hungry to swallow the wounded greatship. There was faint movement in the fire-lit water; some of the crew had gone overboard and were yet alive. He heard the sailors shouting to the civilian crew to swim away from the sinking ship. It seemed bitterly ironic: a person in the water would want only to grasp hold of anything afloat, but the *Pride of the Empress* was now a tomb on the sea, and soon enough it would suck anyone and anything nearby down with it into the deep.

The screams and desperate cries came from all points, but Early lay frozen, unable to help. It was a special sort of hell to be trapped there, fearing not only for his own life, but for all his friends and crewmates. Could he rise from the deck? And, even if he stood, what could he possibly do?

The wind shifted, and a cloud of smoke cleared to reveal a huddled figure nearby. An officer that wore the blue-and-white of the Blueguard lay only a few yards away. Early shouted, but the stricken man, trying to turn his head towards the sound, only coughed and shook with a sudden spasm. Alive then, and hurt. Growing determined, Early rolled onto his front and gathered his strength to push himself off the deck. This man needed his help. That much was within his reach.

His arms and legs trembled, but Early pushed the deck away until he was standing. He was relieved to find it was only shock and not injury that had paralyzed him—he prayed the fallen officer was in a similar condition, because the man was certainly too big for Early to move on his own. As he stumbled over and dropped to his knees at the man's side, he saw it was Matta, the deckmaster. The indomitable terror of Early and his friends had been overcome by smoke, and looked painfully vulnerable. His hat was gone and his face was swollen, and his singed uniform was still burning in several places. Early tugged the deckmaster's long coat away from his body and used its tails to put out the smoldering embers.

Matta's breathing was noisy and labored, and though Early slapped his cheeks—without the joy such an act would have brought him only days ago—the deckmaster barely responded. Early rose and tried to drag the deckmaster to his feet, but while he could imagine someone of Olan's size and strength hoisting the fallen man over his shoulders, Early's head swam with the effort of merely lifting the limp officer's torso from the deck. Early looked towards where the forecastle had been and saw the water had claimed another yard of the deck behind them. Matta was no longer burning, but if Early could neither move nor rouse him, he'd saved the man only to watch him drown.

Then, seemingly from nowhere, Guard-Captain Mestrum was beside him. Without a word, she took one of Matta's arms and gestured for Early to take the other. Between them, they hoisted the deckmaster from the planks and held his body between them. Matta wasn't completely dead weight, but near enough, and even with the captain's help lifting him took all Early's remaining strength. He didn't know what they could do next, but if they just stood there, he'd soon drop back to the planks alongside Matta.

But the captain seemed to know what to do. Seeing Early looking at her, she jerked her head towards the stern of the ship, which still stood high above the waves. Gritting his teeth, Early pressed against the weight of his former nemesis as they dragged him towards the temporary salvation of the sterncastle deck.

The *Pride's* quarterdeck, with the captain's own cabin at the far end, was still above the water. Reserved for officers, Early had only ever stood on its planks twice, but the novelty was lost on him now. They managed to drag Matta up alongside the cabin, where a narrow section of the deck wrapped around and up a steep stairway to the poop deck on its roof. The captain nodded towards the stairs.

"That's the highest point on the ship we can hope to reach, but we'll spare a minute here to rest."

Early, panting, could only nod. He wasn't about to argue with a brief respite, even as the deck was tilting a little more steeply every moment. He and the captain were sitting against the rail on either side of Matta, who was coughing and retching as he slowly came to his senses. The last of the smoke he'd inhaled seemed reluctant to leave his body.

"Could one of the launches still be aboard?" Early asked the captain across Matta's broad shoulders. He knew one of the *Pride's* small boats was usually slung just behind the stern of the ship. "Maybe that's our best bet." In the moment of calm, Early felt his resolve strengthening, and with both the captain and a capable officer by his side, he was even daring to hope they might somehow survive.

Captain Mestrum looked back at him with an unreadable expression. As the *Pride* slowly sank, the flames that had ruined her ship were sputtering out. The tall mainmast still stood high out of the water, and its fire reflected in her eyes, hiding whether they contained hope or despair.

"You may escape yet, deckhand. Once we see to the deck-master, we'll try to gather whoever else is still standing and we—"

The deck beneath them bucked like a horse, and Early tumbled away. One moment the stern deck had been safe and dry, the next a wall of water hit him in the ribs like a maul. Matta's still-limp arm slipped from his grasp, and it was all he could do to scrabble for purchase against the railing as the back end of the greatship spun against the force of the sea trying to tear it apart.

"Early!"

It was the first—and last—time Early would ever see Guard-Captain Mestrum truly afraid. The captain clung to the sterncastle's rail with both arms, her wide eyes staring at the dark air where the deckmaster no longer was. The great wave had receded, and Matta had gone with it. Grief bit deep into Early's stomach, and he sobbed. It had happened so fast, there was nothing they could do... He gripped his section of the railing so hard his hands would have ached had they not been numb with cold. His breath came in gasps and he prayed he hadn't cracked a rib. Sick with shame, he couldn't help thinking at least he hadn't been the one pulled overboard. The unlucky Matta could be here right now, while Early slid beneath the keel of the tossing greatship.

The ship tilted more precipitously in the wake of the great wave. Early and the captain scrambled up to the poop deck atop the captain's cabin, dragging themselves along the rail as much as climbing the steep stairway. Early struggled to keep his feet against the pain in his side and a sudden wave of seasickness. It felt like his body was giving up on him, and he clung desperately to the hope the aft launch, reserved for the captain and the most important passengers, still remained. They struggled to the rearmost rail of the deck, where winches held the small boat in place, and looked down the stern wall of the ship.

The launch was gone.

"They must have taken him away," the captain muttered, half to herself. Early could barely hear her over the pounding of his own heartbeat. "Lord Mardigan and his Redguard," she explained, turning to him. "They must have escaped. Let's hope."

Early nodded. There might have been a world in which the news of the lord's escape and survival pleased him, but at the moment he couldn't imagine it. All he could think was, *There's nothing left for us to do but drown.*

The ship tilted again, and they slid along the narrow deck. Only the railing at its front, where the captain would have stood to observe the running of her ship, arrested them. This forward rail created an impromptu platform, but for how long? Early looked ahead, to where only the still-burning mainmast, and the mizzenmast behind it, still stood above the waves. It was only a matter of time.

As he imagined the forward deck, where his quarters had been, now far below the surface, Early was struck by a terrible, treasonous thought: what had happened to Marie Gold? The ship's brig was beneath the deckhands' quarters, and she'd been locked in the cell... if he'd been in less dire straits himself, the thought of Marie helpless in a cage of wood and iron as the sea rushed in to claim her would have made him panic. As it was, there was only another pang, this one of sadness, as he considered that the brave and beautiful pirate had met a kind of Imperial justice in spite of all her cunning.

The captain put her hand on his shoulder. Early jerked in surprise and shut his mouth, embarrassed by his thoughts. Captain Mestrum was now sitting with the deck at her back, boots against the forward rail, and she'd taken off her hat and set it in her lap. It was strange to see her adopt such a casual posture, like she was just another deckhand.

"Captain?"

She had closed her eyes, and opened them at the sound of Early's voice. She smiled at him.

"Thank you for your service, Wills. You've been a brave sailor." At the resignation in her voice, Early found his throat constricting. The desperation of their circumstances was over-whelming him. His skin crawled with the thought of suddenly feeling the waves lick at his boots when their makeshift plat-form joined the rest of the ship beneath...

"Is there nothing we can do, Captain?" His mouth was so dry, Early wondered if he'd actually made a sound. The captain was scanning the water, squinting into the dark, and it seemed she hadn't heard him. But then she grabbed his shoulder and pointed to starboard.

"See! Something floating. What's that over there?" In his despair, Early had forgotten the world beyond the ship, but now he followed the line of the captain's arm and saw some-thing, dark on dark, bobbing on the waves nearby. Early craned his neck to look, and made out a shattered piece of the main deck, boards which had broken apart but become tangled in a scrap of sail and rigging. It seemed impossible to Early that a storm could reduce a greatship to a pile of wood so rapidly, yet there was the evidence, before his eyes.

He flashed back to the midst of the storm: the terrible force of the wind and water, the *thing* in the sky that seemed to spit lightning and set the whole ship ablaze—had he really seen that? The deck canting wildly underneath him and his crewmates... Early realized he was biting his tongue so hard it hurt, and the captain was shaking him, demanding his attention.

"Early. Early! You need to swim out to that bundle! It's a slim chance, perhaps one in a hundred, but to stay with the *Pride* is surely to drown."

He looked at her, searching her face. Her expression was tired, strained, but her eyes were as stolid as ever.

"Aye, Captain," Early said without thinking. It was easier to obey her orders like a trained sailor than to think about what she actually wanted him to do. "I'll bring it back here, and we can both—" but the captain was shaking her head. She didn't mean to join him. Was she injured? She didn't appear to be.

Captain Mestrum reached into the collar of her uniform blouse and pulled forth a black leather thong. She pulled it up over her head, untangling it from her hair. At the end of the cord was a charm or locket of some kind, gleaming dull gold in the light of the burning mast. She pressed the locket into Early's hand.

"A Guard-Captain cannot abandon her ship, deckhand. My last order to you as a crewman of the *Pride of the Empress* is this: get yourself onto that raft and get *away* from our wake as quick as you can. I don't know how you'll survive, but... you will find a way, deckhand. Is that clear?"

Early's eyes were wide, and his lips moved soundlessly for a moment with the urge to protest. But there was nothing he could say to change the captain's mind. She had given her life to the Imperial Guard, and this was the course her honor demanded. He squeezed the locket, felt the edges dig into his palm. She closed both her hands around his, and pressed them towards him, urging the locket into Early's care.

"And I have a final request, which I cannot presume to make an order."

Early tried to say, "Of course, anything," but his voice broke. His eyes welled up, and he fought to clear them.

"My family, back in Ten Hills. If you... should you ever see Imperial shores again, please find them and give this to them. With my love."

Early gaped for a moment, then shut his mouth and nodded. He took a deep breath and lowered the thong around his head, tucking the locket safely in the collar of his shirt. Captain Mestrum ran a hand through her hair, trying to smooth it down with minimal success, and then replaced her hat upon her head. She rose unsteadily to her feet, walking her hands up the slanted wall of the deck behind them, a captain whose ship was slipping out from under her feet.

"Thank you, Early. Good luck. May the Empress watch over you." It was clearly a dismissal—time was running short, and she meant for him to escape with his life if he could. He looked at her a moment longer, and then gave his best Blueguard salute, right fist against left breast. She didn't look at him, her eyes fixed on the sea, but he saw her nod and even turn her mouth in a small, grim smile. Then Early looked down at the sea waiting just below them. The water was black, glittering orange as it reflected the light of the fire. It looked evil and cold. He dove into it.

There was a moment of total panic as he was sure the sinking ship would drag him down... then his head breached the surface. The floating shards were yards away that seemed like leagues, but, tapping the front of his shirt to make sure the captain's locket was still in place, he swam for them as hard as he could. He didn't dare look back, knowing he would see

Guard-Captain Mestrum holding herself tall and proud in the remnants of the sinking ship, awaiting the end. Early's eyes filled with tears as the first wave lifted him. He didn't bother blinking them away; with the sea full in his face, he'd only be trading one kind of salt water for another.

Stroke after stroke, Early dragged his body, weighed down by his sodden clothing, through the waves. He tried to think of his goal, the raft, and only that—the endless depth of the sea, easy to ignore on the deck of a greatship, seemed hideous now there was nothing separating him from it. Even having the floating debris underneath him would feel more secure. Early considered how irrational this was as he swam, keeping his mind off how the raft didn't seem to be getting closer, and the pernicious fear that the cold black arms of sea monsters were about to grab him from below.

Then he swung his left arm forward and felt a rope in his hand. He grasped it, pulled, and was overjoyed by the simple feeling of resistance. Early raised his head, spat out water, and blinked his eyes. He'd reached the web of rigging holding together the broken boards, and dragged himself up on the sturdiest piece he could find. Early pressed his cheek gratefully to the wet, buoyant wood and let it carry him away into the dark.

When the *Pride* was gone, its fires extinguished, there was only the sea's killing cold. Soaked and freezing, Early clung to his raft of flotsam and tried to get his bearings, but every time he lifted his head he was rewarded by a mouthful of seawater. Even as the storm passed growling away, as though its mission were accomplished, the sea bobbed like an angry crowd, jostling Early and his makeshift raft. He couldn't even call it a raft; he'd have given anything to be able to pull himself on top of the broken planks, if only to keep his head above water, but the wood wouldn't hold his weight, and it was all he could do to hang on and pedal his legs away from the sinking hulk that had been the *Pride of the Empress.*

Bits of the masts and sails were bobbing to the surface, along with pieces of the hull lifted by trapped pockets of air. Some of these burned on stubbornly, in defiance of the chill water. There was a bad moment when a flaming spar emerged right in front of Early, part of the sail still attached, like deadly wings bearing down on him... but it turned and sank again, fizzling like a candle. Still, Early kicked as hard as he could to get away from the wreck. Beyond that, he had no idea where to go. His mind held room only for *"escape"* and *"survive."*

His mind's eye kept returning to Captain Mestrum, imagining her standing in what was left of her ship, like a sentinel who hadn't been told the war was over. He wept, imagining the water rising around her boots, her white breeches, the ornate scabbard of her useless sword. *How can one embrace death like that?* Early wondered, and his shivering was not entirely because of the cold and wet.

He was getting beyond the ring of wreckage from the *Pride* when he heard cries ahead in the dark. He strained to see anything in what little moonlight filtered through the remnants of the storm, but as he drifted closer he could make out another mass of flotsam, and, bobbing in the water among the bits and pieces, human figures!

Early's heart leaped as he saw, among this second mass of wreckage, one of the *Pride's* small boats was intact. He shouted a greeting and heard an answering cry from the boat. Early paddled towards it, bumping debris aside, hoping only to find another living person—not daring to hope it was anybody in particular.

The waves lifted Early, and suddenly he was careening towards the launch. Someone in the boat yelled a warning and Early tried to twist his body out of the way. His flimsy raft crashed against the small boat, and Early was jarred loose. He had a moment of frantic splashing, grasped the slippery wood of the planks again, then lost them. He tried to call out to the other survivor for help, but choked on seawater. He couldn't see and grew desperate as he floundered in the trough of another wave, imagining monstrous shapes rising in the dark water beneath him, drawn by his thrashing. Mere sharks would be bad enough, but he pictured the horrible creatures from his dreams, eager to pull him down to abide with them in the depths.

Then hands grasped his shoulders. Early reached out, found a muscled arm, and clung with both hands as he was hoisted into the boat. He coughed up seawater for a long minute while the man said, "Easy, now. Easy," in a tone so soothing and calm it seemed unreal in the midst of all this disaster. Early wondered if he was slipping into the last delusions of drowning, but at last his lungs and head cleared enough to realize he was truly safe, and he sputtered his thanks.

The man who'd pulled him out of the water was wrapped in a heavy cloak. Though Early couldn't make out its color in the dark, he recognized the shape, and the gleam of moonlight off the buckles of leather armor underneath told him at least one of the Greenguard rangers had survived. The ranger had the hood of his cloak thrown back and in the dark his face was all angular shadows. He looked old and weary, though perhaps Early was seeing what he himself felt; his own youthful energy was long gone, and he wanted only to sleep in a warm dry place—for the next year, if possible.

There were others in the boat. Early couldn't make out their faces, and they seemed as exhausted as he, unwilling to make any great show of greeting a fellow survivor. *A last survivor,* Early thought, looking at the rough sea around the little boat. He saw nothing else in the dark, and there were no other cries for them to answer. Then, two of the others in the boat spoke, and one voice was familiar.

"Here's a torch. Can you light it?" A woman's voice.

"What would be the purpose? Naught to see but water..."

"I would know if our new friend is wounded."

The other voice grumbled to itself, and Early heard fumbling and cursing. The ranger reclining beside him said, "You'll have better luck with my fire-making kit, let me look for it," but Early was already smiling in recognition and shuffling towards the grumbling voice. In the dark, he reached out and poked a big arm.

"Olan! You Gods-Lucky wretch, don't you remember how to light a torch?"

Early couldn't see Olan's face, but enjoyed imagining his shocked expression. "Master Wills!" The big deckhand clapped an arm around him. "You've decided not to drown, then?"

The reuniting of two friends amidst the utter destruction of the expedition was enough to rouse the survivors, and, once Olan had managed the torch, they introduced themselves to each other. The ranger was Isaac Vere, of the Imperial Green-guard, though he gave his formal title without much enthusiasm. Lia, the Imperial Cartographer, was there—it was she who'd asked Olan to light the torch. Early blushed at the thought of her concern being aimed at him, even though she hadn't known who he was when she'd voiced it. Just the idea of the beautiful noblewoman thinking about him, even in the abstract, made Early's ears hot.

Alongside Lia was her assistant, a girl named Rowene who, despite looking haggard and half-drowned, fussed about her mistress protectively. Last, working the oars of the launch, was a Blueguard lieutenant who introduced himself as Mosul Miago. He was a stout veteran of the Guard despite not being much older than Early and had a fresh scar on his cheek where a pirate had slashed him during the boarding of *Black Spirit*.

"As long as we're safe from the wreck, we should wait here till morning," Isaac said to Mosul, once greetings were done and they'd retrieved a few choice pieces of Early's raft. "See if there's anything else to be salvaged once daylight comes." It struck Early that the ranger didn't say "anyone." Despite the joy of finding he wasn't the lone survivor, his heart sank at the thought that, of the many dozens of the *Pride's* crew, only a scant six of them were left. Caught somewhere between excitement and despair, Early tried to let his mind grow still as he huddled close to the others and wished for sleep.

Early woke to a gray sky and choppy sea, realizing he must have dropped off to sleep at last. His whole body now ached, and he was so thirsty he could scarcely remember what it felt like to have fresh, cool water slide down his throat. The sea may have tempted him, but every sailor knew that, should he drink even a handful, his death would not be far away. The others rocked back and forth alongside him with the monotonous movement of the boat over the rolling waves. The boat was crowded with the six survivors, but at least they weren't sinking. The tiny launch that was the only remainder of the Imperial expedition remained seaworthy.

They spent hours that first day paddling around the field of detritus where the *Pride* had broken up, searching in vain for any other survivors—or provisions they could pull aboard the boat. As they rowed away at last, Olan's broad strokes taking them east in the same direction the *Pride* had been sailing, they saw the sleek silver fins of sharks exploring the wreckage of their ship. Early shuddered at the sight and thought it merciful no others had survived in the water.

After that, they took turns at the oars. Olan and Mosul had strength and years of practice, but even Lia, member of the

Court though she was, insisted on her turn and surprised them with her endurance. They knew they could never make it back to Imperial shores, not with their scant food and water, so their only hope lay in being near enough to the hypothetical land claimed by Marie Gold.

If that land existed, Early realized, their predecessors might be waiting for them there, assuming the first expedition hadn't been lost in a storm just like the one that sank the *Pride*. Every patch of clouds was a welcome respite from the glare of the sun, but Early eyed each suspiciously, his imagination filling their dark flanks with menace. Did something huge, ancient, and hateful wait in those vapors, hungry to finish off the survivors?

The truth was, if they didn't find land straight away, no storm would be required to finish them off. Though the Blueguard Mosul had managed to bring a heavy waterskin when he'd launched the boat, the paltry rations they'd salvaged would last only a few days. Without food to keep up their strength, they'd soon be unable to row and at the mercy of the tides.

The nights were bad. Chilled and cramped and scared, Early slept in fits and starts, and the darkness dragged on interminably. Olan snored for a good portion of each night and Early thought spitefully that at least one of them was managing to get some sleep. He spent much of the night restraining himself from kicking his friend—both to jostle the big deckhand into silence, and because Olan deserved it.

In a way, Early's insomnia did have an important purpose: to keep a lookout. He had a sardonic fantasy of land appearing on the horizon only to have them all float past it fast asleep, until their salvation vanished behind them and they were once again hopelessly lost on the endless sea.

Days and nights passed that same way, until all six of them were exhausted and barely able to hold up their heads to look around. There was enough gentle rainfall to keep them from dying of thirst, but hunger was overtaking them. Too tired to converse, each of the survivors brooded over their own dark thoughts. Early spent the time imagining the sight of land. First, he would see a darkness at the horizon, a break in the monotonous lapping of water, a shape swelling in his vision until it became clear that deliverance was at hand; green hills and the promise of soft warm earth under their feet.

Then the happy vision would dissolve, and he'd remember he was lost on the open sea, hungry, shivering, and miserable. Early was not accustomed to sleeping out-of-doors—even his parents' modest fishing boat had a cabin in which to weather long excursions—but now he would have traded even his clothing for a night spent sleeping on solid ground instead of the rolling waves.

As color started to leak back into the sky one morning, Early rubbed his eyes. Surely he could not be seeing the very thing he had just been imagining: a dark line at the horizon's rim, darker than the waves. As the sun began to paint the undersides of the clouds, the far-off waves flashed and dazzled. But the shape on the horizon reflected no sunlight—it couldn't be water. Early shook Isaac by the shoulder. Though dozing, the ranger woke immediately and turned his battered head towards Early, dark intense eyes searching the deckhand's face. Early tried to ask if Isaac also saw the dark line wavering at the edge of vision, but his throat was too dry to speak and his lips could scarcely remember how to form words.

Early nodded towards the horizon, alarmed that he was too weak to raise an arm and point. Isaac gazed at him quizzically, and Early could almost see the ranger's sluggish brain trying to process the meaning of his gesture. At last Isaac looked past Early and squinted at the horizon for a long minute. Then he stiffened, grasping Early's arm so tightly it was almost painful.

Only a cough emerged when Isaac opened his cracked lips, but then he whispered, clearly, "Land."

Energized by the word and what it implied, Early found the strength to force himself up onto his elbows, straining to make out any feature of what loomed up before them. But the dark, hazy blur on the horizon remained just that. Behind him, Early heard Isaac rousing the others, and a groaning complaint that could only be Olan objecting to being shaken from his heavy slumber.

There was a murmur that grew to a tumult on the raft, as the survivors realized, one by one, that the sea had led them somewhere. Lia shouted with joy, and Mosul clapped Early on the shoulder as he passed the waterskin. For the first time in the interminable days since the storm, Early smiled. He and his friends were frozen and starving, but they were alive. As the dawn broke over the Sunfire Sea, hope rekindled in the young deckhand's heart.

4

A tower of clouds massed over the island. With the early morning sun behind their bulk, the shore was gray. Early and the others were curled up on the rough planks of their little boat. Bodies nearly frozen and minds blank with exhaustion, they let the tide carry them onto the welcoming beach. Early rested his chin against the boat's topwale and stared at the land as they approached. The pinnacles of rock Marie Gold claimed to have seen were not in evidence; either the pirate captain had seen some *other* island in the depths of the sea, or she'd lied to save her life. Here, the sand banked gently out of the water for what looked like thirty yards of beach, an easy landing. The beach ended in a low, steep wall of rock, a ridge topped by rushes and other bushy plants, beyond which a great forest of strange trees reared. The forest climbed the slope of a vast hill until in the distance a rocky pinnacle, like a bald head, crowned the island.

A forest, Early knew, meant food and shelter, though the task of acquiring those things seemed impossible as he shivered in the launch. The first thing he and his mates needed was some way to become dry and warm, lest they escape fire and drowning only to die of exposure.

The boat rocked side to side on the breaking tide, slid onto the sand with a smooth hiss, and ground to a halt. Early knew he should scramble off immediately, wanted to kiss the ground and thank the gods he'd survived, but the will to move was simply not there. Olan provided it. The big deckhand muttered, "C'mon, mate. Last stop on the Sunfire ferry service, all passengers debark wherever the Dead Gods this is." He rolled Early over the side and let him sprawl on the sand, climbing out after him. Isaac the ranger leaped over the side and held the boat steady, while Mosul helped Lia and Rowene, both dressed in heavy woolen gowns, to step out of the boat with dignity intact.

As soon as they were on the sand, Rowene started to gather the fringes of Lia's gown, dismayed at the dirt. The cartographer gently brushed her assistant away, and—to Rowene's horror—dropped to her knees on the sand, saying a prayer of thanks. Next to her, Isaac took a bundle carefully wrapped in green oilcloth from his back and set it gently on the ground, then raised his arms above his head and stretched with a quiet groan. The survivors looked up and down the beach as each slowly shook themselves and realized that, yes, they really were safe on dry land. But the ranger's eyes stayed on the line of towering trees, and he began wandering down the beach, clearly wishing to explore.

Early stood, arms crossed and shivering. Olan was next to him, rubbing his hands together, and looking at the sea whence they'd come with a contemplative expression.

"Reckon we'll find food in the woods?" Early asked, hoping conversation would generate some warmth.

"Let's hope. We need a fire first, though. Greenguard!" Olan called down the beach. "Did you say you had a tinderbox, or was that just a dream I had at sea?"

"This whole trip feels like a miserable dream," Early muttered.

Isaac approached, bringing his green bundle.

"I have what we need for a fire. You should quit loafing and get on with collecting brush, though," he said, nodding towards the forest.

Olan scoffed. "Loafing! I'm bloody well freezing and starving, aren't you? Why don't we just burn the bloody boat? That'll warm us up."

"Its boards are soaked with seawater," Isaac retorted. "And the boat's too valuable a thing to burn."

"Planning to row back to the High City, are you? Be my guest." Olan crossed his big arms, a smug look on his face.

"We can use it to explore the shoreline," the ranger said patiently. "And hopefully do some fishing. Now, for the fire, we'll need twigs and brush, then many small branches, then a few larger."

Olan huffed through his nose and narrowed his eyes. Early could see his friend's caustic temper was winning even against the exhaustion of their journey.

"Burning the boat was a jest, obviously. And I know how to make a fire, Greenguard. Or do you take your shipmates for fools?"

Isaac cocked his head slightly at the deckhand but didn't reply, his mouth a thin line behind heavy stubble. Though Olan was bigger and younger, Early had no doubt the ranger would take him easily in a fight. And it seemed like Olan was itching to start one.

Early stepped between them, anxious to defuse the tension. They were all alive, for the Lost Gods' sake, and these two wanted to argue about firewood? He pointed at Isaac's bundle.

"You have flint and firesteel in there? It's good you saved it."

The ranger nodded, his expression relaxing. "It's good,

indeed. I have a tinderbox and other useful tools in here, besides. But that's the least of it..." With a long-practised motion, the ranger stooped and put the bundle on the ground as delicately as if it were an infant. There was a tarnished steel clasp in the center, where two ends of the green-dyed oilcloth came together. The clasp was about as broad as Early's palm, and depicted the Greenguard emblem within a steel circle: the mighty Allevalen tree, symbol of the Imperial Interior, crossed with arrows, hatchet, and sword.

Isaac unfastened the clasp and spread the oilcloth open to reveal his bow. Early had never seen such a weapon up close and was struck by its complexity. Segments of laminated wood gleamed, polished by a loving hand, and the strips of horn and sinew that gave the bow its tension were bound so expertly he could hardly tell where one piece ended and the next began. Beneath the bow lay a long quiver of feathered shafts, a battered tinderbox, and a leather pouch that held Isaac's tools.

He touched the bow with obvious reverence and looked up at the deckhands, smiling.

"What good is a cookfire with nothing for dinner?"

Their meal that day was perhaps the plainest but most satisfying Early had ever eaten. Isaac spent an hour in the woods and managed to shoot two small hares and three plump ground birds with prominent neck fringes, not unlike the three-ringed pheasants of the Interior. The catch made a paltry meal for six exhausted people, but it was a start, and there was fresh water from a burbling stream that emerged from the woods a quarter mile from their landing.

The survivors of Her Majesty's expedition might be stranded, Isaac had reassured them, but at least they wouldn't starve. That was cold comfort once night fell, though, and Early was shivering in his tent. *If you can call this a tent,* he thought, who hadn't done a lot of camping in his life. He wasn't convinced.

Only slightly revitalized by food, they'd spent their first day doing what tasks their bodies would allow. Isaac had them carry buckets of sand up from the beach onto the low ridgeline, reckoning that, while the ridge had more protection from wind and tide than the beach, sand would be softer and more comfortable than dirt and scrub grass. The ranger had taken them into the forest and shown them how to identify suitable branches, and Olan, Early, and the rest of them had taken turns with his one small hatchet until they'd gathered a fair pile. Next was a matter of using the long rushes that grew in clumps along the stream, braiding them together into cord, and tying the branches into triangular frames. They lashed the oddments of sail salvaged from Early's raft across the frames to keep out the wind. The result wasn't much of a dwelling, but Early spent the day amazed at Isaac as the ranger directed them without hesitation. Early had long idolized the Blueguard sailors, but the ability of the Greenguard to wash up on the shore of a faraway land and produce food and shelter from naught but the contents of his oilcloth pack was truly admirable.

Impressed though he was, the day left Early utterly drained, and the tent was not all it was cut out to be. Its walls came unfastened more than once in the night, and Early startled awake at the snap of canvas and the cold rush of wind. He or Olan, whoever rose grumbling from their sleeping bundle first, had to feel their way around the sail and fasten it down again in the dark. Early was tempted to take the renegade bolt of cloth, carry it into the woods, and simply roll himself up in it to escape the relentless sea-borne wind.

The empty grain sacks Mosul had thoughtfully crammed into the launch made a warm enough blanket, but even so, Early struggled to sleep. Shoddy tent aside, his imagination spent the night torturing him; it turned the unfamiliar birdcalls into the cries of lurking monsters, and, when that was no longer disturbance enough, reminded Early of his own soft bed in his parents' home, warm and fragrant from the hearthfire. That hearth was now unthinkable leagues away, across a sea they had no ship to navigate, and which, in all likelihood, Early would never see again.

Never was a hard concept for one as young as Early to stomach. How long would "never" be? Was he to live out the rest of his life on this shore? He wondered in what sort of place fate had left them—he did not yet know even the shape of the land where they'd been marooned. Was it an island, as it appeared from the sea? Or could it be the headland of a far-flung continent with its own strange cities and empires? What would Early's life be like here? Such thoughts seemed a luxury when it wasn't clear to Early, shivering in his sleeping wrap, how they'd live through the next month.

Dreams meshed into waking and into dreams again, and Early found himself walking on the beach with Lia, both of them starving, muddy, dressed in rags, the surf washing their bare, spindly legs as they struggled along, holding onto one another not out of desire or intimacy but from sheer exhaustion. Early stirred awake in the pitch black of the tent, hearing the canvas ripple in the wind. He smiled sardonically at himself; the peril of their situation had his mind twisting even romantic fantasies into horror.

After that, he lay awake listening to Olan snore and resenting—not for the first time—his friend's ability to sleep through anything. Early wished for the dawn, so the others would wake and distract him from the endless cycle of morbid thoughts. He was growing desperate to do something, anything, to relieve the tension: make a fire, have a fistfight, run screaming into the woods. *At least,* he thought, resigning himself to a sleepless night, *I bet the sunrise over the forest is beautiful.*

But Early needn't have worried. After the torturous days at sea, and a hard day's labor on little food, not even his persever-ating mind could maintain its agitation. Early's exhausted body finally obliged him, and he slept quite happily through his first dawn in this new world.

The first morning, the beach was peaceful. Early woke to the sounds of surf and birdsong from the nearby forest. On the second morning, he was awakened by shouting.

Groggy, Early rose and tripped on his sleeping wrap, slipped his trousers on—backwards, the first time—and grabbed the little pocketknife he'd managed to bring from the *Pride*. Olan, the heavier sleeper, rolled and grumbled, tugging a sack closer around his head. Early shook him awake with his foot, then poked his head out of the tent flap. It was not quite dawn, and at first glance the camp appeared to be on fire. At second glance, the cookfire was burning in the pit as usual, but there was commotion beyond it.

Isaac and Mosul were running down the beach, away from the camp. Lia and Rowene stood by the fire, calling after them. Early couldn't make out the words. He emerged cautiously from the tent and moved to follow them, calling back to Olan.

"Wake up, Master Mender! Let's see what's up!"

"Too early," his friend protested. "Leemee 'lone."

"Get your bloody trousers on, swabby!" Early snapped back at the tent, in his best impression of the late Deckmaster Matta. "Something's afoot out here!"

As Olan cursed and clattered about the tent behind him, Early looked up and down the beach and glanced into the looming shadows of the forest. What threat had roused the Guards? Wild beasts? Anything could live in those woods— they'd only been encamped for two days, and had little time to explore their surroundings, as much as Isaac insisted they must.

It was early enough for the full moon to still shine in the clear sky, illuminating in silvery light the beach and the waves beating endlessly on the shore. Isaac and Mosul were featureless black blobs beyond the light of the cookfire, but at least Early could see where he was going.

Olan, awake at last, had the presence of mind to find a torch, and his long legs let him catch up with Early easily. As they approached the commotion in the surf, Early saw Isaac and Mosul with the silhouettes of others, pulling something in from the water—a boat! It was distinctly the prow of a launch, just like the one they'd arrived in, and the person they were helping out onto the sand was none other than Lord Cyrus Mardigan, the Empress's cousin, leader of the expedition. Surreal to see him wearing his fine robes, stained and waterlogged as they were, standing on the shore in the flickering torchlight.

Early felt a curious pang at the sight of him. As much as he admired the proud decorum of the Imperial Court, and the bravery of Her Majesty's Guard, there had been something freeing as well as frightening in their loss. He'd spent the last two days coming to terms with the old structures being gone, how it was now just the few of them, as equals, trying to survive. A new life in a new world, cut off from the Decadin Empire. Seeing Lord Mardigan reminded him of home, and the memory was more bittersweet than he'd expected. The lord's return meant the return of rules and an order to things not dictated by the requirements of survival alone. Early couldn't quite put his finger on it, but it felt as though something new and exciting, gained over the past few days, had just disappeared.

But as he and Olan joined the others around the boat, something did excite him: the sight of Redguard colors on the shoulders and chests of the four who'd pushed the boat in from the shallows. Though the worse for wear from their time at sea, the Redguard were apparently not as devastated by hunger and thirst as Early and his mates had been on their arrival. Sparing only a civil nod for his former shipmates, miraculously still alive, the Redguard captain stepped forward to help straighten his lord's disheveled robes and curtly order Olan to fetch something to warm him. Olan turned at once and ran past Early back to the camp, though Early heard him muttering under his breath. Lord Mardigan, for his part, pushed the captain's hands away, chiding him for making a fuss.

"Please, Morave! I'll keep for the moment. We must express our joy at seeing our crewmates still alive. Well met, Greenguard! Well met, all of you." Lord Mardigan took each of their hands in turn, including Early's, and when Early met the lord's eyes they were warm and abiding in spite of the ordeal; he seemed truly pleased that each of them had made it ashore. When Olan returned with a makeshift blanket, he clasped the big deckhand's arms and thanked him profusely. Guard-Captain Morave Antmar, meanwhile, scowled at the crudely stitched-together sacks as he wrapped them around his lord's shoulders.

"Do you know of any others, my lord?" Blueguard Mosul asked. "Any others that may have survived the wreck?"

Lord Mardigan shook his head gravely. "We know the fate of no other launches, though I recall four upon the *Pride*. When the masts caught fire, Guard-Captain Mestrum ordered my Redguards to get me away from the ship. The Gods' Luck was with us: the boat was neither struck nor swamped. We drifted —I know not for how long—and then we sighted this... this place. It grieves me that, in our haste, we brought no one else away with us."

They were walking back up the beach to the cookfire, and, when Lord Mardigan saw Lia waving to them, he shouted for joy.

"Lady Dracis! And your handmaiden—this is a relief indeed. And how many others made it here? Could the Guard-Captain herself be with you?"

Antmar and Mosul, walking at the lord's side, glanced at each other darkly. Imperial Guards knew the captain would never have abandoned her ship. Early's stomach fell as he remembered Captain Mestrum's last words, and he touched the locket on its cord beneath his shirt.

"My Lord," the Redguard Antmar said, so quietly that Early, a few paces behind, scarcely heard him, "the Guard-Captain went down with her ship, as her duty required." The lord, seating himself on a log by the cookfire, looked horrified for a moment before he regained his composure.

"Of—of course," he said, gesturing that Lia and Rowene should sit beside him. Early and the others, including the three other Redguard, each brought a heavy parcel from the lord's launch: the scant supplies they'd managed to bring in their escape.

Lia reached out and put a hand gently on the lord's knee. "There are only six of us, my Lord," she said. "Myself and Rowene, Greenguard Isaac and Blueguard Mosul, and our brave sailors, Olan and Early." She smiled at them as she named them —last but not least, said her face—and Early blushed in spite of himself. He hoped the heat on his face was hidden by the firelight.

Isaac, inspecting the supplies, grew thoughtful. He stared out at the sea, lost in thought. The ranger's grim, detached expression reminded Early of how much they'd lost, and it occurred to him the sturdy launch meant for the Empress's cousin and his Redguard could easily have saved twice their number, duty be damned. But if Isaac shared this treasonous thought, he kept it to himself.

"I dare to imagine," the Greenguard said at last, "there could still be others as lucky as we. After all, what of the other two launches?" He rubbed the thick stubble on his chin, considering, and scanned the heap of supplies. "Did one of you bring the Imperial pennant?"

One of the Redguard was unwrapping the parcels, and she produced from among them a long, narrow bundle of white and red fabric wound around a staff of roughly her own considerable height. She lifted it as Isaac scanned the ridge and pointed at a spot nearby, where the rock swelled up into a bare pinnacle perhaps five yards above the beach.

"We can fly the pennant from there! If any other survivors come across this island, they'll know we're here to greet them."

Early's heart leaped at the thought of others, tired and dehydrated just as he'd been, seeing the proud standard of the Decadin Empire calling them to safety. He stepped forward, wanting to help, yet found his tongue tied in a knot as Isaac and the Redguard turned to him with questioning eyes.

"I... Um, that is..." He felt suddenly foolish standing next to these two, the Empire's bravest warriors. What could he hope to contribute? If not for the likes of Isaac and the tall, dark-complexioned Redguard—who, despite having just spent days on the open sea, looked ready to fortify their camp and hunt down the day's provisions singlehandedly—Early would stand no chance at survival. Perhaps it was best if he remembered his place—a lowly deckhand—and let his betters take care of things. But Isaac's mouth turned up in a subtle smile, and he took the bundled pennant from the Redguard and hoisted it upon his shoulder.

Isaac turned to the swordswoman. "Redguard...?"

"Taliss," she answered, inclining her head.

"Redguard Taliss, allow me and Early to deal with the pennant. Your duty lies with Lord Mardigan, after all."

She blinked and then shrugged, not quite managing a smile. "Thank you, Greenguard. You say quite true." She gave Isaac a sharp, formal salute, right fist to left breast, nodded to Early, and joined the other three Redguard clustered around their lord as he spoke merrily with Lia and the others. Isaac strolled towards his chosen outcropping, and Early hurried after him.

"Come along, Early," the ranger said. "The Redguard are far too stoic to complain, but they're not used to menial chores." He turned to the deckhand with a conspiratorial smile. "They leave those to the peasants, like you and me. The sun will soon be up, and there's hope yet that more of our crewmates survived. Let's be sure they have a proper welcome."

Early gave his eager assent. He decided then that if he was to be indentured to the Imperial Guard, he'd take being a ranger's assistant over swabbing the decks any day.

Time passed slowly for the survivors. In the week they'd been ashore, Early had volunteered to accompany Isaac on three excursions into the forest—the ranger was interesting company, and Early hadn't found much else to do, besides. Today, on their fourth trip, Lia and Rowene joined them. Their goal was familiarity with the heavily wooded land around their beachfront camp, and the cartographer had been spending her time on a series of increasingly detailed maps of the beach and rocky ridgeline; now she wanted to document the forest.

She'd saved vellum and charcoal from the sea in a waterproof packet like Isaac's, and had wasted no time recording every aspect of their life here. Early watched Lia capture each new plant, bird, and animal they encountered in astonishing detail, marveling at the elegance and subtle precision of her charcoal strokes—it was all Early could do to legibly render his own name. Rowene, meanwhile, the faithful young assistant, was ever at Lia's elbow, ready to provide a new stick of charcoal, or to patiently hold up a leaf as her mistress reproduced every fragile detail.

As for Early, he was becoming a faithful young assistant himself—though it was less that Isaac asked him along on his exploratory trips into the woods, and more that Early followed the ranger and insisted on making himself useful. Isaac indulged his young shadow with a knowing grin. It was obvious Early looked up to the resourceful Greenguard, not merely because Isaac took their dangerous circumstances in stride, but because he was one of the few Imperial Guard left. Blueguard Mosul was little older than Early, and nearly as bewildered. The Redguard were aloof and hopelessly intimidating, with their watchful stares and constant sword-fighting drills. That left Isaac to be Early's guiding light.

Now, after a morning's steady trek through the woods, Isaac motioned for them to stop. Only Lia saw the gesture, though; Rowene bumped into her mistress, and Early bumped into Rowene, so engrossed were the two younger survivors in the surrounding forest. The trees were so strange. The trunks were dark, almost black, and their bark was much rougher than the trees of the Imperial Interior. Mottled with knots and swirls and deep mossy ridges, they looked like nothing so much as the skin of an ancient person. The branches tangled around each other and clawed for the sky, and their leaves were sparse, fuzzy-looking, a pale greenish-yellow. All in all, the trees made Early uneasy, especially as they grew close together not far into the forest, making it shockingly dark only a few hundred yards away from the sunlit beach.

But what really captured Early's and Rowene's attention was not the strange trees but the birdsong playing in their boughs. Whatever was calling out to its fellows from the trees had a strange cry, high and desperate-sounding, as though the birds were warning each other about the end of the world. The way the calls announced the progress of Early and his friends reminded him of the corvixes back home, the handsome and pervasive black-feathered creatures who seemed to watch and report to each other the comings and goings of the Empire (at least that's what Early had entertained himself since childhood by imagining). The cries of these new birds were different and strange enough to make the woods feel even more alien than they looked.

As Rowene smoothed the rumples caused by Early blundering into her, fixing the apologetic deckhand with a glare, Lia scanned the woods carefully and touched Isaac's shoulder.

"Why did we stop?" The cartographer asked.

Isaac nodded at the wall of foliage before them. "I think I see something through there. Something strange."

The ranger had halted them where the path narrowed into a thicket of dark, brambly bushes tall as their heads. Early stepped up beside them and caught a glimpse of blue beyond the tangled vegetation. Water? Had they come back around through the woods to a different part of the shore?

"Early, the hatchets," Isaac said, tugging the small axe from his belt. "Let's make a hole."

Early took up his own hatchet, found in the supplies Lord Mardigan brought with him, and he and Isaac attacked the stubborn hedge. It was slow going, the hatchets biting into the thick bark again and again before the branches split apart and could be cleared away. To speed things up, the four arranged themselves so Rowene and Lia could duck in and pull the dismembered brambles away when Early or Isaac cut something loose. So it was Lia who, pulling an elaborately twisted branch out of the way, first glimpsed the incongruous curve of the greatship's hull through the hole. She cried out.

"The ship!"

"What?" Isaac squeezed in around her, and Early struggled to see past them. "Lost Gods, so it is!" The ranger was laughing.

When Early finally got a chance to see, he couldn't believe his eyes: they were looking down from a cliff towards a part of the beach that must have lain around a bend in the coast, for there was no sign of their camp and the terrain was unfamiliar. He could hear the surf crashing against a rockier shore than where they'd come aground, and upon that shore was the vast shattered wreck of a ship's hull. The blackened and weathered boards still held the shape of the greatship's prow, and the figurehead was unmistakable—the robed seraphic figure of the Empress, crowned in a tenfold crown that represented the ten tribes of the Decadin Empire.

The hull lay at an impossible angle, for the entire midship and stern were gone. The remnant of *Pride of the Empress* had been marooned with what was left of her crew, as though the gods—or the fabled Elder of Storms—wished to tell the survivors what they thought of mortal pride.

It took two hours for Isaac to find them a path through the woods to a section of cliff gentle enough for access to the shore. Once they stood at the wreck, and the ranger was satisfied Early and Lia could retrace their steps, he left with Rowene to report what they'd found. Now Lia was absorbed in her sketching, and Early could only wait and brood.

The once-mighty ship lay with its bowsprit stabbing high in the air. Early stood in its shadow and shivered from the cold wind. The great arc of the bow rose up from the sand, the fore-castle deck tilted almost vertical. Edges of boards hung in ragged splinters. A seabird perched on the broken rail, where the Blueguard crossbows had once fought with pirates, and it watched Early survey the wreckage. The vast body of the great-ship was gone: where the masts, stern, and belly of the ship were, only the fabled *tyrr* might know.

"And how many of my crewmates are those monsters entertaining in their seaweed-draped castles?" Early wondered. He felt grief swelling in his throat and pursed his lips tightly to keep from sobbing, casting an embarrassed glance at Lia. The cartographer was mercifully preoccupied, capturing every detail of the scene except her faltering companion. The tide was low and the rocky beach below the wreck was slippery underfoot. The front of the ship looked otherworldly in its repose, like a hole had opened in the low-lying clouds and it had simply been dropped there on the beach, the discarded toy of giants.

Or dragons.

The wind rose, howling off the sea, and Early cursed in protest. He looked at Lia again, but though her nimble fingers were reddened, she seemed oblivious to the temperature. She was adding to her drawing the seabird, its feathers ruffled by the wind, perched imperiously on the railing high above.

"We'll be a month or more trying to take that apart," Early blurted, needing to break the silence. "Looks like lots of boards still in good shape, though. We'll need the shelter, especially if anyone else drifts in."

"You think many more survived?" Lia asked, not looking up from her work.

Early frowned and looked out to sea. "Hard to say. I... hope so." It seemed an inadequate response.

Early's words hung in silence for long enough he assumed Lia's thoughts had gone elsewhere, but then she replied, "If they're still on the water now, it's the Gods' Luck whether they wash up alive."

"I hope no one else washes up dead!" yelped Early. And added, under his breath, "I couldn't stand it." The day after Lord Mardigan and his Redguard made it to shore, a body washed in, swollen and unrecognizable, only its blue-and-white uniform marking it as an unfortunate member of the

Pride's crew. Early had helped dig a grave in the hard earth of the ridge where they'd flown the Imperial colors, and it had dampened his hopes entirely. After the joy the eleven survivors felt raising their pennant, the drowned sailor's arrival had brought back the stark and terrible extent of their loss.

Now the corpse of the *Pride* itself had washed ashore, and brought the loss back home to Early once again. Rubbing his arms for warmth, he had a grim and absurd vision of them all digging a grave deep enough to bury the hull of the ship, with the figurehead protruding above the sand as a monument. Early shook his head at the dark turn of his thoughts and took a stab at changing the subject. Through no fault of her own, Lia's quiet absorption in her work was getting on his nerves.

"Lady Dracis," he said, "aren't you—aren't you cold?"

At last, she looked up from her sketch. "Lord Wills," she replied with a kind smile, "look where we are. May we abandon ceremony? Please call me Lia, and I'll call you Early. Yes?"

He blushed, was annoyed at himself for it, but at least it distracted him from the wind. Lia was perhaps half a dozen years older than Early, but she seemed to possess a lifetime of sophistication he couldn't hope to match.

"O-of course... Lia. Yes, of course. Please call me Early."

He blinked, stuttered, and realized he was desperate to change the subject yet again. He gestured at the shipwreck. "How do you reckon we'll take that apart?"

Lia glanced at the ship. "I'm no shipwright, but I suppose we'll want axes and prybars, and enough time and sweat will see it done. Is that not so, deckhand?"

She said it kindly, but Early flushed at the obvious answer. His question seemed foolish in retrospect, but witty dialog eluded him. Early felt helpless, like a fish caught in a fisher's net, like the whole world was tilting beneath him. Staring at the wreck, how *wrong* it looked, wasn't helping. He was so overwhelmed by their situation—most of his mates drowned, the rest of them stranded in a strange land—it was all he could do just to stay on his feet. Early resolved to do that much, at least. He turned towards their camp.

"I'm of a mind to head back," he said.

"Almost time for lunch, I suppose?" The cartographer asked. She returned to her sketch to capture a second gull as it joined the one poised on the *Pride*'s railing. The two birds croaked at each other quietly, as though mimicking their conversation.

"I reckon—that is, I suppose so," Early replied. He started towards the path, hoping Lia would follow. He didn't want to leave her alone, but the wreck had become intolerable. He squared his shoulders in determination. "But after lunch, I reckon I'll find an axe and a prybar. Be good to have some work to do, since I see no decks in need of swabbing."

Before Early could make up his mind whether to stay or go, he saw Isaac emerge from the brush on the rocky hillside. The ranger had brought a group of the survivors to see what remained of their ship. Rowene had come back with him, and as they approached, she gave Early a suspicious look, as though she hadn't liked leaving her mistress alone with him. Annoyed, he might have confronted her, but Olan and the Blueguard Mosul came next, and their exclamations took everyone's attention.

"Well, that's a sight for sore eyes," Olan said, clapping his right arm around Early's shoulders while taking in the wreck with a sweep of his left. "*Pride of the Empress*, indeed! Look at her, in all her glory."

He saluted the weathered figurehead. Early would have objected to his friend's irreverence, but the big deckhand gave him a playful shove. "You get that forward deck polished up, swabby, and we can set sail for home!"

"Lost Gods, Olan, you—" Early started to grumble a reply, but Mosul interrupted them.

"Hate to disappoint you, mates, but that isn't the *Pride*," he said.

Early and Olan both stopped and stared at the Blueguard. Lia had tucked her sketchbook under her arm and came to listen. Lord Mardigan himself had followed Isaac to the wreck, accompanied by all four of his Redguard, and the whole group crowded around. Mosul looked at their questioning faces, then back at the ship.

"When the *Pride* sank, the bow went under," he explained. "The weight of water on the decks would press it all the way to the bottom of the sea."

Early imagined the vast forward end of the greatship vanishing into the unknown depths—and the poor pirate captain Marie Gold trapped in the brig, caged like an animal as the water poured in. Something about her predicament horrified Early more than the rest of the greatship's ruin. They had all been at the mercy of the storm and the sea, but being locked up below deck while it happened... The thought made Early sick.

Mosul was still explaining why the wreck in front of them couldn't be their ship. "...and if you look how the boards have weathered—the tar's dried up between the planks. That wreck's lain here a long time.

"It's a Blueguard ship, no doubt of that," he concluded. "But not ours."

Lord Mardigan came forward, clasping Mosul's arm in excitement. "It may be a ship from the first expedition!" he cried. "We must take a look inside and see what proof is left behind."

"Yes, my Lord," Mosul said, with some hesitation. Early noticed how the Blueguard's speech grew more formal in the nobleman's presence. "We must explore the wreck with great care, though, for it's surely unstable."

Olan looked at the waves washing the rocks nearby and snorted. He, for one, was not burdened by formality. "Better have it done before the tide comes in, too. Be easy enough to drown in this little cozy." He pointed, and Early noticed the tell-tale line left on the rocky bank by high tide. The wreck itself lay high enough—and deeply embedded enough in the sand—to avoid being washed back out to sea, but only just. They could easily get stranded inside if their exploration was badly timed.

"Of course," Olan added helpfully, "we've only got the tide to worry about if the bloody wreck doesn't fall on our heads first."

Isaac and Mosul agreed to investigate the wreck then and there while the tide was still out. Early was excited to join them, and Olan—though hardly excited, and grumbling all the while—would not be left behind. As the Redguard quartet escorted Rowene, Lia, and Lord Mardigan back to camp—the lord seemed inclined to poke around the shipwreck himself, but Captain Antmar wouldn't hear of it—the explorers carefully entered the gaping hull.

The tar between the old planks had shrunk or flaked away, leaving gaps that the daylight streamed through in hundreds of narrow shafts. There was enough light to see their way, but the shafts created an eerie effect. The gaps worried Early, too, because they suggested the hull might be none too sturdy. It would be a bad twist of fate indeed if the wreck had waited patiently in the wind and rain for years, only to crash down on the heads of the first people to poke around in it. Feeling the need for luck, Early slipped his hand under his shirt and clutched Captain Mestrum's locket. He felt a bit silly, but none of the others were paying him any attention—they were too busy meeting the greatship's crew.

The lower decks of the ship were partly caved in. Most of the long planks that would once have been underfoot lay at too steep an angle to climb, but wide spaces smashed through the decks by whatever broke up the ship left a series of rooms filled with clutter. It was in the third of these ruined galleries that Early and his friends found the skeletons. Leading the way, Isaac came to a sudden halt. He did not cry out, but the absolute alertness of his body made Early, Olan, and Mosul freeze out of instinct. Isaac waved them over, and they joined him over a jumbled pile of bleached bones.

Early had never seen a real human skeleton before, and he stared at the remains in horrified fascination. Three skulls were intact, and three ribcages as well, but the rest of the bones were scattered throughout the rubble of the room. If the unfortunate sailors had once worn clothing—or uniforms like Mosul's blue-and-white—it was long gone.

Isaac crouched among the bones and pointed out where scavenging crabs had left claw marks, but Early didn't really hear him. He stepped gingerly around the bones—shuddering when, despite his best efforts, something brittle snapped underneath his foot—and he collapsed into a sturdy old chair still upright next to an overturned table. He was glad for the seat; his limbs suddenly felt like water. Early tipped back his head, unable to look upon the bones a moment longer, and gazed at the empty space where the hull curved into darkness above their heads. He felt tears in his eyes.

"This is no good," Olan said in a sharp whisper, and Early was surprised at the fear in the big deckhand's voice. He looked at his friend. Olan was backing away from the bones, his hands up in front of him. "Bad luck, this. Dead sailors in a dead ship? Leave them with the Dead Gods and let's get out of here."

Isaac, who was carefully shifting the bones to see if anything lay beneath, replied with patient derision. "That's a sailor's superstition I hear," he said. "Remember, the point of this little jaunt is to figure out if this ship's truly of the first expedition."

"Curse the first bloody expedition!" Olan shouted, set off as he always was by the ranger's laconic reasonableness. "We survived one shipwreck, what do we want to stay in another one for?"

Isaac stood and faced Olan. "You needn't have come along, deckhand," he said, and Early saw his big friend's hands tighten into fists. He pushed himself out of the chair, ready to intercede, but Mosul got there first.

"Cool off, you two. And be quiet. Hear that?" He gestured in the direction they'd entered the wreck. "Tide's getting nearer. If we want to get a look at the rest of this hulk, better leave these poor sailors to their rest and get on with it.

"Come on, deckhands," he said gently, but it was an order. He led them from the room, maneuvering them so Early stood between the Greenguard and his hot-tempered friend.

By the time they had to flee the wreck—only a few scant minutes before the tide cut them off—the explorers had drawn no conclusions. Between the signs Mosul pointed out and the remaining odds-and-ends they found, the ship was clearly a Blueguard greatship, a ship from their own empire, but whether it was indeed of the first expedition remained conjecture. On his way from the wreck, trying not to slip over spray-slicked rocks, Early clutched the one prize he'd saved: a battered tin mug of the kind Blueguard officers drank their coffee from on morning watch.

As his friends made for camp, Early lingered a moment and considered the ship and its long-dead crew. He felt a certain kinship with those bleached bones. They'd tried to cross the Sunfire Sea, and something had destroyed them. There but for the Gods' Luck would Early be. He raised the mug to the wreck in a salute and hurried to catch up with his friends.

By the time the final group of survivors from the *Pride* washed ashore, Early and his friends had begun to dismantle the remains of the ship, raise frameworks for their tents, and cobble together some sturdier buildings, including a cabin for Lord Mardigan and his Redguard. Having carefully marked the tide's ebb and flow, they now dared a permanent camp on the beach, the soft sand being a more comfortable floor than the barren ridgeline.

The last survivors came in nothing so seaworthy as a boat. They clung instead to a broken congeries of planks and mast, ropes and sail they'd managed to turn into a large raft. They'd done better than Early and the others at scavenging food and water from the *Pride*'s stores before all was lost, but the tide had turned against them and the many days at sea left them in perilous shape.

Early didn't know most of the stragglers well. There were eight of them: two were hands like him, but had served in the ship's galley—the younger of these was Myria, who he remembered from the pirate fight. Two were minor officers of the ship's watch. The other four were civilians brought along for their skill in the trades. These four, with the least experience at sea, suffered worst the effects of cold and exposure. Lord Mardigan, who insisted on supervising their arrival personally, ordered his Redguard to bring them to the modest infirmary they'd finished only that morning—its boards, reclaimed from the wreck, were still covered in dust from their shaping.

Early pitched in, gathering blankets and warm clothes the others had scavenged from the wreck and mended, now willingly given up to their stricken shipmates. It was when he put the fairer-skinned of the civilian women to bed, ensuring she wouldn't cast off the blankets in the delirium of her fever, that

Early realized she looked familiar. Though she appeared to have barely survived her ordeal, there was something in his brief glimpse of her eyes he recognized.

Those eyes were cold and blue, and fixed on him shrewdly despite the shivering and groaning of the body around them. A thrill ran down Early's spine at the sight, but he was called away by Olan to help drag the bits and pieces of the raft away from the water before the sea reclaimed them. Soon Early's mind had wandered to other things. The newly arrived Blue-guard, in better shape than their fellows, were boasting to Lia and Lord Mardigan how they'd made the pile of flotsam seaworthy. Myria, helping her fellow hands wrestle the pieces out of reach of the surf, explained to Early and Olan with obvious pride how she'd rescued enough food and water to keep their party alive for days.

That evening, the survivors, now nineteen, made merry by the fire. Having moved camp to the beach, they dug a shallow pit in the sand, just deep enough to be sheltered from the sea-wind, and arranged cut logs as benches around it. Part of the new arrivals' raft, it turned out, were two watertight kegs. When these were pried open, Early was delighted to see thick dark beer and salted pork: an unexpected bounty! It was a late and raucous night around the fire, and Early kept stealing glances at Lia, hopeful she'd return his warm regard. But in fact his attention kept wandering to the infirmary, where the other woman slept fitfully under layers of blankets, watched over by Redguard Dran Derrish, who was trained in battlefield medicine. Something about that blue-eyed woman wouldn't leave him alone.

Lia had, in fact, noticed Early's glances, and brought Rowene along to join the hands by the fire. She tried to engage Early in conversation, but he kept seeing those cold eyes, stern and commanding in a regal face. In his memory they were framed by thick blonde curls, not the darker, matted hair of the survivor, and—above them—she wore a black captain's hat...

"Early? Early, Rowene just told me the funniest—what's wrong?" Lia had leaned over to put a hand on Early's arm, but now she pulled back in surprise as he sat bolt upright on the log and the bit of pork he'd been chewing tumbled to the sand. Perhaps he was mad, or his imagination was running away with him, but he was suddenly sure: lying in the tent not forty yards off, as unfettered as the rest of the survivors, was Marie Gold, captain of the pirate ship *Black Spirit* and condemned criminal, alive through a twist of fate where the woman who'd sentenced her to death was not.

What could Early do? He looked over to where the Redguard captain, Morave Antmar, conversed with Lord Mardigan. The lord's face was ruddy from the fire, beer, and companionship, the Guard's was as stern and sober as ever, eyes alert for threats even in this company. They were the ones to tell, surely. But he didn't want to cause a scene, and he was fearful lest the stern Redguard rise up and immediately put the woman, sick as she was, to the sword.

Nevertheless, he knew his duty as an Imperial citizen and as a member of the *Pride*'s crew. Early begged Lia's pardon and picked his way around the campfire to where Lord Mardigan and his Guard-Captain sat. He cleared his throat as he approached, and the Redguard turned, unsurprised, but with his hand going by reflex to the hilt of his sword. When Morave recognized Early, he relaxed, but Lord Mardigan saw the worry in the young deckhand's face and his expression became grave.

"What is it, Early?" The lord asked.

"Begging your pardon, my Lord," Early said. He eyed the empty spot on the log next to Captain Antmar. "There's something you must know. May I...?" Morave looked to Lord Mardigan, who nodded, and the Redguard let Early take his seat. "The

woman who arrived today, who's under Redguard Dran's care?
She—she's the pirate that Captain Mestrum sentenced. I
thought I recognized her earlier, and it just came to me. Marie
Gold. I'm sure it's her! She must have escaped the brig of the
ship somehow."

Lord Mardigan looked at Early in disbelief, but then he
nodded and stood. Morave raised his eyebrows, looking to his
lord for instruction. "Let us not cause a general commotion,"
Mardigan explained, "but see to this at once, ourselves. Lead
on, my good deckhand." They excused themselves from the
gathering, saying the lord had been called to minister to one of
the new arrivals. The Blueguard lieutenant who had taken
responsibility for the eight raft survivors, a woman named
Coral Grannic, insisted on accompanying them. Lord Mardigan
obliged, and the four of them crossed the dark patch of beach to
the lamplit doorway of the infirmary.

Marie Gold was paler and thinner than she'd been before,
her hair darkened by the days at sea. But once called by name,
she abandoned the disguise of helpless commoner at death's
door, and looked at each of them with a sly gleam in her bright
eyes. Rather like a cornered animal, Early thought. The
Redguard captain stood between Marie and Lord Mardigan
with his sword drawn, though the pirate was barely holding
herself upright in bed. Redguard Dran, who'd been tending to
her in her fever, stood nearby, abashed at having been fooled.
His sword was still in its scabbard, but he fingered it as though
he expected Lord Mardigan to command the pirate captain's
execution at any moment.

But the Empress's cousin was a diplomat, first and fore-
most. "Our dependable hand here recognized you, Captain
Gold," he said, polite and stately as always, but with a trace of
irony. "You must excuse me imposing on you in your weakened

condition, but I'm sure you understand I was compelled to come at once."

"I would prefer to rest," Marie replied with her own trace of irony. "But I am at your service. What may I do for the Empress's noble cousin?"

"We find ourselves in a strange situation, Captain Gold. The brave Guard-Captain Mestrum suspended her sentence of death, lest you prove a reliable guide. Yet I would say we discovered this new land without your help, more's the pity. Where does this leave us? At the least, Captain, you are still a convicted pirate. You are Her Majesty's prisoner, and must remain in the custody of her Imperial Guard until your ultimate fate is decided."

She looked with venom at Morave and Dran, who flanked their lord. But then the strength left her, and she lay back with her eyes shut. Marie trembled in seeming pain, and Early found his heart going out to her.

"My ultimate fate?" she asked quietly. "I presume my fate is to be hung by the neck as soon as you've gathered enough wood to build a gallows."

From their fierce glares, Early could tell the two Redguard would have assembled a gallows for Marie then and there, just as they'd not hesitate to impale the pirate if she made even a feeble movement against Lord Mardigan. But the lord himself raised his hands in a conciliatory gesture. "Out of a crew of many dozens, only a handful have survived to see this expedition through. Pirate and prisoner though you may be, Marie Gold, you are one of them. It would be foolish, unconscionable, to throw your life away, even if justice demands it.

"Despite your alias, Captain Gold, I know the great name you once bore. And I know what proud family your father brought to ruin. Perhaps the gods have given you a chance to redeem that name."

Marie opened her eyes and looked at him for a long time. Early thought the weariness he saw on her face was no longer feigned in the least.

"Perhaps," was all she would say. She sank back on the bed and shut her eyes again.

"I beg you to consider it," Mardigan replied. "But we must approach this carefully, for not all of our people here will be forgiving as I." His Guards fidgeted unhappily, as if to underline this point.

Early fidgeted as well, but for another reason. The talk of Marie's background and her redemption piqued his curiosity, but this was no time for questions. At least it sounded as though Marie would be allowed to live, and Early couldn't help his excitement at the thought. That excitement was abated, though, by a guilt he didn't entirely understand. As he followed Lord Mardigan back to the fire, he turned for a last look at Marie and felt a chill of fear. Even if she agreed to become a model citizen of their tiny society, could the cunning pirate captain ever be trusted?

For the first time since the watcher remembered, there was light on the shore. Light made by human hand—and not lit by any of his kin. There was no mistaking it: though the gods might conjure fire in the dry brush at the height of summer, this fire was too near the tide line. Nothing grew there to burn, so someone must have gathered wood and set it alight. Someone the watcher did not know.

He had left his routine patrol to investigate, moving from the dense trees of the forest to the lighter tangle of the coastal ridge, bands of blue-gray mud on his skin blending with the night; in the dull moonlight filtered through the clouds, everything was cast in gray. Even the point of his spear was painted to a dull sheen, so it would give no telltale flicker as he moved through the hedges, one silent barefoot step at a time.

When he drew close enough to see dark shapes moving about the fire, he folded into a crouch and became perfectly still. He laid the spear at his side, ready to be grasped at a moment's notice, and unshouldered the bow and arrows. The quiver was tightly bound in cloth to keep the arrows from rustling, except for one dark shaft he kept separate for urgent use. He laid the quiver down and knew by touch, without looking away from the fire, how the arrow lay. He could nock it as easily as grasping his spear.

It was dangerous to look into the fire—it killed his night vision. He swept his gaze constantly from side to side instead, reading the shadows, wary of ambush; these strangers on the shore might have sentries waiting, as he was, in the dark tangle of brambles and scrub trees that clung to the ridge above the beach.

He waited and watched the figures draw near the fire. Bright, flickering light reflected off faces, eyes. Both face and eye were dark, like his own, but in the wavering firelight it was impossible to know the color of skin or eye for certain. A minute's observation of how they moved and the sounds they made confirmed his fears: these were none of his kin. The implication of this loomed at the edge of his mind, too fearsome to be let in. At last the watcher spoke the truth, wordlessly, to himself: the only way to reach this beach in secret was to sail over the sea. The rest of the island was inimical to landing.

A pained expression came unbidden to the watcher's face. He had never been beyond sight of shore in a fishing dinghy, and even that had been uncomfortable. The mere idea of crossing the endless water... but there was no other explanation. He and his kindred had walked the length and breadth of the island, and never before found a trace of others. No one lived here but the Malaspiri. The island belonged to them. Alone.

The watcher absently stroked the feathers of his arrow, and he realized his mind had wandered. He dove back into the present and stretched his keen senses into his surroundings. He saw no movement in the surrounding brush, though his vision was by now too compromised by the firelight to be sure. Bright spots danced on top of the shadows, and he cursed himself for his woolgathering.

Then he heard a step ahead and to his left. A branch cracked beneath a careless tread. Too close now for bowshot—had he really been so preoccupied? Now the watcher saw a large dark shape loom above the bushes, black against the night sky. He wrapped one hand around his spear, his whole body tensing for one great thrust.

The dark shape stopped, belched, and muttered something. Then came a tinkling liquid sound so incongruous the watcher had to swallow a fatal laugh. This was no sentry—or, if it was, not a good one. The sound of the big man urinating went on for what seemed an eternity, and the watcher, still clutching his spear, allowed his body to relax. He need do nothing unless the man spotted him, and there was little chance of that. He crouched in a clump of thick bushes several yards away, invisible in the dark.

At last the man left, picking his way awkwardly down the slope of the ridge, shallow on this part of the beach, and returning to the campfire. Beyond the fire, the watcher could just make out the shapes of crude tents or huts, and, as the wind turned, there wafted to him the smell of just-cooked meat being seasoned and prepared. This seemed to be no transient camp.

If the strangers had meat, they must have hunted for it, and that would mean entering the woods. The watcher frowned. Outsiders could not be allowed to walk the island freely, for not only did their presence threaten his people's security, deep in its wooded heart lay the place where only the *sheenya*, the witch-woman, could go. The haunted place. The thought of these newcomers blundering across that—or what the consequences of their trespass might be—made the watcher shudder, his body wracked by a fear infinitely older and deeper than a simple aversion to foreigners.

With a steadying breath, he comforted himself that these problems were beyond him. They were for the chieftain and the *sheenya* and the Ancestors' wisdom. He told himself he had seen enough, and, as slowly and silently as he'd set them down, he gathered his arsenal and turned his back on the beach and its alien occupants. Once he was back under the trees, the tension started to ease from his shoulders. The watcher could make his way more quickly now, just another sure-footed creature in a forest full of nocturnal life. All he had to do was report his discovery. The chieftain would say whether he and his warrior-kin would return to use the arrows that hung heavy and reassuring at his back.

5

"In the Greenguard we say there are two ways to fight: the way the Redguard do it, and the right way."

Isaac had gathered Early up after breakfast to teach him the finer points of swordplay. Though the deckhand had mentioned his desire to be a better fighter several times, he was still surprised when his mentor took him to a clear spot on the beach and bade him defend himself. Now Early glanced up from nervously studying the blade of his sword. Isaac, standing a few feet away, rested his own weapon casually against his shoulder.

The "swords" were tree branches they'd whittled into about the appropriate size and weight, with a crossguard shaved off and fitted in place with twine. It was entirely possible the mock weapons wouldn't survive the coming encounter, but they could hardly afford to blunt the blades of the few personal weapons that made up the arsenal of their jury-rigged "colony."

"With all due respect, Isaac," Early said, "us commoners always heard the Redguard were the greatest sword fighters in the Empire, or maybe anywhere."

The ranger cracked one of his subtle smiles. His dark eyes glinted. "People get into sword fights for all kinds of reasons and in all kinds of places. The Redguard are peerless blade-wielders, yes, but their traditions and position in the court lead to a certain rigidity."

"You mean... they aren't flexible?"

Isaac rolled his eyes at his apprentice. "In body, certainly, but not in... say, martial spirit. Redguard are not good at fighting dirty. The other divisions of the Guard don't really have that luxury. Ask a Goldguard what's required to keep order in the streets and alleys, or a Blueguard what it's like to fight deck-to-deck with pirates—you've seen that for yourself.

"As for the Greenguard, all we know is we haven't seen all there is to see. Our job is to explore the unknown. That lends itself to a fighting style rich in improvisation."

Early glanced at their makeshift weapons. "So what you're saying is, you're better at fighting with a tree branch than I am?"

Isaac barked a sound that could be interpreted as a laugh. "Let's find out!" And he came in swinging.

The two crosscuts were clumsy, and Early parried them easily. He stepped back, trying to keep his mind on both his hands and feet at the same time, as he'd learned from the rudimentary combat training provided to all the enlisted crew of the expedition. He pushed off his back foot to launch an attack, cursing silently at the treacherous way the sand shifted beneath his feet. He'd tried for a fast stab, but Isaac knocked it aside and stepped to Early's left in one motion, his blade whirling in to smack Early's unprotected arm. Early straightened and backed off.

"So. First 'blood' would be yours."

Isaac inclined his head in a slight bow to his opponent. "Dueling requires you to think a few moves ahead, like a game of Knight's Grace. If I strike this way, they could parry that way, which leaves me open over here. Of course, unlike Knight's

Grace, your move can't wait till your opponent gets impatient and threatens to call the game. Rather, you have fractions of a second. This is why we drill. Because all that thinking ahead has to happen *without* thinking—it must become reflex."

"The question is," Early asked, "how do you survive long enough to develop the reflexes?"

"That is, indeed, the question. You fight your friends with sticks, for starters. Come at me again."

Early did. This time he tried a feint, and it looked like Isaac fell for it. His blade came low, but Early hadn't committed his full weight to the strike, so he was able to stop short and stab at Isaac's face. He had a moment to worry he might actually hurt his friend—a stick to the eye was not as bad as a sword point, but it was still bad...

He needn't have worried. The ranger ducked and, as Early tried to follow through, swinging his blade down on top of Isaac's head, Isaac uncoiled in a tackle. His shoulder caught Early in the stomach, knocking the wind out of him and driving him to the ground. Early's head hit the sand, and he was immediately grateful they weren't fighting up on the rocky ridge. Isaac was on his feet first, of course, and Early was still trying to figure out which way was up when he felt the tip of Isaac's branch rest gently on his windpipe.

Isaac returned Early's furious glare with an impassive face, but humor sparkled in his eyes. After a moment, he offered Early a hand. Back on his feet, Early spent longer than necessary brushing the sand from his clothes, embarrassed.

"That," Early said at last, "must be an example of the Greenguard's prowess at fighting dirty."

Isaac didn't miss a beat. "And now you can see how effective it is."

Early could only shake his head at his friend, who didn't even seem to be breathing hard. Isaac waited patiently for the deckhand to ready himself for the next round. After a dozen sorties with similar results, Early was glad to see Captain Antmar striding up the beach to interrupt them. The Redguard captain had brought half a dozen of the survivors with him to the practice area. Among them, Olan saw his friend's exhaustion and gave him a teasing smile, but Early hardly noticed; Lia was there, watching him, and it was her smile that sent his already-laboring heart racing. The Redguard Taliss stood next to her, the two women having become fast friends since the landing, despite their very different professions—then again, Early supposed with a stab of inadequacy, they had their place in the Imperial Court in common.

"Greenguard," Captain Antmar began, and Early couldn't help noticing the inflection in the stern captain's voice, as though speaking to an inferior. Isaac must have noticed as well, but if it bothered him, the ranger gave no sign. "My Lord has charged you with training each of the colonists in the skills needed to survive our sojourn here. I have divided us into groups, and, in the days to come, you shall take each group into the woods and instruct them as you see fit. You are to start at once."

Early was annoyed by the blunt intrusion on their training session, and, if he was honest with himself, he enjoyed having Isaac's exclusive attention. But he saw the wisdom in training all the few-enough survivors in the specialized skills of the Greenguard rangers. Early admired Isaac's ability to remain stoic while the Redguard captain, younger than the ranger, talked down to him. Antmar's manner reminded Early of how Deckmaster Matta had treated him and his fellow hands—like servants, fit only to be given brusque commands. Much as the notion of belonging to the elite Imperial Guard appealed to him, having to exist in such a rigid pecking order rubbed Early the wrong way.

"Of course, Guard-Captain," Isaac replied, seemingly heedless of what so bothered his apprentice. "If everyone is ready, we can get going."

Isaac considered the scattered clouds overhead, then looked up along the ridge, which climbed higher and higher as it followed the beach. Several hundred yards away, it reared up into a cliff fifty feet or more above the sand, and the forest grew almost to its edge. Isaac pointed there. "Looks like a good day for learning to forage, and I know the place to try it."

"Keep your stick with you, Early," Isaac added, seeing Early jab the training sword into the sand. "It may not be much of a weapon, but after hiking a few miles uphill, you'll be glad for the support."

Laboring up the steep ridge, Early wished Isaac didn't seem so smug. The ranger had been on the mark: as they hiked north the land grew steep, and after an hour Early was leaning heavily on his stick, wishing it were sturdier. He glowered at Isaac, annoyed and envious of the Greenguard's tireless stride. Despite the mild weather, Early was sweating no less now than during their fighting practice.

At least, he thought, *the view is worth the trip.* High above the beach, Early briefly pondered what mysteries the thick woods to his right might contain, but soon lost himself in the endless rolling of the slate sea to his left. Looking over the cliff's edge at the waves crashing on the rocky shore, the uncomfortable thrill of looking down from a high place kept him riveted until Isaac called him into the trees.

The ranger led them into the woods along a path he'd clearly scouted before. A quarter mile from the cliff, the land sloped down into a bowl where the trees grew thinner, and there they stopped. Isaac pointed out how the thinner canopy allowed a profusion of ferns and underbrush to thrive, making this a good spot to forage. He spent the next two hours teaching them to do just that, and also how to notice and follow animal tracks, and the basics of stealthy movement through flora.

As noon approached, the students went off on their own to practice. Early studied the trees near the edge of the bowl, noticing how they differed from the thicker trees only a few steps away. While most of the forest was rugged and black-barked, these trees seemed spindly and pale. He considered what Isaac had told them: perhaps there'd been a fire, and these trees were new, or perhaps something in the bowl's soil kept them stunted. Early peered thoughtfully at both ground and tree. He didn't see evidence of burning, but the ranger said the woods recover quickly, and obvious signs like bare branches and scorch marks get swallowed up by new plant life that rushes into the breach.

Olan, seeing Early looking the trees up and down with intense concentration, snuck up on him with impressive stealth for his size. When he was an arm's length away, he bellowed, "Deckhand Wills! By the bloody seas, why aren't you swabbing the fo'c'sle?"

Early jumped straight up in the air, then whirled around, fists raised. "Dead Gods! I'll mop the deck with you, Mender," he threatened, but dropped his hands and grinned. "Gotta give you that one—you scared me and my ghost. I'm trying to figure out why the trees are so different here than in the rest of the woods."

"Trees!" Olan spat. "Trees indeed. Can't eat a tree, and I'm bloody starving. Help me find some mushrooms won't kill me dead." The big deckhand turned back towards the center of the bowl, scanning the thick underbrush.

"Poison mushrooms are no less than you deserve," Early grumbled, following him. Olan was right, though: the mention of eating made his empty stomach growl. A little foraging might not be a bad idea, though he hesitated to put anything in his mouth without Isaac's assurance it wouldn't lead to painful illness or worse. Olan spread the idea among the others, and soon there was a consensus that the subject of Isaac's training should turn to the acquisition of lunch.

Isaac showed them how tiny yellowstem mushrooms grew in clusters under larger ferns, bursting up from the rich soil around the curling roots, where the fungus could sip the same water that nourished the greenery. He plucked a few mushrooms and gave one to each of them, reassuring them they were safe. Early looked his over thoughtfully, while Olan popped his into his mouth at once. The yellowstem had a golden color, and underneath the tiny rounded cap was dark webbing like the gills of fish. These mushrooms were longer and smaller than the brown buttoncaps they fried up in butter back home, but when Early finally took a bite from the stem, it was less stringy than he'd feared. The meat of the mushroom wasn't terribly substantial, but it had a slight nutty flavor that encouraged Early to eat more. He was glad to know he might find a banquet of these throughout the forest; a handful would go a long way to satisfying his hunger.

Next, Isaac demonstrated how the curly leaves of some of the ferns that shaded the yellowstems were themselves edible, and, while he claimed they tasted much better cooked, one could chew them raw if need be. Early found the fern leaves downright unpleasant to eat, tough and bitter, and when he saw the grim look on Olan's face as the big man ground his jaw, cowlike, to render the leaves tender enough to swallow, Early could not have better summed up the experience of eating them.

Isaac paired his students up to forage on their own, after which they'd make their luncheon with the results of their search. While Early found himself hoping he could be paired up with Lia, the cartographer had already gone off with Taliss the

Redguard. Lia's handmaiden Rowene, usually her shadow, had steadfastly refused another hike in the woods.

As usual, Olan was Early's partner. He clapped Early on the shoulder and said, "Alone in the woods with you at last, matey! Now you'll learn my true feelings." Early rolled his eyes and followed Olan into the trees. It wasn't that Early didn't appreciate the other deckhand's friendship, but the old social hierarchy seemed less rigid now than it had aboard ship, and Early found himself eager to connect with the others—especially beautiful and aristocratic Lia—as an equal.

As they passed by Isaac, who was clearing brush away for a small cookfire, the ranger nodded to Early and said, "Keep the big man from getting lost, eh, Early? You'll soon be more adept in the woods than on the planks of a ship!" Early beamed at the encouragement, and the fantasy of joining Isaac in the Greenguard occupied his imagination as he and Olan hunted for their share of mushrooms. Picturing himself, green-cloaked, nimbly climbing a tree, drawing a bead on some dark forest monster with his powerful bow, not even Olan's relentless teasing could dampen Early's excitement.

After lunch, the afternoon growing late, Isaac pointed them back to camp, intending to go deeper into the forest to hunt alone. Early asked to come along—eager, he said, for more experience tracking.

"If you're not tired of the woods yet, Early," the ranger said with a smile, "you're welcome. Though you may regret it by evening."

Isaac did insist, however, that Early must be armed. Redguard Taliss wore a rapier on each hip, as was her style, and she spared one for Early, showing him how to properly buckle the sheath. Fascinated by the polished, perfectly balanced blade, he could only stutter his thanks.

The rest of the group headed for the cliffside path that

would return them to the beach, while Early followed Isaac deeper into the forest. So excited was he to be on an adventure with his mentor, armed with a real Imperial Guard sword, that even an hour later he was still chattering happily.

"—never seen so many different types of trees, even in the forest back home. And I heard Lia saying—"

Isaac motioned Early to silence with a quick cutting sign of his hand. He didn't turn around. Early froze, crouching down, and peeked around the ranger's shoulder to see what he was looking at.

A bestial face was staring back at them. Emerging from the shadows of the trees not ten yards ahead, its eyes glittered azure in the sunlight as it moved ever so slightly, tasting the air with open jaws. And the jaws were impressive: it had the shallow powerful bite of a hunting hound, but its teeth were pointed and angled backwards like a *sillisith* monitor lizard. Anxious to attack, the beast stood imperfectly still; Early could see the iridescent sheen of scales as it moved its sleek black head. The beast was concealed by the brush, but its head was pony-sized; the body that followed must be similar. Very bad.

Early quietly cursed himself, not for the first time, for his clumsiness in the forest. The thought that Isaac would have been better off alone wouldn't leave his mind as he drew his borrowed sword, wincing at the sound of the metal scraping against the leather sheath. The need for quiet seemed imperative even though the beast had already seen them; Early felt instinctively that any sudden movement or loud noise would provoke an attack.

Isaac seemed to confirm this. He crouched like a statue, bow in hand, one knee out at right angles to his body while the other rested firmly in a clump of leaves. He slowly, slowly pulled an arrow from the quiver at his shoulder and readied it on the bowstring. He didn't draw, and Early wondered why. Wasn't he going to shoot the thing? He wanted to ask, as the tension coiled his stomach tighter and tighter, but he didn't dare make a sound—either to distract the ranger or to spook the beast. Though "spook" seemed the wrong word; the powerful and obviously predatory animal didn't look frightened by the likes of Early.

But the ranger was the one to break the silence. He tilted his head, whispering, and Early had to strain to hear over his shoulder. "There may be more of them waiting," he said, and Early's already-knotted stomach somehow tied itself in another knot. His eyes flicked back and forth to the trees, and he couldn't help seeing another beast huddled in every shadow. Were they surrounded? Was one of the monsters creeping up silently behind them even now? Early could almost feel its breath on the back of his neck... he had to turn, had to run... had to scream...

Early lifted his free hand to his mouth and bit the flesh, hard. He exhaled through the pain, and found some relief: the mindless, animal fear receded, leaving him crouching patiently behind Isaac. Early took a deep breath and looked over his shoulder in one smooth motion. Though his eyes continued to play tricks with the shadows, there was no beast creeping up behind them. So that was something. He still didn't dare speak, merely tried to be ready for the ranger's direction, or until *something* happened.

The beast had been watching them with its long neck outstretched, eerie sapphire gaze fixed on their position. Now, though, it lowered its head and hissed, and then, to Early's surprise, padded backwards into the trees. He exhaled the breath he'd been holding despite himself; there was no reason to think they were safe. He dared to whisper, "Isaac?"

The ranger slowly shook his head. His bow remained undrawn but ready, his elbow bent in preparation. "I don't like this. Early, if I say to run, you make for the camp and don't look back." Early was about to object, but Isaac turned his head to the side and cocked an eye at him. "Understood?"

Early gawked, then swallowed and set his mouth in a straight line. He drew his brows together. "I won't just leave you here, if they... I'll stand and fight."

Isaac turned back to the woods, as though the topic was closed for discussion. "You run back to camp; someone has to warn—"

And then three of the beasts leaped out of the trees.

Isaac loosed one arrow and got to his feet. Early saw the ranger in a blur of motion, saw the dark shapes coming, but though his mind swarmed with impressions—*horse, snake, hound, tiger, dragon*—he had no clear idea what the things looked like. Eyes and teeth and claws flashed, and there was a sharp smell of ozone, like the air in the wake of a thunderstorm. Early stood paralyzed for a moment, sword trembling in his hand. There was no hope for the two of them to fend off three of the things!

Isaac said to run, but...

A snarl to Early's right: a beast was charging at Isaac's open flank. The ranger was turned to the left—somehow he'd traded bow for sword—slashing at the other monster charging from that direction. He didn't see the second beast coming. Early found his blade leading the way. He charged, stabbed, and struck the beast even as it turned mid-pounce towards him. A great weight crashed into his chest, his head hit the ground and his vision swam, but the sleek black shape tumbled past him, howling terribly.

All the creatures were howling now, and the sound made Early want to curl up in a ball. He scrambled to his feet instead, thanking the gods he didn't seem to be hurt, and put his back to Isaac, facing the beast as it turned. It hulked its shoulders, bristly fur rising along its spine in the long patches unguarded by scales. The beast stretched its jaws towards him and hissed, but Early could see black blood dripping from a rent in its neck —he'd *hit* the thing!

Something awoke deep inside him that made him step forward.

Drawing himself to his full height, he shook his sword over-head and roared. The beast's whole body tensed, and Early felt his courage evaporate. In his mind's eye he saw the thing pounce, the lethal body that must have outweighed him many times over launched like a missile at him...

But the beast turned and ran into the trees.

Early lowered his sword, stunned, but a shout from Isaac and a howl from the monster behind him broke the spell. He spun, seeing bloody jaws clamp around the leather bracer the ranger wore to guard his left forearm from the snap of his bowstring. Blood streamed off the beast where Isaac's sword had done its work, but now it came at him in a frenzy, pink-flecked froth dripping from the corners of its mouth. Early plunged towards them, his pulse battering in his temples, and his blade caught the creature in the arch of its exposed neck. It gurgled and bit deeper into Isaac's arm, and the ranger screamed and stabbed with his blade. Early stabbed again, and this time his sword bit into something hard in the creature's spine that held when he tried to pull back. Early lost his grip on the Redguard sword as the beast thrashed, and he tumbled to the ground.

Isaac punched the hilt of his sword into the beast's eye and it released his arm, the bracer brutally creased by its jaws. It weaved backwards, stumbling, back legs trembling as they struggled to support its body. Early's sword hung from its back, the blade embedded in the thick vertebra. Early rose to his feet, shaky, as Isaac, holding his left arm close to his body, advanced blade-first on the beast. Early followed, reaching out for the trapped hilt of his own sword.

"Careful," Isaac mumbled, breathing painfully, "it's hurt. Dangerous..."

Early registered the warning, but adrenaline pushed him forward. His mind was blank, but the need to help his friend, to fight at Isaac's side, drove him to grasp his blade. With a shout, he yanked it free. The monster whirled on him with terrible speed. Its jaws snapped inches from Early's body and he stumbled backwards but kept his footing. He slashed but missed the flailing neck and then danced sideways to avoid its bite. He and Isaac flanked the wounded beast and buried their swords in its sides. It loosed an unearthly howl and Isaac yelled, "Get back!"

Early gladly obliged, stumbling away from the monster as it reared onto its hind legs, jaws stretched high in the air above their heads. Then it crashed to the ground and lay still, Isaac barely dodging its falling bulk.

Early collapsed in a pile of wet leaves, numb to the discomfort as he waited for his heart to slow enough that he could breathe. Isaac came over and slumped to the ground beside him, groaning as he held his mangled arm with his empty sword hand. Early struggled to catch his breath, as the hot rush of adrenaline gave way to a sort of elation. They'd accomplished something primal, something meaningful—that's what it felt like to Early. Something *right*.

"We did it... we... won. Right?" Early couldn't help smiling at the ranger, but Isaac shook his head. He was already forcing himself back to his knees, weariness etching deep creases in his face.

"The other... other one," he panted. "Could come back."

Cold terror struck Early in the gut again, as hard as before. His head swiveled, scanning the clearing. "Dead Gods! There *were* three, weren't there? We only got one. Gods!"

But now Isaac did smile and turned towards the place they'd stood when the beasts attacked. The first one they'd seen —whose movement, Early now realized, had been intentional, distracting them from the others—lay full-length on its side. A long arrow with a green feather stuck up from the head, just behind its eye.

"Lucky shot," Isaac said.

Early smiled and coughed up a laugh from his dry throat. "Lucky! I'm lucky the other one ran away!" He turned to the creature they'd hacked to the ground. "That one, though... that one we earned." Early knew he must go to the beast and retrieve his sword, still embedded in its hide. Truth be told, now that the thrill of battle was wearing off, he feared to go near the thing again. It took him a long time to work up the nerve. At last he approached the carcass and pulled Taliss's bloodied rapier free, sliding it reverently back into its scabbard.

Isaac's weapon, alas, lay under the motionless body. The ranger stood, looking thoughtfully at the heavy carcass, and pulled out his hunting knife. "We did earn it," he said, and held up his shorter blade as though to salute the loss of its partner. "But we paid for it with my sword."

Isaac's left arm bled only a little—the bracer he wore had steel beneath the leather, and there was just one spot where the beast's fangs worried through to pierce the flesh beneath. But he reckoned his forearm was fractured, if not broken, and with their lack of resources that was worrisome indeed. Early helped him gather up his bow, but they had to leave Isaac's sword behind: it was well and truly buried beneath the beast they'd slain. They had no hope of rolling the thing over, not with Isaac's wounded arm. The lizard creature was the size of a small horse and densely built. Isaac would have to hope he could replace his weapon from their paltry cache.

They doubled back along the path they'd followed, wanting

only to return to camp safely. On the way back, they spotted a curious thing. It was Early who noticed it—Isaac was focused on the path, and had retreated inside himself after the battle and his injury. But Early happened to glance to his right and saw something strange through the trees, a flash of color. He grasped Isaac's right arm, and the ranger froze at once, looking where Early pointed.

"What do you reckon?" Early asked.

Isaac shook his head. "Not sure. And perhaps we should pass it by."

Early understood his hesitation but was fascinated. He drew his sword, still black with the blood of their recent kill. "Let me just have a quick look..."

Isaac made an exasperated sound behind him, but Early, still high from the battle, was already stepping gingerly through the undergrowth.

The thing he'd spotted was only a dozen paces off the path, and it turned out to be a strip of red cloth. It was tied around the end of a long branch, stripped of leaves. The branch was stuck straight up in the air. When he got close, Early could see why, and stopped dead still. A number of such branches were bound together with cloth and rough twine, creating a sort of low barrier or platform. The branch he'd noticed was sticking up because something had stepped on the platform and activated its mechanism, dropping it into the pit beneath.

And the thing in the pit was none other than the beast who'd fled from Early's blade. It was as dead as the ones they'd left in the clearing, its body transfixed by other long, sturdy branches embedded in the pit's floor, these sharpened to points and fire-blackened to harden them. Early stood staring until a hand landed on his shoulder and he gasped.

Isaac moved Early aside, inspecting the trap and the cleared space around it: seeking footprints in the underbrush, freshly broken twigs, anything that would suggest the makers of the trap were nearby. Understanding was slow in coming to Early, but the ranger had grasped the implications at once. He didn't explain, but the urgency of his grasp on the deckhand's shoulder and the look in his eyes said everything:

The survivors were not alone.

6

Taliss was sharpening her remaining sword when Lia came by, sketchpad in hand. The tall warrior sat on a log, carefully running the edge of her blade along a dark, rectangular stone. The Redguard must have brought the whetstone in her kit, Lia supposed; no way she'd found something like that on the beach. Lia stood a few paces off so she wasn't looming over the other woman and pressed her charcoal to the paper. The measured sound of the blade hissing over the stone was soothing, and Lia sank into the trance of drawing, her mind wandering while her hands worked.

She didn't know how much time passed before she noticed Taliss had stopped sharpening, but she'd gotten most of the Redguard outlined and was working on the straighter, less-organic lines of her sword. Lia glanced up from her pad to find Taliss watching her.

"Is there a particular pose you wish me to hold, milady?" Taliss asked, a slight smile on her face.

"Oh, I beg your pardon, Guard Taliss," Lia lowered her pad as Taliss slid over to make room for her on the log. Lia sat and showed her what she'd drawn.

"A flattering likeness," the Redguard said, deadpan. "Are you sketching all of us, or am I the only recipient of this honor?"

Lia looked at her sidelong, returning her sarcasm. "Who among us is more worthy of being immortalized by my hand than the mighty Redguard, Taliss Andica?" Taliss laughed, so Lia raised her voice and waved her arms dramatically. "Long may she protect our Empress! Oh, who can count the great feats of bravery and strength for which—"

Taliss interrupted her friend with a mock shove. As always, Lia was impressed by the Redguard's strength. Taliss wasn't that much bigger than she, but could have tossed Lia off the log as easily as tossing aside her drawing pad. Undeterred, Lia shoved back.

"But really, what else have you been drawing?" Taliss asked, plucking the pad out of Lia's hands despite the cartographer's protests.

"Just sketches of our life here," Lia said. Taliss flipped through the sheaf, pausing on a sketch of Early and Mosul laughing at a joke of Olan's in front of the campfire, the warm light on their faces apparent in the elegant tracing of charcoal.

"This is *beautiful*, Lia."

"Hmm, thanks."

"Is all this just to keep you busy?"

"Well," Lia replied, "I don't have a sword to sharpen. And after all, we may yet find our way home, or at least send a message, and my job was always to document the expedition." Lia stared out at the ocean, the surf calm. "We never did know what this voyage would entail. Hopefully, I'm now documenting our survival here."

Taliss wiped the edge of her sword on a worn piece of leather and tested the edge by scraping her thumbnail with minute care. She stood and sheathed the blade in one of the scabbards that hung at her waist. The other was empty. She'd lend that sword to the deckhand, Early, and Taliss figured it would need sharpening once he returned. The eager youth had probably tried felling a tree with it.

"Survival," Taliss echoed thoughtfully, and joined Lia in gazing out to sea. Lia looked at her friend, whose face in profile was chiseled and stalwart as the nearby ridge.

"Do you..." Lia swallowed. "Do you think we'll ever make it home?"

"I hope so," Taliss whispered. Then the vulnerable moment passed, and she cleared her throat, smiling at Lia. "But I leave worries like that to our Lord, and my Captain. As far as survival goes, I take each thing as it comes." She patted her sword hilt. "Benefits of being a soldier."

Her hand tightened on the grip a moment later, though, as a crashing sounded in the brush behind them. Taliss swung her legs over the log and stood, putting herself between Lia and whatever was approaching. She relaxed at the sight of Early, however, scuffed up, panting, and out of breath. A moment later, the Greenguard emerged beside him, clucking at him for making so much noise. Taliss smiled at Isaac's mothering, but her alarm returned when she saw how he held his arm against his chest.

The ranger was hurt.

"Early! What happened?" Lia ran past Taliss, and, once the two men picked their way through the brush and down the slope that led to the beach, she put her arms on Early's shoulders and looked him over. Isaac laid down on the slope with none of his usual grace, clutching his arm stiffly to his chest, and groaned. Taliss dropped down next to him to inspect the damage.

"You were attacked, Guard Isaac," Taliss observed, seeing the teeth marks in the ranger's bracer. "Danger nearby?"

Isaac shook his head. "Beasts in the woods. Stumbled into

them. They got the worst of it, though one of them decided to keep my sword." He smiled painfully. "Something else, though..." He coughed and gestured weakly at Early, that the deckhand should tell the story.

"There's someone here!" Early said, speaking in a rush. "Living here, I mean. We found a hole—a trap! One of the beasts had fallen into it, impaled on sticks."

"A trap?" Lia asked. She looked from Early into the depths of the woods and back, the trees seeming dark and furtive all of a sudden, as though sinister foes were waiting just beyond.

"Hunter's trap," Isaac explained. He turned to Taliss. "Please, fetch Lord Mardigan. And Captain Antmar—we need to make a plan. We're not alone here, and if we haven't been marked already, it's only a matter of time."

The Redguard rose from his side, her gaze lingering on his arm. "I'll bring Redguard Dran as well. You need his attentions." She looked at Early, who clutched the blade she'd given him. The metal was stained with the blood of whatever they'd killed. It annoyed her he didn't know to wipe the blade clean. She saw his hand tremble.

"Best keep that sword for now, deckhand," she said. "Sounds like you might soon have further need of it."

🙂

Once Lord Mardigan and Captain Antmar had accepted the Decadins weren't alone, they set aside every other priority to turn the beachfront into a fortress. The work started at dawn the morning after Early and Isaac found the trap. The next two days, from sunrise to sunset, passed in a frenzy of construction.

The days were clear, sunny, and hot. Most days had been like that in the two weeks since landing. The people of the

Decadin Empire were no strangers to sunshine, yet the sun seemed to burn hotter here, darkening already tanned skin. Early noticed the change most on the arms and faces of the people assigned to turn the salvaged hull of the wrecked great-ship into as formidable a palisade as they could.

Since Isaac was wounded, Lord Mardigan wasn't much up to the rigors of construction, and his Redguard saved the bulk of their strength for keeping a watchful eye on him, there were only a dozen people to do the hard labor. And since hauling felled trees and salvaged planks was heavy lifting indeed, much of it fell onto Olan's huge shoulders.

"It's not fair, Early," Olan grumbled, heaving a plank longer than he was onto a pile. Early winced at the enormous clatter. He looked around the camp, embarrassed, as though his friend had loudly cursed the gods, but everyone was engaged in their own work and paid the blustery deckhand and his woodpile little attention.

"Olan, you sound like you're back on the *Pride*, and Deck-master Matta, rest him, has just given us what-for."

"Rest him on the bottom of the sea!" Olan spat, and Early rolled his eyes at the needless profanity. His friend waxed melo-dramatic when frustrated—which, in the last few days, he perpetually was. Early had seen the deckmaster go over the railing to his death, had been unable to save him; he glowered at Olan but kept silent.

"How many of us are left," Olan continued, "of over a hundred?"

"Not many."

"No, and that means every man and woman is crucial to our survival. Yet we cling to this high-handed order, where you and I are treated like mere deckhands still. Good for nothing but hauling timber. Bah!" Olan cursed as the pile of wood refused to be forced into an orderly stack, and a heavy board slid to the ground, narrowly missing his foot.

"But we *are* mere deckhands, Olan," Early said. "Lord Mardigan has not busied himself handing down promotions. We've been too busy trying to figure out things like food and shelter."

Early did not go out of his way to mention that Isaac, at least, treated him more like an apprentice than a servant. He was even now only pausing to chat on his way to join the ranger for a lesson in arrow fletching. Olan, his great size and strength relegating him to the woodpile, clearly wished to throw off the yoke. Early couldn't blame him.

"I'm not asking for a fancy title." Olan stretched, his great shoulders popping. "I never cared for the pomp of the Blue-guard the way you did, anyway. I'm saying we have talents that are squandered on menial chores. We should be helping shape a new society."

"We're stranded here, Olan, true. But we're still Imperial citizens..."

"But that's just my point!" Olan exploded, gesturing at the sea. "How likely is it we'll ever see the Empire again? Yet we continue to behave like Her Majesty's subjects. We could be anything we want, Early, don't you see? This is an opportunity to start over! An opportunity that's being denied us by our supposed betters."

Early looked nervously up along the ridgeline, where a dozen yards of rocky land separated the thick forest from the beach. Six of their fellows were building a simple watch tower there from trees they'd felled. If anyone heard Olan's outburst, they paid it no attention.

"You haven't shared this talk with others, have you, Olan?" Early leaned in, lowering his voice. "The camp is small, and we don't have the privacy of the *Pride's* brig to air our grievances over your awful rum."

Olan gave Early a withering look. "Do you think I'd rant about this at the cookfire? There are one or two others I trust to share my opinions. Our beautiful Captain Marie, for one. I've met no one as clever and open-minded as she."

Early was taken aback. Since the lord had allowed Marie a chance to be a citizen rather than a prisoner, Early had felt a certain possessiveness towards the pirate captain. Between his brief stint as her jailer and his having been the one to recognize her when they first came ashore, Early thought of himself as having a special relationship with Marie, though he had to admit this was probably unearned... and perhaps one-sided.

He couldn't help feeling jealous that Olan had Marie in his confidence.

"Well, of course Captain Gold would agree with you. She gave up the very Imperial Court for a life of piracy! I'm sure abandoning the social order suits *her* just fine." Early was more dismissive in tone than he really felt, and Olan's face grew stubborn. Early knew arguing with his bullheaded friend was a bad idea, but he couldn't help himself. Not if Marie was involved.

"Are you and the pirate going to stage a little mutiny, then? Is that the idea?"

"Now it's *you* who should keep your voice down, Master Wills," Olan taunted. "If Marie and I were to leave this ruined expedition behind, I'm sure you wouldn't want to be the one swabbing the decks."

"Oh, ho!" Early scoffed. "You're always teasing me for thoughts 'above my station,' Master Mender, but now I suppose you think yourself equal to a captain. If you and Marie Gold ever set sail together, you'd hardly be fit to swab her decks. You and I come from the same place, don't forget!"

Olan took a step back, crossing his big arms over his chest.

His expression was cold, none of the usual sardonic humor in his eyes.

"It's you who's forgotten yourself, Master Wills, so busy licking that Greenguard's bootheels you hardly care about the rest of us peons. I don't begrudge you weaseling a way into your beloved Imperial Guard, now you've got the chance, but it's a poor man forgets who his friends are."

Hurt and angry, Early matched Olan's glare until he realized no clever or biting rejoinder was coming to mind. He turned away and stormed down the ridge, trying not to break into a run. When he reached the far side of the camp where Isaac waited, Early hoped he'd regained enough composure that the ranger wouldn't notice how upset he was.

Early spent the rest of the day fletching arrows at Isaac's direction, trying and failing not to brood over his fight with Olan. At least Isaac was proving unusually talkative, and the string of anecdotes from his adventurous life took Early's thoughts away from his troubles.

"In fact," Isaac said, using a conversation about the importance of foraging to launch into another story, "in Greenguard training, a new ranger is sent into the forest with only knife, hatchet, bow... and loincloth. Before they receive their green-and-white, they must first return clothed in whatever they can fashion."

Early glanced at the ranger's garb, noticing that, unlike the uniforms of the Blueguard or Redguard, there was by necessity no actual white trim on Isaac's clothes. Then he realized what Isaac was saying and looked up doubtfully.

There were similar tales of the initiation Blueguard officers went through, but each Guard division had their own internal culture, and were notoriously tight-lipped. He didn't know much about how the mysterious rangers of the Greenguard were trained, but it was hard to imagine being sent into the wild without even protection against the elements. Surely at least some neophyte rangers died of exposure—as Early imagined he would, if so tested.

"Is that really true?"

Isaac gave one of his enigmatic smiles and looked out into the nearby forest, as though remembering another wooded place where he'd learned his trade. "It is, indeed. Myself, I couldn't catch anything with enough hide to clothe me. So at last I skinned a tree and emerged proudly from the forest in clothes of bark.

"I should say I *hobbled* proudly; raw bark isn't very flexible."

Early laughed. But as he looked back up the beach, his eyes were drawn by the bright hair of Marie Gold. With strength belied by her graceful proportions, she was helping Olan carry his stack of rough boards to where Ander, a leathery survivor of Marie's raft whose trade was carpentry, was shaping and sanding.

Olan and the pirate captain were chatting in a friendly manner, and, though Early couldn't hear what they were saying, he could tell from their relaxed and familiar body language that they'd been enjoying much of each other's company. He felt a pang of jealousy.

Early's rumination was broken by an unpleasant sting on the back of his hand. Isaac's ongoing soliloquy had faded into the background as Early focused on his friends and, when the ranger noticed his apprentice wasn't paying attention, he'd gently poked the head of a new arrow into Early's unguarded hand. Early yelped and looked darkly at the ranger, but Isaac merely grinned with a little more self-satisfaction than usual, and gestured to the pile of carefully cut shafts and sack of gathered feathers.

"No time to dawdle, Early. Captain Antmar wants his fortifications well-supplied, so all these—hi ho," Isaac cut himself off, his smile vanishing, "here comes the Guard-Captain now."

Isaac stood as Antmar, flanked by his fellow Redguard Sander Sund, hiked the slope from the beach to join them. Early stood as well. It seemed proper to rise; Morave Antmar was, after all, second in command only to Her Majesty's cousin. Early found the Redguard far more overbearing than his lord, and—though Isaac never showed it—Early was sure the Guard-Captain got on the ranger's nerves as well.

"Greenguard," Antmar said, the word and a quick salute his only greeting. "How go your preparations?"

Isaac indicated the arrows they'd produced with a sweep of his undamaged arm. "Our archers will have plenty to keep them busy. Once I've taught some of you how to pull a bow properly, that is."

Early was excited to learn how to shoot, but the Redguard barely nodded.

"Good," he said. "Then you are free for a patrol this afternoon."

Isaac blinked. "A patrol?"

"Of course." Antmar looked into the woods. "Our enemy is lurking in there at this very moment, and we must take steps to find them. The sooner we begin..." He trailed off, confident the ranger would take his point.

But Isaac was cross, Early could tell. He saw a muscle twitch in the stubbled jaw.

"I thought fortifying the camp was top priority," Isaac said. "Is that no longer true?"

The Redguard narrowed his eyes. "Of course it's priority. But we can afford no lapse in offense, even as we build our defense. That's the only way we can be secure here."

"But we can hardly spare people from their tasks to go on patrol," Isaac said, "unless you want me to go out myself." He rubbed his wounded arm conspicuously. "Which I will, if I must..."

"Nonsense. I will accompany you," the Redguard captain said, "as will Guard Sund, here, and Guard Andica." He looked down to the beach, where Taliss was in amiable conversation with Lia, as usual.

"The Lady Dracis also wishes to come to record what we find. I thought this a needless risk, but she insisted, and my lord approved." Antmar turned back to Isaac, as though the matter were settled. "We would begin at once, if we may."

Isaac protested. Early understood his concerns—it was too late in the day to go deep into the forest, and, knowing what they now did about the beasts and the unknown Others, it was dangerous to explore. Except in force, which they could hardly afford if they were to finish the defenses. But Captain Antmar was unmoved. All Isaac's arguments could buy was a brief respite. He would lead the chosen party—bringing Early along, to the apprentice's delight—after breakfast the following morning.

Once the Redguards had left them, Isaac sat back down at the newly made table where they were assembling their arrows. He looked tired.

"That's enough fletching for one day," he said, taking a colorful feather out of Early's hand. "Come, get my bow and let's start your practice while it's still light."

Early took the compound bow from Isaac's side with reverence, elated that his archery training was to commence so soon. But the grim look on his teacher's face took the wind out of his sails.

"Bloody Antmar," Isaac cursed, the first time Early had heard him do so. "I wanted more time for this arm to heal. Either you learn to shoot, Early, or you'll have to draw the bow for me."

The strangers on the beach had been busy. The watcher saw they had salvaged piles of wood from the old shipwreck, an impressive feat of demolition. Now they were building fortifications, which worried him. The strangers must have been hunting in the forest, as well: a dozen rabbit skins were drying on a makeshift rack of stripped branches. He glanced into the woods around him, unnerved by the thought of the strangers prowling beneath the trees he called home.

He wondered how they could have caught so many of the quick, frantic mammals, so good were the island hares at vanishing into the undergrowth when startled. They could have trapped, of course, assuming they knew how, but... ah. At the far end of the strangers' camp, the watcher spotted a man in a green cloak. This man was sitting at a table, instructing a youth in what appeared to be fletchcraft—the making of arrows. A fine compact bow was propped at his feet. He was their hunter, then, and he would understand the woods and the tracks that crisscrossed them; dangerous.

Thus far, the watcher had seen no indication the strangers knew of his people, but if any outsider would discover them, it would be this grizzled man. The watcher clenched his own powerful bow, but left it on his shoulder. Nor did he reach for the quiver at his hip. He could land a shaft in the hunter's chest from here, was anxious to remove this threat, but neither the chieftain nor the *sheenya* had given leave to kill. He was merely to watch the strangers each day and remark on the state of their encampment.

The rapid development of the strangers' camp unsettled him. There were nineteen of the strangers now and not all of them engaged in labor, yet every day their camp grew a little more substantial. If the chieftain ordered they be pushed back into the sea, it must be done soon.

Checking that the screen of bushes still properly concealed him, the watcher turned his thoughts from the strangers' construction to the strangers themselves. Though they came from across the sea, their speech and behavior was not difficult to understand—it was comforting, in a way, that they were not truly alien. Over the days of his watch, he had grown sure he could tell who was leader and who was servant, who was warrior and who blacksmith, who hunted and who gathered.

He kept a careful record of their health, as well. Though some of the outsiders had seemed sick or injured on arrival, none were confined any longer to the rough hut that was their infirmary. Even the woman with bright golden hair—impossible not to mark her—even she was now carrying planks of wood on her shoulder, though mere days ago she could scarcely walk on her own.

That woman was strange, and not only for her striking appearance: the others seemed strangely cold or reticent towards her. Perhaps she was diseased, the watcher supposed, or had committed some crime. If there was strife between the outsiders, the chieftain would want to know. It would be to their advantage when the time came.

No sooner did the watcher consider this, breathing softly across his shoulder to discourage a spider that had begun to investigate the gray bands of camouflage painted across his skin, than his attention was drawn by raised voices. The master hunter was arguing with someone.

Two formidable men in bright uniforms of red and white had joined the hunter and his apprentice. One spoke to the hunter in a voice whose commanding, angry edge was clear to the watcher, even across the distance. The attitude of this man in red branded him a leader, perhaps the strangers' chieftain.

Whatever words the two men were saying, it was obvious they disagreed. The man in red gestured to the woods, and the watcher felt his stomach tighten. The hunter, however, pointed to the camp and the watchtower being built on the ridge. When he did, the watcher noticed something that crowded all other considerations out of his mind.

The hunter was injured. The green-cloaked man was trying to conceal it, but, to the watcher—so trained in reading a creature's every gesture—it was obvious: the hunter held one arm too close to his body, and avoided moving it.

Though flushed with excitement, wishing to race back to the chieftain and be honored for his crucial information, the watcher forced himself to relax into the bush. He remembered the spider on his shoulder, now having crawled away to inspect a less dangerous terrain, for the little weavers were symbolic of care and patience. *Be like the patient weaver,* the watcher thought, and smiled to himself, pondering all he'd seen. Was there discord among the outsiders? Perhaps a struggle for leadership? Such a struggle could easily turn deadly. It was dangerous, very dangerous, to jump to such conclusions. But the excitement remained. If the chieftain or the *sheenya* decreed the strangers must die, it would be easier for the Malaspiri if some of them killed each other.

༄

The clearing made Early nervous. His party had been making their slow way through the thick heart of the forest for much of the morning, and he would just as soon have turned back to camp an hour ago. Isaac took the lead, as always. With his uninjured arm, he swung a heavy-bladed machete to clear a path through the dense undergrowth of tangled black brambles. Each of the explorers carried one of the makeshift blades, the work of Ander and Dreanna back at camp—the two trades-people from Marie's raft were anxious to contribute where they could.

Early clutched his machete in a sweaty palm. A cleared space in the middle of this deep and forbidding forest was unnerving enough, but the ancient ruin within left a cold feeling of dread in his bones. Twin lines of standing stones beckoned towards a windowless stone building whose ornate archway framed a black rectangular opening into darkness. Isaac held up his hand before they entered the clearing proper, and the party froze, watchful. This part of the forest was eerily silent, as though the birds and insects understood this place was sacred. *Sacred,* Early thought, his throat dry with fear, *or accursed?*

Satisfied there was no immediate danger, Isaac released them, and the seven explorers walked carefully among the stones. Early stayed at the ranger's side, while the Redguards, Taliss, Sander, and Captain Antmar spread across the clearing in a defensive formation. Only Lia seemed more interested in the stones themselves than in the atmosphere of forbidding antiquity that filled the clearing, and her faithful Rowene trailed behind reluctantly as the cartographer inspected them.

Though some of the menhirs had tumbled, others still reared high above their heads, balanced on narrow points as though dropped like arrowheads from the sky, standing forever where they'd pierced the earth. It seemed to Early such stones must topple at any moment, and he crept along the alley between the two rows with growing unease. The very notion of people, especially ancient people, standing such stones in orderly lines was impossible to imagine, without the intercession of some forgotten elder magic. Each massive stone was carved in intricate relief, but long exposure had blurred the stonework, and moss flourished in the creased and pockmarked surface. Some of the stones had broken into pieces from the slow action of water and plant life.

Lia walked down the aisle of megaliths, stopping at the threshold of the stone building. Early felt Isaac tense in warning, but she made no move to enter, admiring the intricate pictographs cut into the grim, weathered stone of the lintel. She studied the reliefs for long minutes before the rest of the group dared to gather around. Rowene, usually a fixture at her lady's side, stood farther back even than Early. For his part, the young deckhand couldn't shake the intense feeling that they did not belong here.

"This is obviously old," Lia said, her voice hushed. She reached out to the carvings as though to touch them, but stopped just short of making contact. "I wonder if this is the work of the same people whose trap you found?" She looked at Early, and he blushed as he did whenever she regarded him—he couldn't seem to help it, even in such strange circumstances.

"If so," she continued, "they must have been here hundreds of years. By my guess, this stonework is older than the Decadin Empire."

Early gaped, overcome by the notion. He looked to Isaac for the ranger's opinion, but Isaac was crouched down, looking at the long grass at their feet.

"What bothers me is," he said, standing, "these ruins aren't entirely overgrown." Isaac pointed to the boundary of the clearing, a rough ellipse perhaps two dozen yards in diameter at its widest. "If this place were abandoned, the forest would have consumed it. But if our mysterious trappers use this building, you would think they'd keep the entry clear."

"What does that say to you, Guard Isaac?" Lia asked.

He nodded to the low stone bulk with a grim smile. "That's a tomb, if I've ever seen one. If this is where our friends bury their dead, they must be lucky enough to not die very often. Or they preserve this place... but don't dare go inside."

Early looked around the clearing as the others muttered nervously. The Redguards had traded their machetes for their gleaming longswords, as though desperate for an enemy they could master. Apprehension lay against Early's skin like a damp fog, and he remembered waiting on the deck of the *Pride* for the storm to overtake them. The feeling of doom was the same, like he could only wait, helpless, for something to emerge from the black doorway or the surrounding forest, a blight or punishment for trespassing in this forbidden place.

But nothing came. While her companions milled about the clearing, restless, Lia remained fascinated by the ancient ruins. She had her sketchbook now, and was capturing the dimensions of the standing stones in eager strokes of charcoal.

"Perhaps we can come back with torches and tools," she said, her eyes returning again and again to the black aperture with its promise of ancient secrets.

But Taliss, who'd approached hoping to draw her friend away, shook her head slowly. "I don't think that would be a good idea. If the people who reside here shun that doorway, they might do so for good reason."

"What are you thinking?" Lia asked. "That there might be traps?" A sly smile came to her lips. "Or some sort of terrible curse? You bold warriors of the Redguard are a superstitious lot!"

She was teasing, but before Taliss could answer, there came a low hissing growl. Having heard that sound before, Early spun around, glad to feel himself drawing his borrowed sword by reflex. Isaac, next to him, brandished his machete. A beast just like those Early and Isaac had encountered in the woods loped into the clearing, lifting its doglike, reptilian head. A second beast followed, hissing a challenge. Early tensed for battle, but then one of the Redguard shouted a warning behind him. Another two beasts slunk from the trees at the other side of the tomb. Early shuddered as he realized the creatures' malevolent coordination. Circling the clearing noiselessly, the scaly predators had flanked their prey.

7

The strangers had found the tomb. The stones reared by the ancestors lay far from the watcher's village, in a clearing that did not seem to need tending, as though the trees feared to approach the archaic ruins. Tradition said only the *sheenya* came here, to commune with the spirits. Only they could safely enter the space where the greenish pillars of rock thrust up out of the soil like the earth's own teeth. It was not healthy for the living to spend too much time in proximity to the dead.

The watcher shivered just looking at the ruins. The sun seemed dimmer here than elsewhere, the air colder. It seemed proper that the tomb, home to generations of the dead, should feel haunted even at midday. Were it not his duty to play shadow to the strangers as they explored the island, the watcher would never have come here alone.

He slid between the trees like a ghost, always wary lest one of the strangers should turn at the wrong moment. But they were engrossed by the stones, remarking on the carvings left behind by the ancient builders. He watched them reluctantly approach the tomb proper, whose massive blocks blended seamlessly into the ground—as though the building had grown like the grass. He found it hard to believe the site was raised by human hands... if human the ancients truly were.

One of the strangers put her hands against the doorway, touching the carvings, and then tracing over them with paper and charcoal. The watcher trembled at this alien contact with the holy monument, feeling the trespass as an almost physical blow. Though the woman was careful, even reverent in her way, the watcher's instincts told him to charge in and force the strangers off the sacred ground, even at the cost of his life.

But he took a deep breath and flexed his hands around his spear, releasing the tension. He had his orders: no matter what happens, remain unseen. Besides, even if the strangers had not gone about armed—and the ones dressed in crimson had both fine longswords and the warrior's mien—he could not hope to overwhelm them alone, even with the advantage of surprise.

The watcher pondered his next move as he waited, still as the trees. His pulse throbbed in his throat and he realized his teeth were clenched. He was in the midst of forcing himself to relax again when he heard movement in the bush a dozen yards to his left. Something big. He turned his eyes to their limit, unwilling to move his head. A dark shape was moving on a tangent to him. Not stalking him, he understood with relief; it was moving towards the clearing.

He scanned the treeline carefully, saw a telltale rustle on the far side of the open space. The watcher recognized the size and pack tactics of the reptilian *guarni*. The beasts were moving to flank the strangers! Standing in a loose circle, speaking quietly, the prey was unaware of the impending attack.

Should he warn them?

The watcher, every nerve on edge, chose to remain still. As four of the *guarni* stalked from their cover, he considered this may well be the work of the spirits, defending the source of their power from intrusion. The *sheenya* was correct to warn all away from this place. Only she was meant to come here, she who heard the voices of the tomb's ancient guardians on the wind. Others would only earn the ancients' wrath, and here that wrath was in the sleek black shapes that ringed in the outsiders with terrible coordination.

The men and women were all armed, but none had spears like his, so much better for keeping the crushing jaws at a distance. He winced at the thought of what he was about to witness and squeezed the haft of his spear again. Ultimately, the thought of interfering with the spirits kept him from action. But he would stay and watch, and tell his fellow Malaspiri what befell those who trespassed.

Then one of the outsiders was shouting. When the watcher saw why, his blood ran cold: even as the green-cloaked man struck one of the beasts with a heavy blade, he warned the others away from the yawning mouth of the tomb where they crowded. It seemed to the watcher an invisible force was gathering in the air around the old stones, causing the scene to waver. Whether the outsiders saw it, he did not know, but the light of the sun dimmed, and the ground beneath the intruders' feet began to glow in lines of energy, a pattern weaving between the tomb and the standing stones. They had breached the sacred barrier that none but the *sheenya* was meant to cross, and the watcher was more certain than ever of their doom.

He could do nothing but bear terrified witness as, one by one, the outsiders retreated through the doorway, and he prayed whatever punishment awaited them would not be visited on his people as well, for failing to prevent the blasphemy about to occur.

Only the green-cloaked man remained outside the tomb. Even as he slashed the beast who faced him, sending it squealing away to the edge of the clearing, the other three *guarni* milled around the entrance to the tomb. They knew their prey was there, but seemed unwilling to follow them underground. Perhaps the beasts felt the strange touch of the ancients' power, as the watcher did. They began to pace back and forth, an ugly rumble in their reptilian throats. Seeming to understand the prey was cornered, the predators would wait.

Meanwhile, green-cloak approached the beast he'd wounded. His arms were spread wide, machete in one hand and a long knife in the other. The knife hand was trembling, and the watcher remembered noticing green-cloak's injured arm. Bad luck for green-cloak. The injured *guarni* snarled as he drew closer, backing towards the forest.

It happened suddenly. When the reptilian horror sprang, green-cloak skipped to the side with a speed and grace the watcher envied. Heavy paws slashed empty air, and the stranger struck a grievous blow on the elongated snout with his machete. He didn't wait for the beast's response; even as it tried to turn its head, he stepped in and stabbed his dagger in the orifice of the creature's ear. The watcher, caught up in the spectacle, nodded in satisfaction—a mortal wound.

Gasping out a breath he didn't realize he'd been holding, the watcher felt the triumph of green-cloak's kill in his own body. The beast staggered and fell, the twitching dagger protruding from its skull, and its death cry, though brief, was terrible. The sound brought the beasts guarding the tomb to attention. Their heads came up on their sinuous necks, monstrous eyes focused on the stranger.

With a curse, green-cloak froze, and the watcher could tell he was forcing himself not to run, realizing if he provoked the beasts' chase instinct he didn't stand a chance. Instead, with remarkable self-control, he backed out of the clearing, his deep green cloak melting into the shadows of the forest. Growling, hesitating only to cast a wistful glance back at the tomb where other prey tempted, the *guarni* padded from the clearing in single file to hunt him down.

As the watcher tried to slow his racing heartbeat, he silently wished the cloaked outsider the Gods' Luck. The brave man would need it. He considered the tomb and the empty clearing, fingering his spear. The grim place was quiet now, almost peaceful. He thought about green-cloak loping through the woods with his injured arm, the beasts on his trail. After another moment, the watcher cursed and hurried to follow the stranger and his pursuers.

📎

Despite Isaac's warning, Early and his friends cornered themselves in the tomb. It was instinct to find shelter, to have something at their backs so the beasts couldn't flank them, though Early realized they were trapping themselves. It took everything he had to make himself face the doorway along with the three Redguards, weapons ready if the beasts came after them.

But they were safe for the moment. Standing in the dark, narrow vestibule, they could see the creatures pacing in the clearing beyond, their hungry blue eyes never leaving the door. While Early felt a deep foreboding about the ancient place, the creatures evidently felt an even stronger restriction.

But now what? Early wondered. They couldn't stay in the tomb forever, and the beasts were waiting. Worst of all, Isaac was out there, beyond the wall of scales and teeth. Hopelessness left Early almost paralyzed, a bitter taste rising in his throat, and, when Rowene clutched his sleeve to pull him farther into the shadows, he let her lead him away from the door with a sob of despair.

Wonder soon replaced anguish. The tomb was unlike any

building Early had ever seen. The architecture of the High City of Petara was impressive, to be sure, but there was a weight in these great blocks of stone, compounded by their antiquity, that turned a modest resting place into a fearsome pile.

A dozen yards back from the entrance, the narrow antechamber ended in a steep, well-worn stairway plunging into the earth. It should have been pitch dark, yet daylight found its way in; the builders of the tomb had set narrow shafts at regular intervals in the ceiling, providing enough gloomy illumination to at least keep them from stumbling. They filed down the stairway in silence, hands against the rough wall for balance, eyes wide in the gloom. Only Captain Antmar, taking up the rear, looked back over his shoulder every few steps—to be cornered on this stairway would be certain death.

Due to the position of the light shafts, only narrow slices of the walls were visible, but every inch of those was carved in intricate patterns. Their lines resembled nothing Early had seen before, and Lia exclaimed that they were evident of a civilization unknown to the scholars of the Decadin Empire. When the stairs ended, the corridor remained narrow, but the ceiling was twice Early's height, vanishing into shadow. Though they were now far below the ground, enough light seeped down through the ingenious lighting system—and a hint of fresh air alongside—that the dreadful place was at least not stifling.

Still, apprehensiveness weighed on Early more heavily with each step. More so than any place he'd been since washing ashore, he felt distinctly unwelcome, felt they weren't meant to be here—that they were, in fact, intruding on something. He was deep in such brooding thoughts when the corridor took a sharp, right-angled turn, and then widened. Four huge steps, each broader than the last, led down into a large circular chamber. At equidistant points along the curving wall, such that at least a dozen lay there in the dark, were massive stone sarcophagi.

It was a tomb, indeed. And here its ancient residents slept under enormous slabs of stone whose upper surfaces were carved into fantastic shapes. Early couldn't help it: his mind insisted on contemplating what it would sound like if one of those covers began to slide open, the slow scrape of stone on stone... he shivered and cursed his overactive imagination.

But the sarcophagi weren't the most suggestive feature of the tomb. Lia, who'd been murmuring aloud, theorizing about the culture of the people who built this place, went quiet with a gasp. Early followed her gaze to the center of the room, and his mind blanked with horror.

The ceiling spiraled down to a conical point, as though the roof had frozen solid in the act of draining into the floor. A carving rose from the floor to meet the descending point of the ceiling—each was shaped into a monstrous winged figure, one rising, one falling. With only a hand's breadth between their open jaws, the sculpted things were caught in the moment before they crashed together in a catastrophe of stone teeth and talons. They could only be, Lia whispered, an ancient representation of true dragons, the awesome chariots and tools of the Lost Gods.

Neither the exotic expertise of the carving nor its mythological implications were what set Early's head swimming. It was familiarity. The rock was shaped and sanded so the draconic figures gleamed, their intricate scales appearing almost wet in the beams of daylight focused directly upon them by clever shafts in the chamber's roof. The dragon shaped from the ceiling, the one diving downward, as though out of the sky—Early had seen it before. He had seen it, infinitely larger and impossibly terrifying, in a nightmare at sea. He'd been praying what he saw in the storm had been only a frenzy of imagination.

Alas, what his mind's eye had conjured in a moment of panic, and his memory tortured him with ever since, was here reproduced in every hideous detail. Plunging from the roof of the tomb, immortalized in frozen stone, was the Elder of Storms.

❦

The beasts were gaining. Isaac could hear the sounds they made in the brush. He knew if he broke into a dead run, they'd be on top of him in moments. Much as it made his skin crawl, he had to let them stalk him. A branch snapped behind him and he tightened his body, anticipating the terrible weight, the rending jaws—but nothing pounced on him. He dared to turn, poised to defend himself with dagger and machete.

There was nothing there but the path he'd beaten and hacked through the underbrush. He just hoped, completing the thought interrupted by the snapping branch, he could find a defensible spot before the beasts did attack. They could be flanking him even now.

Scanning the forest, Isaac spotted a sturdy tree whose trunk was just about the right diameter for an easy climb. He sheathed his blades and made straight for it, hoisting himself to the first sturdy branch above the ground, and then mounting up higher as fast as he could. He grimaced as he put weight on his injured arm, but it had just enough strength to let his legs push him higher. Where no branches were available, he found footholds in the bark, long practice letting his body cling to the tree by feel.

He was well into the canopy before the first beast padded into the open, its nostrils flaring and slender tongue flickering to taste the air. It did not seem aware of him on his perch, and Isaac dared hope the beasts might simply give up the chase. But he braced himself in the groin of a huge offshoot branch, back against the tree's dark trunk, and carefully, wary of both noise and his balance, worked the bow off his shoulder into a firm, one-handed grip.

He was nocking an arrow, and the other two beasts had crowded around the first, when one of them looked up and saw him. With a hiss, the beast coiled its body and leaped, clawing the trunk of the tree as it tried to find purchase. Isaac grimaced; the thing had jumped fully twice his own height. Luckily for the ranger, he'd climbed twice again so high. With careful aim, he leaned as far out over the branch as he dared, and curled his fingers around the bowstring. He wasn't sure his arm was strong enough to make the draw, but now was the time to find out.

The tendons in his forearm felt as though they burst into flames as he pulled the bow. Isaac groaned in pain through gritted teeth, but forced his weapon to full draw. And let fly. The shaft pierced the beast's flank as it hauled itself towards him, and it slid back down to the ground with a howl. Maddened by the sting of the arrow, the beast turned in a circle and slashed its heavy forepaw at the nearest of its companions.

Isaac smiled, glad to have sown unrest among his enemies. As the two beasts yowled at one another, though, the third took a running start and flung itself into the tree.

This nimbler beast managed to land on the large branch Isaac had first used to pull himself up, and it gathered itself there for the climb, tongue lashing the air at the scent of its nearby prey. Isaac tried to fire a second arrow, but now his damaged arm failed him. The bowstring slipped from his fingers too soon, and the arrow arced to the ground, nowhere near its target. Worse, twisting his body to track the creature threw even the dexterous ranger off balance, and his legs began to slip. Cursing, Isaac caught himself against the trunk of the tree, only just managing not to drop his bow. Meanwhile, the beast in the tree with him climbed steadily closer.

A sweat broke out on the ranger's brow, and a funny thought came to him: he was glad Early wasn't here to see his plight—it wouldn't do for an apprentice to see the master ranger caught up a tree, trying to keep from falling as a reptilian horror came to make him its dinner. He swore he'd make a better show than that. Isaac couldn't get a blade in his good hand without dropping his bow, and he hated to let the treasured weapon fall to the ground... a foolish sentiment, he realized—if he didn't find some way to defend himself now he'd never draw the bowstring again.

He was steeling himself to drop the bow and pull his machete for a last desperate strike at the creature, whose grasping paws were almost arm's-length away, when a terrible cry pierced the air. Surprised, it was all he could do to cling to the branch. But the creature in the tree froze, and, far below the ranger and the beast, the other two stopped snarling at each other and stared into the brush, suddenly alert.

The cry came again, closer now, and the two beasts on the ground actually fled, darting in separate directions. Isaac dared a glance at the beast in the tree and saw it was looking away from him, though it kept its perch with its claws dug into the bark. Its pale tongue flickered wildly between its black jaws, trying to sense what was coming for them. Isaac wondered the same thing.

A man stepped into view. From high in the tree, distracted by impending death at the jaws of the reptile still clinging to its trunk, Isaac got only a passing impression of what the man looked like. The newcomer was tall, lean, and strong, clothed in brief and simple hide next to which his own tanned skin was striped in dusty gray. He held a spear whose head came to a wicked point, and without a glance at Isaac, he drew it back over his shoulder and hurled it like a javelin at the beast.

Isaac tensed by reflex as the stranger launched the missile, as it blurred into the dark body of the creature next to him, as the beast lost its grip. Squirming and howling, it crashed against the sturdy branch Isaac had used to get into the tree, its body snapping at an impossible angle. When the beast had tumbled to the ground, broken and unmoving, Isaac and the man looked at one another.

"Thank you," the ranger said, though he didn't reckon the stranger would understand his speech. He gave the salute of the Imperial Guard, right fist to left breast, hoping his gratitude would come across in the gesture. The man said nothing, yet his eyes widened at the salute and he gazed at Isaac thoughtfully. After a moment, he gave his head a shake as though returning from a daydream, and made a similar gesture in return. Then the man retrieved his spear from the hide of the dead lizard-thing, and, with a lingering glance at the ranger in the tree, turned and vanished into the brush whence he'd come.

Isaac watched the spot where the stranger had been for a long time. The stranger. A native of their new home, apparently, and the man had saved his life. Isaac pondered the import of this meeting and imagined the looks on his friends' faces when he told the story. Then it came to him he was still high up a tree, he was clutching his bow in one hand, and his backside was falling asleep. He laughed at himself. For now, he was glad just to be alive—the ramifications could wait. Shouldering his bow, favoring his wounded arm, the ranger turned his attention to escaping from the tree.

§

For Early, the rest of the tomb and his friends' amazement had ceased to exist. He stood near the center of the chamber, with no clear memory of how he'd come to be there, transfixed by the dragon modeled in dark stone. Lia came and laid a gentle hand on his arm, but even the slight touch made him jump and yelp in surprise.

"Early! Forgive me. This carving is incredible, isn't it? But what's wrong?" Lia saw Early's face had drained of color. Early felt his heart pounding, each beat sending his mind back in time to the tilting deck of the *Pride*, the smoke from the blazing mainmast boiling into the tumult of clouds above. He realized what he must look like, could see his expression was scaring Lia. But he couldn't tell her what he'd seen during the storm, *if* he had seen anything at all.

"Sorry, Lia. It's just..." he tore his eyes from the sculpture and looked around the rest of the tomb, where the others were investigating the huge sarcophagi. The tops of each were carved into scenes of battle, celebration, and rites whose nature was beyond conjecture, and the figures cavorting in those rites had too-long limbs and strange outlines, not altogether human. Between the dragons and these other carvings, the tomb seemed the design of master stonemasons and sculptors all gone completely insane.

"This place *feels* wrong," Early said, quietly, so only Lia would hear. He struggled to explain how his throat felt tight, as though the air were too thick to breathe. "I just... I don't think we should be here."

Lia nodded, and her continued touch on his arm was a comfort, but she turned away to drink in the room, not sharing his sense of dread. "It is a fearsome place, yes. Imagine the civilization that built it! I've never seen sculpture to match this in the Empire. Their art must have exceeded our greatest masters."

Early pulled away. Lia seemed about to reach out and touch the dragon sculpture, and he felt a shuddering trepidation about her doing so. He was sure, without knowing how, why, or what, something dreadful would happen if they persisted in their intrusion. The fear of the unknown Early had felt when he and Isaac discovered the hunting pit, realizing the survivors of the *Pride* must not be alone, was nothing compared to the primal terror of this tomb. Something deep and animal in his mind demanded he run for the stairs and keep running, as fast and far as he could. It took all his effort to remain with his fellow explorers.

As the underground chamber grew more intolerable, Early began pacing near the stairs, unwilling to remain any longer, but likewise unwilling to leave on his own—weren't the beasts still waiting for them outside, after all? A glimmer drew his eye to the floor. Something was lodged right at the foot of the lowest step. Impossible to notice when they'd entered the chamber, he saw it now by the merest chance.

Feeling his eyes must be deceiving him, Early crouched down. Swallowing his distaste at touching anything in the ruin, he tried to make out the shape by touch. What he picked up was small, a scrap of something, and covered in dust—it could not have been dropped by any of Early's party. When he dared return to the center of the room and light from the shafts in the roof fell on the thing, the feeling of unreality that had gripped Early since setting eyes upon the sculpted horror of the Elder of Storms grew stronger. He simply couldn't believe what he held in his hands; it was a torn piece of leather belt, two ragged pieces clasped together by a tarnished buckle, at first glance nothing remarkable.

But the buckle had an unmistakable shape: crossed blade and anchor upon a billowing sail.

The symbol of Her Imperial Majesty's Blueguard.

Unable to speak, Early tottered back to the steps and sat down. Captain Antmar, noticing him, came over. "Wills? What's wrong? The air is terribly close in here, isn't it?"

Early nodded, but held up the buckle. "I found this. It was here, right here at the foot of the steps. Look!"

The Redguard brought the scrap back to the light. When he returned, his face was almost as pale as Early's at the implications of the thing. "This surely must belong to one of us," Antmar said. "We must have dropped it when we came in."

Early just looked at him, eyes wide and fearful, slowly shaking his head. He didn't need to point out the thick coating of dust, or that the only survivors who wore the Blueguard emblem were back at camp. Or that the belt could only have been so torn through an act of violence.

Antmar sighed, and actually smiled at Early's exasperation, though his smile was thin and not comforting. "You're right, Wills. That was foolish of me."

He called the others over, and soon they were all considering the buckle. "It doesn't seem possible," Lia said, "but doesn't this imply the first expedition came here?"

"If that be so," Redguard Taliss said, "if they survived the sea... What's become of them?"

It was Early, remembering the hunting pit and relieved by the notion it might have been dug by familiar hands, who spoke with conviction, "They must have made it here! The lost expedition, the ones we came to find. They must still be living here, somewhere!"

The rest of them were silent, contemplating. The oppressiveness of the underground chamber began to close in again. Rowene murmured something anxiously, and Lia took her young assistant's hand in her own. Guards Taliss and Sander shared a dark look with their captain, as though the elite bodyguards of the Empress communicated telepathically.

Early didn't dare be the one to suggest they ruminate out of doors, so it was a relief when Lia at last took the buckle and wrapped it carefully in a kerchief. Storing the treasure in her satchel, she gazed around the room with longing—she had not even begun to sketch the marvels they'd seen. But she gestured to the stairs and the corridor beyond.

"Let us return to camp at once and report this discovery. It must change what we do next. If the expedition reached this place, this is the first step to unlocking their fate."

She moved to the stairs, but Taliss stood in her way. "My lady. Have you forgotten," she said gently, "what waits for us above? Those beasts may still be there."

Lia blinked, but then gave her friend a cunning smile. "And what's that fancy sword on your hip for, Redguard?"

Taliss laughed and climbed the steps. Lia moved aside to let the other Redguards take the lead.

Happy to brood at the rear of the party, Early found himself suddenly blinded as they emerged into the entryway of the tomb. The narrow doorway was a rectangle of white glare after the gloom below. As vision returned, he saw no beasts waiting for them—but Isaac wasn't waiting for them, either. Though he'd thought himself glad to leave the ancient crypt behind, fear returned to the pit of Early's stomach. He was hesitant to stick his head out into the open air, welcome as the fresh breeze was. Even the close stone corridors and their archaic mysteries felt safer than the forest without the ranger to guide them.

At last, Early followed the others into the clearing. "Seems the beasts have gone," Guard Sander said after peering about. Early also scanned the clearing, remembering Isaac's tracking lessons, looking for telltale signs—not just sight, but sound. He closed his eyes and listened, but heard only his friends moving around him.

"What's become of Greenguard Vere?" asked the Guard-

Captain, and Early wished he knew. There was the huddled corpse of the fourth beast, which Isaac must have killed as the rest of them trapped themselves in the tomb. *Not so foolish a choice after all,* Early thought, hoping that, wherever the ranger had gone, he was okay. Brave and resourceful as Isaac was, Early had no illusions that he could hold his own against a whole pack of the monstrous lizard-things.

They fanned out and searched the clearing, but they were unskilled trackers and found no trace, not of beasts or their companion. "That at least leaves hope the ranger survived," Captain Antmar told them. "We should tarry no longer. Gather your things, and we'll find the path that brought us here."

Finding the path was easier said than done without the Greenguard, but in his absence they turned to his apprentice. Early, trying not to display his pride at being so chosen, was pretty sure he knew which opening in the trees would lead them back along their path—and that he could follow that path once he found it. Grateful for what Isaac had taught him, he only hoped his mentor would be waiting when they returned to camp. The potential survival of the lost expedition would pale beside the loss of his friend.

ঌ৶

Trudging back through the woods, leading his friends, Early had no time to dwell on his fears. Every step forced him to pick his way over roots and branches while making as sure as his neophyte ranger training would allow that they were still following the path, and that all of his companions were still in line behind him.

In Isaac's absence, he'd become de facto leader of the little squad, at least where navigating the woods was concerned. He wasn't used to being so essential, and the burden of responsibility was heavy; what if he got them all lost? What if they ran into the beasts again, or worse? But no one questioned that Early should lead, not even the dour Guard-Captain, who in any other situation would be the natural leader. Antmar had actually encouraged Early. When they'd left the clearing he'd gestured for the deckhand to go first, saying with uncommon diffidence that a Redguard couldn't tell one tree branch or one bird call from another.

Now, preoccupied as Early was, it took many bird calls for him to realize he was hearing not a bird, but a signal. He stopped, held up his hand as he'd seen Isaac do a dozen times while following the ranger's lead. Behind him, Lia and Rowene had been talking softly, but they came to a halt with impressive quickness; Isaac would have been pleased. With only the sounds of the forest left surrounding him, Early listened.

The call came again, off to his left. He turned to face the sound. Lia had opened her mouth to ask what was going on, but, seeing his intent expression, followed his eyes into the forest instead. When the long, high whistling sound came through the trees once more, Early pointed into the woods to fix himself on the direction, and only then turned to his friends.

"It's Isaac!"

"Where?" asked Taliss, her intense gaze scouring the trees around them.

"That sound..." Early waited a moment, and the call came once more. "That's a Greenguard signal! Isaac taught it to me."

"You're sure? It's not just a bird?"

Early shook his head, excitement having overcome any lack of confidence. "Isaac always said you must learn the sounds of whatever forest you're in. We haven't heard that call here before, I'm certain of it."

"Perhaps you've discovered a new species, Early," Lia said, but she was smiling.

Taliss picked up the remark and carried on, "Let's have a look at this strange new bird! Lead on, Early."

Returning their grins, and buoyant both at their faith in his leadership and the thought of seeing Isaac again, he led them off the path, towards the call.

Isaac was sitting in a low depression in the ground, where the enormous roots of two great trees held back other growth. Water must have pooled there waist-deep when it rained, but now the round space was dry and mossy, and even contained a little grove of toadstools the ranger had decided were safe to eat. He had his back to one of the huge gnarled trunks, and his bow, quiver, and machete all near to hand. There were no signs of beast or battle, and, aside from having the haggard look of a man who'd spent much of the afternoon up a tree, the ranger didn't look the worse for wear.

He heard them coming, of course, and gave a lazy salute as the group approached, though he didn't bother to stand.

"Either we've the Gods' Luck that, in all this great forest, you just happened to stumble into my picnic, or Early's actually learned some of his lessons and followed my call. Whatever the case, I'm glad to see you."

Early, grinning from ear to ear, hopped down on the other side of the little mushroom patch, copying the casual way the ranger leaned against the tree, comfortable but able at any moment to leap to his feet. Lia and Rowene sat on the large roots that formed the lip of the pit, happy to be off their feet for a while. The three Redguards loomed behind them, ever alert, ever protective.

"What happened after we went into the tomb, Isaac?" Early asked. "Did you fight off all those beasts yourself?"

"If so," Taliss broke in, "they'll sing your name in the Halls of the Guard, Ranger." Captain Antmar grunted at that, as close as he came to laughter.

Isaac smirked at them, then turned to Early. "You give too much credit to my sword arm. I killed one of the beasts, and the others followed me into the forest. I climbed a tree, hoping they wouldn't be able to follow... Alas, I was wrong."

Early's eyes widened, and he looked at the crooked nodular branches high overhead. "They can climb trees? Lost Gods, how did you escape?"

Isaac looked at each of them before answering. "Brace yourselves for this: I had help. A man came out of the forest, scared off two of the beasts, and skewered the one who'd come to join me in my tree."

There was silence for a moment as they all took this in. Then Lia spoke. "It's beyond doubt, then. We're not alone here."

Isaac nodded slowly. "Not alone. I didn't speak with the man, had he even known our language; he vanished into the trees. By the time I'd climbed down from my nest, he was long gone. I tried to track him, but—and I hate to admit this—he's a better ranger than I.

"There was nothing for it. Back I went towards camp, hoping you'd do the same and either hear my signal... or I'd hear you crashing through the woods like a drove of cattle."

Taliss scoffed in mock outrage. Rowene, who rarely joined in jocular teasing, cried, "Cattle! How dare you?!" Early relaxed against his tree, feeling some of the day's tension melt away.

Isaac rose to his feet, brushing off his leggings and shaking out his cloak. He picked up one of the seed pods dropped from the trees, a black, scaly ball the size of his fist. He turned it over in his hand, thoughtful. "Now we know there are others living here, and if they weren't aware of our presence before, they are now. I'll be curious to see what comes next."

"Well," Early said, "at least we're building a palisade. We can defend ourselves if we need to."

"It doesn't sound like the one you encountered was hostile, though, was he, Isaac?" Lia asked. "If he'd meant you harm..."

Isaac gave a hollow chuckle. "Indeed. He could have had another spear for me. Or just left well enough alone and let the beasts have their dinner."

From his watchful position beside Early's tree trunk, Captain Antmar spoke. "It may not be too much to hope for peaceful relations with these other folk, but we must have our guard up in the meantime. Lord Mardigan will decide how to proceed."

"You're right, of course, Guard-Captain," Lia said. "But I hope we've found allies rather than foes. Perhaps they can tell us more about the fate of the lost expedition."

"Indeed!" Isaac said. "I'd almost forgotten the original purpose of our voyage. It's been hard enough dealing with becoming a lost expedition ourselves."

"We had a stark reminder today," Rowene blurted, blushing as Isaac and the others turned to her. "Well, we found a trace of them in that tomb."

Isaac's eyebrows shot up in surprise. Lia pulled the torn belt and its clasp from her satchel and handed it to him. He inspected it with bewilderment. "The mark of the Blueguard! No doubt about it. And you found this in that old ruin?"

Early nodded. "There was a burial chamber, with these carvings..." He shivered, remembering. "I just happened to notice the belt in the dust. It must have lain there a long time."

Isaac pondered the tarnished clasp, then handed it back to Lia. He ran his thumb over the pebbled surface of the seed pod, lost in thought. Then he tossed the pod against a nearby tree so it bounced off the bark with a solid *thock!*

The ranger quickly gathered his weapons. "Let's not spend all day dallying in the woods after these revelations! Come,

Master Wills. Reckon you can find the way back to camp from here?"

Early beamed. So Isaac was going to let him remain in the lead! He looked to Captain Antmar, who nodded his approval, and the party fell in behind him. As she passed, Lia put an encouraging hand on Early's shoulder. Flustered and excited, he tried to remind himself of the orienteering skills Isaac had taught him. Choosing what he thought was the most likely direction, Early led his friends back into the forest.

8

A week went by after they'd trespassed on the tomb, and nothing. But Early felt the whisper of dread at the back of his mind whenever he wasn't occupied with something else. Whenever he thought back to that monstrous dragon in stone, descending from the ceiling of the burial chamber like the gods' own vengeance, he couldn't help feeling something bad was going to happen.

An uneventful week. And then, in the night, came retribution.

Early squinted against a sudden glare, trying to make out the figure that had come into his tent. He scrambled to grasp his knife—Isaac had warned his apprentice to always leave it within reach—but it lay belted into his trousers on the other side of the tent. Between Early and his weapon lay Olan, undisturbed by the intruder, snoring peacefully.

Backlit by daylight, the figure loomed over Early and he tried to separate the confusion of grogginess from panic. Then the figure spoke, and his relief at recognizing Lia's voice evaporated at the fear in her tone.

"Thank the Gods you're here! They're gone!" Lia cried,

dropping to her knees next to Early's sleeping wrap. "Gone!" Her eyes were wide and her skin was flushed, as though she'd been running.

Early pushed himself up on one elbow. "What—" he asked, choking on his dry throat. "What's wrong? Who's gone?"

Lia put her arms around her knees, bunching her skirts around her body like a shield. She only shook her head and made a sound like a sob. Early thrashed none too gracefully out of his sleeping wrap and put his hand on her arm.

"Hey. Lia, it's okay. We're okay, right? We're safe." He wasn't sure that was actually true, but he spoke as much to calm the tide of his own fear as hers. Lia took a deep breath and shut her eyes, and a tear slid down her cheek.

"I woke up perhaps ten minutes ago," she said. "Rowene was missing from her wrap beside me. I knew she'd gone to say her prayers before the dawn, but she usually comes back afterward and sleeps another hour. I thought perhaps she'd gone straight to break her fast, but I can't *find* her anywhere!"

Early sat up, holding his bed wrap close around him. As the shock of his awakening faded, self-consciousness was taking its place. Circumstances notwithstanding, Her Majesty's Cartographer was in his tent, and he was undressed. Early groped for his clothes, trying to process, with his sleep-addled mind, what she was telling him.

"Did you ask... who was on night watch this side of the camp? Was it Mosul?"

She nodded. "Guard Mosul, yes. And he's gone, too!"

Early gaped at this. "You—you're sure? He's not just somewhere else in camp?"

"I called out for him, as loud as I dared. For both of them. Yes, of course I thought he must have gone to his privy in the woods, anything, but—his post was right outside our tents, Early. He should be there. And Rowene!"

"Could they have... gone off? Um... together?" Early felt his face grow hot, immediately regretting the question. But Lia looked amused.

"If my dear Rowene had taken a lover, Early," she said, as he blushed even brighter, "I assure you, I would be the first to know."

Next to them, Olan snorted in his sleep, pulling the wrap up over his head.

"Okay," said Early, trying to think. "So, they're missing. Have you told Isaac? We should rouse the camp!"

She was shaking her head, eyes wide, the momentary amusement gone. "No. No, I couldn't find Rowene, or Mosul, and yours was the next tent, and I was so afraid I'd find you were missing, too..."

Impulsively, he went to her and hugged her close.

"Okay." He helped her to her feet. "Okay. It's okay. We need to tell Isaac, the other Guards, they'll know what to do. Let's go find Isaac. Let's go, okay?"

"But what if... what if he's gone, they're all gone?" Lia's voice broke. She didn't move. The tent was a refuge, while the beach outside, beautiful in the morning light, had become a place of terror.

Early couldn't shake the exact same thought. His limbs felt weak and his stomach upset, and he was glad he hadn't any food in him. He picked up his machete, drawing strength from the steel, and went to the tent flap. Revealing as little of himself as possible, he looked up and down the beach, but saw no one.

He turned back to Lia.

"We're still here, Lia. We're okay. I don't know where Rowene and Mosul went, but everyone else will still be here. They wouldn't leave us. Right?"

She eyed the tent flap suspiciously, as though doom might

fall on them as soon as they stepped out under the sky. Early reached out his hand, and Lia took it. He nodded encouragingly.

"It's okay," he repeated, hoping he was right. "We'll go straight to Isaac's tent."

After forcing Olan awake and explaining the situation, the three of them left the tent slowly, carefully, peering up and down the beach over and over again. Early's imagination kept producing movement, dark shapes out of the corner of his eye, emerging from the trees. But they reached Isaac's tent without incident, and Early pulled the flap aside without calling to see if the ranger was awake. Isaac lay in his sleeping wrap on his side. His right arm was curled near his face, hand lying inches from the hilt of his hunting knife. Early mentally chided himself for not being likewise prepared, despite the ranger's lessons. He stuck his head into the tent and whispered, "Isaac?"

The ranger's eyes opened, and he turned to look at Early. He seemed to be asleep one moment and fully awake the next, a capability Early couldn't comprehend, and envied. Isaac cast the sleeping wrap open and rolled to his knees and then his feet in a smooth motion, bringing the hunting knife with him.

"What is it?"

"Lia woke me. She said—it's—people are missing."

Isaac's dark eyes flickered with an emotion that didn't reach his face. He picked his belt up off the floor and nodded that Early should leave the tent. Early ducked back from the flap, and, a moment later, the fully dressed ranger joined him, Olan, and Lia near the cold cookfire.

"Lia. Are you all right? Early said someone's missing?" Isaac's voice was low and urgent, and he slid his belt around his waist as he spoke, fastening it without looking. He had replaced his hunting knife in its sheath opposite the hatchet on his other hip.

Lia looked around as though concerned they were being

watched. "Rowene and Mosul. I woke—they were gone when I woke up. I can't find them anywhere."

Isaac raised his eyebrows, as though wordlessly suggesting the same alternatives Early had.

Early spoke up. "Mosul should have been on watch. Lia said she called for him, but got no answer. And Rowene never came back from her prayers. Right, Lia?"

She nodded.

Isaac stroked his graying stubble, turning in a slow circle as he scanned the camp.

"Do you see anything?" Early whispered. He was looking around himself, but the morning light dazzled his eyes and he found himself double-checking every shadow. But Isaac shook his head, already starting to move.

"Nothing seems out of place. Come, we'd better rouse the Redguard, and make sure no one else is missing."

Lord Mardigan was sleeping peacefully in his cabin at the other end of the camp. Taliss and Dran Derrish—the Redguard medic—were on watch, marching quietly around the cabin in an endless circle, while their fellow Guards took their rest within. They saluted Isaac when he appeared, Early and Lia trailing after him watchfully. When they'd explained the situation, Dran went inside to wake the sleepers, while Taliss joined Isaac, Early, and Lia; the four of them roused the rest of the camp.

Mercifully, no one else seemed to have been disturbed. Everyone was in their expected places, either still soundly asleep or just waking up, hoping for breakfast. Once word had been spread that Rowene and Mosul were missing, everyone gathered around the cookfire as Lia told and re-told what she'd seen and heard.

Hearing was at the root of the problem: no one had heard anything. No shouts, no confrontation. Mosul had been on watch at the south end of the camp, while the Redguard around the lord's cabin provided a watch at the north end. Blueguard Coral, having been a watch officer on the *Pride*, had spent the night in the little tower in the center of the palisade. She hadn't noticed any disturbance. Mosul had simply disappeared from his post, and Rowene had left the tent she shared with Lia and vanished.

Lord Mardigan stood and asked for silence around the cookfire before the general grumbling could grow into a dangerous panic.

"This is a matter of gravest concern," he said, "and we must not rest until we find our friends. Likewise, we shall redouble our efforts to guard our camp."

He turned towards Antmar, but before the Guard-Captain could launch into the details of this redoubled effort, Olan stepped forward. "How do we know what happened to them? Makes no sense they'd run off, so were they taken? If they were taken, by what?"

"Maybe it was those beasts you all fought off in the woods," said Sil Edgert, the cook. "Those great lizard-horse monsters!"

The worried murmuring around the fire increased in volume.

"It wasn't," Isaac said, his voice calm but loud enough to carry across the cookfire. By the time of this gathering, he'd scoured the borders of the camp with the Redguard, looking for tracks. "If the beasts attacked, they'd have left some sign." He did not elaborate, and Early was glad; the grim vision of the creatures dragging his friends into the woods in their powerful jaws sprang readily enough to his obliging imagination. "There aren't even new footprints, far as I can tell, leading from the camp."

"What of the stranger you met in the woods, Greenguard?" Marie Gold asked. "You said a man appeared and chased off the beasts that beset you. And before that, you and Early found a trap... if there are others living here, perhaps they took our friends captive."

The murmuring grew again. Isaac looked thoughtful, but shook his head slowly.

"A visit from those others makes the most sense, yet surely they'd have left *some* sign, especially if they'd taken struggling prisoners away with them. We've found nothing yet."

"It's like they vanished into the air," Taliss muttered, gripping the hilts of her twin swords.

"I knew this was a bad place," Ander groaned. The carpenter raised his voice in fear. "A haunted place. This is a vengeance like the one we had on the accursed sea. We'll all be sorry we landed here!"

A tumult of voices rose at that, and Lord Mardigan had to shout to demand calm.

"My people, please! We cannot give in to fear. Instead, let us take action. Greenguard Vere and Guard-Captain Antmar will need volunteers, let us have two or three for each of them, to patrol the woods around the camp and see if any sign of our missing kin can be found.

"The rest of us will begin at once to shore up our defenses." He indicated the low palisade wall that ran along the ridge and the open beach at both ends of the camp. "If we can harvest wood enough, we shall make a true fortress, so no enemy may come upon us."

The crowd grumbled their misgivings. Olan grumbled loudest at the thought of more lumber-hauling. But then he winked at Early and shouted, "Unless they come by sea!"

That broke the heavy dread hanging like a stormcloud over the cookfire. Lord Mardigan smiled at the big deckhand gratefully. Early did, too. At least working on the wall would take his mind off wondering at the fate of Rowene and

Mosul... and worrying that the same fate awaited the rest of them.

But Early's fate was not to work on the palisade wall, and he would not escape being reminded of his missing friends. As Isaac's apprentice, he was assigned to patrol with the ranger and with Olan, whose grousing had eventually bought him a relief from hard labor.

The three of them searched the woods to the northeast of the camp, while Redguard Taliss led Coral and Ereved, the Blueguard watch officers, to the southeast.

In two tense days of searching, neither patrol had found any sign of Rowene or Mosul... or what had happened to them. Early felt the tension growing with every step he took through the thick forest. He kept glancing to his left, in the direction of the camp, and when they'd gone deeply enough into the trees that their palisade—erected by rearranging and bolstering the wall they'd built from the hull of the wrecked ship—was no longer visible, a cold sweat broke out on his brow. Every few minutes, Early realized he was hunching his shoulders, and had to force his body to relax. If they did encounter trouble in the woods, a stiff neck wouldn't help.

He felt the branch beneath his foot a moment before it cracked, but the noise still made him flinch. Beside and slightly behind Early, Olan cursed in surprise, but where he would usually have followed up with a teasing remark, they were both too on edge for banter. Several yards up the trail he was cutting through the bush, Isaac didn't seem to notice the clumsy sounds of his inexpert team, but Early knew he *did* notice their noise, and many more besides that the deckhands were too preoccupied to hear. The ranger was simply well-trained enough to filter out what wasn't relevant.

And Early wished he felt the least bit relevant.

It would help if he knew what they were searching for. They

didn't know whether they would stumble across their friends, or their friends' dead bodies: a thought which made Early shiver. It brought back the intolerable memory of the drowned Blueguard who'd washed ashore weeks earlier, and the awful task of burying the sea-spoiled corpse. The thought of Mosul, brave Blueguard lieutenant, or Rowene, Lia's devoted assistant, stiff and pale and perhaps preyed upon, was too horrible to contemplate. Early struggled with great effort to force such thoughts away, and replace them with something, anything else.

His ranger training told him what he *should* be focused on: the here and now. Orienting himself to the surrounding woods, he tested his senses. Isaac was a dozen yards ahead and slightly to his right. Olan was only a few arm's lengths behind him, a little to the left. The camp was to his left, probably not more than a hundred yards off, though he could see nothing but dark twisted trunks and leaves in that direction. The forest was thick, and the underbrush abundant enough they were obliged to hack through it with machetes as they made their way in a broad arc around the camp. At least it was a bright midday, and plenty of sunlight filtered down through the canopy. The sun-dappled forest was really quite pretty and peaceful, taken on its own; it was only the mystery of their missing friends that gripped Early with dread and made the verdant shadows sinister.

When Isaac wanted their attention, he didn't speak, even though Early and Olan were near at hand. Instead, a quick whistle brought Early, used to the ranger's signals, to an immediate, attentive halt. Olan, less familiar with the protocol, blundered into him. The big man cursed, and Early elbowed him in the ribs. Isaac looked back over his shoulder at the two, and Early could see his body was tense and very still—he perceived danger. Early squeezed the grip of his machete for reassurance.

Isaac gestured for them to move up beside him. When they were close enough to hear him whisper, he said, "Something up ahead. Moving in the trees. Do you see?" He pointed, and Early followed the line of his arm. There was indeed motion among the trunks, but he couldn't tell what it was—animal or man. Though the place where they stood was sunny, the mass of trees to which Isaac pointed seemed darker, as though a cloud had descended only there to obscure part of the forest. As Early watched, the dark edges of the opaque mass seemed to undulate, concealing the trees and bushes behind a bluish-black wall.

"It's like a fog," Early whispered, fascinated. He feared to move or to look away. The dark cloud gathering in the woods only deepened his sense of dread. He found himself remembering the stormclouds churning high above the mainmast of the *Pride*, and how they'd seemed to part like a vast curtain before... something... had set the mast aflame.

Early shivered. Had the woods gotten colder in the last few moments? And darker?

"Is it coming towards us?" Olan asked, as quietly as Early had ever heard him. His big friend was fidgeting, unsheathing his machete with a scraping sound that seemed far too loud.

Isaac took a step forward, bow and arrow drawn. His arm was healing fast, but he still winced as he pulled back the string. Early winced, too. It seemed to him, without knowing why, that remaining still was terribly important—like they were rabbits desperate to avoid the gaze of a predator. The ranger took another step, his soft boots silent in the undergrowth. The fog was moving closer, Early was certain of it. The woods were growing dimmer, as though, up above the canopy of trees, a cloud was passing across the sun.

"Isaac—" Early wanted to warn the ranger to stop, but his voice failed him, coming out in a dry rasp. Isaac, bow at the ready, stalked between two trees, closer to the roiling cloud that was now only ten yards away.

"This is madness," Olan grumbled, standing his ground nonetheless. Seeing his friend's blade from the corner of his eye, Early readied his own, struggling to remain as still and silent as possible. He wasn't sure if he feared alerting something to his presence, or simply that, if he broke the spell of stillness, the unbearable tension would cause him to bolt for camp in a helpless panic. Shoulder to shoulder with his bigger crewmate, blades out, Early felt a little braver. But Isaac was moving farther and farther away, and Early could not bring himself to follow. He wished the ranger would come back to them, but was afraid to call out. He felt sure it was something monstrous bearing down on them, a doom eager to engulf them.

Isaac stopped a mere yard from the trailing edge of the cloud. The thick blackish fog seemed to flicker as it drew near the ranger, and Early swore he could see tendrils reaching out, leaves on the ground swirling in air that was suddenly charged, as during a thunderstorm. The ranger seemed to feel the threat pressing down on him. He raised his bow. But then the cloud billowed outwards as though blown by a driving wind. Its black edges closed around Isaac, and Early's mouth opened in a silent cry as his mentor vanished into the oncoming mass. Beside Early, Olan let out an inarticulate gasp.

The cloud grew as it crawled closer, reaching up into the high boughs above their heads. The whole wood had grown dark, and it was hard to see more than a few yards away. It seemed there was a thrumming sound filling the air between them and the cloud, more felt than heard, and Early found himself shouting over it, repeating the ranger's name: "Isaac! Isaac?!"

There was no reply, and he could see nothing beyond the wall of vapor pouring between the trees towards them. Early and Olan were both backpedaling, afraid to turn, afraid of tripping, afraid with the fear that grips a sailor in the face of an oncoming storm.

But unlike sailors on a ship, they could turn and run. At the last moment, they did.

Early hoped his instincts would serve to take them towards the camp and not, in the panic of their flight, deeper into the woods. His only conscious thoughts were that the fog had taken Isaac, was coming for them, and if it overtook them would surely mean their doom. The feeling in his gut told Early this fog was no mere trick of the weather, but something arcane, dark, and dangerous. He could imagine it boiling forth, black and flickering with unnatural lightning, from the mouth of that great tomb in the woods... or from the jaws of a dragon, plunging from the sky. He found himself running faster, the hours spent navigating the woods with Isaac helping him skip over roots and avoid soft or rotted patches of earth that might have slowed or tripped him.

But Olan, less accustomed to the woods, was not so lucky. The crashing sound he made as he ran behind Early abruptly ceased as Olan tripped and stumbled, cursing. When Early dared look back over his shoulder, he saw Olan, fallen to his hands and knees, swallowed up by the towering black wall that rolled on towards him, devouring.

"Olan!" Early cried. "No!" But he didn't stop, couldn't possibly. Animal fear was driving him. He felt his hair stand on end as the cloud drew near and shivered at the cold touch of vapor on the back of his neck. His lungs burning, Early pushed himself harder, dashing madly through the forest, leaping across roots and great stones that thrust up out of the soil, feet hardly seeming to touch the ground. Isaac would be proud of his agility, Early thought, but Isaac was gone.

When the wall of trees thinned and then ended, and the

spongy floor of the forest became the packed soil of the ridge where their palisade stood, Early barely noticed. Someone on watch in the tower called out to him, but he neither stopped nor slowed until he'd passed through the small wooden gate in the wall, left ajar for the returning patrols. He stumbled down the rough, ungraded slope to the beach and collapsed at the feet of Lord Mardigan and Captain Antmar, gasping for breath and gesturing soundlessly, desperately, that they close the gate.

In the squat tower that peeked above the lashed and sharpened wooden timbers of the palisade, Early should have felt safe. But he could barely bring himself to look over the railing at the woods, which, though the midday sun shone down on their green and golden leaves, seemed twisted and freighted with unseen, unnatural menace. Early knew that, just beyond the line of trees, the malevolent black fog waited, the fog that had swallowed his closest friends. Like Captain Antmar, who stood next to him on the cramped platform of the watchtower, Early had his blade drawn, but he was leaning heavily against the railing. His legs felt weak, and, though he told himself it was from his desperate flight through the woods, Early worried the fear was breaking his resolve.

Olan was gone. Isaac was gone. He'd watched his mentor and closest friend disappear into the land-bound thunderstorm as it rampaged through the trees. Now, though the formidable Redguard captain was at his side, and the dozen of them that remained behind the palisade had taken up defensive positions with all the weapons they could gather, Early felt achingly alone and vulnerable, a child in the dark.

Lord Mardigan had listened with grave attentiveness when Early, bursting back into the camp, told the fate of Isaac's patrol. Guard-Captain Antmar had listened as well, at his lord's side as always. Antmar's sharp face was expressionless, his eyes hard, and Early could tell he would more readily believe a cowardly deckhand had abandoned his patrol than he would believe a black, devouring cloud had rolled in from nowhere, and Early alone had escaped.

But a tense hour passed, and Taliss's patrol did not return, either. Now, even Antmar had to admit something was wrong —especially because, Early thought bitterly, one of his own ever-reliable Redguard had gone missing, not a mere deckhand and the insubordinate Greenguard. The rest of the camp joined in the growing concern, and the lord and his Guard-Captain quickly organized the twelve who were left to guard their camp against possible attack. Taking action, Early figured, must lighten the air of tension in the camp more than standing around. You could believe, while you were shoring up the palisade and handing out the meager arsenal, that you were securing the camp against attack.

But now that he was growing footsore in the watchtower, their wooden wall and smattering of weaponry did not make Early feel terribly secure. He suspected his fellows felt the same way. The man next to him, though, would be the last to admit any anxiety.

Captain Antmar himself had picked Early to join him on lookout, pointing out that Early alone knew what they were looking for. Once, Early might have been proud to be chosen, but he suspected the Guard-Captain just wanted to keep an eye on him; as though, as the only apparent survivor of two missing patrols, Early must have been complicit in their disappearance.

Indeed, after another hour spent in the uncomfortable tower, the silent tension between them was almost unbearable. Early stood as far from the Redguard as he could—not very far, on the small square platform. While Antmar watched the woods, still as a statue, hardly seeming to sweat or even breathe, Early fidgeted. The afternoon was waning, and, though the day remained clear, the watchers were kept in the shade by the tower's peaked roof. Early was clammy with the sweat of his earlier exertions and the shade chilled him until he shivered.

"You said it was like a fog, this menace we're watching for?" Antmar's gruff voice surprised Early, after the long, uncomfortable silence. He had already described what he'd seen, both to Lord Mardigan and the collected survivors, and again to Captain Antmar when they'd begun their vigil. Early looked at the Guard-Captain, but could read nothing on that stoic face. Was Antmar still skeptical of him, or was he just trying to break the tense silence by making conversation?

"Yes, a fog. As I said," Early replied, trying to keep the annoyance out of his voice. The Redguard intimidated him less now—a little less—perhaps through familiarity, perhaps because of the greater threat looming over them. "It seemed to be a billowing black cloud, thicker than smoke, like a wall that rolled towards us." Early gazed out into the woods, remembering the slow but inexorable expansion of the cloud, energy crackling at its edges as it swallowed Isaac. "It was like storm-clouds at sea, but crawling across the ground.

"I know how that sounds," Early added, defensive under Antmar's scrutinous gaze. "I'd never seen anything like it before. But it was there! It came from the heart of the woods, and all we could do was run..."

Captain Antmar held Early with his gaze for a long moment, as though sifting truth from fiction in the younger man's words. Then he looked out at the woods, grip tightening on the hilt of his sword. He wore both long and short blades on his hips, and his hands were never far from one or the other. It must be strange, Early considered for the first time, to have one's life revolve so completely around one's weapons. He remembered Isaac telling him to make his sword like an extension of his arm, but the Redguard, Early mused, acted more like they were extensions of their swords. He had always admired the Imperial

Guard, but now he shuddered a little at how alien the man standing next to him seemed.

"If the cloud was coming in this direction, as you said... where is it?" Antmar wondered aloud, and Early opened his mouth to retort when he realized the Guard-Captain was talking to himself. "Perhaps it is bound to the woods, and cannot emerge from the trees."

Early hadn't considered that. He was surprised to find the captain's words providing some relief. But an objection occurred to him. "If that's true, what happened to Rowene and Mosul? I don't think they would have both wandered into the woods, not at night."

Antmar turned back to Early, who flinched. But the Redguard was nodding thoughtfully. "A good point. I hadn't thought beyond the events of today." Early couldn't help a swell of pride, hearing the older man acknowledge his insight.

"If we could learn more about the nature of this enemy," Antmar continued, "whatever it may be, we might stand a chance of fighting it."

Early nodded, grateful to feel some camaraderie with the Redguard for once. "Yes, and hopefully rescue our friends."

From the beach behind the watchtower, a voice cried out. Early and Captain Antmar both turned to look, and saw Myria, the cook's assistant, standing in the midst of the camp, pointing up at the sky. At first, the source of her dismay wasn't clear. The blue sky was still cloudless and serene... but then Early noticed something strange. The hue of the sky had changed. Though the sun still shone unobscured in the heavens, its light seemed paler, weaker. In the sheltered watchtower it hadn't been noticeable, but now Early understood Myria's shock.

The sky was darkening before their very eyes.

Captain Antmar shuffled behind Early, turning back to the woods. He clutched the deckhand's arm hard and Early yelped.

"Look!"

Antmar hauled him around, and Early's stomach knotted in horror. The edges of the wood were gone. Leaching out onto the open grass of the ridge, its tendrils reaching up as high as the treetops, the stormcloud had come.

It brought the darkness with it. As the fog emerged from the trees, the daylight dimmed, strange twilight falling on the camp. Captain Antmar ran down the steps of the watchtower two at a time, and Early, with one long, terrified glance into the approaching gloom, followed him.

The dozen survivors gathered into a tight circle and moved towards Lord Mardigan's cabin—with solid wooden walls and roof it was the most substantial building in the camp. The lord and Redguard Dran went inside first, and Lia, at the Guard-Captain's insistence, took refuge with them. She protested, wanting to stand her ground against the force that had taken Rowene away, but she was also a member of the Imperial Court, and the Redguard would not be denied their sworn duty.

Early imagined what Olan's bitter words would be at the sight of the chosen few leaving the rest of them outside to face the peril of the fog. But Olan wasn't there with a wisecrack. In his absence, Early found himself simply relieved to know Lia was safe.

His usual companions gone, Early's spirits lifted when Marie Gold appeared beside him, her saber in hand. It was the first time he'd seen her armed since his crewmates stormed the deck of her pirate ship, but now they were on the same side, and she gave him a grim smile. "Well, Deckmaster Wills," she said, "I hear you've faced this... whatever it is before. What should we expect?"

Early wished Marie, teasingly promoting him to deckmaster, hadn't reminded him of his old nemesis Matta being swept overboard. He struggled for some brave, or witty, or even halfway useful response. "I can't really say," he offered at last, "all I know is, Isaac and Olan went into that fog... and didn't come back out."

Marie nodded, the smile gone from her face. But her piercing eyes flashed. "If we have to follow them in," she said, spinning her blade in a flourish to loosen her wrist, "let's at least go in armed and angry!"

The survivors left on the beach gathered at her battle cry. And then the cloud came.

It flowed over the wall and through each gap and crack in the lashed together boards. The palisade, small and crude as it was, would have daunted people, but offered no defense against the fog. It rolled in from all directions save from the sea behind them, the edges of the black cloud impossible to see in the deepening gloom. It had grown dark as night, but no moon or stars could be seen—after all, Early realized, it should have been hours till sunset. Someone lit a torch in the unnatural dark, but it showed only that the camp around them had disappeared, and there was nothing but the eerie, oily movement of the cloud descending on them.

Then the cloud reached them, and the torch was snuffed out. Or Early had gone blind, he couldn't tell which. For a panicked minute he saw nothing, heard only a howling wind that hadn't sounded outside the fog, though he didn't feel its force against his body. He felt only the cool, misty touch of an ordinary fog. But then the hair along his arms and even on his head began to stand on end, a mark of the invisible force that accompanies great thunderstorms. There was a flicker of bluish light somewhere ahead, but he saw nothing and no one else. When he screamed Marie's name, he could not hear even his own voice over the sudden wind. If his friends were still standing beside him, he could not tell. Early feared to reach out, for he could hardly see his own blade in front of his face, though he felt the grip in his fist; his only anchor in a deafening void, he squeezed it so tightly his hand hurt.

The flickering light pulsed again and again, growing until it illuminated a tunnel in the fog. He could not see the camp, but there was a sensation of space, of a passageway before him, walls and floor and ceiling of shifting mist, visible only in the cold, blue, alien light.

Stalking towards him, two or three abreast in the passageway, came tall, dark figures. They were human, but nothing more than inky shadows, their features invisible in the unlight. But Early could see the silhouettes of the long knives and spears they carried. His body tensed and he held his blade at the ready, though he counted three figures coming for him with at least a dozen more behind. He was sorely outnumbered. Even if his friends were still nearby—still existed—they were *all* outnumbered!

Though the figures seemed to approach Early slowly, drifting like the fog itself, the nearest was suddenly upon him. It clubbed him with its spear haft. He blocked and felt the blow against his machete, pain bursting up his arm. As incorporeal as everything here seemed, that attack had been real. And powerful.

Early steadied himself and parried, but his blade cut through empty air. The figure didn't seem to have dodged, but it must have; in the surreality of the fog, disoriented by the dim light and wind, it was hard to tell. Early felt as though his body had detached from the world around him, as though his shadow were trying to fence with other shadows.

But the shadows were solid enough to grab him. A second figure leaped forward and clutched his offhand arm in an iron grip. He yelled, but still heard nothing over the wind. Even this close, he couldn't make out his attacker's face, though he saw the outline of human features against the blue glow. The first figure swung its spear at him again. This time, held off balance, Early swung his blade to block the spear, only to have the machete knocked from his hand with enough force to make his arm go numb. The second figure grappled with him, and Early struggled merely to stay on his feet. The shadow wrestling him was bigger, taller, and much, much stronger, and even had they been on solid ground in daylight, Early would not have called it a fair fight.

The spear-wielder circled him as Early struggled against the grappling shadow, and, unable to turn, he could do nothing but anticipate the deadly thrust, imagining the spearhead bursting through his chest. Instead, a terrible blow fell across his back, driving him to his knees. Breathless, Early felt the fight leaving him. Rather than struggling to free himself from his assailants, now he was struggling to remain conscious at all.

His mind numbed by the wind, the entire assault had the quality of a nightmare. Early found himself hoping he'd awaken in his tent, hear the surf lapping at the beach, realize he was safe. The shadow that had grabbed him was looping a cord tightly around his wrists, but the pain of the coarse rope biting into his skin was so distant.

The shadow who'd struck him with its spear pulled the bound deckhand to his feet. The other tugged on the lead it had tied to his bonds, and the two captors forced him down the foggy tunnel whence they'd come. In no shape to resist, Early could only stumble along with them, vaguely aware of other dim figures nearby, too stunned to tell if they were friend or foe. He could only follow, and fear, as the shadowy figures led him through the unnatural dark.

The howling wind in the strange tunnel battered Early's senses until he was numb and somnolent. He had no sense of how much time had passed, while his captors led him through the dim, flickering gloom, before light—real, natural daylight—appeared ahead. The fog thinned to reveal the familiar trees of the forest, though Early did not know where in its depths he was. He trudged along, one figure leading him by the rope binding his wrists, the other figure pushing him with a firm hand between his shoulders. Then the fog, rather than dissolving like a natural fog, simply vanished. Around them were the sounds of the forest in late afternoon, the sunlight filtering down golden-orange through gently swaying branches. The only signs of any unnatural weather were a chuckle of thunder far out over the sea, and a sudden sun shower that pattered on the canopy overhead.

Before Early could question, or protest, or even properly wonder where they were and how they'd gotten there, he saw a sight that washed all such questions away, and replaced them with even greater ones.

The way the clearing was cut into the forest, you came upon the village suddenly—and sentries would have already heard you coming. Early saw four lean warriors melt out from the trees as though they'd emerged from the bark itself. They wore strangely patterned skins and carried spears, like his captors. Only then did Early realize the shadowy figure in front of him, leading him by his bound wrists, was now recognizable as a person; a muscular young man with long, strangely braided dark hair and tanned skin not unlike Early's own. This man, unlike his kin, was stripped to the waist, and Early could see his shoulders and arms had been painted with blue-gray ink, the elaborate whorls and spirals similar to those etched into the others' leather garments.

The sentries held up their spears to salute the returning captors, but none of the people spoke. The sentries looked Early over with intense dark eyes. In his helpless position, their scrutiny made him distinctly uncomfortable, as did the razor-sharp triangular heads of their well-made spears. Whoever these people were, isolated though they may have been from civilization, they did not appear primitive. But Early wondered what tongue they spoke, and how—or if—they would understand him.

From behind, startling him, came the sound of a tongue he knew very well. Marie Gold cried out from what must have been only yards away.

"Lost Gods!" she shouted. "Where in the Empress's own bloody name have you brought us?"

Early dared to look back over his shoulder, even as he was dragged towards the village. "Marie! Are you hurt?"

Looking past the man who stood behind him, Early could make out the glint of her hair, but little else. He wondered if any of his other friends were nearby. "Do you know what happened?"

"No idea!" she replied, and then cursed at the escort, who must have jostled her for speaking. The man behind Early was grumbling and pushing him forward with greater roughness for the same offense. "That damned fog came," she continued, defiant, "and these fine people grabbed hold of me. I couldn't hear a thing, nor see anyone else. Glad you're alive, Deckmaster!"

"You as well," was all Early could reply, as he stumbled over a root. Their captors were moving them along more urgently now, into the village proper.

A circle of stone huts and wooden cabins ringed a central plaza of fire pits and market stalls. Beyond the clearing, among the towering trunks, Early saw treehouses. At a glance, the wooden structures seemed recently built, of solid construction and in good repair. The stone huts, on the other hand, were of strange shape and their surfaces were pitted and covered in moss, angles worn smooth by the passage of many years. Something in the shape of the huts reminded Early of the standing stones they'd seen near that dreadful tomb.

People moving about the village stopped what they were doing as their raiding party brought the captives into the plaza. Now Early had the chance to look around, and he saw that two others had also been brought behind him and Marie, not fighters but tradespeople: Dreanna the metalsmith and Ander the carpenter. Both of them looked harried and as confused as he was, but none of them seemed badly hurt by their captors.

Marie was glancing from the painted warriors who'd raided their camp to the sentries escorting them into the village, and Early could see the calculation going on behind her sharp blue eyes. Her wrists were bound in front of her, just like his were. It didn't seem to Early they could make any brave moves here, in the midst of these well-armed people, in a village whose location they didn't even know.

Marie and the other captives were pushed into a line next to Early, and bidden through gestures and body language to remain still and silent. Two people were coming from the largest of the stone huts to view the prisoners. One was a man, tall and weathered, about Isaac's age. The other was a girl, perhaps a few years younger than Early, right on the line between youth and adulthood. Both must have held high rank in the village, Early reckoned, for they wore elaborate robes over their well-worked leather garments.

The girl carried a strange totem in her hands, a cylinder of black, polished stone that immediately caused an image to flash through Early's mind: the terrible sculpture in the ancient tomb, cunningly worked so the entire ceiling of the burial chamber culminated in the monstrous Elder of Storms plunging out of the gleaming obsidian "sky." Early looked with alarm from the otherwise innocuous stone rod to the girl's eyes and found them fixed on him. While the older man, apparently the chieftain or leader of the clan, gazed at him with reserved curiosity, the girl's eyes pierced him with a knowing look that seemed entirely inappropriate for her years—as though she saw at a glance all the fearsome things Early had seen, and knew exactly what image the sight of her totem brought to his mind.

Yet of all the shocks Early had that day, none were as great as the utterly ordinary thing that happened next. The tall chieftain looked at the girl, who nodded her head in silent approval. Then he addressed the warriors who'd captured Early and his friends.

"Imprison these with the other intruders. They will be cared for until the ancestors reveal their fate."

At once, with murmured obedience, the painted warriors unbound the captives' wrists. If Early had been inclined to take some violent action, he now found himself too stunned even to rub the numbness out of his hands.

For he'd understood the chieftain's words.

In a proud, clear voice, the tall man commanded his warriors in a tone that reminded Early of nothing so much as Captain Mestrum giving orders aboard the long-lost *Pride*. This stranger, in his lonesome village on its unknown shores hidden amidst the endless sea... had spoken in the tongue of the Decadin Empire!

9

The cell wasn't very big, not with the dozen of them all crammed inside, and Early spent at least an hour or two memorizing every inch of it. They were in one of the small stone buildings near the perimeter of the strangers' camp. The hut had been converted into a makeshift prison by sturdy nets anchored around the windows at two ends of the single room, and a narrow slot near the floor just big enough for a food trough to be shoved in when the prisoners were to be fed.

The slot, when not in use, was blocked by a grating—iron bars, locked in place. The windows were too narrow to let even a child pass through, notwithstanding the nets, and the door was heavy wood on strong iron hinges, barred from the outside. Early and his friends weren't leaving any time soon. At least their captors had removed the bonds from their wrists.

An even greater relief for Early than unbound hands came when, soon after he and Marie and the tradespeople had been left in the cell, the eight others who'd been in camp when the fog came were marched in. Lord Mardigan was there, with his three remaining Redguard, and, relieving Early most of all, Lia followed them. Finally, there were Early's fellow hands, Myria and Sil, with the last of the civilian survivors of the *Pride*: Zek the Luckless, a lean, wolfish man of indeterminate age. Rumor among the *Pride's* hands said Zek was a mere con artist who'd talked his way into the greatship's complement. If that was true, Early thought, he sure looked like he regretted it.

All the newcomers were dirty and disheveled, and the Redguard had obviously put up a fight—Captain Antmar's grim face was made even grimmer by a black eye, and the medic, Dran, was favoring one arm. Still, it seemed their captors hadn't hurt anyone too badly. The strangers must have meant for them to live.

But there was no sign, in the dim, empty room with its straw-covered floor, of Isaac or Olan, or of Redguard Taliss and her patrol, or of Rowene and Mosul, whose disappearance had been the first warning of what was to come. Early could only hope there was another prison hut like this one, in which the strangers were keeping the rest of his friends safe, until...

Until what? Early wondered and worried. He turned to Lord Mardigan, who sat in an undignified heap nearby, his fine robes pooled around him. Early bowed slightly, abashed at seeing their leader in such a miserable state. "Pardon me, my lord," Early said, "praise the Gods you're safe. Do you know what they plan to do with us?"

Mardigan gave Early a tired smile, but instead of answering, he rose slowly to his feet so he could address the whole room.

"Blessings of the Gods keep you, my friends," he said. Despite his rumpled hair and clothes, and the uncharacteristic strain in his face, the lord's voice was as calm and soothing as ever. "Our captors said little when leading us here," he explained. "But what little was said was shocking enough. These people of the island speak our own language!"

"So, it is an island, in fact?" Marie asked.

"They said so," Mardigan replied, but Captain Antmar, standing beside him, spoke up.

"What they said was, we are *trespassers* on *their* island."

All eyes turned to the Redguard captain—it was unusual for him to interrupt his lord. Early glanced nervously around the room.

"There is something strange about these people," the Guard-Captain went on, not even begging his lord's pardon for the interruption. "Beyond the uncanny circumstances of our capture."

From her place in the corner, where her artist's eyes watched everyone carefully, Lia agreed. "There's something otherworldly about them. Like this island itself, that tomb we explored..." She gave Early a meaningful look. "It seems there's a great mystery here, and we're caught in its midst."

Early found a shiver running through his body, and not from the cold. Under Lia's gaze, his thoughts jumbled and he couldn't think of what to say. His ears grew hot as he realized the group was looking at him expectantly.

Marie Gold saved him. She was stalking carefully around the perimeter of the stone hut, poking at the ancient mortar between the rough stones, searching for signs of weakness. "I don't know about solving a mystery," she said, "but if we don't do something clever, I reckon it's only a matter of time before our hosts decide to do away with us. They may speak our language, but they're hardly Decadin citizens.

"And apparently we're trespassing on their island."

There was a general grumbling from the captives, and Lord Mardigan looked uneasy. But once again, it was Captain Antmar who spoke. "She is correct. We must focus on breaking ourselves out of this place."

Breaking out? Early looked around, meeting the eyes of Myria, Sil, and Lia. They all looked as worried and helpless as he felt. Not for the first time in the hours since they'd been captured, he wished Isaac were with them.

As the dozen broke into little knots of people, speaking in hushed and urgent tones about their predicament, Early made his way over to Lia. The cartographer, with a dark look at the heaped straw covering the hard dirt floor of the hut, had lowered herself down into a corner. She watched the others intently, and Early was sure if she had her sketching supplies she'd have been recording the scene for posterity. Not wanting to loom over her, Early crouched uncomfortably at her side.

"You spoke of us being caught in a mystery," Early said. "That's a nicer way to think about this than just one more disaster piled on top all the others. You almost make it sound like an adventure."

Lia smiled. "Yes, that's true. But when I said it I was thinking of what you found in the tomb. The torn belt, remember?"

Early sat back and banged his head painfully against the wall. He'd forgotten, in fact, in all the action since the tomb. The belt and its clasp, with the unmistakable emblem of the Blueguard. A definite link between this island in the midst of the Sunfire Sea and their far homeland. And now the even more inexplicable identity of language between the Decadins and a group of people who must have been indigenous here.

"Lost Gods," Early muttered under his breath, grasping at the implications. "You're right. There *is* a great mystery here!"

"Great enough to take your mind off our impending doom?" she asked with a sardonic smile. "To give you back your sense of adventure?"

Early blushed. "I did hope this trip would be a great adventure," he said. "I don't think I actually knew what that meant." He felt silly admitting it to a noblewoman of the Imperial Court, but he could see in Lia's face that she understood. He dared a personal question.

"What made you come on this voyage?" he asked. "What were you hoping for?"

"I came because Her Majesty asked me to. To discover the fate of her first expedition."

Only that. Though neither Lia's expression nor voice changed as she answered him, Early felt pushed away. He chewed his lip, his thoughts grim. "Given what's happened to us, if the first expedition made it here at all... I wonder where they are?" He lowered his voice. "What these people did to them?"

Lia nodded, no longer smiling. "I suppose we must wait and see how they treat us. We've not been handled too roughly so far."

Early hunkered down in the straw, trying to find a comfortable position. "Not *too* roughly, no, but none too kindly, either. If only this lousy hut had bunks!"

The straw did little to keep the hard floor from growing cold as night fell. The hut grew dark quickly as the sun set, and, without lights of their own, there was little for the prisoners to do but huddle in the dark and talk, or try to sleep. Early attempted the latter and gathered the straw into a meager bundle for a pillow. At least the straw was clean, but it poked and scratched at his cheeks. It seemed he'd never find a comfortable position, but at last boredom and exhaustion caught up with him and he fell asleep.

He *must* have fallen asleep, anyway, because the next thing Early knew he was being shaken awake in the dark.

No sooner had he opened his eyes, but a hand was pressed to his lips to keep him from speaking. He stiffened, but the hand was small and warm, and pressed only gently. Someone was leaning over him in the dark, silhouetted by a faint blue glow. A voice, young and female, whispered urgently by his ear.

"Come! You must get up and come with me! No time to explain, and you must make no noise. We cannot rouse any others... hurry, it's the only way to save them!"

Early hardly understood, but the small woman was pulling him to his feet and, half-awake, he followed. He'd have stumbled over three people in the dark if his guide hadn't held him close by the arm as she pulled him—pulled him into a dimly lit tunnel of roiling black fog, just like the tunnel through which Early and his friends had been captured!

It was good Early thought he must still be asleep, for he didn't try to ask questions. As the stranger pulled him into the fog, she simply shook her head at any attempt to speak. The sensation of moving through a space larger than the hut in which Early had been sleeping was surreal; how could he have taken this many steps without running into the stone wall? And, since he hadn't run into the wall, that meant they'd somehow walked right through it...

Early's head swam, disoriented by the impossibility of it all. The dull blue twilight that suffused the fog, brightened only by the muted flicker of lightning deep inside the vaporous walls, was replaced by the homely orange glow of a proper fire. As though waking from a dream, Early heard his feet step onto the wooden floorboards of a small stone cottage. Its walls resembled those in the prison hut, but closer and more inviting, warmed by the fire in the hearth.

Now Early could see his savior was the young woman who had looked so knowingly at him when he'd first been dragged into her village. She still held her strange black totem, and it glowed with a bluish light. As the fog vanished, so did the totem's glow—so quickly it was hard to tell, a moment later, if

Early had seen a glow at all, or if it had only been a trick of the fire playing off the polished facets of the stone.

There was no denying, however, the strangeness of what had just occurred; if Early was indeed awake, he'd just been rescued from prison! And he had at least one ally among the strange people that held his friends hostage.

☙

The Revered Captain Tion Zanda stood at the prow of his ship, both for the unhindered view of moonlight on the midnight sea, and because it was the farthest he could get from the Holy Mother. With her retinue and the infant they protected, she had taken over his own quarters in the stern of the ship.

There was a strong wind at their back, and the sails snapped and whistled overhead. Though the cold wind blew the captain's curly hair in his eyes and forced him to huddle deep in his thick overcoat, he was glad for its favor. The sooner they crossed the sea and brought the royal child to Stormheart Isle, the sooner the Holy Mother could perform the ancient rite, investing the heir to the Holy Kingdom of Rzhan with the blessing of the Dragonlord of Darkling Skies, etc., etc., and so on.

More important to Tion, the sooner they crossed the sea, the sooner the whole mission would be over, and he would have control of his ship, *Blazing Emblem*, once again.

Six ships as mighty as *Emblem* sailed in convoy several leagues behind them, as tradition demanded only the ship carrying the Holy Mother could approach within sight of holy Stormheart Isle. His was the flagship, and the Scaly King had personally selected *Blazing Emblem* to carry the heir to the throne. Captain Zanda knew it was his place in his king's favor that led to the assignment, yet with the Holy Mother aboard, he felt no more meaningful than the wooden figurehead mounted below him on the ship's prow.

And, he thought bitterly as he shivered in the night wind, that massive carving of a fire-breathing dragon seemed substantially more fearsome than he felt.

Steps on the deck behind him brought the captain from his sour reverie. Judging by the heavy tread and the confidence with which they approached the master of the ship, it could only be Bohr, his second. Most likely come to tell him the royal child had woken squalling from its sleep, had wet itself, or some other crucial update.

"Revered Captain," the huge man rumbled, coming up close beside his master to be heard over the wind. Captain Zanda did not mind the proximity; he hated to shout across the deck, and his oldest friend exuded heat through his coat and scaled armor as though he were not man but furnace.

"Good night, Bohr," Captain Zanda said, calling his second by name rather than rank. While the big man was a brutal enforcer of formality among the crew, Tion knew his friend must indulge him. "What have you to report? I trust all goes well with His Tiny Eminence?"

Bohr Inzon grimaced slightly at his master's impertinent reference to the royal child, his dark brows knitting themselves even darker. His small, fierce eyes were hidden in the shadows of his rough-hewn face. "His Majesty sleeps peacefully, the watch tells me. Holy Mother Myrnaz wishes to discuss the procession of the landing ceremony. Will you go to her?"

Captain Zanda turned back to the dark miles of sea, as though enjoying the play of moonlight on the waves. It hid the rolling of his eyes. "Have you told the Holy Mother we are yet days from the island? I should think the ceremony can be arranged tomorrow. In daylight, perhaps. Does the Holy Mother never sleep?"

"I am not privileged to know, Revered Captain," Inzon said gravely. "She merely expresses her wishes, and her servants must hasten to obey." Bohr Inzon never did respond to Tion's sarcasm. The captain had never figured out whether his friend was too blunt to pick up on it, or chose to ignore it. But now there was an edge in the second's voice that Captain Zanda disliked. He turned and glanced sharply at the bigger man.

"Indeed, indeed," the captain replied, scouring his friend's dark face for insubordination. "And I suppose at this late hour we can discuss ceremonial arrangements without the distractions and intrusions of daily life aboard ship."

Captain Zanda turned back to face the water, making a short gesture of dismissal as he folded his hands behind his back. "Tell the Holy Mother I will be with her shortly. The duties of a captain never rest, however, and I must be sure of our course."

Bohr Inzon hesitated, brow furrowed. Captain Zanda knew the big man was staring at him, contemplating a rejoinder. Obviously, he'd expected to return to the Holy Mother with the captain in tow. But Zanda wasn't about to show quite that much deference to the woman who'd displaced him from both his cabin and, in all but name, his command. After a moment Bohr mumbled, "Very good, Revered Captain," so low it would have gone unheard had Zanda not been listening for it, and his heavy footsteps receded along the deck.

Captain Tion Zanda waited a while, after he was alone once again, calculating the precise interval that would maintain his dignity but would not subject him to too much of the Holy Mother's ire. Her righteous anger was so very tiresome. Tion watched the dark line of the horizon, where the moon glittered on the open sea. The waves lapped at the *Blazing Emblem*, with its weapons of war and invaluable cargo. The shape of legendary Stormheart Isle could not appear soon enough.

❧

Early was reeling from his sudden awakening, and even more from his sudden transit into the young woman's hut without passing through any doorway. When he opened his mouth, a stream of questions tumbled forth. His rescuer only shushed him, though, and went to one of the hut's small windows, motioning for him to duck his head. Seeing how fearful she was, he crouched in the corner, trying to turn invisible, as she made her way from window to window, making sure no one was around to overhear them.

At last, she turned to Early, and motioned to a carved wooden chair. Its sturdy frame and well-oiled wood, luxuriously carved and cushioned, were incongruous in the spare old hut. Early had the strange notion the chair belonged in the officer's cabin of a ship. His weary limbs, however, didn't care about the chair's provenance. After spending the last day on the dirt floor of the prison hut, Early dumped himself into the seat with a sigh of relief.

The woman paced in front of the fire, nervous, her large dark eyes darting to the windows when she wasn't examining Early with an intensity that made him uncomfortable. She was small and delicate, but there was obviously more to her than there appeared. Whatever strange power her people used to capture the Decadins, she'd done the same to pluck Early from the prison and deposit him here.

Was she the source of that power? Was she some sort of... witch? He'd heard tales of such powers, but never imagined they might be real.

The questions crowded his mind, jostling for space. The woman was someone important to her people, but now she was obviously acting in secret, unsanctioned. Why? And why had she grabbed *Early*, of all people?

"What's going—" Early began, but at the sound of his voice the woman gestured violently for quiet, glancing at the windows again with alarm.

"What's going on?" he asked again, lowering his voice to a whisper.

"I'm sorry," she whispered back, crouching near the arm of Early's chair. "There are night guards, we must be quiet. I had to act before it was too late."

"Too late?" Early could only imagine what she meant, but her manner suggested she was afraid of her own people, and that terrified him. "What's going to happen to us? To me and my friends, I mean?"

She put her small hand on his forearm. Despite her youth and her worry, her hand was dry and steady. Early wished he felt the same.

"My chieftain decided, since you and your friends trespassed in the tomb of our ancestors, their spirits will not be appeased unless you are put to death." Early stiffened, but she tightened her grip, warning him to keep silent. "Though it is up to me to hear the voices of the ancestors and speak for them, in this matter they have said nothing... except that you are important."

"We are?" Early asked, no less confused than before.

"*You* are," she corrected. Her gaze was more penetrating than ever and made Early shiver. The firelight made her girlish face seem ancient and strange.

"Since I could not say what the ancestors intend for your people, and whether your trespass truly offended them, the chieftain has bowed to the fears of our people, and to his own fears."

"I don't understand," Early said, in protest. "I don't understand what we did. We were trying to escape those beasts—"

She was shaking her head, dismissing his reasons. "You

come from outside, and that means danger. They wish to be rid of the danger, so they will kill you and your friends, in the ancestors' name."

Early shuddered, trying to process what she was telling him. He felt in shock, like what was happening couldn't possibly be real. He wished—not for the first or last time—this was all a dream he was having at sea.

How he and this witch-woman shared a language, and could have this conversation in the first place, was merely one baffling question among many. But he asked her a different question. "Why did you take me away? What do you mean, I'm important? I'm not a leader or a warrior. I'm just a sailor. Just a deckhand."

She took a deep breath, exhaled, shut her eyes. "When I hear the voices of the ancestors, sometimes their words are very clear. More often, though, it is just a feeling, here." She touched her chest. "I feel it so strongly, I know they are speaking to me." She opened her eyes, and they were deep and mysterious in the dancing firelight.

"When I saw you among your friends, the ancients told me the survival of both our people depends on you."

"But—" Early began to protest. They all depended on *him*?

"That's all I know," she interrupted. And, with a slight smile, "They did not even tell me your name."

"Oh. It's... Early," he said. He felt dizzy, realized he was clutching the arms of the chair as though he might slide to the floor. "And you?"

"My name is Kori," she said.

"Kori," Early repeated, and nodded. Pleasantries escaped him. "I should thank you, but... there's so much I don't understand. I don't even know why you and I can speak to each other!"

She glanced to the window and back, impatient. "I wish I

had time to answer all your questions. But as for the first, why should we not be able to speak to each other?"

Early blinked. Wasn't it obvious to her? "Well... we come from different lands. My friends and I came by ship, from the Decadin Empire across the sea. In the Empire there are many languages, and the Emperors had to give us a shared one so we could all live together.

"I didn't expect people who lived here, far beyond our borders, would speak it, too."

Kori considered this, her face thoughtful. "I've never thought about it. I've never met people from... other places. My people all understand each other, so why would your people be any different?"

Early wasn't sure how to explain; it just seemed obvious to him. People from different places spoke different tongues. But he had grown up in an empire formed from many tribes. If everyone Kori had ever known all spoke the same language, it made sense that she had different assumptions.

But that brought Early back around to the original question, the one that had tickled the back of his mind since he first heard their chieftain speak: why *did* the people here speak the language of the Decadin Empire? The first expedition must have arrived here and taught them! What other explanation made sense?

"Do you remember any... others, coming from across the sea?" Early asked. "Before we arrived, maybe years ago. Other people from my land sailed this way, but I don't know if they ever found this island."

He hesitated. Was it safe to tell her this? "Those people... never came back."

Kori looked at him, and for a moment, he saw something in her eyes. But she blinked and it was gone, had perhaps been only a trick of the firelight. "I don't remember any others, Early, no. We've always lived here by ourselves, and have no tales of strangers coming from across the sea. Not until now."

Early chewed his lip, unsure. Was she lying to him? If the first expedition had arrived and taught their language to these people, what had become of them? They must have had good relations at first, if they exchanged languages, but... could those relations have fallen apart, and the Decadins been put to death, as Kori said Early and his friends would be?

Despite his misgivings, Early decided that line of inquiry had to wait. "What should we do now? You rescued me. What about the rest of my friends?"

Kori shook her head. "I've interfered as much as I can. My chieftain and his warriors will set fires inside the prison huts, and they may do it soon. They haven't told me their plans."

Early felt his blood freeze in his veins. His mouth was suddenly dry. The idea of his friends, locked in that small stone hut, fire and smoke... it was too terrible to imagine. He had to *do* something.

"We have to save them!" Early shouted, and Kori flinched.

"Please! Be quiet. We must—"

He sprang out of the chair. "No! I can't sit here when they're all in such danger."

"Early! We mustn't be overheard," she said. Her small, warm hands were on his forearms, pushing him back into his seat. "If you're discovered here, I won't be able to protect you. They'll put you to death."

"I have to do something," Early said, his face set in determination.

"I know you do," Kori nodded, "and you will. You will warn your friends. I'll help you get a message to them. I'm not sure what more you can do, but you can at least give them a chance to escape."

Early looked at her, unable to understand her motivations. "You want us to escape, then? But you can't help us do it?"

She nodded. "I do not believe the ancients want to see you burned, and neither do I. Even were I not certain that you, Early, must survive, I would not want to see that. But I also have no power to dispute my chieftain's commands, not if the ancients refuse to show me a different way."

Early stood, slowly this time, taking her hands in his. "But you can give me a chance to help us escape. I see it now. Thank you, Kori."

Though she was small and scared, Kori's eyes held steely courage. Early tried to draw it into himself. Whatever he was about to do, it would be dangerous.

"Show me how, then," he said. "Show me how to save my friends."

The village was much darker than the Decadin camp on the beach. Dense forest blocked much of the moonlight, and, while Early and his friends had kept a watchfire burning, tended by whomever was on patrol, the village was silent and dark. If a villager needed to be about at night, Kori had said, they carried a torch. Early saw no torchlight now, save a flickering some distance away in the trees, where guards were posted outside the prison hut. Watchful guards with spears.

And that's where Early had to go.

Though he felt blind and vulnerable, Early was glad for the darkness; it would be easier to move through the village unnoticed. For a long time, he pressed himself against the cold stone wall of Kori's hut, telling himself he was waiting for his eyes to adjust to the dark. He was also waiting for the intense fear to release its grip enough that he could move.

It helped to think of Isaac, and what the old Greenguard had taught him. It helped to imagine he was a weathered ranger himself, a protective cloak wrapped around him for camouflage, bow strung and ready, on the hunt and at home in the wilderness. Early imagined that fantasy as vividly as he'd once daydreamed about captaining a Blueguard greatship. Where that had been an idle fancy to keep his mind occupied while swabbing the deck, imagining himself as a fearless ranger, a hero of the Imperial Guard, was the only way he could overcome his terror.

Early dropped into the half-crouch Isaac had shown him, and slipped into the shadows. He tried to be aware of both the ground under his feet and his surroundings at the same time. At least the packed, well-trod earth of the village was unlikely to throw up a root or pothole to trip him, or, worse, twist his ankle and leave him helpless and waiting to be speared by a guard. Still, he moved with his hands held out defensively. In the dark, he might not even see one of the stone huts before he walked right into its wall.

Every few steps, Early patted his trouser pocket to be sure the message was still there. Kori had given him a scrap of paper and a stylus and he'd written to his friends in an unsteady hand: *You are in mortal danger and have to attempt escape right away.* He told them to meet him by the river to the northeast. He'd never seen the river himself, but Kori told him it was there, and that it flowed to the same side of the island as the Decadins' palisade.

She assured Early that, if he could get to the river, he'd find the fishing boats and could stage an escape for his friends. What choice did he have now but to trust the strange young witch-woman?

As he made a quiet arc around the intervening huts towards the clearing where the prison stood, Early thought of Isaac, the person he was struggling to emulate. He wondered what had become of the ranger, and of Olan, Taliss, and the others who were taken before the evil fog had rolled over the rest of their camp. He still thought of the fog as a monster, unearthly and horrible, though he'd now seen it summoned on his behalf.

The only people imprisoned with Early were those taken from camp alongside him, and they were sentenced to death. What did that mean for Rowene and Mosul, and the others taken before? Were they still alive and captive? And, if they were alive, where?

Out of the dark, Kori's words came back to him: her chieftain was going to set fires in the prison huts. *Huts*, he was sure she'd used the plural. If Early's memory was true, Isaac and the others *were* still alive. He just had to find them!

Creeping behind a particularly large trunk, Early noticed something. The prison hut loomed a dozen yards away, the trees and brush surrounding it cleared, but only roughly. Before him was a front corner of the hut, and he could see two sentries flanking the heavy door, silhouetted by their torches. He would have to sneak around the edge of the clearing to reach the small rear window where he could deposit his message unseen.

But he noticed something else: another flickering light, deeper in the trees. After a long time watching, trying to remain as still as the tree he crouched behind, Early was sure it was the light of another torch. With the bulk of the village behind him, he wondered what that torchlight could be.

A patrol? Perhaps. Kori had been worried about patrolling guards overhearing them. But the only sentinels Early saw as he crept through the sleeping village were here at the prison. The flicker was stationary—if it was a torch, whoever held it wasn't moving... Which meant they might be standing guard, perhaps outside a hut just like the one in front of him. The hut containing Isaac, Olan, and the rest?

Early knew every moment he spent out in the dark was another moment in danger—he didn't stand a chance of fighting back if he was discovered by spear-wielding warriors, the only people likely to be out at night. But he had to at least confirm his other friends lived. He wasn't sure what he could do to help them escape, but he couldn't just abandon them.

Steeling himself, imagining Early the mighty Greenguard, he changed his plans. He snuck back into the trees, fighting the urge to race towards the far-off light, reminding himself that silence was most important. Dawn would not come for hours yet; he had some time. Time enough to be cautious.

Away from the prison hut, it was harder to see his surroundings. Early had to step very carefully, embody the apprentice ranger as best he could. Fortunately, the enfolding dark made it that much easier to see the light he'd spotted. As he moved closer, he was sure it was a torch. Now and again the light was blotted out, but only until he moved again—Early realized a large dark shape was coming between him and the light. It must be another hut! That it was guarded by torch-bearers now gave the excited Early hope instead of fear.

The hut seemed interminably far away. His thighs ached from the semi-crouched walk, and despite prowling slowly over flat ground, Early found himself breathing hard as if he'd been running uphill. The night air was cold against the sweat on his face. As he reached the edge of the trees, the bulk of the hut loomed, dark on dark, the flickering torchlight on the far side. The brush and undergrowth were thick here. This hut was even less maintained than the prison from which Kori had rescued him.

More by touch than sight, Early found the rear wall and was relieved to feel a window-slit identical to that in the other prison. He stood on tiptoe and strained his eyes, but it was darker within than without, and he could see nothing. Standing very still and trying to listen over the sound of his own heart-beat, he made out the sound of heavy breathing in the hut. There were people inside, and they were asleep.

What should he do? Early considered the stone in his pocket, and the message tied around it with twine. He only had the one. If he threw it into this hut, he'd have no good way to warn the others: Lia, Marie, Lord Mardigan, and the rest. As much as he longed to see Isaac and Olan again, he didn't even know for sure they were in this hut. It made sense that, if the main prison was the only building he'd seen guarded, this other hut—similarly lit and watched over—also held prisoners... but that was just an assumption.

He couldn't spend the message on an assumption. And he didn't dare push his luck and go back to Kori for more paper! If he called out to the people in the hut, the guards on the other side of the building would surely hear.

Early stood in silence, shifting his weight from one foot to the other, indecisive. He was painfully aware of the proximity of the guards. His ears were pricked up for any sound of footsteps coming around the hut.

At last, the soft night noises among the trees gave him an idea. One of Isaac's lessons: use natural sounds as a signal that would only alert those who knew to listen for it. Isaac was a master of this, showing Early how to not only mimic the calls of birds, but to mimic birds that were not native to their surroundings. Early wasn't particularly adept, but it was all he could think to try.

Early tried to force the reflexive worries from his mind: what if no one woke to hear the call? What if the guards came to investigate the strange sound?

But he had to act; Early couldn't crouch in the dark all night long, not if he meant to deliver his warning to the other prison. He took a deep breath, cupped his hands around the sill of the window-slit, and gave—quietly as he could—the call of a corvix. The large black birds were common in the Decadin Empire, but he hadn't heard any similar birdcall on the island.

The noise he made seemed intolerably loud. He waited on edge, not daring to breathe, listening for the guards. But there was nothing. No sound from inside the hut but the steady breathing of the sleepers. Gathering his courage, he tried the call once more.

Now, moments after his second call, came the sound of someone stirring. A voice within murmured, and Early swallowed a shout of triumph.

Instead, he made the call of the corvix again, praying it truly was his friends inside the hut.

The stirring within the hut continued. After a moment, a male voice, thick with sleep, startlingly close to the window slit: "Who's there?"

The voice was different from Isaac's and wasn't Olan's. Unable to see who spoke, Early thought it might be Mosul. His heart leaped.

"It's Early!" He cut off their reply with a rapid whisper. "There's no time! We've all been taken captive, and tomorrow they'll burn us alive if we don't escape. Everyone else is in another hut, you have to break free..."

He thought he heard muttering on the far side of the hut, and all his instincts were telling him he had to vanish into the trees before the guards fell on him. Early desperately hoped the listener would understand, and not ask questions.

"I have to go. Good luck!" he dared to add, then padded quickly into the forest. He hadn't gone a dozen steps when the torchlight swelled behind him, and he froze against the trunk of a tree, his face turned away from the light. Isaac had taught him nothing was more recognizable to a watcher than a human face, even in the dark.

"Who's there?" an unfamiliar voice asked, near where he'd been standing mere moments before. "Quiet in there! You should be asleep."

Mosul, if that was indeed who Early had spoken to, said something in retort, and the sentry growled again for silence. The distraction gave Early the opening he needed to disappear into the trees. He didn't look back.

As Early returned to the first prison hut, his original target, a wave of exhaustion washed over him. It wasn't merely the late hour. The terror of sneaking through the woods, trying to be stealthy, sure that armed guards would step out from behind the next tree, to lay hands on him or simply run him through... it was almost too much. He was just a simple deckhand, not a heroic Greenguard. Early longed for his uncomfortable bunk aboard the *Pride of the Empress*, its great sails carrying him swiftly away from this terrible place, carrying him home.

He shook his head. This was no time for despair, or for fantasies of home. If there was any hope of escape from this strange island and its murderous inhabitants, it would only be possible if Early kept his wits about him.

The larger prison hut was just ahead in its less overgrown clearing. After all the fumbling about in the dark, finding the rear window-slit in this hut was easy. The orange torchlight was on the far side, meaning the guards were as far away as they were going to get. Early reached into his pocket, felt the stone with its paper wrapping. He pulled it out and ran it through his fingers carefully, trying to make sure the twine was intact; it wouldn't do to toss the stone without its precious cargo.

Early crept up to the window-slit, holding his breath. He reached up, made sure the stone was above the sill, and flicked his wrist. There was a muffled thud, which could have been the stone bouncing off the straw-covered floor, or an unfortunate sleeper. He almost laughed at the notion of Guard-Captain Antmar clonked on the head by his rock, but Early hoped there would be no actual commotion. The last thing he wanted was another narrow escape from the guards.

His mission complete, Early retreated from the clearing. He made it back to Kori's hut without incident, and gave the gentle knock she'd taught him. Cracking the door barely wide enough to admit him, Kori looked worried. Her face was drawn and tired in the light of her small fire, banked low to keep the hut warm for the night. She looked as exhausted as Early felt.

"All is well?" she asked once he was safe inside. Early dragged himself towards the chair he'd sat in before, but she put a hand on his shoulder and pointed towards her small straw-filled bed.

Early collapsed on the bed with a groan. His whole body ached from the tension of his adventure. "I think so. I found a second hut, too, and warned my other friends. The ones you—your people—took before the rest of us."

Kori nodded, unsurprised. This at least reassured Early that Rowene and Mosul, Isaac, Olan, and the others were indeed still imprisoned, and his warning had not been in vain.

Not if the Gods' Luck let them find a way to break free.

"In the morning, when it's safe, you must go to the river," Kori told Early, as she filled a mug from the kettle which hung over her fire. "If your friends can free themselves, you'll have one chance to help them escape. Just a little chance, but that's all I can give you."

She turned to hand Early the steaming mug of fragrant tea, but after a moment she smiled and sipped it herself, holding the mug between her small hands for warmth. Early was beyond her tea or her consolation now. He was snoring softly on her bed, already fast asleep.

❦

Marie woke as the sky outside the prison hut was just beginning to lighten. All around the pirate captain were the huddled bodies of her sleeping "friends," if that's what the crew of the Imperial ship that put an end to her piracy career could be called.

Friends? She had no better word at the moment for a group of people bound together by tragedy and a struggle to survive. And now, bound together in a more literal sense; held captive in this drafty room by strangers for an unknown purpose.

Across the room, the cartographer Lia was waking also, rising from the heap of straw she'd gathered for her bed, and picking sharp yellow bits out of her hair. Marie watched her, noticing Lia was already focused and scanning the room, as though she'd been awake a while before opening her eyes. When Lia's gaze reached hers, Marie smiled politely and looked away.

Aside from Lord Mardigan, the cartographer was a reminder of the Imperial Court, and the high station Marie had given up. Abandoned, not that she'd had a choice, for the life of a seaborne outlaw.

Marie rose to her feet and stretched, and tried to shake some of the worst tangles out of her hair. During their confinement, it had begun to resemble the straw on which the prisoners slept.

"Good morning, Captain Gold," Lia called quietly, with just a trace of irony in her tone. "I've noticed that sailors are early risers. Though I've also heard pirates can't afford to sleep?"

The noblewoman's jibe annoyed Marie, but she let no emotion show on her face. "You've taken to sleeping on the ground like a sailor yourself, Lady Dracis. A credit, no doubt, to your family name."

Lia only shrugged, and if Marie had hoped to draw her into an unwise remark about Marie's own heritage, the pirate was disappointed. She turned away from Lia, letting her mind wander.

The others were still sleeping deeply, filling the room with the sonorous rhythm of sleepers' breathing—punctuated by the occasional snore. When Lia gasped, Marie spun back around instantly.

"Early's gone!"

Marie blinked and stared at the empty patch of straw where the young deckhand had curled up near Lia for the night. She stepped nimbly around the bodies of the sleepers, some stirring, roused by Lia's cry, and crouched next to the cartographer. Together, they counted the bodies of their friends again and confirmed it: Early was missing.

"Where..." Marie paused in mid-sentence, turning over the possibilities. "Where can he have gone?"

Lia scanned the small room, taking in the heavy door, the solid walls of ancient stone, the small slit windows.

"Escaped? But how? Taken away? But how, without anyone noticing?"

"If someone opened that door during the night, at least one of us would have woken up," Marie said. "Those hinges are hardly quiet, and the draft..." She turned to Captain Antmar, who was already on his feet, brows knitted in concern.

"Who's missing?" Antmar asked.

Lia nodded at the place where Early had slept. "Early was lying right here, Guard-Captain. He's gone."

The Redguard looked around the room, where others were starting to stand and stretch, awakened by the commotion but slow to shake off the lethargy of uneasy sleep in their uncomfortable prison. "You're sure? How could he go missing?"

Marie snapped at him impatiently. "We've already counted! He's definitely gone. The question is, how? And where? And... *how?*"

Lia, with her keen eye for detail, was the first to notice the little bundle lying in the straw. Lord Mardigan had disturbed it as he rose, blinking the sleep from his eyes as he shook out his fine cloak, which he'd lain under as a blanket.

"Look! What's this?" Lia moved to snatch up the stone, untangling the twine that bound the scrap of paper around it.

"Someone's gone missing?" Lord Mardigan asked, only half awake. "And what's that you've found, Lia?"

She was already reading the note. "It's from Early! He says someone from the village... remember the girl who came with the leader to have a look at us?"

"I remember her," Marie said. "She carried a strange stone rod and wore colorful robes. Hardly more than a youth— perhaps the leader's daughter."

"Perhaps," Lia said, "or something more. Maybe a shaman or witch-woman." When she saw the others watching her intently, she elaborated. "Someone who advises the tribe. She appears young, yes, but it's common in primitive cultures to—"

"What does Early say about her? She let him loose?" Marie, impatient to learn what happened, gestured for Lia to share the rest of the note.

Lia cocked an eyebrow at Marie's interruption, but nodded. "It seems so. Early said the fog came again—the same thing that happened at the camp, when we were captured. The girl told him we're in danger—Gods!—The tribe plans to burn us alive right here in this hut!"

Everyone spoke at once, their startled exclamations jumbling together. Marie stepped close to Lia and called for quiet. Her heart was already starting to race; not from fear, but from the clarity of knowing what came next and the thrill of danger.

"Quiet, all of you! Lia, what else does he say? Where'd he go?"

Lia finished reading the note and answered, "There's a river nearby. He says we need to break out—somehow—and meet him there."

"And the sooner the better, I reckon!" Marie was already moving. "Those bastards could show up with torches anytime. We need to figure a way out of this damned hut!"

A few of the other prisoners muttered, but most of them just stared at her. Marie ignored them, looking at the walls, scanning slowly, taking in every detail. She noticed Lia doing the same. Marie had already spent hours staring at the worn stone walls and the slit windows, long hours contemplating a way out, but it had always been with idle indecision, not knowing what their captors intended. Now their situation was dire, and, with the need to act, every detail of the prison leaped out at Marie.

She couldn't help feeling it was a bit unfair that, just as she was struck by the solution, Lia pointed it out.

"The hatch they use to pass in the food trough," Lia said, kneeling by the low, narrow opening at the bottom of the wall, where the guards delivered the prisoners' meals. "It isn't barred like the main door, merely fastened with a lock."

Marie dove into the straw by the opening to verify what Lia said. Sure enough, the rectangular frame of iron bars blocking the hatch was fastened at both sides by heavy locks.

But locks could be picked.

Lia looked around at the other prisoners as everyone crowded in to peer at her discovery. "I'm not sure the largest of us can fit through here, but... if we get past these locks and a few of us can crawl out—Marie and I, at least—we can pull the bar and open the door."

"If the sentries aren't about," Captain Antmar said, his voice sharp.

Marie looked him up and down. "If you can manage to

wriggle through that opening, Guard-Captain, you can help us make short work of them."

He gave a short, barking laugh. Before he could reply, Lia cut in.

"If there's a way out, this is it. And we'd best be long gone by the time they bring the morning meal... so who's the best locksmith among us?"

Marie grinned, already settling down to work. She retrieved a long hairpin and a slender twig from the thick mass of her hair and then plucked a blonde strand from her head. Setting twig, pin, and strand carefully on a clean patch of dirt floor, she began to carve a tiny channel into the twig with the delicate point of the pin.

Captain Antmar hovered nearby and made to speak, but Lia put a finger to her lips, warning him not to disturb Marie. The pirate slowed her breathing to steady her fingers as she slid the pin into the channel in the twig and bound it tightly in place with the strand of hair. With the makeshift lockpick in hand, she confronted the barred gate.

The first lock only took a minute of careful concentration. When the shackle snapped open, the crowd of watchers gasped, and Marie turned to her audience with a look of smug satisfaction on her face.

Remembering the pirate captain's highborn station, Antmar muttered, "Where did you learn to be so handy with locks, Captain Gold?"

"A necessity of my chosen profession, dear Redguard." Her look became sly. "How did you think I survived the wreck of your greatship? When the storm struck, I was still locked in the brig..."

Antmar's face darkened, but Lord Mardigan himself stifled a laugh, and Marie turned her attention to the second lock, which still held one side of the grating in place.

"A patrol!" Zek the Luckless, watching out the rear window of the hut, hissed in warning, and the audience went abruptly silent. Marie shut the hasp she'd opened as quietly as she could, and slid the lock back into place, leaving it unfastened. Hopefully, her handiwork would survive a casual glance.

"Are they coming here?" Lord Mardigan asked. Zek watched for a long moment, then shook his sallow head. After another moment, he nodded with satisfaction. "Nay, my lord. They're headed off into the woods."

At once, Marie was working on the second lock. After a few tense minutes, it was clear she was having trouble.

"What's wrong?" Lia asked, putting a hand carefully on the pirate captain's shoulder.

"This one's sticky..." Marie chewed her lip, turning the pick with infinite care, knowing either twig or pin could easily bend or break under too much strain. "Doesn't want to tumble. Rust, maybe, inside the lock. I mustn't break the lockpick, can't make another."

Noticing the daylight growing outside, Zek whispered, "Hurry! Soon enough, they'll be here to deliver breakfast!"

Marie cursed. Lia reached in and gently put her hand over the pirate's. "Will you let me try?" she asked. After a moment, Marie moved aside.

Lia worked slowly but steadily, moving the pick inside the lock even more gently than Marie had. She made subtle adjustments to the depth and pressure, and, with a click, the lock released. Next to her, Marie couldn't contain a cry of surprise, but cut herself off quickly. Her audience was likewise hushed by a harsh word from Captain Antmar. Only the first, easiest step of their escape was complete.

They wasted no time. Marie and Lia, already in position, were the first ones out after the unlocked grating had been pulled aside. Once they were sure the coast was clear, Lia kneeled to help pull Captain Antmar through. He was a much tighter fit, and a great deal of squirming (and pushing from those behind him) were needed before his powerful shoulders were through the hole. He uttered a colorful stream of profanity as he got to his feet, dusting the dirt and straw from his raiment.

Marie smiled at the stoic Redguard's uncharacteristic bluster, but her thoughtful gaze never left the Imperial Cartographer. When Lia turned and noticed Marie's questioning look, the pirate captain turned away and scanned the woods around them. "Early said the river was northeast, right?" Marie asked and pointed. "Pretty sure it's that way."

As the escaped trio helped the others out of the hut, Marie said nothing else to Lia. But she resolved, the next time the cartographer was alone with her, to pose the same question Captain Antmar had asked her.

What circumstances made a lady of the Imperial Court so adept with the tools of housebreakers and thieves?

10

Early crouched in the brush on the long bank of the river. It was not quite dawn. He hoped he'd timed it right. Kori had told him when the sentries usually left their night posts, and there was a window between then and when the village rose for the day when he was least likely to be spotted.

A wide empty strip cleared through the ranks of trees sloped down to the water. The tribe had built a small jetty where their fishers tied their boats. It was quicker to get moving that way than if they had to carry the boats down the embankment every time. The danger, of course, was that an unexpected current would smash the boats or carry them away downriver.

Or that an escaped prisoner would steal the boats and use them to rescue his friends.

Early tried not to dwell on what he was about to do, and how inadequate to the task he felt. He tried to resist the urge to ruminate on Kori's motives for freeing him and abetting the prisoners' escape in defiance of her own leader. If she truly had the shamanic powers she claimed, and was not simply a madwoman indulged by her people, why could she not convince her chieftain of what she'd told Early?

He tried not to think about these things and failed. Isaac would have scolded him: *You're thinking when you should be acting.*

The memory returned Early to the present. His legs burned from moving in a crouch, but it kept the thick bush above his head, screening him from sentries. One sentry in particular dawdled with his spear across his shoulders on the other side of the open strip that led to the water. Early hoped the man would leave soon—he could try to creep through the bush parallel to the cleared strip of land, but he feared the noise he would make in the attempt. Even if he reached the water unnoticed, the sentry could hardly miss him taking the boats. Raised by fisher-folk, Early could do many things with boats, but stealing one in complete silence was not among his talents.

Better to wait and hope the sentry's shift was coming to an end, but he could only wait so long. Already he could hear people moving about in the village a short distance away. He needed at least a few minutes with no one in sight or hearing range to abscond with the boats—it had to be done in secret to give the escapees the benefit of surprise.

If Early had to break his friends out of the guarded huts themselves, he knew he wouldn't stand a chance. He could only hope his warnings spurred them into a jailbreak while he provided the getaway. Slim odds, but what else could they do? Kori was certain her kin would snuff the prisoners out today, without time for debate.

With the Gods' Luck, Lord Mardigan and the others had seen his warning, and Isaac's group of prisoners had gotten the message as well. Early tried not to think about what his friends would have to do to overcome their guards; one more reason to focus only on the task in front of him.

Early heard a voice and tensed in the bush, trying to shrink to the size of a field mouse. The sentry across from him was turning and talking to someone—*Ah, this might be it!* Early thought, excitement building inside him. Another sentry had come, a tall woman who leaned against her spear shaft with casual strength. Early couldn't make out their words, but he could tell by their body language she was cajoling him to come away from his post. The first sentry seemed hesitant, and Early clenched his teeth in frustration. But then the man gave his companion a playful grin. After another minute's flirtation, the man picked up his spear and the two sentries left with their arms intertwined.

With a sigh of relief, Early waited until the sentries had disappeared, and then forced himself to wait even longer. When he heard nothing more, he emerged into the narrow clearing and, still in the crouching posture of stealth Isaac had taught him, hurried down to the water.

The boats were smaller than Early had hoped. The tribe's fishing boats were long and sleek, but had a shallow draft and narrow beam that would make them easy to tip. Early didn't see any boats sized for more than a few people, and realized he would need to steal the whole flotilla. His stomach churned with fear and he cursed softly—it would take extra time to lash the boats together, and maneuvering the convoy down the river would be difficult.

He looked over his shoulder, where the village lay hidden by the woods. There was no more time to hesitate. He chose the boat that would lead his little convoy, and set to work unmooring four others and using their mooring lines—sturdy thongs of leather—to fasten the prow of one boat to the stern of the next. Handling five boats by himself would be touchy, but if all his friends arrived at the rendezvous—as Early desperately hoped—even five boats meant four people in each, and that would be a near thing.

The river water came up to his knees. It was shockingly cold, but at least, Early thought with a grimace, it numbed the pain in his cramped thigh muscles. He had no time to pause for calisthenics, after all. Early kept peering into the gloom of the woods as he worked, listening for the sound of anyone coming down the bank. But there were only the sounds of a forest in the morning. Soon, chilled by the water, the rising sun warming his brow, Early pulled himself into the lead boat. With its pole and oar, he guided the boats out of the breakwater, towards the middle of the river.

The river was perhaps twenty or thirty yards wide at its widest, and less than half that when it narrowed, leaving little room for error. But this was the sort of boating Early had grown up with, and though the task was arduous, he managed to keep the moored-together boats in line as the current swept them along. It brought him back to his days as a boy in the lush river-lands of the Imperial Reserve, helping his mother and father haul the catch of their various crews to market.

There had been enough demand for fish in that district that Early's parents, enterprising fisherfolk, bought more boats and hired them out, selling the entire catch at market, and reimbursing the fishers for their work. Early was imagining the long market stalls, row after row of colorful fish scales glimmering in the sunlight, when a human shout brought him back from his reverie.

Returning to the present, Early was suddenly aware of the boats bumping and jouncing in the current, of the chill in his body, his soaked trousers clinging to him—and now the sound of people shouting upstream whence he came. Peering along the bank, he saw the village passing by in the shadows of the forest. He would soon reach the place where he expected his friends to meet him, but the cries echoing down the river made it clear his theft had been discovered, and sentries were no doubt piling into canoes to give chase.

Grimacing at how stiff his body had become, Early thrust his oar into the water and urged his boats to greater speed, at the same time trying to aim the convoy away from dangerous shallows. He had to hurry, but couldn't afford to get reckless; the trailing boats could easily be dashed against the rocks and he'd turn up to the rescue—if he turned up at all—with nothing left but the oar clutched in his hands.

Then he saw the place where the trees thinned, and a sight that made his heart leap. It was none other than Marie Gold, her hair glistening in the morning sun, beckoning him towards the shallow bank. Early had to fight the urge to jump to his feet, instead carefully working oar and pole to slow his boats and direct them towards the shore.

He let his years of practice take over, and had soon run his boat gently aground, his comrades racing to pull the other, empty boats to shore. Early tried to count the small crowd and reassure himself they were all there. Isaac, smiling, stepped forward to offer Early a hand, and he took it gratefully, only to be lifted off his feet as the ranger grabbed him in an unexpected bear hug.

No sooner had Isaac put Early down than Olan was there, embracing his friend with an even more crushing grip. It was, he assured Early, not a gesture of affection, but only to confirm the smaller deckhand was in one piece.

Early was still recovering from the manhandling when Marie, Lia, and the rest of the prisoners said their thanks, wary of speaking too loudly or enthusiastically. Early longed to hear the story of their escape, but the others were already sorting themselves into the boats, and he knew his work was not yet done.

"Sentries are coming down the river," he said to Isaac, who nodded, squeezed his arm, and turned to the others to let them know. Soon, all the fugitives were back out on the river, Early leading the way. His fellow hands, Olan and Myria, joined his boat, and—Early felt a swell of pride—the Blueguard lieutenant Mosul, one of the first people captured, climbed in behind him.

Early had made sure each boat had oars of its own. Now that each was untied and manned, they would make much quicker time. And they would need haste—no sooner did the escapees turn the first bend of the river, then angry shouts on the water brought their heads around and they saw four canoes bearing down on them. Each boat had one person paddling while another stood behind them, balancing with impeccable skill in the shallow craft. The warriors had traded their long spears for wicked-looking javelins. Each thrower had a dart in hand and a quiver of others at their waist.

Early watched a javelin whistle past Marie's boat and vanish into the water with hardly a sound. Lord Mardigan sat behind the pirate captain, with his Redguards Captain Antmar and Sander Sund huddled close around him. The Guard-Captain yelled in outrage when he saw how close his lord had come to being struck. Their boat rocked dangerously as he and Sander shifted, and Marie cursed at them to sit still.

In the lead boat, Early paddled as hard as he could, and Mosul joined in. Behind them, Olan was grumbling about the lack of a third paddle so he could make himself useful, and Myria watched their pursuers, calling a warning as each javelin arced towards them. Each shot hit the water closer to their boats than the last.

Ahead, the river forked, and the left-hand path foamed with a dull roar. *The rapids!* Early couldn't find the words to explain to his friends—and there was no time to shout them, regardless

—but he knew if their pursuers followed them into the turbulent leg of the river, they would be too focused on keeping their boats upright to throw their deadly javelins. Early didn't know how he could shake off the pursuit, but at the moment the most important thing was not being skewered.

His friends in the other boats seemed to understand his intentions, though he saw fear and doubt on their faces as they followed him. Early's boat began to rock in the whitewater. Olan, taking up the long pole, barely pushed them away from a jagged rock, and made a biting remark drowned out by the growing roar of the rapids. Early was happy to miss Olan's words—he felt his own fear and doubt steadily gaining on his confidence and resolve.

The fugitives flew down the river, but their pursuers were right behind. Javelins whizzed into the river between the boats, disappearing into the froth—it was a miracle none had yet found a mark. Behind him, Early heard Mosul cry out, "Hah!" and feared he'd been hit. Instead, he turned from watching the white churning water to see the Blueguard holding up a javelin with a look of exultation.

Early was confused, until Mosul yelled to Olan, "Take the oar, Master Mender! Early managed to nick a boat with its own armament! Keep us steady, and I'll give them a taste of their own medicine!"

The Blueguard, whose sea legs were even better than the deckhands', swiveled to face aft and stood up, hefting the javelin. He'd retrieved it from a quiver just like those their pursuers wore. Early hadn't even noticed it under the seat! If all their craft were likewise equipped, they might actually have a chance at escape.

Mosul aimed as true with the javelin as he had with a crossbow from the forecastle of the *Pride*, and his shot struck the pilot of the nearest pursuing boat. Seated with oars in hand, the man had no defense against the dart, and it pierced his chest. His cry carried over the roar of the rapids, and his boat was immediately tipped by the unforgiving current, causing the javelin-thrower standing behind him to tumble into the water.

There was general turmoil now amongst all the boats, as the pursuers redoubled their efforts to strike the fleeing prisoners, and Early's friends searched their stolen boats for weapons. Isaac found a javelin and stood to take a shot. Another Blueguard, Ereved, was piloting his boat with a steady hand, but the ranger was less sure-footed in an unsteady boat than Mosul. His first dart struck neither pilot nor thrower of the next pursuing boat, and he stooped quick as he could for a second shot. Whatever happened next, Early didn't know—Olan shouted at him to watch where he was going, and they fought a particularly tough stretch of the rapids.

Behind them, Isaac and his target had traded darts. While the ranger's throw wounded his enemy, the answering dart missed him and hit Zek, who'd been huddled low between the seats, moaning with fear and seasickness. The pursuing boat, with its javelin-thrower out of commission, dropped back in the current, but Isaac had to turn his attention to his wounded crewmate.

As the rapids smoothed, Early dared to look back again. There were now only four pursuers left in two boats, but they came on doggedly after the fleeing prisoners. As another javelin came close to striking Lord Mardigan, Captain Antmar cursed and yelled for Marie to slow down. He motioned to Taliss, in the next boat over, and the Redguards came to some agreement. Taliss got to her feet in Blueguard Coral's boat, cautioning Lia and Rowene to stay low behind her. As their respective pilots slowed their craft—not without reservation—Taliss and Captain Antmar each jumped into an enemy boat.

The maneuver took the pursuers by surprise. The prisoners

they'd been racing to catch were suddenly alongside them, and, though the Redguards were hardly at home on the water, their agility was nearly inhuman. At the same moment, Taliss and her captain forced the javelin-wielders into the river. The pilots, armed only with knives they had no time or space to draw, both took their chances in the water rather than face the fearless Guards.

The defeated warriors swam for the shore, hoping only to escape from the dangerous rapids. Taliss and Captain Antmar, the adrenaline of their attack wearing off, now found themselves trying to pilot their enemies' canoes. Marie Gold laughed at the wide-eyed look of fear on Antmar's face as she deftly came alongside and beckoned him back into her boat.

"After a stunt like that, Guard-Captain, don't tell me you're afraid of a little water!"

His comeback went unuttered. He clambered back into her boat, accepting a steadying hand from his lord, and sank bonelessly to the floor. Lia and Rowene were likewise helping Taliss back into their boat.

Early looked back over the convoy—everyone was present, only one seemed to have been hurt, and their pursuers were now scattered in the river. The turbulent rapids stretched ahead of them, but that was the least-threatening thing Early had faced in days. For now, he allowed himself to whisper the word, "safe."

The river gave out in a shallow stream, as though exhausted from its whitewater tantrums. Here the escapees beached their boats and hastened into the forest. The Redguards took the lead, while Isaac hung back to cover their tail. The fighters kept the javelins they'd found in their boats; none of them preferred the weapons, but they were better than nothing.

Zek the Luckless, in spite of his sobriquet, had survived the javelin meant for Isaac. His wounds hastily bandaged with scraps of cloth, he stumbled along between Olan and Ander, the big men practically dragging him on their shoulders. Early paused at the treeline, anxiously gazing upriver for signs of pursuit, but Isaac put a steady hand on his shoulder and tugged him into the woods.

"No time, Early. If we stand and worry that they'll catch us... they'll catch us. Run!"

It was a dizzying, wearying race through the trees. Early's arms felt like heavy sacks at his side; in the thrill of escape, he hadn't noticed the toll his desperate paddling had taken. At least his legs still felt strong, but his tired arms were too clumsy to keep low-hanging branches from hitting his face. He tried to stay fixed on the backs of the other deckhands, Sil and Myria, running in front of him, glancing at their feet to see where to put his own.

The labored heartbeat Early felt along the sides of his face up into his ears kept most of the anxious thoughts away: thoughts of a javelin in the back, of twisting his ankle and being left behind, or—worse—of the rest of the party stopping to help him, being surrounded, and slaughtered.

Early didn't expect a standoff if they were caught. No questions, nor another tense but harmless trudge back to the tribe's village. If their pursuers caught up to them, it would be a fight to the death, and Early had neither a sword nor strength to swing one. Making it back to their palisade was the only hope. And, even then, Early knew a final confrontation with Kori's people was only a matter of time.

The trees thinned. At the same time, the rush of the surf rose over the sound of the fugitives' pounding feet and ragged, panting breath. Early yelped in joy when they broke out onto the low ridge above the beach. The sight of their modest fortification and the Imperial colors flying from the top of the watchtower gave Early and his friends a resurgence of strength.

The palisade gate was fastened from within, since their captors' strange power had taken them right through it. Clapping arms around each other's shoulders, Early and his friends hurried around the side of the palisade, through the narrow gap between the wall and the water. Soon everyone, even the dignified Lord Mardigan and his guards, had collapsed in the warm sand. Early felt the grit against his face and heard the water crashing on the shore, and he buried his boneless arms down where the sand was cool. He heard joyful speech from the people around him, but he was too tired to make out the words.

He was too tired, and grateful to be safe at last—even if only for a few blessed hours. All Early wanted was to burrow deeper into the sand, and sleep.

Lia roused him. She pressed her toe into Early's ribs, and he rolled onto his side with a groan. She was sitting on the sand next to him, arms around her knees, her features outlined against the light blue of the sky. Early couldn't help smiling shyly at the sight of her.

"Lia?" he asked, propping himself on his elbows. He looked around the beach. They were alone, the others having moved off to the tents and the fire pit.

"Was I asleep?"

Lia nodded. "Come along! It won't do for the architect of our escape to roll about in the sand when our lord wants an audience."

Early scoffed, but saw she wasn't kidding.

"He does? Um, with me?" Early pushed himself painfully to his feet, Lia moving to brush sand off his shoulders and his face. Without thinking, he pressed her hand to his cheek, feeling her soft skin against the grit of sand and stubble. Something danced in Lia's eyes that Early knew was reflected in his own. She looked down, then, smiling, but left her hand where it was.

"Why, Early, our lord asked for you by name." Her tone was

half-teasing. All Early noticed was how warm his face remained once Lia removed her palm. "'Bring me the brave young man whose cunning saved us all,' those were his words."

Early was sure his face was glowing red and wished he could bury it back in the sand. "I can't claim responsibility for our escape," he said. "It was Kori, she—uh, it's hard to explain. She helped me. We couldn't have done it without her."

Lia looked at him thoughtfully, her brows drawn together. "I remember you mentioning her in your note. Kori. She was the tribe's shaman, I thought."

Early blinked. "Shaman? What's that?"

Lia took Early's elbow and led him towards Lord Mardigan's cabin. "A sort of witch," she explained, "someone who talks to spirits. A woman who can, perhaps, summon a fog to let her friends step through solid walls..."

She raised her eyebrows, and Early nodded, confirming what he'd experienced when Kori rescued him.

"A shaman would be a very important person in her tribe," Lia continued. "That she would help us escape from her kin is remarkable."

They were nearing where the cabin stood, at the far north corner of the palisade. Early could see Lord Mardigan on the stoop, surrounded by a ring of people.

"We need to discuss this with our lord at once," Lia concluded. "You deserve his congratulations, of course, but this thing with Kori... it might be the key to our survival."

Lord Mardigan was waiting outside his cabin—waiting impatiently, as it turned out; his Redguard, insisting on protocol, wouldn't let him in until they'd secured the inside. Meanwhile, he was talking to Rowene and Mosul, the first two people captured. Several others were standing there, and they all turned and looked at Early as he approached. He felt heat rising in his face again as Lia pushed him gently forward. But Lord

Mardigan smiled, stepped down from the stoop, and placed his hand on Early's shoulder.

"Here's our riverboat captain himself! After the wreck of the *Pride* and now this adventure, I'll be happy if I never set foot on the water again in my life. But you've proven a fine sailor indeed. Gods bless you, young man."

Early, not used to being the center of attention, glanced nervously at the faces of the others, but everyone was smiling at him. He turned quickly back to Lord Mardigan.

"Uh, thank you, my lord. I was…" Early considered saying something like "only doing my duty," or "doing what anyone would have done," but those words didn't capture how he actually felt. Early *was* proud of his actions, now that they were safe and he could think straight, and parroting words of humility from tales of legendary heroes would only make him feel phony.

Isaac was in the crowd, and Early tried to imagine how the stoic ranger would respond.

"Thank you," Early concluded, and bowed deeply.

"Early the Brave!" Mosul the Blueguard gave a friendly laugh. "But you should rest, Early. We all should rest, I reckon, while we can. No doubt an attack will come soon."

"I'm sure you're right, Lieutenant," Lord Mardigan said. "But when they come, I will seek to make peace with them."

Captain Antmar, having just emerged from the cabin to stand next to his lord, tensed when Mardigan said this.

"I know what you think, Morave. But you, my faithful Guard-Captain, are here to fight when battles need be fought. I am here to speak, if any ear will listen. And making peace is the only road to survival, you must agree."

He swept an arm across the shore, raising his orator's voice. "We have the sea at our backs, and, while I know you will all fight bravely when you must—" Early felt as though the lord were looking right at him as he said this, "—in time they will drive us back whence we came, and with no ship to carry us."

Captain Antmar looked unhappy, but did not refute his master. And Lord Mardigan was surely correct, Early thought. As skilled as the Imperial Guard were, there were only eight of them. He and the rest of his friends could hardly be called warriors, brave or not.

The truth was, Kori's people were already entrenched here. They had access to weapons, a self-sustaining village, and there were far more of them. Even had the Decadins a stomach for conquest, they could not hope to take and hold the island from the people who lived here.

Early returned from his thoughts to realize Olan had just voiced something very similar. Captain Antmar was answering the irascible deckhand's protest about being outnumbered.

"We must rely on our fortifications to be a force multiplier," Captain Antmar explained. "Even if they come in greater numbers, from behind the walls we will push them back." He had unsheathed his knife and was considering its edge as he spoke, in the meditative way Early had noticed many of the Guard treat their weapons. "Much as I prefer a sword fight, our goal is to protect each other and to survive. And," he nodded grimly at Lord Mardigan, "to give our lord a chance to buy peace, if he—*if there is* peace to be bought."

"And what if they come in the fog again?" Ander the carpenter asked, shuddering at the memory of how he'd been taken. "Our walls will do us little good!"

"That may be," the Guard-Captain replied. His patient tone was uncharacteristic, and Early wondered about it. "But they took us unawares and unprepared; they won't have that luxury again. From now on, every one of us will go about armed and in groups. We'll be ready for battle at all times.

"Whatever strange witchery they used before," Antmar

continued, "their warriors still had to incapacitate us hand-to-hand, taking advantage of our disorientation. If they try again, we'll give them a nasty surprise."

Captain Antmar had never given a rallying speech before, but his words seemed to work. Olan had been brooding during much of the conversation, but now there was a familiar edge of humor in his voice—it lightened Early's spirits. "I don't much like fighting in the dark," the deckhand said, "but I'll lay them out all the same if they come! The first time, I thought death had come for me... comforting to know it's just someone I can punch."

This gathering broke into hesitant laughter. Given the circumstances, any levity was welcome, and Early basked in it. Lord Mardigan wished them well and went into his cabin to rest. The others broke into groups, and Early found himself with Olan, Marie, and a few others as Isaac recounted for those who'd been in the large prison hut how the earlier captives had made their escape.

"Mosul woke me before daylight and told me what he'd heard in the night—from Early, as it turned out. Once we convinced ourselves we had to act, it was easy enough to fake a fight. Deckhand Olan here staged a proper fracas, and the sentries opened the door and walked right into our ambush.

"I gather your prison was closer to the village, but we were off in the woods and no one heard a thing. Once we'd locked our former guards in their own cage, we made for the river Early mentioned. Ran into the rest of our friends near the shore where you retrieved us, Early. They were crashing through the brush noisy as elephants."

"We made a stealthy escape for not having a Greenguard leading the way," Marie teased. "When you came out of the trees, I thought for sure we were caught. You're lucky we had no weapons, or I'd have skewered you before I realized who'd stepped onto the path."

"You never had the chance!" Olan challenged playfully, "Not when we came on you silent as—"

That was as much irreverence as the Gods' Luck would allow.

There came a shout from the watchtower, where the Blue-guards Coral and Ereved were keeping a lookout. Early felt the tingling excitement he'd known during their escape take hold of his body once again. Though scared, he was glad for that icy thrill. He had feared the lassitude of hopelessness would descend on him when the fight came.

All around the encampment, people scrambled to ready for battle. Those of the Imperial Guard had rearmed themselves as soon as they'd returned, but Early and some of the others had to hurry to the camp's stores.

Though part of him wanted to hide in his tent, Early found himself grasping a sword and running to the watchtower with the others, almost eagerly. It surprised him how far away the paralyzing fear now seemed. Perhaps he was finally getting used to danger.

The thought gave him mixed feelings. But they, too, were swept aside as he and his friends followed Isaac to the tower. The ranger called up, and Guard Coral, a salvaged crossbow in her hands, leaned over the railing to tell them what the alarm was about.

"Shadows in the trees!" Coral called down to them. Early saw her gather a handful of the steel-tipped bolts he'd helped Isaac make before she turned back towards the forest. He hoped the crude projectiles would serve. Following Isaac's direction, Early and several others clambered up the ladders to the low platforms that let them see and shoot over their simple palisade.

Shadows emerged from the trees all at once. With no fog to conceal them, the warriors of the tribe nonetheless appeared smoothly and silently, like a wave rolling onto the shore. Each of them, man and woman, had a spear lashed diagonally across their shoulders with a leather thong, freeing their hands so they could nock sleek arrows to the short bows they held.

Early's legs were shaking, perhaps just to give him an excuse to lower his head behind the safety of the wall. He didn't know what he had expected. He'd guessed the tribe, when they appeared, would charge and be repelled by his friends' arrow fire before they reached the wall. He had been trying to imagine shooting an arrow at someone as they raced towards him, and that thought had been frightening enough.

Realizing the warriors were going to soften up Early and his friends with an arrow volley of their own, that he could only crouch on the rickety ledge and hope an arrow didn't drop on his head, brought back the same terrible, trembling weakness that had seized him on the deck of the *Pride*. Early tried desperately to keep from remembering the *thing* he thought he'd seen dive out of the stormclouds to attack his ship—the thing he'd seen for a second time frozen in stone in the ancient tomb. The current situation was quite frightening enough.

Lord Mardigan stood bravely in the watchtower, his Redguards crammed around him. But the tribe's warriors, at least two-dozen strong, did not give the lord the chance for his desired parley. They came in two lines. The archers came first, emerging from the trees already drawing their bows, and Early ducked beneath the top of the shielding wall just in time.

As the dark arrows whistled overhead, Early put an eye to a knothole drilled into the wall. He tried to stay calm enough to make out faces in the throng of tribespeople emerging from the woods. In particular, he sought the face of Kori, who might be their one ally among her hostile people—though what help she could give in the face of all this, he had no idea.

It was when the second line came, the warriors armed with spears charging past the archers, charging the palisade gate, that Early glimpsed the contrasting figures of the tall chieftain and the little shaman standing back in the last rank of trees.

Early didn't have time to ponder Kori's presence. At a shout from Isaac, acting as lieutenant for this section of the wall, Early and the half-dozen others on the platform picked up the bows and arrows that had been cached on the ledge. Aiming over the wall, Early tried to draw a bead on the line of warriors forcing themselves against the gate.

The gate of the palisade was no great bulwark, just a sturdy door made of logs lashed and tarred together, barred shut from behind by a large crosstree. At a command from Captain Antmar, half the defenders leaped down from the archery platforms and hurried to the gate to brace it against the onslaught. Early stayed near Isaac, feeling safer up off the ground. He wasn't turning out to be much of an archer, though. Early drew and let fly until his shoulders were aching, but he wasn't sure any of his arrows had struck the body of an enemy.

Then Early looked back at the woods, and what he saw filled him with dread. Kori was holding her strange totem aloft, her eyes wide and staring in a way that scared him, her lips working as though beseeching the sky above. Beside her, the chieftain had thrust forward his long spear with a streamer of cloth tied just below the head, its trailing edge dyed bright red.

At this signal, there was a hollering chant from within the trees, and Early saw eight stout tribespeople crash out of the forest, carrying a massive log. There were four people on each side of the log, holding ropes slung underneath it, so it rocked from side to side as they ran across the open ground of the ridge. The end of the log nearest Early had been carved to a point and blackened in fire to harden it.

A battering ram!

No sooner did Early realize the danger than Isaac was at his back, yelling to him and the others near him, "Shoot the ram! Hurry! Before they reach the gate!"

Isaac demonstrated, shooting an arrow that arced high over the wall and hit one of the rammers as they drew near the gate. The arrow struck the man's side and he stumbled with a yell, but somehow managed neither to fall nor to trip the others running with him. Another tribeswoman, shadowing the runners, threw down her bow and took the injured man's place at the ram with a practiced ease Early marveled at. She plucked the rope from the injured man's hand an instant before he threw himself out of the way. The former runner crumpled to his knees, looking down at the arrow that pierced him.

The defenders redoubled their efforts, and Early loosed an arrow that, though he thought it off the mark, dropped on one of the rammers and slashed their shoulder. Alas, though the ram rolled precariously to one side, the attackers steadied their siege weapon and did not slow. They reached the gate, and their fellow warriors, who were hammering on the reinforced logs, stepped aside to give the ram an aisle in which to do its work.

"Lean over the wall! Loose! Loose! Stop the ram!" Isaac was calling, trying to muster his undisciplined crew. Early was not the only one caught up in watching the fray at the gate, frozen by the fear of having their defenses breached. On the other side of the gate, Mosul was shouting at his own crew, trying to keep them from giving in to the stupor of despair.

Early forced himself to reach out over the wall, balancing his body so he could fire towards the gate. The angle was awkward and his palms were sweating. He struggled not to drop his arrow or tumble over the wall himself. He began to pull back his bowstring.

He never loosed the shot. Some of the tribe's archers, not needed at the gate, heard Isaac's call and sent a hail of arrows at the ranger and his crew. Early dropped to the platform, fumbling his bow. Sil, the galley hand, was not so quick. He fell backwards from the wall with a strangled yell.

Early, heart pounding, hiding behind the wall like a snail cowering in its shell, looked down to the beach where Sil had fallen. The hand's eyes were open, unseeing, and on his shirt a bright red stain spread around the shaft in his heart. Beyond the terrible sight, Early grew aware of a curious thing. A bank of fog had formed over the water, creeping up behind the defenders like a silent, sneaking army. Beyond a few feet away, the beach was obscured.

Early thought of Kori and her ritual behind the lines. He scanned the forest, trying to find her, but there was no time. The shouts of the tribespeople outside the gate and the defenders within rose to a climax, and above the noise came a terrible cracking sound... and the great door shattered.

The defenses were breached! Unthinking, Early followed Isaac and the others down from the platform. His bow left behind, he drew his short, sturdy sword. Their ram's work complete, the waiting warriors charged through the gate, the spears of the vanguard forcing back the defenders. Early heard an awful scream from someone whose retreat was too slow. The tribe's remaining warriors followed with heavy-bladed machetes.

It was a fearsome, desperate melee, the likes of which Early had never been caught in before. Perhaps the fight on Marie Gold's pirate ship had been like this, but, on the relatively safe deck of the *Pride*, Early had faced only one foe. The memory of stabbing the pirate was horrible enough, but now there was a tumult of bodies everywhere, friends and foes, overwhelming noise. When a tall warrior thrust a spear at him, it was almost a relief to have a clear focus.

Indeed, Early could afford to think of nothing else. His vision narrowed to the woman and her spear, and though he managed to deflect a thrust with a hard swing of his sword—a swing which numbed his arm—he realized immediately that he was overmatched. Perhaps a balletic Redguard could spin inside the spearwoman's reach, but Early felt clumsy, half-dazed, and stood no chance against the tribeswoman and her long weapon.

He backed off and ran awkwardly away, trying to watch where he was going without entirely giving his back to his enemy. Fortunately, as the spearwoman stalked him, looking for an opening, Taliss and Lia appeared. The cartographer held a short sword like Early's, though her blade was wet with blood. The Redguard had both her long rapiers.

Taliss did not hesitate; she charged even as the spearwoman turned to the new attackers. The warrior twirled her spear with a deftness Early could scarcely believe for such a long, heavy weapon. She deflected the Redguard's strikes and forced Taliss a step back for each step forward she took, always keeping the long spear shaft between her body and the rapiers.

Lia stepped in to harry the spearwoman, and Early stepped in beside her, bolstered by the presence of his friends. Despite her obvious mastery, the spearwoman could not fend off all three of them. Hampered by Early and Lia, she let Taliss slip inside her guard. She cried out in rage as much as in pain as one of the Redguard's thin, deadly blades ran her through.

Early had no time to contemplate their victory. The fight had taken them down the beach, away from the gate, and now Captain Antmar was calling for Taliss, his scarlet uniform standing out among the general mayhem. With the gray fog rolling in off the sea, the mayhem was only getting worse.

"Taliss, here!" the Guard-Captain shouted. "To me! Get His Lordship to safety!"

Captain Antmar and the other two Redguard were fighting desperately to keep the tribespeople away from Lord Mardigan. Early could just make out their leader through the encroaching fog. The lord could do nothing now but try to stay behind his defenders, a shocked look on his face that Early could relate to.

Taliss looked to Lia, hesitating; the Redguard had obviously taken to being the cartographer's defender. Lia was, after all, also a member of the Imperial Court, and the two women had become close friends. But her first duty was to the leader of the expedition. Lia nodded, her expression grim, and waved Taliss towards the spot where Lord Mardigan and his Guards had blurred back into the fog with the rest of the fight.

Taliss never reached them. Another group of warriors emerged from the obscuring mist, coming in their direction. Tall even among his chosen, the tribe's chieftain was there. He wore a battered steel helm not unlike a Decadin soldier, but enhanced with a tall headdress of woven branches and other decorations Early couldn't make out. As his companions grappled with a handful of the Decadins, the chieftain strode towards Early and his friends, a fierce light in his eyes.

The chieftain raised his spear. Though beneath his helm he looked not unlike a soldier of the Empire, he spoke words in a language Early had never heard before and his spear began to hum, a low and dangerous sound. Early, Taliss, and Lia spread themselves out instinctively, swords held ready, on guard for the tall man's attack.

He seemed to correctly judge Taliss to be the most dangerous combatant and jabbed at her. The Redguard side-stepped the thrust and blocked with her rapier, but there was a flash of violet light as metal struck metal, and a horrid sizzling noise. Early's mind was once again thrown back to the deck of the *Pride*, where he swore purple lightning had set the main-mast on fire.

Taliss cried out in pain and fell to the ground. Lia leaped at the chieftain in a desperate attack, given the much shorter reach of her weapon. Early was shocked by the ferocity of her battle cry. Despite his fears, he found himself following her. Their sudden move caught the chieftain off his guard. Somehow they wrestled the big man to the ground, and Lia had her blade at his throat as Early tried to restrain his powerful arms.

Seeing the bright sharp blade so near the chieftain's neck, Early swallowed hard, believing he was about the watch his genteel friend decapitate their enemy before his very eyes. But Lia mastered herself and bellowed into the rest of the fray, spread out across the foggy beach in a hopeless tangle of fighting shadows.

"HALT! Or your chieftain dies!"

At least some of the tribe's warriors heard, and they *did* stop. More and more of the melee turned to see Lia standing over the chieftain. He resisted Early's grip on his arms only weakly, as the cartographer pressed the point of her blade to his throat. Early was amazed at Lia's control, drawing not a drop of blood. Her years of illustration must have lent an incredible steadiness to her hand.

Early managed finally to knock the spear from the bigger man's grip, more because the chieftain had ceased to resist than from any might of his own. After seeing the shock Taliss had received, Early was careful not to touch the spear with anything more than the toe of his boot. The Redguard lay still in the sand nearby, and Early didn't know if she was alive or dead.

Now that the fighting had stopped, the beach was oppressively silent. Tribal warriors and Decadin survivors stood at arm's length from each other, watching Lia to see what would happen. Some of the nearer warriors glared at her dangerously, and Early feared they might risk a charge that would either free or doom their chieftain, but the Imperial Guards in the crowd began to disarm their adversaries to prevent such mischief.

In the sudden silence, the fog-shrouded beach was a spectral place. The heavy gray bank of fog, natural or not, had formed over the sea and was now so thick you couldn't even tell the surf lay mere yards away. Early heard the ever-present beating of the waves on the sand, and he realized he heard something else, something so incongruous his mind refused to process it.

Somewhere in the blank wall of fog, he heard the creak of a ship's rigging.

He stared into the fog as Captain Antmar and Isaac came to take charge of the captive chieftain. Lia kept her blade at the man's throat until the two Guardsmen had their longer swords trained on his chest.

"Her Majesty's Imperial Cartographer bested their fiercest warrior," Isaac said, giving Lia a mock salute. "I didn't see that coming."

"You were wise to drive him into my arms, Greenguard," Lia replied with a smile, but she looked back, worried, to where Taliss lay unconscious.

Closer to the water, Lord Mardigan was returning to them, leaning heavily on Redguards Dran and Sander. They had gotten their lord most of the way to the safety of his hut before the sudden reversal of fortune. Nearby, Mosul and his fellow Blueguard Coral had been fighting three of the tribe, and the combatants, bruised and scratched by each other's swords, now stood apart in the surf, each side eyeing the other warily.

Lord Mardigan looked pale, but Early could see the diplomat composing himself, preparing to negotiate peace now that the Decadins' position had unexpectedly strengthened.

But the lord had not yet reached them when Early, looking past him at the shrouded sea, saw a strange and terrible sight: two lamps, like vague glowing eyes, suddenly kindled in the air above the lord and his Guards. The lights seemed high off the ground and some distance away—but distance was hard to perceive through the enclosing fog.

As Early watched, the lights grew from a pale yellow gleam to a fierce orange glow, and a deep bellowing sound rolled across the beach, like a vast, monstrous creature drawing in a great breath.

The fighters on both sides of the battle began to turn towards the lights and sound. Early heard their murmurs and cries, but couldn't look away. Mardigan and his Guards, focused on the tribe's captured chieftain, were still walking towards them. Early was looking at the lord's honest face, his kind, determined expression, as the lights behind him suddenly blazed ascendant...

And the beach exploded into fire.

11

The air around Early roared in outrage as a wall of heat forced him onto his back. He threw up his hands to shield his face. The world in front of him, where Lord Mardigan, Mosul, and the others stood, had transmuted into flame. Stunned, mind blank with horror, Early could only crawl backwards through the sand, digging himself in towards the cool relief he felt below the surface. Trying to heap sand over top of himself, he felt like a tiny creature burrowing for safety in the earth. Blind and deaf, he waited for oblivion to roll over him.

But he would not escape the terrible spectacle that easily. The light dimmed, and the scorching heat became less intense, and when Early dared lift his head out of its protective cover of sand, he saw the fog was almost dissolved. And then he was captivated by the strange black ship almost beached on the shore before him.

The ship must have a shallow keel, Early's sailor instincts told him, if it could come up so close to the shore. It was much smaller than the *Pride of the Empress* had been, similar to the low galleons that made up the bulk of Imperial commerce.

Indeed, the ship had a bank of oars like a galleon, but Early also counted three masts, whose sharp lateen sails were dyed red and green. Clearly, a ship meant for speed. The vast mainsail bore a strange emblem: a dragon whose scaly body curled about itself, engulfed in yellow flames.

The ship's prow pointed straight towards him, and Early saw the hull rearing up out of the water was carven into scales. Arranged in overlapping rows like the skin of a reptile, they swelled out into the head and maw of a great beast, from whose derisive snarl the bowsprit protruded. Strangest was the figurehead's lack of color; despite the masterful carving, the entire bow of the ship was black, where the figureheads of Decadin ships were lacquered in bright colors representing their owners, or the blue-and-white of the Imperial Blueguard.

Two long, burnished horns with flared ends, like huge trumpets, curled out from behind the draconic figurehead. These two outlets were still burning with the residue of what they'd unleashed.

Early had eyes only for the ship, trying to ignore the awful sight that lay between him and its black hull.

Along the beach, the survivors had been reduced to huddled figures, shielding their eyes and bodies. The air was filled with soft moans and cries of pain. Nearby, Lia, Isaac, Captain Antmar, and the tribe's chieftain lay in a heap, their arms around each other in instinctive protection. Taliss lay next to them, dazed but moving. Early was glad, at least, to know his friends were alive.

But everyone closer to the water—Mosul and Coral, Lord Mardigan, and his Guards...

The sand was glassy where the wall of fire had passed over it, and upon that strange surface were dark misshapen objects that did not bear inspection.

A hatch banged open in the upper deck of the ship, and a

sturdy ramp was lowered into the water. Soon a line of warriors clad in dark armor marched down the ramp, splashing up to their thighs in the shallows.

As the shaken but unburned survivors of both tribe and Decadin Empire got back on their feet, the newcomers in their fearsome armor formed two rows on the beach. There were more than enough of them to stand sword-to-sword with those who had been fighting, and they were heavily armed and clad in steel.

At the head of their company stood a man of no great stature, but his black-and-gold helm curved outwards into great wings, the shape of a dragon's head at the peak breathing a plume of red. A dark cape was pinned to one of his shoulders by the emblem of a red dragon. At his right hand stood a vast armored figure, perhaps the largest man Early had ever seen, and this man bore their standard—from his quarterstaff flew a long banner of cloth in red and green, marked with the same draconic symbol as their ship's sail.

The leader's voice was high and clear, a voice used to addressing crowds from a position of command, like the late Lord Mardigan. Early marveled that, like Kori's mysterious people, the captain of the fireship spoke Early's own language, though with halting words and a strange accent that made it clear the tongue was foreign to him.

"I am the Revered Captain Tion Zanda, of the Holy Kingdom of Rzhan. Greetings!" Beneath the gilded helm, Early could see a cold, ironic sneer on Zanda's face. "I invite you kindly to drop your weapons, whosoever you are, and surrender! You trespass in a forbidden place, for is not this Isle of the Storm's Heart the dominion of the Scaly King? Who are you? Let he who dares speak!"

Both Early's people and the tribe's warriors stood blinking for a long, tense minute, trying to process this latest and strangest event. At last, Captain Antmar, holding his sword in a formal salute, stepped forward. His voice was carefully controlled, but Early could see the deep well of rage churning inside him as he addressed those who had murdered the lord he'd sworn his life to protect.

"We know of no Scaly King, nor the name of this isle! We are survivors of a shipwreck, and did not choose to come here. Who are you, beast—" he spat, "—to attack us without provocation, claiming trespass? How do you speak my tongue?"

The huge man next to Zanda shuffled uneasily at the tone of challenge in the Redguard's voice, but the foreign captain himself seemed not to notice, or care. He took a step forward, though twenty paces still separated the men.

"I have learned your speech, for the Eyes of the Dragon see all who go upon the Great Sea. If your people have marked us not, then you are poor in knowledge! The reach of the Scaly King is long upon all the shores south of the Iron Mountains."

The names Zanda used were unfamiliar to Early. He supposed the "Great Sea" was the body of water surrounding them—what the Decadins called the *Sunfire*.

The captain went on, his voice rising in anger, "But I have not sailed across the sea to be schoolmaster to heathen brutes! This isle is holy and we must cleanse it! You—"

But now the chieftain of the tribe stepped up beside Captain Antmar. The shock of the sudden attack had changed everything, and the foes of just a few minutes earlier found themselves both on the defensive. Antmar gave the tall man and his spear a long look, but was content to face the newcomers with the chieftain at his side.

"Twice now you have claimed this place as your own," the chieftain said. "But my people have called this isle home since forgotten days, when the stones that lie now in ruin were first raised by our ancestors. How do you presume to come here and deny our existence?"

The foreign captain stared at the tall chieftain, bewildered.

"I came last to *our* holy isle twenty years ago, a junior officer of the watch," Zanda said patiently, as though indulging a child. "Of course, we came to invest the Scaly King. So the tradition has always been for the People of the Dragon, since long before my fathers' fathers were born.

"And, twenty years ago," Zanda continued, scornfully, "we had not the pleasure of your acquaintance. Indeed, *no one* lived here, and who would dare? The sacred 'ruin' you speak of, the Altar of Storms, was made in time immemorial by those who are gone, the scions of the Lost Gods and first worshippers of the Great Elder.

"Their time passed before the days of our forefathers... or yours. You lie, heathen. Or you are mad."

"No!" Captain Antmar objected, "No, this is ridiculous. We found these people here when we arrived, they already lived here!"

The foreign captain scoffed. "Enough of this! I don't know your game, but I am not deceived! The two of you look enough alike that none would mistake the tall one for *our* race, and he speaks your language better than I do! Do you take me for a fool?"

The chieftain and Captain Antmar looked at one another, and all the while both Decadins and the tribe had been gathering in an uneasy crowd. But there was no more time to wonder. Revered Captain Zanda gestured to his huge standard bearer, and the big man stamped his staff in the sand. At once, the ranks of armored warriors snapped to attention and clashed sword against buckler.

"This charade is over!" barked Zanda. "Will you surrender, or stand and die? It is your choice, but you must make it now!"

At the foreign captain's challenge, Early looked to Captain Antmar and Kori's chieftain with tense expectancy. He could see from the barely contained energy in the Redguard that Antmar preferred to stand and fight, avenging the death of his lord until the invaders cut him down. Though he may have been Early's leader now that Lord Mardigan was gone, the welfare of all the Decadins was not, had never been, Antmar's first concern. More so than any of the Imperial Guard, the Redguard were singleminded in purpose: protect the Empress and her inner circle. With violence.

But the tribe's chieftain *was* a defender of all his people, and he put a steadying hand on the Guard-Captain's shoulder. Though Antmar turned with a snarl, reason returned to him when he saw the expression on the grave, proud face of his foe. The chieftain raised his spear in the air, and the People of the Dragon shuffled in anticipation of combat, their dark armor clinking.

But the chieftain yelled, his voice carrying along the beach, "Fly! Fly to Sanctuary!"

And, though he ground his teeth in frustration, Captain Antmar swung his sword around towards the forest and shouted, "Retreat!"

The shouts roused Early and the others on the beach. Churning the sand beneath his feet, heart pounding, he joined the crowd fleeing towards the sundered gate of the palisade.

There was a great battle cry from behind, and the clangor of the armored warriors charging in pursuit. Early imagined the giant standard bearer looming behind him, and it gave fresh speed to his legs. His muscles complained at the exertion of running over the sand, but fear drove him.

At the gate, Isaac and a few others who had kept their bows, including three of the tribe's archers, shot arrows over the heads of their retreating friends. Outnumbered by so many, it was a desperate stand, and Early quailed as he approached—to join the archers was to stand and certainly die so some of his friends might escape, yet he was divided by guilt and the fear Isaac would be torn from him, for good this time.

But Isaac made the decision for him. As Early approached, the ranger saw his indecision and shook his grizzled head.

"No time to stand around, Early! Help them!" Isaac pointed over Early's shoulder, where Lia and her handmaiden, Rowene, were supporting Taliss, who'd survived the shock of the chieftain's spear. The Redguard was limping, dazed, and her arms were around the other women's shoulders. Abashed, Early ran back to them—how could he think only of his own safety, when Taliss had fought to save his life? He took hold of Taliss's boots as the three of them, with Taliss protesting being handled like a sack of grain, carried her bodily from the field.

Facing the beach as he helped pick up Taliss, Early saw the flock of black-armored warriors bearing down on them. At least their heavy armor made them clumsy in the sand, and the few arrows Isaac and the other archers had time to loose made them pause for a moment—but only a moment. Early and his friends still had to make it off the beach, up the steep bank of the ridge, through the ruined gate of their palisade, and across the open shoulder of land into the trees... and then hope they could somehow lose their pursuers.

Once he had a firm grip on Taliss, Early's reflexes mercifully took over; fear clouded his thoughts, but his legs pumped underneath him. He could feel his heart pounding beneath his jaw, and was nagged by the worry he was leaving something behind. His hands around the Redguard's boots, he realized: *You lost your sword*—but the weapon would hardly avail him now.

They climbed the slope and passed the palisade gate. The trees were ahead, but Early's strength was almost gone. The ridge separating forest from beach seemed like leagues of wasteland. But there was no stopping, not when Lia and Rowene were right behind him, and the three were carrying their injured friend. He could only hope Isaac and the others didn't fall in the last defense of the palisade. Early didn't think he could ever forgive himself if the ranger died for him.

Shoulders hunched painfully around his ears as though to protect him from the killing blow he expected at any moment, Early made it into the trees. Only when the protective green shadows had enclosed them did he dare slacken pace enough to release Taliss and glance back.

Isaac and the tribe's archers were sprinting across the ridge towards them, and the armored head of the first invader was framed in the palisade's ruined gate. The archers and the sand had bought the survivors valuable time, but not much.

Early reached once more for Taliss's boots, but the Redguard objected. "Enough! Enough. I can walk. Bless all of you, let me walk!" She managed a laugh, and Early, Lia, and Rowene were relieved she was recovered enough to crack a smile—and, Early thought, relieved to not have to carry her farther. Taliss stood and, though a bit unsteady, drew her swords. She positioned herself between two trees, between the oncoming invaders and her friends. Clearly, she meant to fight so they could escape.

This time, Early would join her. He could not think of making a getaway while his friends stayed and died, and even though he had no sword, he would—but a familiar voice interrupted him.

"Early! Bring them along! Hurry!"

He whirled and saw, among the trees yards away, Kori standing with two of her tribe, beckoning to him. Once she had his attention, she turned her own to the totem in her hands. Lifting it for the second time that day, Kori shut her eyes and began a chant that, though Early did not understand the words, sent a chill through his entire body.

Gloom enveloped them. Not like the sun had gone behind sudden clouds, but like night had fallen on the forest all at once. Early heard the voices of Isaac and the others crashing into the woods, but all was dark... and then a weird bluish light lit the void.

By now, the strange fog was familiar enough; Early was in the same liminal space as when the tribe had captured them, as when Kori had plucked him out of their prison. He stood in a corridor whose walls were shifting fog, and the figures around him were gray and indistinct. Kori's squat black totem was limned in a fierce purple-blue light, and the young shaman's face looked alien and ancient in the strange illumination. Her eyes were open wide but seemed solid black.

Early was gripped with unreasoning dread, as though the power gathered around them held a malevolence barely contained, but he hurried towards Kori, nonetheless. He dared not look back, but could only hope, whatever the properties were of this supernatural transport, that somehow the invaders would not be permitted to follow them.

When the world reappeared around Early again, he was lost in the forest, but not alone. Kori was sitting against the slender trunk of a young tree a few yards off, leaning her head against the bark, eyes closed. Remembering how black her eyes had seemed in the fog, how alien her face, Early shuddered. But now Kori only looked like a tired young woman resting against a tree. Overhead, clouds had gathered, darkening the day. Early heard a threatening rumble of thunder.

Then he heard a voice behind him: "Well, Master Wills? Can you tell where we are?" It was a gravelly voice with a note of humor Early had sorely missed. He turned to see Isaac. The ranger and a tribesman were helping Zek the Luckless to walk.

The disreputable little man's clothes were singed, but he was very much alive, joking with his helpers.

It was strange for Early to see one of his friends and one of the people who'd tried to kill them working together. Isaac was helping a wounded comrade, but the tribesman was helping a former enemy, who, before the devastating arrival of the invaders in their monstrous ship, would have stuck a spear through Zek without a moment's hesitation.

The unspoken truce gave Early a sense of relief; from his time with Kori, he did not think her people were malevolent. They saw the Decadins as invaders in the same way that both groups together now saw the "People of the Dragon" as invaders...

That's hardly a fair comparison, Early thought, *since we were shipwrecked here and just wanted to survive, while they claimed the island as their own and tried to kill us all!*

Fearful as he was of the heavily armed invaders and their fire-breathing ship, horrible as their losses had been, Early found himself glad of this outcome. It felt correct that his people and Kori's should come together, even if only against a common enemy. There was the mystery of their shared language, among other things, that perhaps they could now explore, assuming they made it to safety.

Isaac's question to Early had been an idle one—the ranger had already returned to bantering with Zek and their new companion—but Early pondered it, nonetheless.

Where were they?

He'd been basking in the silence of the forest, a relief after days of battle and fear. Now he looked for the signs Isaac had taught him, trying to mark the angle of the fading sunlight through the canopy, to become aware of the wind and the sounds around him, to remember the direction in which moss grew on bark. Still new to the ranger's way, the forest was a sensory overload to Early once he opened himself to it. He knitted his brows, trying to filter through the various facts and understand what each told him.

They were now far from the beach. That was obvious when he thought about it: he could neither smell nor catch a glimpse of the sea, and he heard no sound of combat—or, thank the Gods, pursuit. However Kori's magic worked, a few paces in the fog had taken them a great distance. They were on the slope of a hill, and, though they rested for the moment, the tribespeople seemed to be leading them from lower ground to higher.

The tribe's village had not been much higher than the beach, as they'd descended no great height during their escape on the river, so Early concluded they must *not* be heading to the village. Or, if they were, it was through some hidden way that curved around the tall hills to the north of the beach.

As he pondered, Early began to worry; only five other people were with him and Kori. There were three of Kori's folk, Isaac, Zek, Early, and Kori herself—were these all that escaped the beach? Where were Lia, Rowene, and Taliss? They'd been right behind him! What about Olan and Marie Gold?

He was still fretting over his lost friends when three figures swept out of the woods, out of breath. Early was ashamed of his own disappointment when he saw they were members of Kori's tribe. Two were warriors, a man and a woman, both tall and muscular, carrying their long spears. Their leader was a shorter woman, not much bigger than Kori, though perhaps a dozen years older. She held a short bow—and the quiver on her back was empty.

The newcomers were tense at the sight of the Decadins, but, seeing Kori and their kin mingling with Early's people, they soon relaxed into the general relief of escape. The archer hurried to Kori's side, and Early noticed the effortless way she moved over the uneven ground, very much the same way Isaac moved. Kori was still sitting against the tree, and the woman kneeled and touched her shoulder, speaking just loudly enough that Early could make out her words.

"*Sheenya*... we must be on the move. The fiery ones will soon find our trail."

Kori took a deep breath and opened her eyes, her face composed. She gave the older woman a tired smile and accepted the tracker's help getting to her feet. The survivors, having accepted Kori as the instrument of their escape, followed her lead as she started up the slope, deeper into the forest. The tracker, looking back over her shoulder, gave Isaac a long, curious glance before she began to move swiftly up among the trees.

Early pondered the way the woman looked at his mentor as he hiked and pondered the word she'd called Kori in a reverent tone: *Sheenya*. There were so many mysteries here, large and small.

An hour of steady marching later, Early was out of breath. He was soggy, too: the thunder heard when they left the fog had become a mild rainstorm, only just ended. Miserable, Early could focus on little now other than the trees ahead and the ground beneath, having learned enough forestcraft to always be aware of his next step. It wouldn't do to trip and slow everyone down when their pursuers could be close behind. He felt panic rising inside his belly at the thought and forced himself to think rationally.

The invaders had all been wearing heavy armor, which would slow them down and deny them stealth. And, though they obviously knew *of* the island, they might not know the trackless woods as well as Kori's people did. At least some of the survivors—himself included—had the fog aid their escape... though Early again wondered what had become of the rest.

So, he told himself, while the threat was dire, if the escapees kept moving, they should be able to stay ahead of anyone that followed them into the forest. Early hoped his unexpected comrades-in-arms truly had a safe haven somewhere.

And, he added to himself, wincing at his sore feet, *I hope it's not too much farther away.*

As the day wore on, Early kept glancing back, hoping to see more familiar faces joining them. He badly wanted to see blustery Olan again, and even the sight of stern Captain Antmar would have been a relief. But Early did not quite want to admit to himself it was Lia he really longed to see, her unknown fate that made him most uneasy.

What if she hadn't made it into the fog and been stranded on the beach? He imagined the giant, black-armored standard bearer looming over her, his quarterstaff raised...

Early cursed at himself, almost aloud. Such anxious rumination would help no one! Through his shirt, he clasped the medallion given to him by the lost Captain Mestrum, what felt like a hundred years ago. She had worn it for luck, and Early supposed it *had* given him luck, if only enough not to die a half-dozen times since the shipwreck. Early felt his resolve return—he would continue to survive, and help whoever of his friends remained, too. He could only leave it to the gods that Lia, Olan, and the others had escaped the beach.

Lost in his thoughts, Early realized the company had stopped only when he saw the tracker's upraised fist out of the corner of his eye. The woman had become so still so suddenly, Early would have thought she'd disappeared if Isaac hadn't trained him to notice the familiar hand signal for *stop*.

One of the warriors who'd joined Kori's escort now moved silently to the back of the group to check the others were all accounted for—and were keeping quiet. He made a strange whistling noise to signal all was well, and the tracker moved her hand again, this time beckoning. Early could see her gripping a drawn knife as she moved forward in a crouch. Isaac, leaving Zek to lean on his companion, moved with fluid stealth up the line to join her, his own knife in hand.

There must be something up there the keen-eyed tracker saw that Early could not. He scanned the ground and picked up a heavy stone whose tapered end fit into the palm of his hand. If need be, he could bring it down on an enemy's skull, though he felt a little sick at the thought.

The line moved forward again, wary of threats in every direction. They had closed their loose rank together, so Early was bunched between Kori and her escort in front and the two warriors who'd followed the tracker behind him. When a bird-call sounded from the trees to their left, Early tensed. But then he felt the tribespeople relax, and the warrior behind him even breathed a sigh of relief!

Kori's people now hurried on confidently, beckoning Early and his friends towards the thick clump of trees whence the birdcall had come. Early glanced at Isaac, noticing the ranger still clutched his knife, and his own hand tightened on the stone, not knowing what to expect.

Murmuring voices came from the clump of trees, and the tracker, peering around the trunks, looked back excitedly and waved them all forward. They passed between two huge, ancient trees that grew together like a gateway and stepped carefully down over the tiered roots into a clearing. The spongy, leaf-covered ground was divided by a tiny stream, and gathered around the stream was a group of a dozen people.

The group was evenly mixed between Kori's tribe and Decadins. Early's heart leaped. There was Olan! And Marie Gold was beside him, looking exhausted but amiable, and there was Myria Sorrel—the galley hand—and Ander the carpenter.

In the middle of the circle sat the tribe's chieftain with Captain Antmar, both badly beaten and bloody, but alive. The

Redguard's scarlet tunic was tattered and covered in mud, and a tribesman was carefully winding a bandage around the chieftain's shoulder. Great warriors though they were, Early didn't know how they'd made it out, let alone how they'd gotten here *before* Kori's group. The magic she'd summoned must be chaotic indeed. But all that really mattered was his friends had survived.

Early stood at the edge, looking over the gathering. Most of the people were resting or tending to their wounds, or watching the chieftain scratch a map in the mud as he showed Captain Antmar the route to their sanctuary. Kori joined them. Isaac had fallen in with the tracker, whose name Early overheard as "Bristi." Much as Early wanted to join his friends in their leisure, a terrible worry nagged at him.

Like Early, Rowene was also alone at the edge of the clearing. He approached where she sat, huddled in her skirts. Rowene's perpetually serious expression often made her look more girlish than she was, like a child pretending to be an important grown-up, but now she simply looked miserable. Early stood by her side, taking in the implications of Lia's faithful handmaiden being here alone.

Rowene noticed Early looming and looked up at him, prompting him to speak.

"Rowene, I'm so glad to see you... but what happened? Where—"

Her story spilled out as though she'd been holding it in.

"The fog came again," she said. "It was terrible! I could see nothing but shadows. I called out to Lia again and again, but heard only a horrible wind." Her eyes were wide, and Early remembered his own fear of the dark, spectral place. Rowene continued, "I saw a light, far away. All I could do was stumble towards it. When I reached the light, I was here, with everyone else."

Rowene looked at the company, chatting happily by the stream. So did Early. *There are so few of us now,* he thought. Rowene had sunk back into silence, and Early had to force himself to ask, though he dreaded her answer.

"And what about Taliss, Rowene? And... and Lia?"

The handmaiden looked up at Early sharply, as though startled by her mistress's name.

But she only shook her head.

After Captain Antmar, Kori, and the chieftain had finished their discussion, they agreed it was safe to rest before moving on to the sanctuary—but only for a scant half-hour. The sanctuary, Kori explained, was a network of caves whose only entrance was high on the northward face of the hill they were climbing, the highest point on the island. All the survivors from the beach would come; to Early's relief, none of Kori's people objected to sharing their hideout with the Decadins. He supposed having a common enemy made all the difference. Still, he worried at every dark glance and muttered word from Kori's people.

All the survivors were hungry. They didn't dare a cooking fire, but the tribespeople carried dried provisions with them, nuts, berries, and some strips of dried meat. A few of the Decadins had been wearing their packs before the battle had broken out, and they produced more of the same. Everyone shared the paltry meal.

Sitting next to Early, Kori saw him glowering at an earthy-tasting tuber, and reassured him there was more than enough food in the sanctuary for a proper meal.

"Would it be rude to ask how much farther we've got to go?" Early asked, lying back in the grass as he finished chewing. He felt he could sleep the night right there on the ground.

"Not to worry, Early," Kori said, and Early heard the touch of humor in her voice. "The caves are just through another mile or two of wild trees and brush, and then a hard climb up the crest of the hill... we'll be there before you know it."

"Kori," Early groaned, not opening his eyes, "just leave me here."

A few minutes passed in silence, and Early began to worry that Kori *had* left him. But when he opened his eyes, she was still sitting there. The mirth had left her face. Her gaze was far away, focused on something in her memory. Something painful.

"What is it, Kori?" Early asked softly.

"I was just thinking about..." She waved her hand in the direction she'd come.

Early tried to imagine the terrible shock of the attack from Kori's point of view. She'd been safe in the forest when the fire-ship struck, but it still must have been a terrible sight: the sudden flames, the heat, the bodies burning. Early shifted awkwardly across the spongy earth and put a hand on Kori's shoulder. The tribesman standing nearby, who'd quietly taken to guarding the shaman, shot Early a suspicious look. But Kori gratefully leaned forward and hugged Early, and the guard visibly slumped against his spear shaft, as exhausted as the rest of the fugitives.

Kori rose to her feet, and Early rose with her. She slipped her arm around Early's waist. He felt embarrassed at the familiar, intimate contact, and couldn't help wondering what his friends would think, how Lia—but Lia wasn't there, of course. He didn't know if she was even still alive.

Early swallowed hard and looked into the gathering gloom. There was a question he'd long wanted to ask, and it would take his mind off the horror.

"That darkness, that fog," he began. No words for the phenomenon seemed quite correct. He was, after all, asking about magic, stuff that belonged to old tales, not the proper, civilized life of the Decadin Empire. "I've seen the fog twice, before today."

Kori nodded patiently. At last, Early simply asked, "How... how do you... do it?"

She returned his gaze steadily, as though deciding how much to tell him. Then she took the black, carven totem from the leather sling over her shoulder and cradled it in her lap.

"You entered the tomb of the Ancestors, didn't you? I mean, I know some of your people... went there," Kori paused, and Early sensed she had thought 'trespassed' but avoided saying the word. "But did you see it yourself, Early, with your own eyes?"

Early nodded, shuddering at the memory of what he had seen in the tomb.

Kori held up the totem. It looked dead black in the failing light, but Early knew it was a highly polished glassy material, much like the fearsome carving in the center of the tomb.

"This is called a stormshard," she said. "It is held only by the *sheenya*—the shaman of the Malaspiri, and passed from her hand to the next sheenya when she dies." Kori's eyes clouded, as though remembering something sad.

Early perked up, however, excited. "Malaspiri! That's the name of your people?"

"That's right," Kori said, smiling. Then she looked back at the totem, turning it in her hands.

"With this, I call out to the... the *power* in the storm. If I am devout and faithful in the rite, that power may answer with aid.

"Or, it may answer..." she trailed off, then shook her head.

"Certain arts the storm taught to our Ancestors," Kori continued, "and the sheenya whisper them only one to the other. To call up the great black fog in which we can walk between worlds, that is an art I know. As you can see, we have had great need of it."

"Walk between worlds?" Early asked. "What worlds?"

Kori looked upwards, where beyond the canopy of trees the vault of the sky darkened through blue towards indigo. Early knew the far elder stars sparkled there, said to be part of the shattering that created the world, but just now there was still too much daylight to see any. He wondered about worlds beyond the one he knew; or perhaps *beside* it, worlds into which he may have stumbled without even realizing. He shivered at the thought and rubbed his temples.

Kori replaced the totem in its sling, where it hung below her left arm. She touched Early and gave him a grave smile. Her voice was low, confidential. "It is never wise to speak too long or openly of the storm and its powers. We do not willingly draw it near, except in greatest need... which may yet come."

A fearful look came over her young face. "I hope it will not."

Early could not help remembering the shocking and terrible sight of a dragon's great maw, flickering with purple lightning, descending on him from a boiling sky. He ran his hand over his eyes, silently cursing the memory, and shook his head at Kori's concerned glance.

"I'm tired. It feels like this day has been a year long."

She nodded and took an offered handful of dried food from her bodyguard. She gave Early a strip of meat and a palmful of berries. He appreciated the berries' bright pop in his mouth better than the dry, chewy flesh.

"You'll be able to sleep when we reach the sanctuary," she said, smiling. "We'll be safe enough there. It will not be easy for the invaders to find, and even if they do, they cannot come upon it in secret or in force."

Early looked around at the survivors once again, as though hoping Taliss and Lia would suddenly turn out to have been among them the whole time.

"I'm glad to hear it," he said, "but will any of our other friends be able to find us there?"

She saw at once what he meant. "If they are with any of the Malaspiri, they'll find the sanctuary. They would have to cover much ground on foot that we stepped across in the fog. But who knows, Early? There is always hope."

Early looked at her, at her face that was somehow both so young and so old—a girl of less than his own slight years but holding in her mind a heritage of such strange, ancient wisdom. And magic. In his haste to just survive, Early had not thought much about hope. But with these mysterious people alongside his own, instead of arrayed against them?

"Who knows?" he whispered back to her, allowing himself to smile.

12

As Kori promised, it was a long and difficult hour at least before Early and the other survivors reached the Malaspiri sanctuary. They hacked through a thick and uncooperative part of the forest, the ground ever steeper beneath their feet, until they reached the sheer wall of a gray cliff. Kori's tracker, the woman named Bristi, showed them a steep, hidden path they had to climb with hands as much as feet.

As they wound in single file around the jutting tooth of rock that capped the island, Early could see the forest canopy in all directions vanishing into darkness. It was a clear night, but there was not enough moon to illuminate the waves—nevertheless, he knew the trackless sea lay beyond. He imagined he could hear its deep, eternal rumble. Despite his fear and exhaustion, Early hoped he could return and admire the view from here in daylight. Then Olan's big hand prodded him between the shoulders and the big deckhand scolded him to quit holding up the line.

At last, they came to a black slash in the rock wall and, winding around a tight corner by touch more than sight, Early found himself in a cave. Kori's chieftain, with Captain Antmar beside him, had led the way, and now they lit torches left piled in a crate just inside the cave's entrance. When a dozen torches had been distributed among the two-dozen survivors, they started down the curving passage into the heart of the hill.

The sanctuary was more than a mere cave. As they rounded a curve of the passage, Early saw the light growing instead of diminishing. Artfully carved sconces appeared in the walls at regular intervals, and these were all lit. Some sort of fragrant herb or oil gave the flames a strange tint and a pleasant, comforting aroma, and they burned without filling the hall with smoke.

Studying the walls in the sconces' light, Early saw that the rough, uneven passage was supported by stone ceiling beams, and these rested on massive stone pillars. All were covered in strange designs. The passage bent around a tight corner similar to the entryway that must by now be far above, and Early stepped into a large chamber whose ceiling was comfortably above his head. The walls here were even more clearly shaped by human hands, being roughly square, and lined with reliefs in a wide band from hip to head height. The carvings reminded Early very much of the tomb he and his companions had so fatefully explored.

As the group spread out in the chamber, Early found Kori. He whispered to her, for something in the air of the place demanded quiet.

"Did you make this place?"

He realized how childish the question sounded. But the massive stonework and the simplicity of the figures in the carvings gave him a feeling this sanctuary was old indeed.

"Not any among us today, or even their grandparents," Kori replied. "The Ancestors showed the sheenya this place a long, long time ago. The stories passed down to me are vague about who actually made these caverns. And I've not," she concluded with a smile, "had the chance to ask the Ancestors myself!"

They followed a farther corridor into another large chamber, this one lined with bunks. The beds, stacked in two tiers, were clearly modern additions, well-made out of dark wood. They reminded Early of the officers' berths aboard the *Pride*, roomier and more comfortable than the tiny bunks or hammocks allotted to mere sailors like him. The beds looked almost out of place in the ancient hall with its cryptic carvings, but Early was overjoyed at the sight of them.

He realized his mind had wandered. Kori was explaining that everyone in the tribe had some part in maintaining the sanctuary for times of need. They needed it sorely now; Malaspiri that Early hadn't seen before, who must have been awaiting their arrival, were helping their wounded companions into the beds. Early looked on enviously. He was grateful not to be wounded, but wanted nothing more than a long sleep under clean, warm covers. Finally, Isaac hauled himself into a top bunk, and the battered ranger pointed Early to the bottom, telling his apprentice they needed to rest up. With that permission, Early felt he could claim the bunk without guilt. He'd hardly pulled off his boots before sleep took him.

Waking brought a moment of confusion and fear. But then Early peeked out from the blankets he'd bundled like a fortress around his head, saw the cozy, sconce-lit room, saw the faces of friends lying peacefully in sleep, and breathed easy. He felt better than he had in... he couldn't even remember.

No natural light made it down to the bunkhouse—though the twinkling flames in the sconces meant there must be shafts running to the surface for ventilation, at least—so Early did not know the time. But he felt he had slept as long and deeply as he ever had since arriving on the island. Or maybe since before the expedition had ever set sail.

He pulled his boots on and left the bunkhouse for an adjoining chamber of similar size, where several long benches were gathered. There sat the chieftain of the Malaspiri and several of his warriors, heads close together in low conversation. Early wondered what they were planning and hoped there would be no return of animosity towards him and his friends, now that the danger of the invaders was behind them. There were only nine of the Decadins left, Early realized with a pang, and here they were completely in the power of Kori's people.

But he was not quite correct about their number. He was touring the sanctuary, whose halls and chambers seemed to go on without end, when a hand touched his arm. He spun around, and his eyes widened.

"Lia!" he shouted, and then, when the other people in the chamber all turned at his shout, ducked his head in embarrassment.

"Lia, I'm so glad to see you," he whispered to the cartographer. "I didn't know..." His voice broke, and he felt tears in the corners of his eyes. Lia smiled widely and nodded, putting her warm hand on his cheek. On a sudden impulse, he embraced her, a wave of exhaustion and relief flooding through him—and then, realizing what he was doing, took a hasty step back.

"Oh! Sorry, Lia. I, um... sorry."

But she smiled at him, and there was a certain light in her eyes—though it may have been only the warm flicker of the sconces—that made Early's face feel hot.

"I'm glad to see you, too," she assured him. "Glad you made it here safely." Lia's gaze became keen. "How *did* you escape, Early? I saw some very strange things when we left the beach."

He explained as best he could. "Kori summoned this—this fog, and I went inside, and ended up far off in the woods. But you and Taliss weren't there! What happened to you?"

"I saw that black fog billow out of the woods and surround

you," Lia confirmed, "but it came and was gone so quickly. Rowene was standing just in front of me and she disappeared in the cloud, but Taliss and I were left behind. You said Kori— that's the shaman, right? The young woman?—She... *summoned* it?"

"Yes, she told me she calls on this..." Early paused. He thought of the 'Elder of Storms' and how close the whole adventure had him to believing in the fable Olan told him on that long ago night in the brig of the *Pride*. "Well, she calls on some power, and it makes this fog appear, and you can step through it to cross great distances in an instant! They used it when the tribe took us captive," he continued, "and Kori used it to take me out of our prison, so I could rescue the rest of you— err, I mean, warn you to escape..." Lia laughed politely as Early blushed at his unintentional boast.

"And now Kori used it again," Lia took up the story, "to help us—well, some of us—escape certain death from those... those dragon warriors. Whoever they are."

Early nodded. "I'm sure Kori didn't mean to leave you behind!"

"I'm sure you're right," Lia agreed, soothingly. "I don't imagine a strange power such as that fog can be easy to control. Once the fog had gone, Taliss and I could only make a run for it."

Early raised his eyebrows. "A run for it? Taliss? She could hardly stand!"

"Hand it to a Redguard," Lia shook her head, smiling. "She set a fearsome pace through the forest. I could hardly keep up! I think she was determined if anyone slowed us down, it wouldn't be her."

They had wandered the hallways back to the doorway of the bunkhouse. Lia pointed to where Taliss was now sleeping. The Redguard was dead to the world, her proud face pale. One of the

Malaspiri healers had wrapped her in a special blanket, warmed over the fire and scented with exotic herbs.

"She's paying for it now," Lia said. Her face creased with concern. "I hope she'll be all right." Turning back to Early, she said, "Despite my Redguard's valiant pace, we'd have been caught sooner or later, not knowing where to go. But we crossed paths with one of the tribe's warriors, a man named Goran. He brought us here—I think somewhat reluctantly."

Early looked into the adjoining chamber at the chieftain and his advisors. Their conversation had grown tense, despite their quiet tone.

"Seems we've all got Kori and her people to thank for our lives," Early said, watching them. "I just hope they don't regret their decision to save us."

Lia put her hand on his arm. "I know what you mean."

As Lia and Early spoke, Captain Antmar, having gathered Isaac and Olan, stormed out of the bunkhouse, obliging them to flatten themselves against the wall in the narrow corridor connecting it to the room where the chieftain sat with his advisors. Antmar looked ready for a fight, longsword and dagger both prominent on his belt, the colors of his Redguard uniform still blazing like the plumage of a fierce bird despite the battering he'd taken the past few days.

"If you wish to corral us in this cave," he boomed at the chieftain, "you'll not have secret councils behind our backs! What are you planning in here?"

He stopped mere inches from the seated chieftain, whose three advisors all began scrambling to their feet in protest.

But the chieftain waved them back to their seats. He turned and looked steadily at Antmar, his voice low and placating.

"Why do you speak this way?" he asked. "Have we not brought you safely to our sanctuary, revealing its secret at great risk to all my people? Do you accuse us of treating falsely with you now?"

Early and Lia had come into the small conference chamber to watch the scene. A handful of others appeared at the doorway on the other side of the room, Kori among them.

The chieftain's advisors stared down Isaac and Olan warily as their leaders confronted each other. The ranger and the big deckhand glared right back. The tension in the room made Early's hair stand on end. The chieftain stood slowly, carefully, trying not to antagonize the hot-headed Redguard captain. Since he fairly towered over Antmar, his standing up was antagonism enough. The captain's right hand tightened on his sword hilt, though the unwanted thought came to Early that he'd have better luck trusting his dagger in the close quarters.

"Don't think we've forgotten," Antmar snarled, "before those newcomers came, we were fighting you to the death! You assaulted our palisade, shot us with arrows, battered down the gate! And now you detain us in this cave. You call that, what, an alliance? Friendship?"

"You are not detained!" The chieftain gestured to everyone in the chamber, his patience depleted. "Take your people and return to the beach if you prefer the outdoors. It is not my choice, but the sheenya's council and, through her, the voices of our Ancestors, that brought you here. Here to safety," he added bitterly.

At the mention of her title, Kori left the crowd and joined the men. At least a dozen people had crowded around Early and Lia, along the wall opposite the arrangement of benches. Whether the onlookers would prevent the outbreak of violence or participate in it when it came, Early did not know.

It seemed madness that Antmar should confront their saviors like this; it was clear enough to Early that everything Kori and her people had done since the devastating fire on the beach had been in service of saving the Decadins alongside themselves. What was the use of bringing up their previous animosity? Early remembered seeing his crewmate, Sil, die, pierced by a Malaspiri arrow, but... he found himself less angry about Sil's death than about Antmar ruining their budding alliance, jeopardizing the survival Early had fought for since the moment they washed ashore.

Early could not understand Antmar's behavior. Perhaps the Guard-Captain felt a need to prove himself a worthy leader? Early knew how fiercely the man had tried to protect Lord Mardigan. Yet he'd failed in that duty—through no fault of his own, Early thought; who could have predicted the newcomers and their terrible weapon? It had *seemed* the lord was moving away from danger, not into it.

Early turned his focus back to the argument going on in front of him. The whole entourage had joined in. While some were trying to soothe and appease the others, there was enough shouting to show suspicion and accusations were winning the day. Needing to escape the rising tension, Early's mind kept wandering. He noticed the way the chieftain carried himself, reminiscent of no one so much as the Blueguard Captain Mestrum, how she used to stride the deck of the *Pride of the Empress* with an attitude of confident command. It made sense, Early supposed, for someone who had been a leader of men and women for years to display that mastery in their every movement.

But the thought nagged at him more than such an idle observation deserved. There was something else, something about how the chieftain kept tugging the hem of his leather shirt to smoothe it over his chest, that made Early imagine him wearing the blue-and-white uniform, with a Blueguard captain's peaked hat, and a cutlass in its scabbard clasped to his belt—

The clasp! Early thought back to the strip of tattered leather they'd found in the tomb, with its Blueguard insignia. Baffling to find it there in an ancient ruin on this unknown island in the middle of the sea. The past few days had given Early too much else to think about, but at the time it had seemed they must be on the trail of the first expedition; the whole reason for their own doomed quest.

Early had felt the same way once before, when he recognized the familiar style of the chair in Kori's hut. With the urgent need to help his friends escape, he'd had no time to think about the strangeness of finding such an object in such a place. But now, when he could do nothing but watch the chieftain and the Redguard captain argue, the chair was a welcome distraction. It was of a style of furniture he'd seen often in his homeland. And, come to think of it, so was the bunk he had just slept in so gladly. The bunks were shaped from the dark trees peculiar to this island, but the style was unmistakably Decadin. How had they come here? Had the Malaspiri salvaged them? Or taken them from survivors of the first expedition, who'd also been shipwrecked here?

But if that was so, why did the Malaspiri deny ever meeting anyone like Early and his kin?

Early watched the chieftain as the tall man spoke, his eyes flashing with anger but his voice carefully controlled. This was a man used to command, used to giving orders but also to navigating conflict. That was to be expected of anyone in his station, but why did he remind Early so much of the lost Guard-Captain Mestrum in particular?

Then, the way his thoughts sometimes shifted to forge an unexpected connection, Early's mind leaped back to their escape through the forest, how he had noticed Bristi, the nimble tracker, moved so much like Isaac: crouching, fluid, the same silent and sure-footed steps. Isaac had told Early how rangers used each part of the foot to muffle noise and be sure of their tread. The technique stood out to Early because he had been at such pains to learn it—next to shooting a bow with any sort of accuracy, the ranger's gait was the Greenguard skill he'd struggled with the most. He could explain away all these similarities—of course a huntress for a tribe such as this would move in a way similar to a Decadin ranger. Of course the chieftain of the Malaspiri would have similar bearing to the captain of a Blueguard ship.

But the broken strap, and the furniture, and... and they all spoke the Decadin language, by the Gods! That was the hardest thing of all to explain. Early had tried to just accept it, because, after all, it was the case—and there'd been little time to sit and ruminate, until now.

The truth, impossible as it seemed, flashed from its disparate parts into Early's mind like the recognition of a constellation in the night sky.

Antmar and the chieftain were dangerously close to one another now, the Redguard's pointing finger mere inches from the chieftain's chest. No blades had been drawn, but everyone armed was gripping their weapons. The din of their shouting, and the crowd's concern over their shouting, was a blanket of noise.

Into which Early swore, and loud. "Lost Gods!"

The blanket of noise vanished, replaced by an even heavier silence. Early cursed whatever part of himself caused him to shout, effective as it was in pausing the ruckus. He felt the deadly momentum in the room shift, knew it could tilt back at any moment into its headlong plunge.

"K-Kori," he fumbled, most comfortable addressing the shaman, "you—your people, I mean. We, and you... we're the same, from the same place."

"Early?" Kori probed. The others watched him with confusion on their faces.

"We came here to find an expedition lost at sea," he explained. "We DID find them. It's... you! You're them!"

"Deckhand Wills," Captain Antmar growled, "what in Her Imperial Majesty's name are you talking about?"

Over Antmar's shoulder, Isaac was looking at Early with deep concern. Olan was trying to keep a straight face, but Early could see the big deckhand found this delightfully amusing. *You've stepped in it now, Master Wills,* Early imagined him saying. *Better you than me!*

All eyes were on Early, and his face was burning. What if he was mad, or simply wrong? But it was too late. There was nothing to do but stumble along the path he'd committed to. He was relieved to feel the words come more easily as he explained himself.

"We've found the first expedition, Guard-Captain, though it seems they've forgotten who they are."

He turned to Kori. "Kori, you—your chieftain, your people —you haven't been living here for generations, you can't have been! You came here on a ship, just as we did. A ship from the Decadin Empire!"

Early's declaration was followed by a long, crushing silence. Then everyone in the crowded room began to talk at once. Early's hold on their attention was gone, just like that, and he wasn't sure he could get it back. He wasn't sure he wanted it back; he could feel his legs shaking and wished the crowd wasn't blocking him from collapsing on a bench.

He looked around for anyone to verify or support his conclusion. Kori, close at hand, had a thoughtful look on her face. He made eye contact, pleading with his expression, but she turned away.

Captain Antmar and the chieftain had resumed their

debate. Kori made her way between them, slid her totem from its sling around her shoulder, and stamped the heavy black stone with great force upon the bench three times. She didn't wait for silence to fall at her signal, but stepped up on the bench, so she stood taller even than her chieftain.

"Hear me!" she cried.

A hush fell on the Malaspiri. A moment later, it fell on the Decadins, too. Everyone turned to face her and Early shrank gratefully into the back of the crowd.

"What is it, sheenya?" the chieftain asked. "Is it the voice on the wind?"

Kori shook her head, but the Malaspiri murmured. They looked at their shaman with reverence.

"The shepherd of storms came to me and said: Sheenya, yours is the duty—remember the voices of your Ancestors." Early heard the power of ritual in Kori's words and marveled again that the slight young woman was so much more than she looked.

"Indeed," she continued, "I hear those voices on the wind. And," she touched her chest, over her heart, "in the stone. What Early has claimed, how can it be? Yet the voices do not deny it. I don't see how it can be true; have we not always lived in our village? Can our very memories be... false?" Kori's voice faltered, but she looked at Captain Antmar, returning his skeptical gaze with calm resolve.

"The ways of the Malaspiri are not your ways," she said to him, "but I must ask you as I ask my own chieftain: will you make peace, at least until the Ancestors have shown me the way?"

Early saw Captain Antmar look around the room. On the faces of their people and Kori's people was anger and confusion, but also wonder and curiosity. Antmar and the chieftain both locked eyes, looked at Kori, then at each other again. And, hesitantly, both men nodded. Early saw Kori smile, felt a weight lift from his shoulders. If there would be a final confrontation between their people, at least it wouldn't be here and now. Whether Kori actually could learn the truth, Early didn't know —but he understood she had bought them all a reprieve.

❦

Two long days had passed since the first tense standoff between Antmar and Suran—Kori had told Early the Malaspiri chieftain's name—and Early took to eating his lunch alone, just inside the hidden entrance to the caverns. He chose the spot as much to get away from the brooding tension of his fellow survivors as to feel the breeze and see the open sky.

There was much talk among and between the Decadins and the Malaspiri since his revelatory outburst, but no one was sure what to believe. There was less fear of open conflict between the two groups, as far as Early could tell, but more uncertainty. What were they to do about the powerful invaders, who were probably scouring the island for them even now? And what were the Decadins to do if the Malaspiri *were* survivors of the first expedition, their memories somehow replaced by alien lives? And what were the Malaspiri to do?

It was all quite beyond Early. It seemed every day brought more questions and no answers. Long after he'd finished eating, he leaned against the rock, feeling the breeze on his face and staring out over the sloping, wooded hills to the endless mirror of the sea. Kori found him there.

The young shaman had spent much time with Early since defending him in the debate. They had spoken about his theory, and the feelings it stirred in her. She knew only the life she'd led here on the island, she insisted, and Early believed her; yet she agreed his deductions made sense, and had a lingering feeling, in the place usually reserved for the voices of the Ancestors, that told her to pay attention. Her practiced reflex for trusting her intuition made her more willing than anyone else to accept Early's outlandish theory. He was grateful for it.

Now she touched Early on the shoulder, bringing him out of his reverie. He looked up at her, appreciating the casually intimate way she could enter his personal space without feeling like an invader. She smiled and did not ask what he'd been thinking.

"You should come back down," she said. "Suran and Captain Antmar are making plans for an offensive. You should be there, too."

Early disagreed with her assertion but got to his feet. "Thank you, Kori, but I'm sure they can come up with their plans without me. Captain Antmar and Isaac, and your tribe's warriors, they—I mean..."

He glanced downwards and muttered, "I'm just a deckhand."

She shrugged and smiled, turning back down the corridor. She didn't wait for him to follow, and, with a moment of anxiety, he hastened after her.

"I guess you're right, though," he added. "I'd rather hear the plans with my own ears."

He couldn't see it from behind, but Kori had a knowing smile on her face.

"We can't let those invaders keep a foothold," Antmar was saying, with his characteristic intensity, when Early and Kori returned to the conference chamber. "If we allow them to scour the island at their leisure, it's only a matter of time before they find this place."

Suran, the chieftain, nodded. "We know we cannot suffer them to stay. My trackers have already spotted them searching the woods for us. We must push them back into the sea. But that's easy to say, less easy to do."

The tall chieftain sat with his back to the chamber's carven wall, perpendicular benches on each side. A small table had been placed in the middle, and Early saw a map of the whole island there. Captain Antmar was sitting to the chieftain's right. Isaac and Bristi, the tracker who was Suran's top lieutenant, were seated to his left. Suran turned to them.

"You've scouted the fortifications on the beach. What have the invaders done with them?"

"We've seen them at work strengthening the wall," Bristi said. "Clearly they are happy to use what you left them," she nodded wryly at Antmar, "and launch their search parties from there."

"We can't allow that," the Redguard captain insisted. "We have to take the fight to them, now!"

"You're right, of course, Guard-Captain," said Isaac, his voice low and reasonable. "But what's the way to victory? They are well armed and armored, they outnumber us, and they have that fire-breathing ship."

Early, watching the conversation from behind his mentor, was amused to see Captain Antmar stroke his chin like the ranger did when lost in thought. The younger man must have picked up Isaac's habit, though he lacked the ranger's beard.

"If we could take control of that ship..."

"Hah! Indeed," Suran scoffed. "How would we do that without first fighting our way through every last one of them?"

Captain Antmar gave him a dark look and shrugged his shoulders.

Isaac leaned back and chewed thoughtfully on the stem of a long thin pipe Bristi had given him. The tracker had one of her own and shared with Isaac the purplish woody leaves she and the other Malaspiri trackers smoked during their long vigils in the forest. Neither of them were smoking now, under-ground, but the pipes gave them something to occupy their hands while they worked over the problem of attacking the beach.

"Aside from the ship," Isaac said at last, "a more likely target is their captain. Bristi and I noted he was in the camp, over-seeing things—not hidden away on their ship. He could be vulnerable."

Antmar leaned in eagerly, pouncing on the idea. "I see it! A careful raid, one precise stroke, and we cut the head off these invaders. It could work."

Suran, more cautious, nodded slowly. "It could. If we take him alive, as a hostage, and force the rest of his people to surrender."

As the group discussed, Kori sat without invitation next to Suran, who nodded to her respectfully. But Early hovered behind Isaac, avoiding notice, wanting to know the plan without feeling he had a voice in it.

"How best, then, to carry out such an assault?" Suran pulled a vellum sheet from the piled papers on the table and began a rough sketch of the beachfront defenses. "I keep hoping to hear that, as the builders of the palisade, you know of some secret entrance, or weakness."

"Alas," Isaac replied, "our design included no such thing."

Beside him, Bristi snorted with laughter.

"Indeed," Captain Antmar sighed. He leaned forward, tapping the sketch on both sides of the wall Suran had drawn. "The weakest points are at the sides of the palisade. We never extended the wall all the way down to the water. Our best bet is to feint at the wall, while entering the camp in stealth from each side."

"A three-pronged attack?" Bristi asked, tapping her pipe impatiently against the stone table. "We have perhaps two-dozen people suited to an assault. That's no great force to divide three ways. They've at least twice that number."

Antmar glowered at her, but said, "You're right. We have whoever can stand and hold a weapon, and it's hardly enough. Our best chance is to take them by surprise, lay hold of their captain, and spirit him away. We must strike quickly, at night, around the wall. As I have said."

They sat in silence for a minute, and Early felt the tension in the air. He knew Captain Antmar was probably right, but it was a desperate plan with slim hope of victory.

"What about," Isaac asked, "using the black fog Kori summoned?" He looked at her. "If you have that power, it seems by far the best way to mount a surprise attack."

Suran and Bristi went silent, obviously uncomfortable. They looked at Kori, who leaned her head back against the stone wall and shut her eyes.

"You are right to think so, Isaac, but I'm afraid there is... a cost to that power. We did not use it when we attacked the beach, you recall."

"Yes," Isaac said thoughtfully, "that did strike me as strange. Though you did use it during our escape."

Kori nodded, patting the totem slung beneath her arm. "To attack, we relied on force, because I dared not summon the fog again. I did so after the invaders came since it seemed our only hope of survival.

"There is a power I call upon to bring forth the fog. The power is a thing outside, not within me." She gestured up at the ceiling, at the sky beyond. "It abides in stormclouds. We have all heard its voice: the fury of thunder that rends the very air."

Kori looked at the Greenguard, her eyes wide. "It is no small thing to call upon the storm. To touch it without invoking its wrath is delicate work, an art passed down from each sheenya to the next. Do you understand?"

Now it was Isaac, not Antmar, who rubbed his chin. "I'm not sure I do, but please continue."

She touched the totem again, staring off into space. Early saw an expression of fear on her face and shivered.

"In short," Kori said, "if we call on the storm's power too often or too boldly, we risk an unthinkable retribution. The malice of the storm will be upon us. I fear that doom more than I fear even these horrible invaders."

As Kori spoke, Early thought of the frozen image in the tomb, of what he thought he had seen on the night the *Pride* was destroyed, of Olan's second-hand fable—of the Elder of Storms. Was that story true? Was some behemoth of the ancient world the source of Kori's strange powers? And is *that* what would come down on their heads if she continued to use those powers? His mind recoiled from the thought.

"We dare not risk this," the chieftain said, grim and quiet. "We will simply have to use what cunning we possess to kidnap the captain of the invaders, and hope we can thus compel them to leave us in peace."

The room was quiet as everyone digested this. Captain Antmar looked like he wished to argue, but he said nothing. Early could think of many objections to the plan, but he understood the need to do *something* to save themselves, rather than await extermination.

Bristi broke the silence. "Our people know the woods well enough we can assemble even at night without alerting the enemy. We'll need to time everything perfectly to sneak in from both sides while distracting them at the wall."

Captain Antmar nodded, his voice betraying excitement at the prospect of action. "We will arrange our people in groups with yours. It won't do to have half our force crashing about— or, worse, getting lost."

"No," Suran sighed, "instead, each of the groups will be

crashing about. We have no time to teach your people the art of moving quietly in the woods."

"They will do their best, I'm afraid," Isaac said, returning his pipe to his mouth. "I've tried to teach what I know of wood-craft to these poor souls, but they're quite hopeless."

The ranger smiled sardonically. Early let out a nervous chuckle, but the chieftain and the Redguard did not seem amused.

"Let us arrange everyone without delay," Captain Antmar said, rising from the table. "And let our strike fall no later than tomorrow night. Once action is decided, there is naught to gain by staying idle. We have little time to lose."

Suran nodded in agreement, though Early noticed the strained look on his face. Isaac and Bristi shared a glance, then stood with the same graceful motion.

"Come on," the tracker slapped the ranger's shoulder. "Let's divvy up whoever of this riff-raff can still work a sword."

Isaac chased Bristi as she left the room. Early envied the eagerness in his mentor's stride—he envied all of these warriors their enthusiasm in the face of danger. All he could think about was the black-armored invaders; their great cruel swords, how many of them there were. And, even worse, the wall of fire from their terrible ship. Willingly going up against those people again? Early didn't think he'd been less enthusiastic about anything in his life.

13

The night of the attack came too soon for Early. Not that a month to prepare would have felt sufficient. As his group broke free of the woods and he stumbled for the hundredth time in the gloom, Early wished Isaac was with him. Rather, it was Suran, the chieftain of the Malaspiri, that led the dozen of them. To his credit, he was almost as cunning in stealth as the Greenguard. He had them sneak across the ridgeline and down to the beach well north of the palisade. Most of the group were Suran's hand-picked warriors, but at least Olan was there with Early. The presence of his ever-grumbling friend helped Early keep his mind off the peril they were sneaking into.

The transition between bluff and beach was much steeper here than near the palisade. Early found himself preoccupied climbing down the cliff in the dark, more by touch than sight, unable to worry about anything for the moment beyond his footing. They were several hundred yards north of the enemy camp—and it felt terribly strange to think of the place where he'd slept, surrounded by the wall he and his friends had built with their bare hands, in those terms.

But that's where they were going: the enemy camp.

The beach was cold in the night, but at least the sand muffled their footsteps and there were no tree roots to trip over. At Suran's signal, Early's party drew sword, knife, or spear in silence. They were still some distance from the palisade, whose dark walls were outlined by watchfires glowing within. Early remembered when those fires had given him a feeling of safety, as he slept in his own tent on the other side of those walls. Now the fires helped their enemies, and the only thing waiting on the other side of the palisade was a desperate fight against fearsome warriors.

No sooner had Early drawn his short sword, a new blade he'd taken from the sanctuary, then there came a shout and a clamor from the palisade. Isaac, with his team of archers, must have begun their diversion: shooting arrows over the wall from directly in front, where the Malaspiri had so recently attacked the Decadins. Early imagined the ranger and the others concealed among the trees, awaiting the appointed time, then loosing their barrage.

The walls loomed as his team crept nearer, and Early tried to sort through his varied feelings of fear and excitement, doom and hope. With any luck, Captain Antmar's team, guided by Bristi, would at that moment be reaching the gap between wall and water on the south side of the palisade, just as Suran's team came from the north. With the archers drawing the enemy's attention, Early hoped the sentries at those gaps in the wall, where a narrow strip of beach lay between the edge of the wooden palisade and the tide line, would be distracted. Or, better yet, he hoped the sentries would be called away entirely, so he wouldn't have to fight them.

Suran led the way through the gap, followed by nine of his warriors, with Early and Olan bringing up the rear. Their intent was to go directly to the late Lord Mardigan's cabin, that being the most likely place to find the enemy captain. They encountered no sentries, but the sight inside the palisade was dizzying. All the invaders in sight were already armed and armored—so much for catching them off their guard. But they were focused on the wall and the deadly rain of arrows, another volley of which came even as Early watched. Several of the invaders lay on the ground, unmoving shadows between the watchfires.

Everyone was shouting. Beyond the din and confusion, Early saw a flash of red and white; on the far side of the fray, Captain Antmar and his team were already locked in combat. Early saw Marie Gold's bright hair flashing as she knocked aside the blade of her enemy, her sword seeking a gap in the dark armor. Early thrilled to see the sly, brave pirate captain in battle. But he felt a guilty relief that he wasn't on her team, already hard-pressed by the enemy.

His turn came soon enough. A pack of the invaders came around both sides of the cabin. Suran raised his great spear, and the spearhead blazed with unnatural energy—Early remembered the purple glow and the wicked crackling sound that accompanied Suran's thrust. But the sight of the arcane weapon did not deter their enemies. Early and Olan fought side by side, then back to back, and Early was again glad the big deckhand was with him; this time for his size. With his much longer reach, Olan blocked the sword of a warrior who would have been on top of Early in two more steps.

As the fight pushed them away from the cabin, along the water's edge, Early looked up at the invaders' black ship. It loomed above them, its prow a grotesque silhouette in the firelight. Though he had much to hold his attention on the ground, Early couldn't help glancing fearfully at the brazen horns on each side of the carven dragon figurehead. At any moment, the terrible light and heat of the fireship could be turned on them. That the invaders were unlikely to roast their own people along with the attackers did little to relieve Early's anxiety. Rational thought was abandoning him to gut fear and reflex.

There was a grunt to his left, away from the ship, and Early turned and blocked the enemy's thrust without thinking. The force half stunned him, but his blade found the crease of the other man's armpit, and Early thrust his sword into that unprotected spot, beneath the invader's armor. His enemy's sword fell from suddenly nerveless fingers, and Early saw the man's eyes and mouth go wide beneath his helmet. The attacker's momentum had carried Early's sword deep into his body, and suddenly the man was in his arms, sagging against Early as he breathed his last.

The battle shrank down to that awful moment. His foe's dead weight brought them both to the sand, Early on his knees, swaying in shock. He was conscious of the need to free his sword, but also of the numbing horror of taking a life. A bellow from nearby brought Early back, and he saw Suran and Olan both confronting a giant figure who, with dark armor and horned helm outlined in firelight, looked like a demon of the ancient world. While Suran's glowing spear had a long reach, this creature—the Revered Captain Tion Zanda's standard-bearer, Early remembered—bore a poleaxe equally long. As Suran attacked, his spear gleamed and crackled with lightning, but the huge warrior was undaunted.

As Early watched, Olan waded in, thinking he saw an opening as the standard-bearer fended off the spear. But the giant turned with surprising agility and caught Olan's sword on the haft of his axe. The pole snapped up and caught the big deckhand in the forehead. Early cried out as his friend dropped bonelessly to the sand. He wrenched at his own sword, buried under the weight of his fallen enemy, and finally grabbed that unfortunate man's blade instead. It was longer than Early was used to fighting with, but at the moment all that mattered was rejoining his friends.

Suran and the standard-bearer faced off across the sand as Early closed in, heart hammering in his chest hard enough to distract him from the madness of what he was doing. But then a clash and cry farther down the beach brought the standard-bearer around. The giant dashed away, again with surprising speed given his massive size. Early saw Captain Antmar circling the captain of the invaders; he recognized Tion Zanda's winged golden helm. Though Zanda used his longsword and buckler well, he was no match for an Imperial Redguard. Early cried out in excitement. This was their chance! He didn't see where the enemy captain had come from, but they had him now.

Another moment, and Antmar would force the man to surrender... but then the standard-bearer crashed down on him like a tidal wave. The poleaxe lashed out, and Captain Antmar, with a grace born only of constant training, dodged the blow just in time. Seeing all this, Suran charged after the standard-bearer, calling to three of his nearby warriors. Early wanted to follow, but Olan was lying in the sand at his feet. Early crouched by his friend, overjoyed to see he was still alive. The big deckhand rolled in the sand and groaned, then put his palm to his forehead and swore. He blinked several times before he recognized Early's smiling face.

"Very well, then," Olan said with some detachment. "Is it time for breakfast?"

"Not hardly," Early laughed. "Can you stand? We're in bad trouble here! Gods only know why you chose this spot for a nap."

Olan accepted a hand getting back to his feet and picked up his sword. The focus of the combat had split between those defending the wall—firing arrows back into the dark where Isaac and the Malaspiri archers still harried the palisade—and a knot of desperate fighting around the enemy captain. The warriors in Early's group had followed Suran, and all were locked in combat. Early knew duty required he and Olan join them, though it was awfully tempting to creep back down the beach and into the peaceful dark, away from the madness of battle.

Though the giant standard-bearer fought like a beast, Suran and Captain Antmar together would have bested him. But a horde of invader warriors swarmed into the melee. As Early and Olan cautiously approached, Early counted eight enemy fighters, plus Captain Zanda and the giant. He saw Antmar switch from fencing with the enemy captain to fending off two other soldiers, all while dodging swipes from the standard-bearer's axe. The Redguard's sword, dagger, and body blurred in a dance that was somehow coordinated despite its apparent chaos. Early saw Zanda's sword arm falter, and the enemy captain stumbled away with a cry.

Early and Olan waded in. Though he hardly felt capable of engaging these warriors—or anyone at all—sword-to-sword, Early's reflexes were young and keen. He managed to pull one of the invaders away from the fight between their leaders, and, with Olan's help at the critical moment, dispatched the armored man. Catching his breath, it seemed to Early the assault was going well; there was still fighting throughout the palisade, but there was no overwhelming press of foes. There were fewer of the invaders than Early had feared, and they were spread between those still fending off Isaac's archers, the group defending their captain from Antmar and Suran, and a few scattered one-on-one and two-on-two fights throughout the Decadins' former camp.

Early let himself believe they might win the day. But his thoughts were interrupted by the standard-bearer's roar. Without quite realizing it, Early and Olan had come into combat with Captain Zanda himself, the injured captain attempting to escape from his more formidable enemies. Seeing a new threat to his master, the giant pulled away from Suran and his spear and charged at the deckhands!

Early froze, and for a moment he forgot how to breathe. A black iron mountain was about to drop on top of him. The man's vast bulk was all he could focus on—rather than the incoming swipe of the deadly poleaxe.

"Early! Lost Gods!" Olan swore and leaped to put himself between Early and the berserker. Sword met haft of solid steel. Sparks flew as, despite Olan's strength, the great blow slowed but did not stop. Olan's sword arm drooped, shattered, and he clutched it against his body with a grimace. Early realized the swing of the poleaxe would have cut him in half had his friend not intervened.

The standard-bearer, wielding his huge weapon with surprising agility, tugged the axe towards himself, shortening the distance with a practiced eye, and caught Olan across the thighs with a powerful stroke. For the second time in as many minutes the big deckhand fell, but now Early saw his friend's blood on the sand, black in the firelight.

Early screamed at the giant, half in terror, half in rage, and prepared to fling himself at his enemy, though he would surely be crushed. Before he could, Suran charged in, the distraction of Early and Olan giving him an opening. The chieftain aimed his spear for a killing thrust, but the standard-bearer seemed to sense the danger and spun. A hasty swing of his poleaxe took the spear off a course that would have pierced his heart, but the point of the weapon crunched through chainmail and plunged into the huge bicep. Purple lightning sparked and cackled around the giant's body, and the huge man fell to his knees with a howl.

Early's heart leaped with joy—but then his ears rang with

terrible sound. Captain Zanda was blowing a stout horn of polished bone. From this close, the sound was painful, but it was the answering shout from the fireship that truly frightened him. He imagined the terrible blast of heat...

But it wasn't fire that came to the enemy captain's aid. From the gloom beneath the ship's black hull came first the tramp of feet on wooden planks, then the splash of many boots in the shallows. A tide of black-armored warriors, longswords flashing with reflected firelight, swept up the beach to answer their captain's call.

At once, Suran's commanding voice rang out to call for retreat. Early could not object: in an instant, the attackers had been overmatched at least two-to-one, and by fresh warriors not yet wounded or even tired from battle. Early looked to the nearest opening where the palisade ended and the tide line began. He was now closer to the south end, where Captain Antmar's team had entered the fort. The way was clear, if he ran, but Olan lay in the sand in front of him. His friend was alive... but surely unable to walk.

"Help! Help me!" Early shouted, simply hoping anyone would come to his aid. "We can't leave him!"

Captain Antmar and Suran both met Early's eyes, even as a dozen of their companions abandoned the fort. Perhaps, Early thought, with Antmar and the chieftain both, they could carry Olan away...

But Suran shook his head, and Antmar shouted, "Early! Run!"

He looked down at his friend and saw Olan's eyes, usually sparkling with sly humor, were fixed on him with a grim stare. In the firelight, he looked strange and old.

"Go on, Early. Get out of here."

The wave of reinforcements was almost on top of them. Fighting a strange paralysis that told him he should stand and

14

Early's body went rigid, ready to fight, but Isaac's familiar voice whispered urgently, "Don't move. We've found you, but let's not startle... them."

The hand over Early's mouth was the wrong size and shape for the ranger. Early turned his head, saw Bristi the tracker watching him. She let him go, but pressed a warning finger to her lips and turned to watch the gathering of phantoms. Isaac crouched on Early's other side, and, also releasing him, patted him on the back.

The three stayed very still, watching the ghostly figures form a line and drift, rather than walk, into the black rectangle of the tomb's entrance. Their pale light lingered in the opening for a few moments, then was gone. The clearing now contained only bright moonlight on eldritch stone.

"What in the name of—" Early bit his lip, feeling it would be wrong to curse. "What *were* those?"

Isaac shook his head. But Bristi said, reverently, "Ancestors."

A dozen questions rose in Early's mind as he looked at her,

Early heard no sound. He wondered if they gathered here every night, or if their appearance was somehow related to the terrible battle just fought on the shore. They must be connected to the Malaspiri, he supposed, and some of those brave warriors hadn't survived the night. Early's speculations were interrupted without any warning. Arms seized him from both sides, and a hand clamped over his mouth.

of light with as much stealth as he could. He wished Kori was with him. The wise young shaman would know what to make of this. If the glowing figure was, indeed, a spirit, she might even be able to communicate with it. Early was too afraid to try. He kept glancing down to check his footing, but only for a moment at a time, fearing the presence would vanish. He was so focused on silently trailing the figure that when he followed it into the clearing of the ancient tomb, he gasped in surprise. Instantly, he froze and slapped his hand to his mouth, cursing his carelessness.

But the apparition did not react. It drifted underneath the great standing stones, the carven pillars looming up black and terrible in the stark moonlight. As the figure meandered into the alley of the menhirs, towards the mouth of the tomb whose trespass had set in motion such a strange chain of events, other glowing phantoms appeared. Early hunched in the bushes at the edge of the clearing and watched.

Seven lambent figures coalesced between the standing stones. They hovered in a loose circle, as though in casual conversation. The carven pillars seemed to focus their unnatural light like a lens, for Early could see the figures more clearly than when he'd followed the first through the woods.

They were humanlike, but alien. Their limbs were elongated while their bodies and necks were stocky, and they were covered all over with thick fur or hair. The faces that were turned in his direction had inhuman, bestial features, yet were marked with a sort of calm intelligence that made Early less fearful and more curious. Their eyes were huge, round, and featureless. What color were those eyes, or hair, or bodies, Early could not tell—the apparitions seemed to be formed of nothing but ghostly light. He could, he realized, see through the figures to the pillars behind them, and the black wall of trees beyond.

Though the ghosts seemed to be speaking to each other,

he knew which way to go. What really mattered was not getting turned around and ending up back at the beach, in the arms of his pursuers.

Then again, Early thought, remembering the snapping branch, *not ending up in the jaws of a giant lizard is also a priority.*

He brooded over the crude map in his head, made his best guess at the right direction, and began loping forward, his eyes and ears peeled. He dared to break into a trot when the moonlight grew bright enough, often slowing to step gingerly through a shadowy tangle, or to listen for sounds other than his own footfalls.

As the night wore on, Early's mind grew numb. He kept pushing away his anxiety at his predicament, but there was nothing to replace it save the moment by moment awareness of each step. He didn't know how long the faint blue glow had been dancing in the trees ahead before he noticed it. Realizing the glow was not moonlight, he stopped. Early stared, unable to quite believe his eyes. Pale, neither flame nor moonlight, the light was moving on its own; he wasn't simply drawing closer to it. Was someone looking for him, perhaps? Friend or foe? Early realized even that explanation was nonsense. His friends would not dare light a torch, and the light did not resemble torchlight. Was it a strange artifice of his pursuers? With a ship that breathed fire, Early would not put anything past them.

Creeping from tree to tree, Early peeked around the trunks at the glow. It was perhaps twenty yards from where he stood, drifting slowly in a single direction—currently away from him. The diffuse light was concentrated into a bright center. As Early drew close as he dared, this radiant blob seemed to move like a human figure. A thrill ran down Early's spine. This forest of black-barked, witchy trees had always felt haunted, and by more than *guarni.*

Early dared not make any noise, but only followed the wisp

absorb. Merely twisting an ankle on a root might mean certain death. He thought not only of the pursuing invaders, but of other foes in black armor—the dreadful lizard-beasts the Malaspiri called *guarni*, that had once seemed the greatest danger on the island. It was ironic, Early thought, to find himself wishing for those simpler times. They had still been shipwrecked and uncertain of survival, but now...

Not for the first time, Early scorned his past eagerness for adventure. Since joining the crew of *Pride of the Empress*, he'd been attacked by pirates, shipwrecked, almost eaten by beasts, almost set on fire by both the Malaspiri and the terrible dragon warriors from... what had their captain called their kingdom? Zan? Rezzan? Something about a Scaly King? In all the turmoil, Early couldn't remember.

Of all those travails, this was the worst. Now he was all alone, maybe for good. Early tried not to let himself think about leaving Olan behind to be captured or put to death by the invaders. He didn't know where Isaac was, or Marie Gold, or their leaders—there hadn't been time to stop and wait at the rendezvous points to see if anyone came. Early didn't know who had survived the disastrous attempt to capture the enemy captain.

He didn't even know what direction he was stumbling in anymore.

A branch snapped behind him and Early froze, peering back the way he'd come. The moon rose high enough, after his first blind flight into the woods, to let dull light filter to the forest floor, enough to see his surroundings. He strained his eyes, but there was no movement among the dark shapes of the trees. He didn't dare call out. Instead, Early held perfectly still, trying to listen past the roar of his pulse.

After a few minutes, perceiving only the night sounds of the forest, he looked in each direction and tried to convince himself wait to die, Early turned and ran to catch up with Suran and the Guard-Captain. An enemy soldier stepped into the latter's path, but the precise slash of Antmar's sword put him out of the way. Early swerved around the falling enemy without breaking his stride. Beyond the wall of the palisade ran the stream the Decadins had used for water, and beyond that the dark beach climbed up to the ridge. The black forest lay beyond. The attackers had planned for the contingency of retreat and Early knew roughly where the southern rendezvous point was.

If he could find it in the dark.

He had an advantage over the pursuing soldiers, aside from being unarmored and nimble: he'd lived on this beach for weeks and knew the terrain better than they did. Even as three soldiers closed on him, he jumped over the narrow stream. Then, without warning, he changed course and ran straight towards the ridge, knowing by feel where the path upwards lay. In the dark, it took a few crucial moments for his pursuers to realize he'd changed direction, and by then he was almost among the trees.

The forest that had once seemed full of unknown dangers closed protectively around Early, and he felt almost safe. However, after many long minutes of picking carefully through the darkened woods, hearing the lumbering and curses of the pursuing invaders fade behind him, Early realized he didn't know where he was. Or where the beach was. Or where the rendezvous point was. He didn't dare double back to find out.

All alone, hating himself for leaving Olan behind in his primal need to escape, Early lost himself in the forest as night deepened around him.

After what felt like an hour of pounding through the woods, not hearing pursuit, Early let himself stop running. The brush had grown thick and the ground uneven. He crept instead, calling on all the apprentice ranger training he'd managed to but she was still watching the tomb with a rapt, serious look on her face.

Isaac squeezed Early's shoulder. "We should move. The woods are dangerous, and we've a long way to go. We can ponder this vision once we're safe in the sanctuary."

Bristi took the lead, taking them around to the edge of the clearing where the alley of standing stones began, then plunging back into the woods on a swift northerly course that would take them to the sanctuary through the Malaspiri's abandoned village. The terrain was difficult, but Bristi knew exactly where she was going, and Early could not have been more relieved to have a guide.

"How did you find me?" he asked Isaac.

The ranger sighed, and Early saw even he was on the verge of exhaustion. "When Suran called for retreat, those of us harrying the fort with arrows had it easier than you. No one pursued us. We gave you cover for as long as we could, then fell back as a group. The Malaspiri know their way from beach to sanctuary, even in the dark, so we partnered up and went hunting for survivors.

"Or," Isaac added, resting his hand on the grip of the bow slung over his shoulder, "hunting any invaders that followed you into the woods."

Early thought of the fearsome armored warriors from whom he'd narrowly escaped. He thought of Olan, lost, and guiltily hoped the ranger had shot them all. "Did you... find any?"

Isaac shook his head, throwing an arm around Early's shoulder. "Bristi and I found only a poor sailor, lost in the forest. I'm glad you escaped."

Early let himself slump against his friend. "So am I. And you, too."

As they hiked, Early was mostly occupied keeping pace with the ranger and the tracker, both of whom moved effortlessly through the thick forest, even in the dark. But he also found himself peering into the surrounding gloom, watching for spectral figures. He wondered about just what he had seen and wished Kori were there to explain it to him. He knew she hadn't been part of the raid, but Early found himself unreasonably worried about her safety. He wouldn't be comfortable until they reached the warmth of the sanctuary, its sconces glowing with mellow, fragrant flames, and he could see the faces of his friends and know they were all right.

He thought of Olan again, lying bleeding in the sand. *If* they were all right.

The ground had been getting steeper as they went, and at last the trio reached the long, hard climb up to the crown of the island. At the entrance to the sanctuary, found at night only by the failure of the moon to illuminate the fissure, Bristi gave the birdcall that signaled friends returning.

The sentries waiting just inside the cave did not confront them, but asked only, "How many?"

"Just the three of us," she answered. "Bristi, the ranger, Isaac, and the sailor, Early."

The sentry grunted a satisfied acknowledgement. They couldn't risk light in the vestibule of the sanctuary lest it be seen from outside, so the three felt their way along the wall in darkness. As he navigated the corridor, Early felt a sense of safety he had never before associated with the darkness of a cave. As they came around the bends of the hallway and entered the first lighted chamber, friends were waiting for them.

"Lia!" Early almost sobbed her name. The cartographer rose from her seat and embraced him. He felt an urge to kiss her and began to stutter nervously. She stepped away with a demure smile, her hands still on his arms.

As they hiked, Early was mostly occupied keeping pace with the ranger and the tracker, both of whom moved effortlessly through the thick forest, even in the dark. But he also found himself peering into the surrounding gloom, watching for spectral figures. He wondered about just what he had seen and wished Kori were there to explain it to him. He knew she hadn't been part of the raid, but Early found himself unreasonably worried about her safety. He wouldn't be comfortable until they reached the warmth of the sanctuary, its sconces glowing with mellow, fragrant flames, and he could see the faces of his friends and know they were all right.

He thought of Olan again, lying bleeding in the sand. *If* they were all right.

The ground had been getting steeper as they went, and at last the trio reached the long, hard climb up to the crown of the island. At the entrance to the sanctuary, found at night only by the failure of the moon to illuminate the fissure, Bristi gave the birdcall that signaled friends returning.

The sentries waiting just inside the cave did not confront them, but asked only, "How many?"

"Just the three of us," she answered. "Bristi, the ranger, Isaac, and the sailor, Early."

The sentry grunted a satisfied acknowledgement. They couldn't risk light in the vestibule of the sanctuary lest it be seen from outside, so the three felt their way along the wall in darkness. As he navigated the corridor, Early felt a sense of safety he had never before associated with the darkness of a cave. As they came around the bends of the hallway and entered the first lighted chamber, friends were waiting for them.

"Lia!" Early almost sobbed her name. The cartographer rose from her seat and embraced him. He felt an urge to kiss her and began to stutter nervously. She stepped away with a demure smile, her hands still on his arms.

but she was still watching the tomb with a rapt, serious look on her face.

Isaac squeezed Early's shoulder. "We should move. The woods are dangerous, and we've a long way to go. We can ponder this vision once we're safe in the sanctuary."

Bristi took the lead, taking them around to the edge of the clearing where the alley of standing stones began, then plunging back into the woods on a swift northerly course that would take them to the sanctuary through the Malaspiri's abandoned village. The terrain was difficult, but Bristi knew exactly where she was going, and Early could not have been more relieved to have a guide.

"How did you find me?" he asked Isaac.

The ranger sighed, and Early saw even he was on the verge of exhaustion. "When Suran called for retreat, those of us harrying the fort with arrows had it easier than you. No one pursued us. We gave you cover for as long as we could, then fell back as a group. The Malaspiri know their way from beach to sanctuary, even in the dark, so we partnered up and went hunting for survivors.

"Or," Isaac added, resting his hand on the grip of the bow slung over his shoulder, "hunting any invaders that followed you into the woods."

Early thought of the fearsome armored warriors from whom he'd narrowly escaped. He thought of Olan, lost, and guiltily hoped the ranger had shot them all. "Did you... find any?"

Isaac shook his head, throwing an arm around Early's shoulder. "Bristi and I found only a poor sailor, lost in the forest. I'm glad you escaped."

Early let himself slump against his friend. "So am I. And you, too."

moving, but her voice had blended with the other sounds in the room into a low burbling, like the sound of a river heard from underwater. Darkness was closing in on him. Lia called Rowene over and the two of them helped Early stumble to the bunkhouse. He didn't even get his boots off before collapsing into bed.

For a night and a day, the survivors nursed their wounds. With Olan gone, there were only ten of the Decadins left, and perhaps three times that number of Kori's people. Though Early would have liked a week in the peace and quiet of the sanctuary, the leaders were unwilling to wait. Early came from breakfast in the chamber set aside for eating and found Kori in conference with Suran and Captain Antmar, both men bandaged and looking exhausted. Marie Gold was with them, of all people. Not even Antmar could ignore the pirate's experience, despite his hatred for outlaws. There were few enough people left who could fight.

Isaac and Bristi, now close companions, were also there. In what seemed to be Greenguard fashion, they listened to the conversation but didn't participate until asked. Early brought Isaac coffee in the battered tin mug he'd rescued from the wreck on the beach so long ago. The ranger, inhaling the warm, homely scent, smiled in gratitude. The Malaspiri had a great cache of the roasted beans, so similar to what was grown in the Southlands of the Decadin Empire it deepened Early's conviction that Kori and her people must be survivors of the first expedition.

"There aren't enough of us left to break their hold on the beach," Captain Antmar was saying, and the undercurrent of defeat in the stolid warrior's voice scared Early as much as any battle. "If we attack again, we'll be destroyed."

"There never were enough of us to break their hold on the

"I was worried we'd seen the last of you, deckhand," she said.

"I was—was worried I'd have to spend the night in a pile of leaves!"

She laughed. "Good thing our ranger was able to run you down!"

"I owe my hide to the Greenguard, once again," Early said. He was starting to realize how deeply tired he was, but couldn't help smiling. He felt almost giddy to be out of danger. "I hate to think what I owe him by now. And Bristi, too.

"But how were things here?" Early's smile faded. "Did... many others make it back?"

Lia told him what she knew, but Early's mind kept wandering to the ghostly conference at the tomb, and his eyes sought Kori. From where she sat, cross-legged in a corner of the room, she smiled and lifted a hand in greeting. He would have to tell her later, in private, what he'd seen. Perhaps Isaac or Bristi would bring it up to the group, but Early didn't dare. Kori seemed like the one to tell, especially after the claims he'd made about the Malaspiri's true identity.

At her touch on his arm, Early turned his attention back to Lia. She asked if he was listening, and he gave her a sheepish smile.

"Sorry. Just thinking about everything that happened tonight. The battle, it was... terrible."

She nodded and took his hand. Her grip was strong and comforting. It gave him the courage to ask, "Olan. Did he make it back? Do you know if he's...?"

Lia shook her head, and Early felt himself sinking. Suddenly, he wished he'd gone straight to his bunk.

"Early, they told me he never made it out of the palisade. We don't know—"

But Early could not listen any longer. He saw Lia's mouth

beach," Suran pointed out. "Our raid was only a desperate hope, and the Gods' Luck was against us."

"We can't stay in these caves much longer," Marie said. "The dragon-lovers might be clumsy in the woods, but there's only so much island." She smacked the tabletop with her palm. "After our attempt on their captain, they'll have redoubled their efforts to find us. And what if they get reinforcements by sea? I'm betting their navy has more than one ship. We need to finish this, somehow, and soon."

Suran and Antmar both grumbled uneasily, but neither disagreed with the pirate captain. Isaac and Bristi traded dark looks as they chewed their pipestems.

Kori, meanwhile, had fallen into herself, saying nothing. Early wondered what she was thinking. The sheenya sat with her hands in the folds of her thick robe and she stared at the floor, where her sandals made small circles in the dust. As the others equivocated, she rose from her bench and drifted out of the chamber. After a moment of hesitation, Early followed.

Kori made her way to the cluttered armory chamber and slipped into a narrow passage on the far side. Early had been in the armory, but never noticed this exit. He followed her into a dark, narrow space, with no sconces illuminating it. Early guided himself along the smooth wall for a short distance before the way brightened—with natural light. The passage took a sharp cut to the right and, turning this corner, Early saw a great square of light five yards away, where the narrow hall opened suddenly on empty sky. Kori was sitting on the floor with her back against the carven jamb of this opening, and as Early joined her, he saw the passage ended in a narrow shelf of rock, a precarious balcony above unclimbable cliffs plunging down to the sea.

He gaped at the view, unable to speak. This side of the island, unexplored by the Decadins, curved out in two long horns around a deep inlet. The spits of land that embraced the dark blue water were steep, uninhabitable, but lush with trees. Multicolored birds circled above the treetops; the hidden cove must be a paradise for them. Beyond the jagged headlands of the inlet, Early saw the Sunfire Sea, its Eastern reaches still unexplored by any of his people.

Kori nestled against the rock wall, her knees pulled up almost to her chin, and looked out at the far-off waves. Amused by Early's astonishment, she said, "Welcome to the back door, Early. It doesn't see much use."

"I... I guess not," he stammered, breathless. He'd looked straight down over the jutting stone balcony, and the vast drop made him dizzy. He turned to Kori, and, though she still smiled, he saw doubt and sadness in her eyes.

"Early, since you brought up the idea that we—that I, and my people—might be your kin... the thought has weighed heavy on me."

Early found a place against the wall opposite her. Unlike Kori, he felt the need to stay well away from the balcony and the unguarded drop beyond.

"I'm sorry if it troubled you," he said quietly.

"No, it..." Kori shook her head and laughed. "Well, it *did* trouble me. It does trouble me. But you need not apologize. It's a mad notion, yet I can't seem to dismiss it as the others have."

"I know it seems impossible..." Early looked at the floor, unsure what to say.

"It's not just that I don't remember living in the Decadin Empire, Early," Kori continued. "I remember my entire life here. I remember *Tho'see*, the old sheenya. I can see her face, she—"

"What did she look like?" Early interrupted.

Kori stopped, closing her mouth and staring at him.

Early felt his face grow hot. He wasn't sure what impulse made him ask. "I'm sorry, I just... wondered."

Kori stared into space, sifting through old memories. "She taught me to listen to the voices of the Ancestors. But her face? Hmm... what are you thinking, Early?"

He was, in fact, thinking of the ghostly figures he'd seen gathered in conversation outside the ancient tomb.

"I saw something, Kori, on our way back to the sanctuary. A spirit, or ghost, or—I don't know what it was. Isaac and Bristi saw it, too. We ended up near your tomb, and there were..." he trailed off, remembering the strange, translucent figures, humanlike but not human.

"Yes? You saw... spirits?" Kori looked at him intently.

"I think so. Some kind of creatures, anyway. They didn't look like us, I don't think." Early was no longer sure he trusted his memory. Perhaps the terror of that night had lent monstrous shape to the apparitions.

"I think they had big eyes that looked blind, and strange long limbs, and... fur. They were furry."

Kori gazed into the ground between her feet again, introspective. "Furry. Big blind eyes. Now that you prompt me, Early, my old sheenya... Yes. She looks this way, in my memory." She raised her head and fixed him with an intense gaze. "But how can *that* be, Early? How can I be human, like you, yet remember ancestors who... were not?"

He nodded slowly. The air between them seemed charged with a possibility too bizarre to acknowledge aloud.

Kori huddled in her blanketlike robe, as though the sea breeze beyond the doorway had brought a sudden chill. "I have always heard the voices of the Ancestors, Early. The voice on the wind, that speaks words only I can hear, and the voice in the stone, a feeling of guidance deep in my heart. I have no memory of a time when I didn't hear them. Yet *whose* ancestors have I been hearing?"

Early moved from the wall, sat carefully next to Kori, daring the opening and the drop beyond. She pressed against his side for comfort. He felt he had little to give. Their situation seemed hopeless and this revelation, amazing as it was, hardly changed it.

"Whoever they are, can't these Ancestors give us a hint?" Early asked. "Because it doesn't seem like anyone knows what to do. I certainly don't." He smiled, embarrassed. "Then again, I can't remember the last time I *did* know what to do."

Kori grinned at him. "Poor Early, with no voices to guide you. Just that old ranger."

Early laughed. "Isaac said he wished he could get his hands on the fireship, threaten the invaders with their own weapon. But I don't think he was serious. We can't *get to* the ship through all those warriors."

Kori grew quiet, gazing thoughtfully out to sea. They watched the wheeling birds in silence for a long time before an idea dawned on Early.

"Kori, I know you said summoning the fog was risky..." Early began. Kori sighed, shook her head, and huddled even deeper into her robe. "I know," he persisted, "but couldn't that be the way? We could pop right onto the deck of the fireship!"

"We've used that power too much already," Kori said, and Early got the feeling she'd had the thought long before it occurred to him. "The wrath of the storm has drawn very close. Calling on that power even once more... may unleash destruction on us all."

"I understand," Early said. "Well, sort of. I believe you when you say it's dangerous. But what if it's our only chance? It seems like the invaders mean certain death! Isn't the *possibility* of something better than that, even if the thing is terrible?"

She turned to him, and he saw a haunted look in her eyes.

"It's one thing to die at the hands of people," she said. "It's another to bring the doom of the Ancestors upon us."

Early thought back to the tomb, to the sculpture of the monstrous thing diving from the sky. To the Elder of Storms.

"So this power of the storm," he said, struggling to understand. "It's connected to your Ancestors somehow? Is there any way you can just... *ask* them? Ask if they're willing to help?"

Kori stiffened.

"I'm sorry," Early said quickly. "Maybe that's a heretical idea."

She took a deep breath. "It's not so much heretical as it is... a thing of last resort. It is one thing for a spirit to reach across the gap and for you to listen. It is another thing to reach across yourself, across the gap between life and—and death."

"It's dangerous?" Early whispered.

Kori was looking out to sea, but her wide eyes were unfocused, seeing some inner panorama. She sighed.

"Dangerous? Yes. In a way, it's dangerous. It's dangerous to the woman who presumes to demand the Ancestors' attention, and it may be dangerous to all of us, if we provoke the wrath of the storm."

Early slumped against the curve of the wall. He felt leaden in body and mind, wanting only to sleep and forget the gravity of their situation.

"I'm sorry, Kori. I just thought... I don't know. It's a fantasy, I suppose. A fairytale."

Kori continued to stare out to sea. When she turned back to him, the young shaman looked old indeed.

"It's not a fantasy, Early," she said. "Just a choice of one danger among many. I said your idea was a last resort. Perhaps now is the time for last resorts."

At the foot of the cliff far below them, one wave after another crashed in, painting the rocks with sea-spray; the power of the storm venting its eternal anger on the obstinate earth.

15

Once resolved to a course of action, Kori did not hem and haw or second-guess herself. Early envied her. Having decided that daring to summon the Ancestors—whatever they actually were—was their only hope for victory, Kori began preparing for a journey to the tomb. Early did not relish the prospect of exploring that fearsome place again, but it was the only place to accomplish their task, Kori said; the tomb was the anchor that connected the island with the terrible power brooding in the clouds above.

When it became clear Kori intended to sneak out of the sanctuary without telling anyone, and that she wanted Early to come along, he grew doubtful indeed.

"Shouldn't we tell your chieftain, at least?" he asked. "And isn't—isn't it awfully dangerous to trek across the island by ourselves? The dragon-warriors are probably crawling all over the forest..."

The two conspirators were in the long, low chamber where the Malaspiri kept their stores. It was one of the few places in the sanctuary caverns where no one was likely to intrude, as the evening meal was already going on in the dining hall nearby.

Kori was changing clothes, trading her voluminous robe for the leather garments appropriate for the woods. She was hidden, for privacy's sake, behind a stack of rough sacks stuffed with dried fruit. Early sat on the other side, his back to the stack, eyes straying nervously to the door of the chamber.

"If this dangerous path is the right path," Kori replied, "then we must walk it. None of my people—and, I think, none of yours—will want to do this. Telling them only invites obstacles. No, we've made this choice, and we're making it for everyone."

He could hear the determination in her voice, supposed it came from being a shaman, a guide to all her people. For once, Early thought about the real magnitude of Kori's responsibilities. He could hardly imagine taking that all on himself, at their young age.

He envied her again, this time for her confidence.

"I think that's what scares me most, Kori: we're choosing for everyone. What if we're wrong? Do the... the voices of the Ancestors, have they said anything?"

There was a pause, and Kori's response was quiet. "No, Early. No voices on the wind." He despaired, but after a moment Kori spoke again, with a hint of her usual mirth. "But in my heart, the voice in the stone, it tells me we're doing what we need to do."

"I wish I had a voice in my stone," he said.

From the other side of the sacks, he heard Kori snort with laughter.

"You know what I mean!"

Kori, now dressed for the woods, totem slung under her shoulder, came around the stack and offered Early a hand. He got to his feet and handed her one of their small packs. They only planned to be gone overnight at most, so he'd packed only the minimum they might need in an emergency.

"I think everyone hears the voice in the stone, whether

they're in touch with the Ancestors or not," Kori said, tapping Early over his heart. "You've done brave things these past few weeks, just like all of us. Something told you what to do, even if you didn't *hear* it speak."

Early caught Kori's hand and held it a moment. "I'll have to think about that. But thank you, Kori."

She smiled at him and held his eyes until Early grew shy and looked away. He said, "So it's really just you and me doing this?"

She nodded with calm serenity. As always, Kori didn't seem like a girl several years Early's younger. If anything, there was an air about her older and wiser than even Isaac.

"Then can we start right now?" Early laughed nervously. "I think the voice in the stone is telling me to just get this over with before I lose my nerve."

"Soon," Kori said, ushering Early to wait with her near the chamber door. "We'll bide our time until the guards at the gate come for their supper. They eat after the rest of us do. When their shift changes, we'll have just a little time when we can leave unnoticed."

Their departure happened as Kori predicted, though with every step along the winding, sconce-lit hallway to the sanctuary entrance, Early expected them to get caught. But the guards had left for their meal, and their replacements lingered, chatting with them in the dining hall. Early suspected Captain Antmar would disapprove of this lax discipline, but the sanctuary was, after all, well-hidden—and the point of the guards wasn't to keep people in.

The sun had almost set, and from the hillside the sky was vast and clear. The endless swell of the sea glittered, blinding, while above a dust of stars was already visible at the dark blue zenith. It promised to be a clear and moonlit night; at least they wouldn't have to stumble through the woods in the dark. Once they'd climbed down the difficult path from the crown of the hill and entered the woods—Kori headed straight for the tomb along a path obviously familiar to her—Early felt a growing dread. His jangling nerves warned him some nameless fear crouched behind every tree. At any moment, he expected a great reptilian beast to bar their path, or a band of men in black armor, or a swarm of ghosts. Some doom felt close at hand, and Early kept his shoulders hunched close as he walked, until his neck was aching and he cursed his own nervousness. But the feeling of tense anticipation refused to let go.

The darkening forest was quiet, and the sounds of night replaced the sounds of evening as they emerged into the ancient grove. The moon was not quite high enough to illuminate the clearing, so the looming stones were indistinct presences, felt more than seen. Early knew it was mere imagination that made him feel the menhirs were watching with stern disapproval, but he remembered the ghostly meeting of nonhuman shapes he'd seen in this very spot, and he shivered even though the night was warm.

Soon enough, they stood before the black, forbidding rectangle of the tomb's entrance. Early realized he'd been dreading this moment, and it had come upon him too soon. He wished the trek through the woods had been three times as long, or that the avenue of standing stones stretched ahead of them for miles.

But the moment was here. Knowing the answer, he still asked Kori, "Must we go in there?"

"Yes," she said, standing beside him. She slipped her hand into his. It was the only reassurance she could give.

They each lit a torch, holding the lights high as they entered the narrow antechamber and descended the steep stairway beyond. Early caught glimpses of the carven walls in the flickering torchlight, and the strange symbols and figures leaped and writhed, highlighting how alien they were. He thought again of the ghostly Ancestors and wondered if the hands that shaped these images had been at all akin to his.

But it was the final image he most feared to see again. Kori led the way silently to the lowest chamber, where the sarcophagi and their ancient tenants waited with eternal patience. And the Elder of Storms also waited, captured in stone, that horrible sculpture frozen in its cataclysmic dive.

Early tried to resist the memory, but it was no use. He was back on the burning deck of the *Pride*, dazzled and horrified as the great mainmast burst into flame, then feeling Deckmaster Matta slip from his numb fingers to disappear into the churning sea. The image of Captain Mestrum's grave and fearless face as she bid him Gods' Luck and went to await the end... dissolved into Kori's face, and he remembered where he was.

Kori squeezed Early's hand, and he realized his face was wet with tears. She asked him only, "Can you go on?"

He couldn't. He had to. Whatever happened next, the unforgiving sea lay between him and home. Turning back would bring neither solace nor safety.

He nodded. They came to the center of the chamber, the heart of the tomb. Kori handed him her torch and took her totem out of its sling, holding it in front of her with both hands. Early saw what had occurred to him unconsciously the first time he had seen her holding the totem—when he'd been marched into her village what felt like a very long time ago. The totem and the sculpture of the great dragon were carved from the same glossy black stone. Carved, he had little doubt, by the same long-dead artisan.

Kori began an incantation, her voice at first quiet and quavering in the stillness of the tomb, but gaining in strength with each syllable until Early found himself glancing around at the silent sarcophagi, fearing insanely that something might awaken in response to her voice.

"Ya-lan kay-aton, ita-lan pemer-ay ton!
Spiri-an seemay-ton ala-tan tanna-lon!"

The air in the tomb seemed to stir as she chanted, and the hair on Early's nape stood on end. He could have been imagining it, but the dark stone of Kori's totem—her *stormshard,* she'd called it—appeared to pulse with an inner light, and the sculpture of the dragon responded in kind. The rest of the room sank into shadow. Even the two burning torches Early held grew dim. They weren't burning out—Early could see the flames flaring and guttering as high as before—but the light itself was subdued as the colorless radiance waxed. The glassy totem and sculpture looked almost wet, and Early imagined oily waves lapping against a beach of dark stone.

He felt strange, queasy, like the world was turning sideways, and he hoped he wouldn't fall to the floor and drop the torches. The notion of the flames going out and leaving him and Kori down here with only the witchlight was unbearable. He wanted to shut his eyes, but couldn't bring himself to look away from the totem... or, rather, from the sculpture.

The hated countenance of the Elder of Storms was starting to move, Early could swear it; the shape of the dragon was rippling, as though soaring amongst sinister clouds. Was it real or a hallucination? Just torch smoke in his eyes and the horrible tension assailing him from every angle of the room?

Kori's voice faded into a background drone in Early's consciousness as he wrestled to understand what he was seeing. The rest of the room was lost in darkness now, as though the torches *had* gone out, though Early still felt their heat against his face. The totem and the dragon were blazing, though he could not describe what sort of light they emitted; it was without color or heat, a frozen fire.

The chant rose to the forefront of his mind again, and though he could make no sense of Kori's words, there was something of fearsome climax in them. He was filled with a desperate desire to run, to flee, to escape what was coming, but the world that contained his body was gone and movement was impossible.

"*Maya-enna sumay-ton! Ella-enna maray-ton!*
Satra-senya kamay-lon! Arna-enna tumayyy—"

The rest of Kori's chant was lost to Early's ears—somehow, he could hear the wind outside the tomb shriek to a crescendo. In his mind's eye, he saw the trees of the forest creaking in the tempest, and even the mighty standing stones seemed to shift, muttering darkly to one another. High above, the moonlight was smothered by a growing mass of clouds, blacker than the black of the night sky.

Even as his disembodied vision saw all light outside the tomb extinguished, Early was back in the chamber far underground. The sculpted dragon and Kori's totem both glowed silver, as though the moonlight had all been sent down here to light them. Kori was a mere silhouette, haloed by the gleaming totem. She held the stormshard high in her outstretched arms, as though offering it to the sculpted dragon... or shielding herself from it.

Through the tons of solid rock above their heads, Early heard thunder. The walls shook, ever so slightly, and Early swore a groaning rose from the huddled sarcophagi around them. But what truly gave him a shock of fear were the small chips of rock flaking from the ceiling overhead. He saw them drift down in the torchlight, once, then again.

He was quite sure he wasn't hallucinating *that*.

Kori turned to him, and he saw the fear in his eyes mirrored in her own. She mouthed a word Early didn't need to hear to understand: *Run.*

He turned to the exit, gestured that she should precede him up the stairs. Kori did not argue, slinging the totem back under her arm, its unearthly light winking out. Early followed close behind, his torches bathing the close walls in a chaos of orange light. They hurried up the stairs as though pursued, Early praying not to trip on the steep, worn steps. With his hands full, a fall would be no minor inconvenience.

Then the open mouth of the tomb loomed ahead. From the chamber now far below, Early thought he heard a rumbling building in power until it was a terrible roar, but it was probably only thunder, echoing from outside.

They emerged into a storm. Howling wind bent the trees surrounding the clearing, and rain hammered down in gusts. There was no stopping to dwell on what they had done; Kori sprinted for the trees and Early ran after her. They faced a difficult path back to the sanctuary in the dark, for the promised moonlight was hidden by menacing clouds that were limned in lightning.

Had Kori actually summoned all of this? Early was eager to know, but Kori obviously wasn't stopping to chat. He focused on reaching the protection of the thickest part of the forest canopy. Something in the fury of the storm chilled Early beyond the mere cold of wind and rain.

They'd been running almost blindly through the forest for what felt like ages when the torches blew out. They stopped to rekindle their lights and catch their breath.

"Did you—did this storm—was it—?" Early could hardly string together a sentence, let alone force it past the burning in his chest. He was panting for breath. But Kori understood.

"I called out, and something answered," she said.

They were huddled together against the trunk of a tree. Around them, tempestuous winds roared through the forest, swallowing all other sounds. Kori leaned in to shout, but this time her closeness brought Early no comfort.

"All we can do now is get back to the sanctuary," she said, adding, "and hope whatever has come means doom for our enemies, not for ourselves."

When they were finally in sight of the sanctuary entrance, Early did his best to mimic the correct bird call to alert the sentries. Kori had lapsed into a daze as they made their way back from the tomb, slowing her pace until she was drifting aimlessly through the woods. Early took her hand and did his best to lead, despite being much less sure of the right direction.

When he'd asked her what was wrong, the young shaman had merely shaken her head, and could do little more than nod to confirm Early's guess about which way to go. Her work in the tomb must have exhausted her, and she'd pushed the overpowering weariness aside just long enough to flee the storm that work had summoned.

Two sentries, seeing Early and Kori in the mingled light of their own torches and the one brand Early still carried, came quickly out of the cave mouth to help. They brought Kori into the sanctuary, and put her to bed in the chieftain's chambers, a quiet room with a large and comfortable bed, away from the bustle of the public spaces. When Suran arrived, he found Early watching Kori anxiously from a finely carved rocking chair in the corner of the room. The sheenya seemed to be in an uneasy sleep. Outside the room huddled a group of both Decadins and Malaspiri, worrying in hushed voices.

Suran shut the room's heavy door and stood at the side of his bed, looking down at his young shaman. "What's happened to Kori?" he asked Early, his voice quiet but grave. "Where did you take her?"

"We went into the tomb," Early said, and the chieftain

raised his eyebrows. His stoic face showed little sign of how he felt, but a tremor in his voice suggested outrage.

"The tomb? Only the sheenya alone can enter the tomb, for only she can speak with the sleepers there. But that was true when we lived freely in our village. With those invaders on the loose, it's much too dangerous for her to make that journey. Did you take her in secret? Why did I hear nothing of this?"

"I didn't *take her* anywhere," Early said. There was an accusatory tone in Suran's voice, and Early found it made him angry instead of fearful. "She decided to ask the Ancestors for help, and I went with her. She asked me to."

"But why would—" Suran raised his voice, curiosity warring with anger.

Kori laid a hand on his arm. He looked down at her, surprised she was conscious.

"Suran, there was no other way. We need the power only the storm can give, so I asked the Ancestors to grant it. And I needed Early's help."

Early flushed at this and avoided Suran's suspicious glance. He didn't understand why it had been so important to Kori to have him along, either.

"But Kori," Suran asked, still glaring at Early, "who gave you leave to go outside the sanctuary?"

"I am sheenya, am I not?"

The chieftain considered her unhappily.

"You are. But it was terribly dangerous. Did the Ancestors demand this of you?"

She shook her head. "They have been silent since the invaders came. But my heart told me we had no other hope. Now I have awakened a great power, and we must ride it to victory."

"A great power..." The chieftain looked at the wall of the room, as though seeing through the candlelit rock to the storm boiling outside. "The sentries told me of the sudden storm. Is this what you've brought us? The anger of the Elder?"

Kori sank into the bed, seeming to shrink from the name. After a long moment she gestured to Early, and he brought her water from a cup and pitcher at his elbow. When Kori had wet her lips, she replied, her voice thin.

"Perhaps. But its anger may be our only hope. If we can turn its wrath on our foes."

Suran pulled a stool close to the bedside and sat, pondering. His gaze returned to Early, who was watching them both with apprehension.

"You may go now, Early."

Early gripped the arms of his chair to rise, but stopped. He looked at Kori, drained by their ordeal. Though she had always seemed older than her years, now she seemed old in truth, wasted by exhaustion. He wondered if she would recover. She'd sacrificed something, part of herself, to save all of them.

Early sat back down. His grip on the chair now had a hint of defiance in it. He shook his head. "No. I want to stay with her. She's given everything for us."

Suran considered this, then nodded. He looked weary suddenly, as weary as Kori. The sheenya had shut her eyes and seemed to be sleeping. He stroked a lock of hair back from her forehead, a fatherly gesture. "She may have done, yes."

But Kori was not asleep. "You both fret over me like my grandmother used to," she said quietly, smiling. "I'm not gone yet."

The chieftain gave a soft laugh of surprise, and Early felt his heart lift for the first time in ages.

"So be it, Early," Suran said to him. "Stay by Kori's side. But first, please find Captain Antmar and bring him here. It seems we must have a council of war, and I assume our not-gone-yet sheenya will insist on being involved."

For one so exhausted by her ordeal, Kori's smile seemed to Early awfully self-satisfied.

There was not much room in Suran's bedchamber for a council, but once it became clear they had to use whatever power Kori had summoned in a final, desperate strike against the invaders, the decision-makers crowded in. Bristi and Isaac, the lieutenants of the united Malaspiri and Decadin force, stood around the bed. Kori still lay beneath the blankets, though she had propped herself up with pillows and her eyes were open. It seemed her youth and vitality would prevail.

"The storm rages on," Bristi was saying. "I've never seen anything like it before."

"I have, but once," Isaac said, looking meaningfully at Captain Antmar and at Early. The deckhand had been trying not to dwell yet again on the storm that sunk the *Pride*, but of course that's what the ranger meant.

The tracker ignored the Greenguard and spoke to Kori. "Sheenya, is this what you intended when you called to the Ancestors? Is this storm meant to aid us somehow?"

Kori shook her head, her tone apologetic. "I did call on the Ancestors, but it was a gamble to do so. I have used their power much these past weeks, and there was always the chance that... another would answer. That may be what this storm is: the Elder's wrath."

Early shuddered at the idea.

"Still, we have an opportunity," Kori said, and looked at the ranger. "Isaac, Early told me you had an idea: we could capture the invaders' ship and use it against them."

Early had rarely seen Isaac look taken aback. "Well, I—" he stuttered, "that was more of a lark than anything. Capturing the ship would be a master stroke, but I don't see how we can. After our last attack, I hardly like our chances of catching the enemy unawares."

He chewed his pipe thoughtfully. "Maybe we could row a boat around the island under cover of darkness and use grapnels to climb up onto the fireship's deck. But we'd need more than a few of us to take the ship, even with the advantage of surprise."

Kori nodded impatiently, as though expecting his objections. "But there is a way to put our entire force on the deck of their ship directly: the same way we took your people captive the first time."

"That awful fog?" Early blurted.

"That's right," she said. "I know I declared it too dangerous to use again so soon, but if the storm's wrath has already broken loose…"

"Do you think it will work?" Early asked, doubtful.

Kori shrugged and managed a smile. "With all the power of the storm gathered here, it may work better than it ever has. Or it may devour us all instead of delivering us to our goal. I can't say. And," she said, looking at Suran as though to preempt his question, "the Ancestors remain silent. I suspect they've gone away somewhere to watch us and judge what we do."

The chieftain thought this over for a long time. "However we came to this," he said, "with invaders on our shore and the Elder raging overhead, it seems we're at our last throw. We have to drive the enemy off the island. I can think of nothing else to do but try to take the ship. If you, Kori, can open the way for us, I'll lead the strike myself."

He looked at Captain Antmar. The Redguard stood silent and brooding, leaning against the wall with his arms crossed. But he answered the chieftain quickly. "I don't understand the powers at work here," Antmar said, "but if this is the way we may prevail, all our swords will be at your side."

"Thank you," Suran said.

Antmar gave a short, sharp nod. "Very well. How do we do this thing?"

"We'll gather everyone at a place in the woods nearby," Kori said, "and I will call up the fog. I don't know if it will come, or if it will be safe to enter. So I will enter with you."

"Kori," Suran reproached, shaking his head.

"Our last throw, you said," she reminded him. "This is how it must be.

"If the Ancestors favor us, we'll step out of the fog right onto the deck of their ship. From there..." she looked to Early.

He cleared his throat, realizing the others in the room had turned to look at him as well. "Um—" he began, faltering. "I—I think Marie would know better than anyone how to assault a ship. Why don't I go get her?"

He stood and made to leave the room, but Captain Antmar cut him off. "Leave the pirate out of this," the Redguard growled. "She can't be trusted."

Early began to protest, but Antmar waved him back to his chair. "We have no more Blueguard officers to help us plan this attack. You're in the room, deckhand. Surely you know your way around a ship?"

"Well—right." Early slumped back in his chair. His ears were burning, and he felt a little sick. But the leaders were all waiting for him. "Well. Taking a ship. I remember Mosul telling me this, once: you want to take the stern deck first, that's where the officers are. And try to capture the captain. Then you can force the rest of the crew to surrender."

Antmar grumbled at the mention of capturing the captain —they'd failed at that once already. But Early ignored him. He stared into space, willing the wisdom to come. "Oh! And make sure to guard the hatches, um, because if most of the soldiers are belowdecks, they've got to come up one at a time, and you can trap them there."

"A choke point," Isaac added, helpfully.

"Exactly!" Early said, grateful, and felt a stirring of hope that they might actually be able to do this. Then the thought of being lost forever in the enchanted fog crowded out his hopes. He leaned back in his chair, worrying as the others took over the conversation.

"We'll take every last one of us who can fight, as well-armed as we can make them," Captain Antmar said.

Suran agreed. "If we take the fireship, we can force the invaders to terms. If we fail..." He turned his palms upward, and they all knew what he meant. If they failed, it would not matter who went on the attack and who stayed behind.

Early noticed Captain Antmar's face darken at the mention of "terms." But the Redguard did not challenge the chieftain. In fact, he said nothing more as they finished their council. As the leader of the Decadins, he left the room first, taking Isaac to ready the rest of their people for the attack. To Early's relief, the Greenguard was quietly arguing with Antmar about Marie Gold's position in their ranks.

Suran and Bristi went to gather the Malaspiri, and the chieftain put a hand on Early's shoulder as he left the room, letting Early know he could stay with Kori.

When they were alone, Kori looked at him. "You're afraid, Early. Of the fog, the wrath of the Elder, or the invaders?"

"All of it," Early said, and scoffed bitterly at himself. "I'm as afraid as I've ever been. It feels like I've been afraid constantly ever since sailing away from home, though I suppose that can't really be true."

Kori threw the covers off her body and swung her legs over the side of the bed. Her totem stood on a side table, its sling on the floor below. She gathered up both, touching the glossy black stone with reverence.

"I know what you mean," she said. "I'm afraid of it all, too."

"But here we go anyway, right?" Early said, rising from his chair. His legs felt weak. He took a deep breath and forced his shoulders, hunched with tension, to relax. "We must be mad."

"Maybe we are," Kori said, and her eyes flashed with the mischievous humor Early admired. "But have you considered we might simply be brave?"

Early blinked at this, then smiled at her. "I can honestly say," he said, "that thought has never occurred to me."

16

The storm did not abate while Early and his companions worked out their plan. If anything, the fury of the elements grew as the night drew on, and when he had stepped out of the sanctuary cave and looked down the wooded slope towards the sea, Early saw a maelstrom swirling above, visible only in the frequent flashes of purplish lightning. The evil light illuminated the wet forest and the choppy sea beyond, like it was a vista from another world.

As the company made their way into the woods, Early tried to ignore the rain already soaking him to the skin. Even more, he tried not to dwell on the images the storm conjured from his memory: the deck of the *Pride*, the chaos and fire, the hated deckmaster he couldn't save, his beloved captain ordering him to leave her to drown. The thought of actually being on the deck of a ship again in such a storm, even a beached ship, was becoming intolerable.

And once we're aboard, Early sulked to himself, *then it gets* really *bad.*

Climbing down the treacherous path to the forest in the rainy dark was frightful, and the Decadins clung to their

Malaspiri companions, who were used to the path. Once they reached the shelter of the trees, things got better. The ground was much easier, and the canopy cut the wind and rain enough for them to light torches.

They hiked for perhaps an hour before gathering in a clearing to wait. Bristi and Isaac had left on their own as soon as the plan of attack was finalized. The tracker and the ranger would return to the beach and examine the enemy's defenses, to give the attackers as much detail as possible about what they would face—if, Early couldn't help reminding himself, the fog Kori summoned didn't simply swallow them all up, to be lost forever.

The group of three dozen—about two Malaspiri for every Decadin—broke up into tense clumps of fours and sixes. Lia had come along on the attack, and even her handmaiden Rowene was there, uncomfortable in patched-together leather armor and clutching a short spear. Early hung around with them near the distinctive row of five trees whose fiery red foliage marked their rendezvous point with Isaac and Bristi.

"You'll be just fine," Lia was reassuring Rowene. "Stay close by my side and remember what Goran showed you."

Goran, the Malaspiri who'd kept watch on the Decadins since they first landed, had spent the past day giving his civilian allies a crash course in spear fighting. Spears, with their long, solid shafts, would be better on both offense and defense for untrained fighters than the close-combat finesse demanded by swords.

"I will do whatever fate demands to keep you safe, Lady Dracis," Rowene told her mistress, but she regarded her spear doubtfully, as though its point might transform into a serpent and bite her.

Early rather envied Rowene. Being able to keep his enemies at spear's-length was awfully appealing, but he had trained with his sword and it seemed best to fight with it. Lia seemed to agree, for she'd armed herself with a short sword. Early wondered where the noble-born Imperial Cartographer had developed a preference for the blade and was just screwing up his courage to ask her when Suran called to everyone from the clearing's center.

"Now is our last chance to prepare body and mind," the chieftain warned. "Our enemy's force is larger, better armed, and dug-in. Once our attack is underway, our only hope is momentum. We must capture their captain, take over their ship, and force the invaders to surrender."

The attackers had all heard the plan, but the reminder of its exigency set many of them grumbling with agitation. One voice rose above the rest.

"What chance do we have?" Zek the Luckless asked. "Is there no better course than to throw our lives away?"

Captain Antmar, standing next to Suran, strode forward to reprimand the old scoundrel. But Marie Gold appeared first, answering in a voice the whole clearing could hear.

"Maybe we win and maybe we lose," she said, and flipped her cutlass end over end. Early held his breath as he watched the blade flash above her head, but Marie caught the bucket hilt with practiced ease. She winked at Zek. "I'd rather test the Gods' Luck blade-to-blade than wait to be hunted down and wiped out like a rat!"

Several people cheered at this and Early felt his spirits lift. Marie Gold was a captain, after all, and knew how to rally a crew. Zek didn't look convinced, and might have objected—but he never got the chance. With a whistled signal, the scouts came out of the trees.

The sight of his friend and mentor eased Early's anxiety as always; he could not feel quite so hopeless if he was fighting by Isaac's side. The ranger and the tracker came straight to where

their leaders stood, and the various little groups gathered around to hear their news.

"We may be in luck," Isaac said with a tired smile. It was strange to hear him out of breath, whether from exertion or excitement. "The storm has forced our enemy off the beach, and I reckon they're huddled belowdecks in their ship. Easy pickings, if we can get command of it."

"I'd rather they were scattered around the beach," Marie Gold said. "The more of them onboard, the more we may have to fight."

"That's why we have two goals," Captain Antmar retorted, annoyed by the outspoken pirate captain. Though Early's name wasn't mentioned, it pleased him to hear the Guard-Captain, chief of the mighty Redguard, echo his contribution to their plans. "We must hold the hatches so the crew below cannot press us in force, and we must quickly take their captain to force their surrender."

"Oh, silly me!" Marie laughed, tossing her head carelessly. "That's easy enough, then."

Antmar scowled at her sarcasm, but Isaac barked a humorless laugh; clearly, he had been thinking the same thing.

For Early's part, the mention of the enemy crew belowdecks made him think of Olan—was his lost friend still alive? Could he be held on the ship? Early prayed they'd find the big deckhand safe and sound, and let himself imagine how he'd tease Olan when he released him from the enemy's brig.

Kori stepped forward, taking her totem from its sling. "Nothing we are about to do will be easy," she said, smiling patiently at Marie. "But the time has come to try." She bowed slightly to Suran, who nodded and addressed the gathering in a booming voice.

"Prepare yourselves! The time has come. Look to Kori and follow only her lead."

Kori walked to the gathering's edge. She turned to look at the company, all of whom had enough faith in her to plunge themselves into a danger from which they might not return. Her eyes met Early's, and he saw her fear and her hope. Then she turned and faced the forest, beyond which lay the beach and their foes.

Her small shoulders squared as she took a deep, steadying breath, then she held the stormshard aloft and began to chant. Above the canopy of trees, thunder boomed, as though outraged at the presumption of the tiny woman below. Wind howled in the branches all around them, and Early felt his body tighten as though expecting a killing blow.

Then the light in the forest clearing changed. The torches seemed to dim, and Kori's totem glowed as it had in the tomb. Its eerie light shifted from deep blue through purple to white and back, pulsing with the tides of the storm high above. Early realized, with a stab of alarm, he could no longer see Kori or even the people standing next to him. Everything had sunk into darkness but the light of the stormshard. The fiendish wind swelled until it deafened him, and he started to panic. Then he heard Kori's voice, clear and serene even as the storm winds raged around it.

"Don't be afraid! Follow me. And be ready!"

The sound of her voice, anchored in the world he understood, broke the spell of fear. Early drew his sword and imagined his friends doing the same, though he could no longer see or hear them. He stepped towards the glowing totem, tenuous at first, then, reminding himself he was not alone, with greater intent and speed. Soon he was charging through the fog, and Early spared little thought for fears of what he might be charging into. In the distance, though she couldn't have been that far away, Kori's totem burned brightly, the light's color

now a blend that surpassed description. The light flared like a cold star...

And Early heard many feet stomping a wooden deck. He was running down the black planks of the fireship, and his friends were with him.

Kori led them. Beyond her, stumbling in the thick dark cloud that delivered the horde of strangers to their ship, the dragon-warriors of Rzhan were drawing their swords.

"Kori!" Early shouted, and his charge became a sprint. The shaman was leading their attack, yet she herself was unarmed. A warrior in black armor charged at them, and Early's heart raced as he sought to throw himself between Kori and the blade of their enemy. It was a relief to find Captain Antmar beside him; Early was happy to be a mere distraction as the Redguard's flashing sword dispatched their foe. And then Suran was there, too, his great spear crackling and humming with violet light. Those warriors unfortunate enough to be within its reach were thrown down shrieking and twitching to the deck, their armor unable to protect them.

Early heard a familiar cry, and he peered through gusts of rain towards the bow of the ship. Flashes of lightning illuminated the battle in a series of still images. Marie Gold was dueling one of the enemy crew, wild light in her eyes as she worked her cutlass. Nearby was Ander, the carpenter, overpowering a baffled invader, and Redguard Taliss, forcing another warrior to the deck at the crossed points of her rapiers.

Isaac strode from the fog with his bow already drawn, spiking an invader who was charging down the stairs from the stern deck. Bristi the tracker was at his side, an arrow nocked to her bow, scanning for targets. She had her long pipe clamped between her lips, and blew a puff of smoke as she loosed her shot.

The ranger urged his friends onward with a swing of his hand.

"What're you waiting for?" he yelled. "Let's find that captain and his fancy hat!"

Early looked around for Kori, but she was already next to him, touching his arm in greeting. She had slung her totem and drawn a long knife.

Suran turned to them and said, "You heard the ranger! Captain Antmar, will you take control of the deck?"

The Redguard shouted affirmatively and called Taliss to join him. He did not look pleased when Marie came along, too. The pirate was already ordering their people to cover the hatches at the bow of the ship, so they could stop any of the crew who tried to come onto the deck.

There was no time to argue over who was in charge, and Antmar had to satisfy himself by fending off a sudden rush from two dragon warriors. Early was just glad to see Marie imposing some order on the attack—he'd forgotten his own advice about the hatches in the excitement of battle.

Suran prompted the rest of them—Isaac, Bristi, Kori, and Early—and they ran for the stern deck, where, similar to the *Pride*, two tiers of wide steps led up to the officers' cabins. The captain's cabin was at the very top, its heavy black door decorated with gold. Beyond that portal, Early hoped, waited a quick, decisive end to this perilous adventure.

Following Isaac's lead, Early and Kori were running up the steps to the captain's cabin when a door slammed on the tier behind them. Suran, guarding their backs, let out a shout. There was a terrible clash of steel and bodies slamming together, practically at Early's ankles.

He spun around to see the enemy's standard bearer, that huge man made even larger by his heavy black armor and high, sturdy helm. The warrior had driven Suran to the ground with a

blow, and the axe he held—a short, cruel one this time, not the long poleaxe he'd used to cut Olan down—was stained with blood. He looked inhuman, looming over the chieftain, visage obscured by the faceguard of his helm, a giant shadow in the fog that still rolled over the deck.

The giant was trying to drive the blade of his axe through Suran's neck. The chieftain had his spear shaft between them, but even with all his strength, he could barely hold the massive warrior back by the crucial inches.

There was no time to think. Early jumped down the steps and swung his sword at the foe's axe arm as hard as he could. Though the blow jolted him and hardly dented the mottled plates of armor, the standard bearer reared back, ready to fend off a second attacker.

A third attacker came. Kori sprang down the stairs alongside Early with a cry of rage, and as the standard bearer drew up to his massive height, she thrust her long knife at his armored hip. With surprising agility, the big man jumped back from the wicked jab and swept down his left forearm, so the black buckler strapped there could shatter Kori's arm. But the shaman was even quicker than he, and she danced aside before the blow fell.

Early despaired of either of them actually injuring the huge warrior, but they'd given Suran time to get to his feet. The quarters were close for spear work, but he handled his long weapon expertly. Its broad triangular spearhead still flickered with eldritch energy to match that which crackled and boomed in the stormclouds above. With it, Suran forced the standard bearer down the steps onto the main deck.

Early's heart rallied. Not even the giant could stand against all three of them. He was no expert at coordinating his attacks with his allies, but Early found an opening as the giant swung his axe at Suran, and he pressed in to block the weapon. The

shock of the blow knocked Early's sword to the deck... but the standard bearer's axe clanged to the planks beside it.

The big man was in cautious retreat now, swatting at Kori with his small round shield as though she were an insect. She tried again and again to sting him, to take his attention away from Suran's deadly spear. But the standard bearer was obviously a master of armed combat and, though he was slowed by his heavy armor and the narrow, slippery deck of the ship, it was no easy thing to land a stroke on him. Dodging the spear thrust once again, he turned and made a dash to the mast, against which were mounted several long gaff poles barbed with hooks.

The big warrior came on again, and now his reach was greater even than the chieftain's. The pole he held was meant for spearing fish, but, as it whipped across, Early was forced to scramble out of the way nonetheless, lest he catch an iron barb in the face.

Suran crashed his spear against the great pole, and lightning danced and hummed angrily between the two warriors. But even though purple energy cracked and sang in the joints of his armor, the standard bearer fought with strength and resolve that seemed more than human. He sidestepped a spear thrust that sizzled against his elbow, and, in a moment that seemed to slow into an agonizing eternity, Early watched him thrust the pointed tip of the gaff between Suran's ribs, high up on the chest.

Screams sounded in Early's ears as he froze in the act of picking up his sword; he couldn't tell Kori's from his own. Suran did not scream. His breath burst from his lips in one great exhalation, and his legs gave way beneath him. His spear rolled towards Early, its deadly glow fizzling out as soon as it left the chieftain's failing hands.

The standard bearer pressed his thrust until the pole

punched into the wooden deck, and Suran, who'd stood against the giant more than once, conceded the fight. The chieftain of the Malaspiri lay still.

Kori and Early drew back, stunned and wary. Mixed with sorrow at the brave chieftain's fall, Early felt the gnawing fear that he and Kori now faced the huge warrior alone. In desperation he looked around the deck, but Marie Gold, the two Redguards—all were busy elsewhere. No help was coming.

The standard bearer, seeing his enemy would not rise again, stepped away carefully and considered the two smaller foes. As he sized them up, Kori and Early reflexively moved closer together in front of their fallen leader. They watched for an opening, but the giant didn't give them one. The huge warrior drew a short sword from his belt. Then, watching them intently from behind his faceguard, he crouched to the deck and retrieved his axe.

Rearmed, he stood and brandished his weapons. Early quailed at the sheer height of the man—they may as well have challenged a tower to hand-to-hand combat. As a fresh gust of rain hammered them, the giant charged.

Early went to step in front of Kori, but she was already ducking and rolling to the deck, a movement that would have made graceful Isaac proud. Early himself barely dodged the arc of the heavy sword, deflecting it off his own raised blade. This close—too close—to his enemy, Early could see the details of the man's faceguard. It was carved into an image out of nightmare—a dragon of old—and Early couldn't help imagining the face beneath the mask wore that same derisive, hateful sneer.

Early backpedaled, grateful his old boots felt at home on the rain-slick planks of the deck. The giant, on the other hand, was clearly more warrior than sailor and less sure of his footing. If they'd had to face each other on the beach, Early knew he'd have been snapped in half by now. He saw no opening to attack,

knew he had to try; he couldn't just wait for the bigger man to overwhelm him. Dodging the deadly swing of sword and axe, he realized he didn't know where Kori had gone—it took all Early's attention to avoid being gutted on the planks like the day's catch.

He leaped back, barely parrying a sideways swing of the axe, his hand and arm shocked dangerously numb from the powerful blow. But then his enemy screamed in pain. Early was baffled, but for only a moment. Kori appeared from behind the giant, her long knife buried in his side. She'd circled around and found a gap in the man's armor.

The standard bearer stumbled away from them both, going down on his knees for just a moment, and a better warrior than Early would have had him. But Early was no Redguard, and by the time he found himself leaping forward, leading with the tip of his sword, the giant had recovered enough to knock the weapon aside. Still tall even on his knees, he clubbed Early in the shoulder with the fist holding the axe; fortunately the crescent-shaped blade swung wide of his head.

"Gods' Luck," Early muttered as he fell back on the planks, pain bursting in his shoulder, while the big warrior surged back to his feet.

But the giant didn't attack Early. Instead, he stalked towards Kori, who held her dripping knife down and away from her body as she backed away. The standard bearer was limping but menacing, nonetheless—he was twice Kori's size. The fight had taken them to the edge of the deck, and soon she had the railing at her back. Early saw her eyes widen.

Seeing his opportunity, the giant swung his axe. But the shaman proved too nimble once again. She dropped to the deck as the axe clove the railing, showering them both in splinters.

Early forced himself to stand, his body aching in a dozen places but burning with the need to save his friend. He got his

feet firmly beneath him and, not letting himself think about what he was doing, he charged. The standard bearer managed to turn just in time, leaving his axe embedded in the railing. He put all his strength into turning Early's thrust with his short sword, and, instead of gutting him, Early's blade merely dented the armor over his stomach.

Kori cried out, and Early saw she'd thrown her arms around the giant's waist. She yanked him backwards with all her might. His free hand closed over hers and Early knew he'd soon toss her aside, or worse. Acting on instinct, Early hurled himself at the huge man, coming in low and plowing his shoulder into the giant's belly, a solid wall of armor and muscle. The collision almost stunned him, but Early made himself push, trusting to momentum and praying this impromptu wrestling match would work...

It did. Kori dropped to the deck behind the giant's knees and the huge warrior lost his balance. Early drove him into the rail, and then up, over. The giant's weapons clattered away as he clutched at Early, at the railing, at the air.

Early gave one last heave, and then the rail was driving hard into his stomach, and Kori had grabbed his legs to keep him from toppling after their foe. The standard bearer dropped into the shallow water at the fireship's side and disappeared with a tremendous splash. Early watched, panting, for what felt like ages, Kori standing up beside him. He couldn't see anything in the dark water, not with the rain in his eyes, and he heard only the thunder overhead.

"Even if he survived the fall," Kori said between ragged breaths, "he can hardly climb the side of the ship. The monster is gone."

Early gathered his sword again, having dropped it when he tackled the giant. Walking was painful, and bending down even more so, adrenaline perhaps the only thing keeping him on his

feet. Kori dropped to the deck at her chieftain's side and cradled Suran's head in her lap. His long, powerful body lay limp on the deck, a dark stain soaking his leather armor. But, as Early approached them, he saw the chieftain's life had not quite fled.

Suran's eyes could not focus, and he looked past Kori as though seeking answers in the stormy sky. She brushed his hair and the rain from his face again and again. Early knelt beside them, and he heard the chieftain whisper his last words.

"So strange. I remember sailing a ship. Sailing away from the docks of a great, gleaming city..."

Early was thrilled to hear this, even as exhaustion and sorrow threatened to overtake him. Was Suran remembering the High City of Petara, when the first expedition set sail? Had Early been right?

"The storm," Suran croaked, and Early wondered if he meant the storm raging overhead even now, or another storm, one that wrecked a Decadin greatship years before the *Pride of the Empress* met a similar end.

Suran looked at Kori, managing with great effort to lift his head. "But what... was my name?" Kori shook her head, gave a single sob, and Early saw the chieftain lie still.

Kori tenderly closed Suran's eyes and looked up from his face. Early's mind was full of questions, but Kori was staring straight through him, lost in her sorrow and her own private thoughts.

Before either of them could speak, the cabin door at the top of the stern deck opened, and Revered Captain Tion Zanda emerged. Early struggled to rise, sword hand trembling with exhaustion; then he realized the captain, haggard-looking and missing his golden helm, had his hands bound. He was being shoved through the doorway by none other than Bristi, with Isaac right behind them.

The enemy captain looked the way Early felt. Now that the

terror and thrill of battle was passing, Early was chilly and tired. Only the need for further action kept him on his feet. Likewise, Captain Zanda shivered and grumbled to himself as he surveyed the deck of his hijacked ship.

Early's victorious allies and the enemy captain noticed Suran lying on the deck at the same time. Bristi leaped down the stairs to kneel at her chieftain's side. She let out a terrible cry, bowing her forehead against his cold, unmoving chest. Kori laid an arm across her shoulders, murmuring words of comfort. Early felt he should leave them alone in their grief and hurried up the steps to help Isaac with his captive.

"I suppose you've killed Zir Inzon, heathen," Captain Zanda said to him quietly, once he saw his giant second in command was not on deck. "But you have paid a steep price." Zanda's face was a carefully controlled mask over the hatred and fear Early could see in his eyes.

"What—who? Zir Inzon?" Early gaped at the enemy leader. Zanda was neither bigger nor taller than Early, and without his winged helmet and great cloak, fair hair falling in his eyes, he wasn't an imposing figure. But Early still felt intimidated by his strange words.

"Zir Bohr Inzon," Zanda repeated with weary patience, stretching out each word of the giant's name and honorific. "He was my friend, and the greatest warrior the world has ever known."

"I—we, we didn't—" Early stuttered. The captain hadn't asked for an explanation, but his tone and his bearing seemed to command one.

Over Zanda's shoulder, though, Isaac shook his head.

"That's enough," the ranger said, forcing Zanda down the steps to the main deck, carefully skirting around where the Malaspiri mourned their chieftain.

Early and Isaac walked Captain Zanda the length of the

ship to the bow where the rest of the attackers waited. As they passed the mainmast, Early tried not to let his gaze linger on the bodies slumped in dark heaps about the deck. With shock and surprise on their side, not to mention the mystical fog, his friends had easily overcome the few sentries on deck.

At the foot of the ship's shallow foredeck—Early could not quite bring himself to call it a forecastle, like on the *Pride*—were two large hatches, one to port and one to starboard. Marie Gold and Captain Antmar had stationed themselves and a dozen others around these. The largest and strongest attackers were sitting on overturned wooden benches laid across the hatches to keep them shut. Even as they approached, there came a great shouting and battering from below, but, as the attackers had hoped, the ladders leading up to the hatches were so narrow the crew could only press against them one or two at a time. The dragon-warriors were effectively trapped on the lower decks.

"Do you really think they'll surrender at their captain's command?" Early asked Isaac quietly as they brought Zanda to the scene.

"It turns out we've something better than this fellow's command to bring the crew to heel," Isaac replied, and Early was surprised by the wry smile on his weathered face.

"What do you mean?"

"We found others hiding in the captain's cabin."

Zanda shook angrily at this and said something in his own language that required no translation.

"Be quiet," the ranger said, without anger. He didn't so much as jostle his captive, but he must have gripped Zanda's arm much harder, because the captain grunted painfully, and his rigid, defiant bearing slackened.

"Imagine our surprise, Master Wills," the ranger continued,

"when we broke into the cabin and found not only the captain here, but an unarmed woman and an infant child."

Early was indeed surprised; this seemed like a ship of war. "What, really?" he asked. "Are they his family?"

"Oh, much more interesting than that," Isaac said. "The woman would not speak, but from what I coaxed out of the captain, I think the two are quite important. The woman is a religious figure of some kind, and the baby..." Isaac paused dramatically, "I believe he's their royalty."

Early didn't know how to respond. Holding such hostages must have great implications, but the immediate needs of the moment were all he could think about. He was pleased to hear, at least, that they might have enough leverage to demand a true surrender from the ship's crew.

They brought Captain Zanda before Captain Antmar, who inspected him with a mixture of animosity and contempt. The Redguard held his sword unsheathed, point lowered, and Early saw the tip of the deadly blade rise slightly, as though it was only with effort that Antmar resisted the urge to kill the leader of their foes here and now. Isaac motioned Early to take a guard position a few steps away and put himself between Zanda and Captain Antmar, perhaps to ensure his counterpart didn't do anything regrettable.

"As you can see, we've taken the ship's captain," Isaac reported. "And something even better: in the cabin we found a woman—some sort of priestess—and a baby. If I'm not mistaken, the child is of very great importance to these people."

Antmar looked closely at the enemy captain. Their captive was trying to remain impassive and do nothing that would confirm Isaac's voiced suspicions, but the Guard-Captain must have seen something in his eyes. Antmar smiled. The smile was thin and lethal, and it chilled Early to see it.

"You understand my speech," the Redguard said to Zanda. It

wasn't spoken as a question, but he waited until the other man gave a curt nod.

"You will call to your people below and tell them to abandon the ship. None will come up on deck. We will hold you and this woman and child as hostages to ensure your crew's cooperation."

Zanda held his opponent's cold stare for a moment, then exhaled with a sigh. "They will need to see me to trust what they hear is true," he said. In the weariness of defeat, his accent was thicker than usual. "Will you not open the hatch? Take what precautions you see fit."

Captain Antmar considered this. "Kneel down," he said. Zanda glared, and it seemed the two men's wills struggled wordlessly with each other, but then he took one knee on the deck. Antmar lay the blade of his sword against the back of Zanda's neck. Only then did he gesture to Marie and the others to remove the bench barricading the hatch. The turmoil below had ended at the sound of the conversation above; perhaps the crew already sensed their captain was there.

Early, Isaac, and all the others gathered around the port-side hatch, their weapons ready. At last, Marie and Taliss lifted the wooden cover gingerly, as though uncovering a nest of snakes.

The crew beneath did not leap blindly out, however. The warrior at the very top of the ladder looked rapidly from one strange face to another. His eyes widened when he saw his captain kneeling—and glittered with anger at the sight of Antmar's sword poised to strike. But Captain Zanda spoke to his man in their own language, and, though Early couldn't understand the words, the voice and manner were calm. It could have been a trick, of course; the captain could have been telling his men to do some mischief, and Early and his friends would find out about it only too late.

But for the moment, the man in the hatch merely nodded his assent. He replied quietly. With a last dark glance at the attackers, he turned and barked a command to the gathered warriors crowded behind him, like so many insects in their black armor. The man must have been an officer, Early supposed; he had a decorative red ribbon at his shoulder that probably signaled rank. The warriors obediently began to disperse.

The attackers left the hatch open and stood, tense and wary for a while, prepared for trickery. Zanda, still on one knee, said to Captain Antmar, "They'll do as you wish. I've ordered them to gather on the beach. Is that acceptable?"

Antmar nodded, but they all remained wary. After a few minutes, there was a crashing sound from first the port, and then the starboard side of the ship, as the ramps were lowered to offload the crew. Marie went to the rail and confirmed, with eagerness in her voice, that the warriors were leaving.

Captain Antmar stood back from his captive at last and sheathed his sword. Early could see Zanda's body relax, and he stood up when ordered. As the victorious attackers began to discuss what to do next, their spirits lightening, Captain Antmar interrupted, "Where is Suran?"

Silence fell. Isaac leaned close, gazing back up the deck towards the aft section of the ship, where Bristi and Kori still sat with their fallen leader.

"I'm afraid he fell in battle, Morave," Isaac said gently.

Early had never heard him use Captain Antmar's given name before. "Early, you saw it, didn't you?"

The eyes of both men fell on him, and Early's heart, which had begun to feel buoyed by their victory, sank again.

"Yes," he confirmed. "That giant warrior, if you remember him? He attacked us, and Suran was mortally wounded."

Captain Antmar was silent at this. But Isaac asked, "What became of the giant, then?"

"Kori and I managed," Early could not quite believe the words even as he spoke them, "to throw him overboard."

Isaac's eyes widened, and a smile started to break across his face. But Antmar had turned away and was walking up the deck. They fell in behind him, leaving Zanda in the care of their friends.

When they reached the spot where the chieftain lay, Kori and Bristi were sitting beside him. The tracker had her arms around her knees, pipe clutched in one hand. Her staring eyes were red, and tears shone on her cheeks. Kori had taken out her totem and laid it on the planks between her and Suran, and she was pondering it, whispering words to herself—and perhaps, Early thought, to the Ancestors.

Captain Antmar picked up the chieftain's long spear. Early watched him as he looked up and down the length of the weapon, his gaze coming to rest on the point. Early seemed to see an electric glow begin to dance once again along the head of the spear. Its dangerous light reflected off Antmar's dark eyes, and his face looked pale as Suran's in the glow.

Bristi rose to her feet. "Kori says he fought bravely against their mightiest. If we've won the day, we owe victory to him."

"Have we won the day?" Antmar asked, though he seemed to be speaking to himself. His eyes stayed fixed on the tip of the chieftain's spear. Thunder cracked overhead as a purple flash lit the deck, reminding them the fearsome power of the storm Kori summoned was not yet appeased. "It seems to me there is work to do still."

Something in Antmar's words, his tone, or his manner frightened Early. The young deckhand's fear was growing again, to match what he'd felt when they'd entered the fog to begin their assault on the ship.

Finally, the Guard-Captain let go of the spear, and it fell to the deck with a jarring clang, like its own miniature clap of thunder. Antmar's face was impassive as he spoke to them, but the eerie glow remained in his eyes.

"Isaac, Early, come with me. We'll interview our prisoners first, and then... I want to know how the weapons of this evil ship function."

17

With the fireship secured, Early went with Isaac, Captain Antmar, Marie, and several of the other Decadins to tour their prize. And, Early hoped, find some sign of his friend, Olan. Kori had gathered the Malaspiri together on the deck to perform the last rites appropriate for Suran.

What rites *were* appropriate? Early wondered. It sounded at the last like Suran had remembered being someone else. Away from the chaos of battle, with time to contemplate, Early felt his wild theory developing into a tenuous certainty: that the people who called themselves "Malaspiri" were in fact the survivors of the Decadins' own lost expedition, somehow living out the lives of an ancient race who'd inhabited the island long ago. But would Kori and her friends only remember their true identities at the moment of death?

Another boom of thunder reached Early through the solid planks of the ship, and he remembered that ancient race had some strange connection to the terrible power in the skies above. The fearful storm still boiled overhead, awaiting some climax yet to come. Early hardly felt he could celebrate victory over the invaders with that potential doom so close at hand. But what a victory it was: they had a ship! For the first time in weeks, Early dared to think he might see Petara, his city, again.

He wondered what would become of Marie Gold when they got home. Early and the pirate were scouring the lower deck for Olan, while the others explored the deck above with their hostages.

"Marie, what—" Early asked haltingly, as she emerged from another storeroom, "what do you reckon you'll do after we sail this ship home?"

She gave him a strange look and continued up the passageway. Early hurried after her.

"Reckon I'm at the mercy of Her Imperial Majesty's justice," Marie said over her shoulder. "Or have you forgotten old Captain Mestrum's sentence?"

Early winced, realizing what an awkward topic this was. He did remember the scene on the *Pride*, when his captain had sentenced Marie to hang from the mainmast. But he remembered something else.

"But Captain Mestrum pardoned you, didn't she?" Early asked. "I mean, you helped us get to the island, and—"

"Early, grow up." Marie whirled on him and he stopped short. She was very close, her eyes very bright. "Your captain let me live because I told her I had information she needed. And it didn't matter, because a bloody great storm sank your gods-cursed greatship and we *washed up* here."

Early opened his mouth but didn't know what to say. In the emptiness of the lower deck, only the persistent drip of water intruded on the silence.

"It's the Gods' Luck you and I are still alive," Marie said, and turned back to the passageway. "I hadn't a bloody thing to do with it."

"Well, yes," Early conceded, "but I—that is, you know, you—"

"If we get back to the High City," Marie said, in a tone that made it clear this was her final word on the subject, "your beloved Blueguard will tie me to a rock and throw me in the Bay of Moonlight."

As Marie said this, she passed a doorway on her right. A voice boomed out. "Anyone tries to throw you anywhere and they'll answer to me, Marie Gold!"

The self-possessed pirate captain jumped with an undignified yelp, but Early recognized the voice.

"Olan?! You great sluggard!"

He ran past Marie into the room. Sure enough, the tiny room contained an iron cage that stretched from floor to ceiling. Inside the cage, his arm in a sling, legs bandaged but on his feet, was Olan Mender.

"Figures you'd be hiding down here," Early teased, "while the rest of us are capturing the whole ship ourselves!"

He was surprised he could speak so lightly about the terrible battle they'd just fought. But Early realized he hadn't expected to find Olan alive.

Marie pushed past him, smiling, and pulled her lockpicks from the golden cloud of her hair. Olan's cage was fastened shut by a stout but simple lock, and the pirate had him free in moments.

Olan picked Marie up in a one-armed hug, and she kissed him on the lips. Early felt a pang of jealousy, but forced it down —it was no time for rivalry. The huge deckhand crushed Early to his chest next, then led the way, in spite of his stiff-legged walk, back to the stairs that ran up and down the stern of the ship. He was so eager to be out of his prison, it was a minute before Olan thought to ask how—"by the Lost bloody Gods!"— they'd taken the ship.

"It was Kori," Early said. "She summoned up this storm—you can still hear it—and we used her black fog to fly straight onto the deck! We took them all by surprise!"

Marie was the one who said, "Sorry we left you behind, big man. What happened on the beach after we quit the field?"

"For fighting like bloody monsters," Olan groaned, not relishing the memory, "I figured these dragon-worshippers would cut my throat. But they didn't. Patched me up and threw me in here, didn't bother to say why."

Olan winced and grasped at one of his bandaged thighs. Marie came up beside him and put a hand on his uninjured arm, and he leaned against her shoulder as they carried on. It was the first time Early had seen his stubborn friend accept help like that. Walking down the fireship's narrow passageway behind his friends, Early tried to ignore the envy whispering in his brain.

The trio of Early, Marie, and Olan rejoined their companions on the middle deck of the fireship. Just behind the bow was a chamber, its thick metal walls insulating it from the rest of the ship; or, rather, insulating the rest of the ship from its contents. Taking up much of the space in the chamber, so the newcomers were obliged to squeeze their way around it, was a bronze furnace. Thick pipes ran from the round body of the furnace through ports in the chamber wall. These pipes all ran towards the front of the ship, and the Decadins had no doubt these had their outlet in the two great horns below the carven dragon figurehead, and were the source of the ship's terrible fire.

The furnace burned low, giving off a strange smell from the black stuff smoldering in its belly. The closeness of the room forced Early to stand no more than a foot away from the radiant metal, and he began to swelter almost as soon as they'd entered the chamber.

Though Captain Antmar had been only mildly interested by the rest of the ship, he now turned on the captive Zanda with urgent questions. How did this weapon function? What was its fuel? How was it released? But the captain's reticence turned into stubborn silence at his captor's urgency, and he drew himself up with a dignity Early recognized from Captain Mestrum's final stand on the *Pride*; this was a line the man would not be pushed across.

Seeing his words could not move the captain to explain the fire weapon, Antmar's eyes darted dangerously to the priestess, and the child wrapped in her full crimson robes. He had insisted all the hostages be brought along as they toured the ship. Now the Redguard considered the woman, tightening his grip on the hilt of his sword.

Marie Gold spoke up distractedly, but Early could tell by the look on her face she was trying to take the increasingly volatile Redguard's mind from a terrible course.

"Were this merely a furnace," she pondered, "you would expect smoke to come from the pipes, not a great burst of flame. There is some trick we cannot see from here to make the fire explode with such force."

"Perhaps it's to do with what's being burned," Isaac said, catching onto Marie's intentions. He pinched his nose to indicate the powerful and unpleasant odor that filled the room. "Whatever mixture they've got in there, it must burn with unusual violence."

"It seems calm enough now," Antmar retorted.

Early saw the Redguard had turned from the captives to consider the furnace and the conversation. Early sighed with relief, blinking a droplet of sweat from his eyes.

"If you're right, Greenguard," Antmar said, glancing back at Captain Zanda with annoyance, "there must be a store of it we haven't discovered. Certainly, it can't be hidden in this tiny room."

"Guard Andica," he continued, calling Taliss by her last name, "kindly scour the rest of this ship for whatever fragrant substance they're burning in here."

"If you find it," he added, as Taliss left the room, "be careful with it."

"Learning how this weapon works is certainly important," Isaac said casually, but Early could tell he was wary. "We might need it when we put back to sea. But perhaps we'd best discuss how to handle this ship's crew. I reckon they're growing restless out there on the beach, and there aren't near enough of us to guard them."

Early wondered why Isaac bothered pointing out this obvious fact. But the ranger was clearly directing his remarks at Captain Antmar, as though trying to gauge the Redguard's thoughts.

"We will deal with them soon enough," Antmar replied, and turned his attention back to the furnace. "If it were only a matter of burning with great violence," he said, "this room would be a deathtrap, would it not? What directs the fire out of the ship?"

Something occurred to Early, and the answer burst out of him. "A pump!"

"What?" Antmar demanded.

Early's face immediately grew hot with embarrassment—hotter than it was already—as the focus of the group fell on him. But he saw Marie nodding slowly with a smile as she, a fellow sailor, caught his reasoning.

"I've seen before," Early explained, "at the Imperial Docks, they'd use these things to get water up on the decks of ships without having to carry it up in buckets. A team on the dock works a great lever, and it builds up a force that carries the water upwards!"

Captain Antmar's face bore an expression of astonished curiosity; he'd clearly never imagined such a thing.

"It's a useful tool for fighting fires, funny enough," Marie added. "I suppose you might find a way, using the same device, to *direct* a fire... a stream of flaming liquid."

They all looked to Captain Zanda to see if their speculations would be confirmed. Seeing their expectant faces, he scoffed and turned to the priestess at his side, who busied herself, as she had during the whole conversation, murmuring to the child in her arms.

Olan clapped Early on the shoulder. "If what this clever sailor says is true, I reckon the likeliest place for pumps is directly below this room. Come on, Early, let's go find them."

There was no chance to object—Early's big friend fairly shoved him out of the room. He complained to Olan once they were on their own, headed back down the narrow passageway to the curving stair that led from the top deck to this one, and spiraled farther down to the deck below where Olan had been imprisoned.

"I suppose we should do our part, Olan," Early said, "but I wanted to know what Captain Antmar is planning to do... I wish we'd stayed."

"Whatever it is, you know he means these dragon-worshippers harm," the big deckhand said with his typical carelessness. "I just wanted to get out of that bloody boiling-hot room. I suppose it's too much to ask I get a nice soft bed to lay down in. There's work to be done, but I see no reason to roast alive while we do it."

As Olan suspected, they found a larger chamber directly underneath the furnace room. It was filled with strange metal contraptions in rows, each with wheels and a lever and just enough space for two people to stand and work the lever up and down. A network of pipes ran up from the machinery to the

ceiling, where they must have fed directly into the furnace in the reinforced chamber above.

"This looks like a fun job," Olan said with spite, resting his hand on one of the levers. He pulled it only slightly, testing the tension.

"Olan, don't!" Early shouted in alarm, eyes going to the ceiling. He imagined a sudden burst of hissing steam in the chamber above, blinding his friends...

"I'm not an idiot, Early," Olan said. "Surely it takes more than a little tug at just one of these levers to cause the *conflagration* they hit us with when they arrived."

Olan drew out the syllables of the word 'conflagration' as though demonstrating his intelligence to his doubtful friend.

"Ah, sorry. You're right," Early conceded, ashamed. "I wasn't thinking."

Olan grumbled his agreement and turned back to the pumps. "They must have a crew working these when they go on the attack. How'd you like to be one of those poor souls?"

"Better that, I reckon, than feeding the furnace above with that awful-smelling fuel." Early remembered the heat of the furnace chamber, and that was without its fires being stoked.

"So probably the fuel gets fed in above, and burns in some form suited to being pumped," Olan thought aloud, eyes tracing the gleaming bronze pipes that filled so much of the room. "And then I reckon the crew in here pumps their little hearts out, till the pressure forces the flaming stuff out the front of the ship."

"Same way they fight fires on the docks," Early said, able to picture the whole process in his mind. "Except... sort of in reverse."

Olan gave a scornful chuckle. "There's no magic to pumping water! The question is, what's their fuel? If we could learn that, imagine a fleet of Blueguard ships armed with this!"

"That's probably why Captain Antmar is so hot to learn how it works," Early said.

"Maybe," Olan granted, "but he—"

But the big deckhand's objection was fated to go unspoken. An immense boom of thunder echoed through the walls, loud even on the lowest deck. The fireship shook to its keel. The two friends looked at each other, eyes wide, both having grabbed by reflex onto the nearest pipe.

"Your friend, the shaman—did she know what she was doing when she summoned this storm?" Olan asked.

"She didn't summon the storm, not on purpose," Early said, though he despaired of explaining the entire thing to Olan. The ritual in the tomb, the terrible visions, Kori's fear of a doom waiting if she asked too much of the Ancestors and their power. Fortunately, Olan's mind had moved on to more practical matters.

"I wonder what's the safest place in this ship to ride out the rest of tonight's nonsense?"

They'd both taken a step towards the door. Early, his sword now in hand, turned to give his friend a skeptical eye.

"Surely you're joking," he said. "We must go up and see if they need help!"

Olan shook his head at Early with a long-suffering expression. "Lead the way, Master Wills. But just you wait and see if my idea isn't the better one."

18

As the two deckhands climbed the stairs to the top deck, they heard nothing as loud as the terrible crash that had shaken the ship, but there were sounds of boots tramping the deck and inarticulate cries. They reached the top of the narrow stair that led out onto the stern deck, where Early, Kori, and ill-fated Suran had fought the giant standard bearer, and they tried their best to survey the deck without letting themselves be seen.

There was no one nearby. Everyone was gathered on the far side of the ship, towards the bow, where they had confronted the crew and made Captain Zanda order them off the ship. The stormclouds were roiling violently overhead, and flashes of lightning—now white, now unnaturally purple—lit the deck with stark angles of light and shadow.

Early and Olan snuck across the deck. Even though the ship now contained only allies, something in the air drove them to be furtive. When they reached the low railing that separated the ship's raised foredeck from the main deck, they saw their friends in a tense circle around Captain Antmar, whose sword was drawn. The captive Zanda, his hands still bound, stood

behind Isaac. Though the Greenguard's weapons were sheathed, he seemed to be shielding Zanda from the Redguard's fury.

That Antmar was furious was clear, though no one spoke; the Redguard captain's eyes were wide and gleaming, his dark hair plastered to his forehead by the rain, and his face, pale when the lightning illuminated it, was twisted into an almost inhuman expression of outrage.

"What's going on?" Early whispered to Olan. The big deck-hand only shrugged. They saw Kori up there, and Marie Gold, and most of the others. Early didn't see Lia or her handmaiden, and Zanda's priestess with her infant charge was nowhere to be seen.

"This won't do, Guard-Captain," Isaac said, and though his voice was loud and strong over the constant thunder, his tone begged for reason. He used Antmar's formal rank as though trying to remind him of his duty. "Killing this man will only set his people against us with resolve. Can't you see he's more valuable to us alive?"

Antmar took a step towards Isaac, his deadly sword gripped tight in both hands. Isaac stiffened but didn't move. Behind him, Captain Zanda stepped back, eyes wide with alarm.

"Alive? Alive?" Antmar's voice was terrible to hear. It boomed forth like thunder, and its hollow ferocity matched the storm overhead. He spoke the words as though they were foreign to him. "Why should we leave *any* alive? See how they treated us, coming out of the fog like cowards with their flame.

"Flame... flame..." Antmar muttered, seeming to fall into himself. When he raised his head again, his eyes were wilder than ever.

"Flame!" Early could have sworn the thunder waxed louder above as Antmar shouted the word. "They should all die in flame!"

"We cannot turn their weapon against them," Isaac said, a pleading note in his voice. It must have seemed to him—to all of them, as it did to Early—that their leader had gone mad. That something dark and terrible inside of him had finally overwhelmed his disciplined Redguard spirit.

"It's monstrous," Isaac stated, quietly.

Early imagined the fireship's crew gathered on the beach below. Hated foes, fearsome in their black armor, but the thought of them consumed by fire, flesh blackening as they cooked inside their steel shells, smoke rising through the faceguards of their helmets... it was a demonic, nightmare vision. And while Early couldn't help feeling a hint of grim satisfaction, of a justice desperately desired, a final triumph after so many long weeks of struggle and doubt, Isaac was exactly right. They could not make the same despicable choice their enemies had.

They must not use the fire-weapon. At least, Early thought —though it did little to relieve his tension—Captain Antmar could hardly work the great machinery himself, if the rest of them defied him.

Early returned his attention to the drama unfolding on the raised platform of the foredeck. Antmar was not listening to Isaac's entreaties. He turned and walked slowly to the very prow of the ship, his back to the rest of them. The enemy crew must have been gathered on the sand below, for Antmar shouted as though addressing a great crowd.

"Flame!" he roared. "You burned my lord on this very beach! At that moment, my life was forfeit. It should have been I who burned. It should be *you* who burn!"

As he raged, Early and Olan crept up the steps onto the foredeck to join the others. They had to fight their way against the wind—the storm was reaching a fever pitch. All the timbers of the masts behind them were creaking and groaning. Early made eye contact with Kori and Isaac, both of whom quickly turned back to the raving Redguard captain. Early saw terrible fear in their eyes. What must they do about this madman who, now that the even-tempered Suran was gone, was their only leader? Antmar's whole body was rigid and shaking as he lifted his sword higher into the air, and it seemed with every flash of lightning his figure grew larger and more terrible.

"Die in flame, People of the Dragon!" he screamed. "Enemies of the Empire! See how all who challenge Her Imperial Majesty burn. Burn! *Burn!!*"

At this last demand, there came a great flash of lightning. In its wake, Early's vision swam, but he would swear the blinding stroke stabbed down from the sky and touched the very sword that Captain Antmar held in the air. But before Early could consider the impossibility of such an idea, or that the man so struck could still be standing before him, he heard a terrible roar from *below*. The deck shook beneath his feet and, visible above the high prow of the beached fireship, he saw a familiar infernal glow.

As though a spell had been broken, Early and all his friends rushed forward, Captain Zanda among them. They crowded to the rail to look down at the beach, but almost all of them turned away with cries of horror. Early, though he desperately wanted to look away, could not; for he looked down at the nightmare he'd been imagining mere moments earlier.

The beach was on fire. The invaders were burning. Impossibly, the ship had unleashed its killing breath at Antmar's command. An intolerable frenzy of screams rose from the writhing black figures on the sand, matched with deafening rage from the stormclouds above. It sounded as though the storm wished to drown out the madness taking place on the beach. Rain hammered down on ship and sand, but the sticky, pungent fuel of the weapon was immune. The inferno continued.

Early backed away from the railing at last, slipped in a puddle, and fell hard to the deck as his legs gave way beneath him. He looked up and saw Captain Antmar standing at the prow, face contorted like the ship's own draconic figurehead. Noise still poured from the Redguard's mouth, but Early heard no human words. Antmar's voice and the voice of the storm had become one and the same.

Unable to rise under the suffocating cloud of horror, Early saw his friends scattered about the foredeck in a similar state of shock and dismay. Only Captain Zanda stood by the railing, unmoving, his bound hands gripping the black wood with white knuckles, solemnly watching as the people under his command burned and died. Something in Zanda's absolute stillness frightened Early.

It was Guard-Captain Antmar, not Captain Zanda, who first turned away from the hellish spectacle. And at the sight of his leader, Early's terror grew even greater.

The man who'd led them since the death of his lord was gone. A monster wore his skin. Antmar looked at each of his companions without recognition, and Early saw nothing human in his eyes, his movements, or the sounds coming from his open mouth. He moved with weird, jerky steps, as though unused to his own body, so unlike the graceful Redguard he had been. Antmar raised his sword as he approached Captain Zanda and challenged him in a deep, thunderous voice, but Early could not understand a word.

Zanda backed away from the madman, raising his bound hands in supplication. With an inhuman hiss, Antmar gathered himself to strike... but then Isaac was there, sword upraised. Their blades met with a flash and shower of purple sparks, like when Suran had wielded his enchanted spear. Isaac cried out and collapsed, his sword ringing on the deck, but Antmar only howled in rage at being kept from his prey.

Antmar raised his sword again, this time above the Green-guard's slumping head. Early, his stomach tightening, found himself on his feet, his sword in his hand. But he had no time to interpose himself, as Isaac had just done, between death and his mentor.

Kori shouted from behind him, and Early turned to see her lift her totem just as Antmar raised his sword to kill Isaac. The black stone she held was gleaming, limned in blue light, as she cried out words like those she had chanted in the tomb. Her voice, belying her small body, rang out clear and commanding above the chaos of the storm.

Antmar shivered, turned to face her, and roared. It was the sound of a beast blinded by pain. The Guard-Captain, forgetting Isaac and Zanda, charged across the deck at Kori.

As he charged, Early saw not a man but the great dark shape of the Elder of Storms, as he'd seen it from the *Pride*: batlike wings outstretched, monstrous jaws split wide, crystalline eyes burning black with hatred. In the face of that alien wrath, Kori would be destroyed as utterly as the greatship had been destroyed.

Early threw himself forward, sword raised. Marie Gold got there first—she leaped between Antmar and the shaman, only to be swept aside with a flash and ring of steel. Like Isaac, she cried out in pain and crumpled to the deck. Though Kori and the monster unleashed by the storm were mere yards away, it seemed to Early they were all moving so slowly, as though trying to stride into shore out of waist-deep water, the swell of the tide resisting each step.

Everyone was shouting, but Early's head rang with thunder and even words in his own language fell unheeded on his ears. Kori stood bravely, rooted to the deck, totem held high, pouring all her will into a desperate exhortation. Antmar came for her, sword in one hand, arms outspread like wings.

And suddenly Early stood in the monster's way, not knowing how he'd gotten there in time, knowing only that he must protect his unarmed friend—the young woman who'd risked and fought to save both her people and his, and who believed him when he said those people were one and the same.

Mercy or adrenaline deadened the pain of Antmar's strike. There was a blinding flash of light as their swords met. Early's arms went numb and his blade shivered into pieces in his hand. He shut his eyes as he felt the shards touch his face, a rain of metal that felt almost delicate even as it tore his skin.

When Early's eyes blinked back open, he was lying on the deck. Though he hadn't felt himself hit the planks, he hurt all over. Above him, backlit by lightning, a blurred shape strained towards the tiny shaman. Was it Captain Antmar? The Elder of Storms? Early could not tell. The monster struggled to engulf Kori, but, on all sides, a ghostly glow was growing, flowing outward from Kori's stormshard. The glow coalesced into a ring of alien figures whose grave faces and huge, blank eyes were familiar to Early.

The phantoms of the Ancestors raised their long arms towards the thing that had been Morave Antmar. The storm above reached a whirling crescendo of noise and light. The stormshard glowed brighter in Kori's hands, and brighter, and shattered. The sky itself seemed to scream, and that was the last Early remembered as he lay senseless on the deck.

19

Early woke from feverish dreams. Where was he? A strange keening sound beat upon his left ear, and he tried to swat it away without success. He felt disconnected from his body, unsure of where his limbs lay in space. Ahead of him was a dark blur. He blinked, his eyes watered, but the blur refused to become a shape. A bright light from off to his left made his head pound, and Early closed his eyes again.

Time passed. A hand pressed on his shoulder and he flinched, but the hand was gentle. It anchored him. His shoulder was connected to his arm, his arm was next to his head, and his head lay on a pillow. He was lying in a bed, gloriously warm and soft compared to the sleeping roll on hard-packed sand or hard bunk in a cave he'd gotten so used to. He opened his eyes again and saw the dark blur was the ceiling of Kori's hut.

As though a puzzle had been solved, the world unlocked itself to Early's senses. The repetitive sound became farther away and less unpleasant; it was merely the chirp of a squaffinch preening its colorful feathers on the windowsill. The light was the late-morning sun, and when the figure whose

hand was on his shoulder saw Early squinting painfully, she went to the window and drew the curtain. Early's voice returned to him and he spoke—or, rather, he croaked.

"Kori?"

"You're alive," she told him, smiling. "The storm is over."

Sunlight leaking in around the edge of the curtain made a corona of her hair. Early's recollection was fuzzy; how had he come to be in bed? Was he wounded? He crawled back through his memories, scrabbling for purchase on something solid. When he found it, he wished he hadn't.

"The fireship? Captain Antmar?"

Early tried to look around, but pain lanced through his torso and pressed him back against the bed. He moaned. Kori hurriedly put her hand on his shoulder again, then touched his forehead, urging him to be still.

"He's gone," she said.

There was an image in Early's mind of the brave Redguard turned bestial, towering over Early and Kori with his sword raised, its blade crackling with lightning. The incongruous mental impression of great wings spread wide. And then a swell of light and sound, and nothing else.

"Gone?"

"He vanished, Early. I prayed to the Ancestors, and... they answered. The stormshard burst apart in my hands, there was a great flash, greater than a lightning bolt, and..." Kori spread her hands. Only then did Early notice they were bandaged.

Early finished her sentence. "And he was gone."

He focused on Kori's face, noticing a gash above her eye, another across her cheek. Several smaller scratches marred her skin. He ran his hand over his own face, felt similar marks that stung under his fingers. And he remembered his sword breaking into pieces from the force of Antmar's stroke.

So he and Kori had both been marked by the forces

unleashed in the storm.

"He was gone," she repeated, "as though he'd never been there. Only a great scorch mark was left on the deck. I think lightning might truly have struck, right in front of us."

"That's like something out of a story," Early murmured, and shut his eyes as a wave of pain and dizziness overtook him.

Early's breathing became labored, and Kori added fresh leaves to the small brass bowl standing next to the bed. She crushed the glossy green leaves with her fingers, then lit a taper and set them smoldering. As the sharp, smoky aroma burst from the leaves, Early tried to look, grimacing as he turned his neck.

"What's that?"

"They're called *jouma*. The smoke will help you feel better. Just relax," Kori said, touching his forehead again.

"You saved me from his sword, you know." There was gentle humor in Kori's voice. "Threw yourself in harm's way like some sort of hero."

Early managed to laugh. "If I'd known I could be hit so hard my sword would break, I might have thought twice."

"Do you remember the power Suran had in his spear?" Kori asked. "That was a power granted to us by the storm, so his thrust would strike with the force of lightning. Your captain had the same power, it seems. And you stood in its way."

Early nodded. Memories were coming back to him, but they were still images, frozen in time, like the pictures in Lia's sketchbook.

He wondered where Lia was. And others.

"Isaac, and... Marie? They were struck down, too. Are they —?" He started to rise, or try to, but Kori stroked his hair to soothe him.

"They were hurt, but no worse than you were. The Gods' Luck was with us, Early, we..." She looked away, out the window. Added only, "it could have been much worse."

Her use of *Gods' Luck*, that common Decadin expression, was odd, but at the moment Early couldn't think clearly enough to question it. As his mind groped slowly backwards over the events of the past night, he remembered something else.

"Could have been much worse for us, yes. But... for *them*..."

Kori nodded gravely. "Yes. The woman—their priestess—and the child, they are safe. Lia took her and the baby back into the cabin before all the rest happened."

"But their crew?" Early knew the answer to his question, but couldn't help asking it.

"They burned."

Early shuddered, as what he'd seen from the prow of the fireship returned to him.

"All of them," he whispered. "Just like that..."

It was only when Kori sat on the stool by his bedside and lay her head against his shoulder that Early realized he was weeping. The People of the Dragon had been merciless, had been first to use their terrible flame weapon, would have killed him and Kori and all their friends. Yet he felt only sorrow for how they'd died.

And for their captain. Early remembered him, the Revered Captain Tion Zanda, silent and stoic as Captain Mestrum had been in the last moments of her doomed greatship, watching it all. He imagined how helpless Zanda must have felt, as those who had followed him paid the ultimate price.

"What happened to their captain?" Early asked.

"I'm not sure," Kori said, shaking her head slowly. She looked towards the window, as though seeing through the curtain the expanse of the island beyond.

"After everything, we couldn't find him. No longer on the deck, nor anywhere on the ship. Guard Taliss took the lead in her captain's stead, and she insisted we search every corner. The ship was far too precious, she said, to allow the possibility of sabotage.

"But we never found him. Perhaps he threw himself overboard and was washed out to sea, or perhaps he escaped," she nodded towards the woods beyond the village, "and is lost somewhere in the forest."

Kori let Early sleep a while, and in the late afternoon he was awakened by a bustle at the door. Lia, Olan, and Taliss had come to see him, though the little cabin was hardly large enough for them all, and they crowded the space around Early's bed. The patient was thrilled to see them—especially Lia.

"Taking all the glory for yourself, Master Wills," Olan began to bluster as soon as he saw Early was awake. "Running into death like a fool out of his wits. You belong in the Imperial Guard, after all."

Taliss, the only Guard present, objected to this, but she was smiling.

Early tried to say something witty, but a fit of coughing overcame him. Kori quickly brought a cup of water, and he held himself up painfully in bed long enough to drink it. It returned his voice to him.

"Where," he said with attempted nonchalance, "is the old ranger we used to keep around here?"

"He'll be back on his feet soon enough," Taliss said, with a tender smile at the obvious worry in Early's eyes. "He and the other wounded are resting in other huts."

The Redguard took the stool by the bedside and leaned close to Early. "I'm glad you're on the mend. With Captain Antmar gone, we are but ten."

Early considered that. He'd come to think of Kori and the

Malaspiri as his kin, and had avoided counting just how few people who'd set out on the *Pride of the Empress* were still alive. But something a little more hopeful occurred to him.

"Are you now our leader, Guard Taliss?" Early asked.

"What—me?" The Guardswoman sat up even straighter than usual, surprised by the question.

"Well," Early said, "the Redguard outrank the Greenguard, right? So I figured..."

He trailed off. Olan had muttered something to Lia, and the noblewoman was snickering.

"Hey!" Early protested. "I'm just trying to understand what —" He looked at each of them. "What happens now?"

Taliss moved out of the way so Kori could refresh the *jouma* leaves again, and force her patient to lie back against the pillows.

"What happens now," Kori said, scolding him only mildly, "is you rest and heal. Such matters can wait, besides, until we've all decided what to do next."

Days passed, and Early grew stronger with each, until at last Kori allowed him to leave her hut. His body was whole, if bruised and scarred, and he still felt a certain distance from everything around him, like a cloth was wrapped around his head. He heard a slight ringing in his ears when other noises fell silent. He hoped it would all pass.

But at least, Early thought, looking at the ruin on the beach, *I'm alive.*

The fireship still waited there, ramps down, and the expanse of sand below its prow was glassy and fused from heat. There, in a black and horrible tangle, lay what had once been the fireship's crew. Wisps of white smoke still hung about the remains, even days after the great burning. The exhausted survivors, Decadin and Malaspiri both, had not been up to the task of moving the dozens of armored bodies to solid ground for burial, but some work had been done to heap sand over the awful pile.

Realizing he'd been staring at the great pyre of their enemies for long minutes, his mind's eye flashing back to the terrible, almost unbelievable events of the past days, Early turned to Kori. The shaman had brought him down to the palisade at his request. Wishing to look upon the carnage no more, he offered Kori his hand. She took it, and they passed through the open gate of the palisade, climbed the steep ridge, and found a seat on its grassy top against a large tree at the edge of the forest.

From here, they could see the great black mast of the fire-ship above the jagged wall of the palisade, but the charnel scene below the ship was concealed. Early looked long at the mast, and beyond it, contemplating the sea across which he had come.

It felt like another lifetime, standing on the deck of the *Pride of the Empress*, his heart leaping with the thrill of adventure. He had even found the object of their quest; for he was sure now that the Malaspiri *were* the lost expedition. During his convalescence, Kori had told him how the voices of the Ancestors had gone quiet. She had felt them leaving her behind since the moment on the ship when she'd called to them, her totem had broken, and they appeared to stop Captain Antmar's rampage.

He'd been debating what must have happened with Kori ever since, and, after they'd sat in silent thought for a while, he broached the topic once more.

"The first expedition—your expedition—must have landed here, just as we did," he said. Kori looked at him but said nothing, letting him unwind the story.

"And you found the tomb, and, somehow, the *spirits* of the things that lived here once before—the Malaspiri—got into your heads, and replaced your memory of who you are, of the Decadin Empire, with their own lives."

As she had every other time Early described these events, Kori neither accepted nor denied.

"But the problem is," she protested, "if I don't remember being a different person, and all my memories of being Kori are as vivid and real as your memories of being Early... how can Kori not be my identity?"

Perhaps it was his still-weakened state, but the question made Early dizzy. Was memory all that made any of them who they were? Just memory? And if you lost your memories—or, somehow, gained the memories of another—then who *were* you, in truth?

He looked at Kori, not knowing how to answer her. Who was she? What had her name been, and who were her kin?

"The *Pride* had records of the lost expedition," Early told her, not for the first time. "We had the names of everyone who set sail five years ago. But I never read them, nor did anyone who's still alive. And those pages are at the bottom of the sea now!"

"Early, stop this," Kori said, tired. They'd been over this ground before, and it led nowhere but frustration. She took his hands in hers. "There's nothing we can do about the *Pride*. And it's not helping."

"It's just—" Early sputtered, the injustice getting the better of him. "Maybe the *tyrr*, if they really exist, can tell us what your name is. Who your mother and father—"

That thought stunned Early most of all, but too late—he saw the pain on Kori's face. He tried to imagine not even remembering your own family, as you lived each day right next to them.

"Kori... I'm sorry. I'm such a fool."

She shook her head, then slumped it heavily against his shoulder. "Never mind, Early. Just, never mind."

They sat like that for a long time, and, though Early's thoughts were dark, at least the sunlight filtering down through the branches overhead was warm. After a while he dozed, and woke to find Kori standing a few yards away, her hands on her hips, looking out to sea. When he joined her, he saw a look of determination on her face.

"Early, I don't know how or if it will help, but I'm coming back with you. We're going to sail that ship. You're going to take me to the Decadin Empire, and see if we can learn who I was. Who I am, if I'm not Kori."

There was little he could say to that. As always, Kori's inner strength made him embarrassed for his fear and doubt. But it also inspired him.

"Of course I will, Kori," he said. They walked back to the village, hand in hand.

❦

Whether it was hard or not for Kori to convince the rest of her people, the two dozen that were left, to join the return journey, Early didn't know. The Malaspiri had invited Early and his friends to stay in their village, where once they'd been captive, as honored friends. But the Decadins wanted to go home, and spent the next several days inspecting the fireship and making it ready to sail, loading it with the provisions they'd need for the journey back across the Sunfire Sea. It wouldn't be easy to sail the ship with such a scant crew, Early knew, so he was much relieved when the entire company of Kori's kin resolved to join them.

Some of the Malaspiri now felt, like Kori did, that they had lost something of themselves to the influence of the island. Though it was hard for them to believe they could have been born and lived whole lives in a different country they did not remember, they were determined to cross the sea and learn the truth if they could.

Others may have been less convinced by Early's theory, but the island which they believed their ancestral home was clearly no longer a haven—who could say when the invaders might return with even more ships, even more black-clad warriors, to learn what had happened to their own lost expedition? So the Malaspiri decided, reluctantly, that their island must be wholly abandoned.

When the entire company returned to the ship, Early was a little baffled to find himself giving instructions. He and Olan, along with the pirate Marie Gold, were now the most experienced sailors available. It was strange—and not entirely comfortable—for Early to find even his mentor Isaac looking to him for the right way to splice a line. The ranger, at least, accustomed to fending for himself in new situations, mastered the basics of seafaring quickly.

While the two deckhands and the pirate captain were hardly the Imperial Blueguard, it did not take long to whip their crew into shape. Most of the Malaspiri, in fact, took to their various tasks naturally, as though their bodies remembered how to move and work aboard ship from long practice.

Early was perfectly happy to look to the future as they prepared the fireship to set sail; a future in which he'd be safe again in his own homeland, the fear and danger of the past weeks no longer a reality to withstand but just a tale to tell.

But there was one issue they could no longer put off, and Isaac brought it up as he stood with the ship's other "standing officers"—Early, Kori, Marie, Lia, and Olan—on the ship's stern deck, just outside the captain's cabin.

"We know now there's another kingdom, far across the sea," the ranger said, indicating with a sweep of his arms the evidence: the ship on which they stood. "And, though we never meant to, here is the truth: we've stolen one of their ships, destroyed its crew, and taken as hostage a priestess of their people and the very heir to their throne." Isaac nodded to the closed door of the cabin a few steps away, where the priestess now stayed, minding the child under Rowene's watchful eye.

"But it was they who attacked us," Early protested. "It was only the Gods' Luck things turned out as they did."

"Of course," Marie replied. "But Isaac has stated the case as *they* will see it. For what can we possibly do to mend the situation?"

"Well—" Early began, but Marie wasn't finished.

"We can't very well sail this ship back to its home shore," she said, "and tell them, 'Don't worry! We've returned your heir and your ship, less its crew,' and then expect them to give us harbor, or perhaps *lend* their ship to us so we can go home."

Olan scoffed at the notion, agreeing, "Hardly. We have no choice but to take this ship back to the Empire or live the rest of our lives on this island. And I would much rather get back to my poor, abandoned barstool at the Darby Crow."

"Then we must decide what becomes of our accidental hostages," Isaac said. "Do we leave them here, marooned on this island, or take them back with us?"

"We can't just leave them here, alone!" Early cried. "Especially not an infant child!"

Isaac nodded to him, but his face was very grave.

Lia spoke. Her voice was soft, but her words carried a deadly weight.

"You're right, Early," she said. "But if we bring them back with us, then we—not just *we*, but the Decadin Empire—have kidnapped this kingdom's heir. How can they see that as anything but an act of war?"

Early stared at her as the implications crashed in on him. His excitement and anticipation for the journey home were threatened by a sudden stormcloud.

"Then... what do we do?" he asked.

Isaac patted his apprentice on the shoulder, then took a step past Early, towards the cabin door. "We go home," he said, "and we take the woman and child with us, and then we deal with whatever comes."

They entered the cabin. It was spacious, but so richly decorated with art and furniture it felt cramped. Early had seen a Blueguard captain's cabin, and this was very different from those spartan quarters. The priestess, a woman of striking presence even when silent, looked up from the book she'd been reading and regarded them with an unfriendly stare. The royal baby's elaborate crib stood beside her chair, and Rowene was hovering as nearby as she respectfully could. The priestess ignored her guardian completely.

As Lia went to the priestess and tried to explain their intentions to bring her and her tiny ward safely to the Decadin Empire, Early started poking through a large inlaid chest of narrow drawers, the type in which ship captains kept their maps. The large sheets of vellum were laid flat in the wide drawers, and one in particular caught his eye as he flipped through their edges. He removed the heavy sheet carefully and spread it on the table which stood nearby.

Now that he could see the whole map, Early's suspicions were confirmed. And his blood ran cold, for it was a map of the coastline near the Free Cities of Antebar, not forty miles south of the High City. These people had maps of Early's own coast! Hadn't Captain Zanda said something, during that first terrible confrontation on the beach, about being familiar with the

Decadin shores? Certainly the enemy captain had spoken their language, so his kingdom had some advantage in terms of intelligence, but the sight of this map brought it home so starkly. As far as Early knew, the Decadin Empire was unaware of any kingdom of dragon worshippers with fire-breathing ships; the idea that such powerful enemies had visited their very doorstep was chilling.

He returned to the chest of drawers and pulled out another map. It appeared to show the whole Sunfire Sea, though in much less detail than the map of the coastline near Antebar. Early focused on the alien coast on the other side of the sea from the Decadin Empire, the land that was the Holy Kingdom of Rzhan. He couldn't fit the fact of it into his mind alongside the superstition, long held by Early and many of his kin, that beyond the sea was only the deep dark void at the end of the world.

He drew Lia quietly away from where she was admiring Rzhan's royal baby, sleeping in his elegant crib of dark wood framed with gold, tiny golden robes piled around the little pink circle of his face.

"Lia, come look at this," Early said. She came, and her eyes widened at the sight of the strange maps. She bent over the table, smoothing the supple vellum with a reverent touch.

"So, this proves there is a land across the sea, as some of the Empress's astronomers guessed," Lia mused. "And the people from that land have no need to guess what lies beyond their own horizon. They've seen it. They've mapped our shores."

She traced the Decadin coast with slender fingers, her face grave. She called Isaac and Marie over to join them. Kori came, too.

"And where are we?" Kori asked once she'd seen the map, scanning the various blobby outlines of islands scattered across the empty breadth of the sea.

Marie scrutinized the map thoughtfully and reached past Lia, pointing to a large, oblong shape nearer to the Decadin Empire than the opposite side of the sea. "I'd say we're probably here. It's hard to tell how far apart these landmarks are— or, for that matter, how wide the sea actually is—their indications for distance are different from ours."

"But if this is the island," Marie tapped the shape again, "and we sail back home from here, the length of that journey will tell us much about this map."

Lia stood back from the table, an eager expression on her face. "Guard-Admiral Bacay will be beside himself when we show him these."

At the mention of the Blueguard navy's commander, the dread of the unknown in Early began to turn into excitement. Whatever dark implications these maps held, he and his friends *were* going home. And perhaps they'd even have a heroes' welcome. Early imagined climbing the great Tower of the Guard where the heads of all the Imperial Guard divisions held council, and receiving a commendation for bravery from the Guard-Admiral himself. He felt a little ashamed of the grandiose fantasy, glancing around at Lia and the others as though they could hear his thoughts. But, given the adventure their expedition had turned out to be... perhaps he was within his rights to indulge himself.

Isaac, who'd been leaning over the table studying the maps intently—especially the detail map of the Decadin coast— dropped gracefully into a wide chair and rubbed his eyes. It struck Early that his mentor looked old and tired, as though that last battle on the deck against his own fellow Guardsman had drained whatever reserve of strength usually kept the ranger going.

"So, we have a ship," Isaac said. "And its cargo?" He nodded to Kori, "A group of people who may be our own kin, the reason for our quest, their memories lost. We have the royal heir of a fearsome and heretofore unknown kingdom from across the sea; a kingdom who already knows far more about us than we know about them."

He looked across the cabin. The priestess of Rzhan doted over the child, sending her captors occasional dark glances; though, as far as Early knew, she didn't know what they were saying. Unlike the missing Captain Zanda, she'd given no indication she spoke the Decadin language.

"Oh, and she seems to be an important religious figure of some kind," the ranger continued with sarcastic nonchalance. "So we have not one but *two* important political prisoners from this dangerous kingdom."

Early's elation had faded in light of Isaac's grim synopsis. He imagined an entire fleet of fireships, black shapes with red sails cutting through the waves, surging closer and closer to the Bay of Moonlight and its great Imperial harbor... and then, he saw the Blueguard greatships and the docks all in flames, as black-armored figures swarmed into the High City like an army of crusader ants.

"We have to go home," Early said, slumping heavily on the table, staring at the map. The thought of what might lie ahead, not a hero's welcome but a desperate race across the sea and war on the very doorstep of his city, sapped the last of Early's strength. He let the sturdy table support him.

"It's not just that we want to go home," he explained. "We have to. We have to warn the Empress. Don't we?"

Early looked to Isaac, to Lia, to Marie, with a sort of desperate hope they would somehow deny this terrible responsibility, tell him this was all just a dream.

But all of them nodded. "You're right, Early," Lia said, squeezing his arm. "There's nothing left to do but go home."

"Yes," Isaac agreed, rising heavily from his seat with none of the easy grace with which he'd sat. "And no time to lose, either."

"Come on, Early," he said. "You, too, Marie. Let's find Master Mender. You sailors need to help us get this floating lamp ready to shove off."

20

Early stood on the foredeck of the ship they'd named *Hope of the Empress* and looked out across the sea. His crew had pushed the shallow-bottomed fireship away from the beach with its long oars and turned it so the prow, with its snarling dragonhead, faced west. Somewhere beyond that horizon, blue-gray with low clouds, Early's home awaited him.

Kori stood nearby, her small hands rubbing the grain of the black wooden rail. Since the loss of her totem, Kori always seemed to have something in her hands—a walking stick, the leather strap of her pack—as though she felt something was missing. Today, she was as focused on the sea as Early. Though he felt the anticipation of seeing his homeland again, Kori had the deeper mystery of not knowing what to expect. Feeling Early watching her, she turned and met his gaze. She smiled, but Early saw something else in her eyes.

"It must be sad," he said, crossing the deck to her side, "leaving behind the home you knew."

She accepted his hand and squeezed it in hers. "It is sad," she nodded. "But it's also exciting to know there's something waiting out there. Some new life I can't predict. It must be how you felt when you set off on the journey that brought you here."

Early thought back to those days—mere weeks ago, though he felt years older. He remembered the giddiness of simply standing on the docks gawking at the mighty *Pride of the Empress*, and then being part of the crew making her ready to sail. He had never in his life felt anything to match that sense of impending adventure. Even the mixed anxiety and relief of this return journey didn't match it.

He was glad Kori could know that sort of excitement for herself.

There were shouts from the ship's rigging, and Early turned to see Bristi, clinging to the lines high above the deck, catching in one hand something Olan tossed up to her. She'd become a capable sailor, learning quickly along with most of the other Malaspiri how to maintain the decks, handle the sails, and everything else Early and the other sea-savvy members of the company could teach them about sailing a ship. They were by necessity under-crewed, and they were racing against time. It would be a hard journey, and they would depend on the wind and the Gods' Luck more than anything else. At least everyone seemed enthusiastic for the voyage, whatever it would bring.

Isaac and Marie came to join Early on the foredeck, and he could see Lia watching them from the high stern of the ship, sketchbook and stylus in hand, ready to immortalize the moment when they cast off for the journey home. At Lia's side, Rowene was fussing over her mistress as usual, enjoining her to don a warmer cloak. It made Early smile to see the young woman, who took her duty as Imperial Cartographer's assistant so very seriously in spite of all that had befallen them.

"All appears ready on your ship, Guard-Captain Wills," Isaac said, and Marie chuckled at the eager grin Early could not keep from his face.

Early reached up and touched one of the tacky spots on his cheek where the ranger had painted simple blue marks. They were the nearest he could come from memory to the Blueguard's ceremonial face paint, since there were no Blueguard left to correct the pattern. It had been Isaac who first suggested Early be made Guard-Captain of the fireship, for the bravery and selflessness of his service on the island. It was unheard of to be both inducted into the Imperial Guard and given such a rank all at once, but the only objections came from Olan—and he was only giving his friend a hard time.

The big deckhand grudgingly admitted *someone* had to command the ersatz crew.

Since Isaac and Taliss were the only members of the Imperial Guard left in the company, they'd invented a ceremony, cobbled together from the respective rituals of their own divisions. It was never how Early had imagined joining the Empress's devoted elite, but it was still his dream come true.

Now he stood at the bow of his ship, *his*. And all he could do was beam at his friends with a grin unbecoming of a stern Blueguard captain.

"The marks of the Guard suit you," Isaac said. "Or, anyway, you'll grow into them."

Isaac tapped his index fingers against the green slashes that curled like blades of grass among the stubble of his own cheeks. He'd worn the paint for the occasion of their departure, claimed to hardly remember how it was meant to look.

"To guard the Empire," the ranger said.

"To serve the Empress," Early replied, returning the formal Guard-to-Guard salute.

"Forever she reigns," Isaac said.

"Forever it stands," Early concluded.

Olan had left Bristi to her work and joined them. He cleared his throat loudly and tapped his own conspicuously bare cheeks. "To leave this gods-cursed island, already," he said, mocking them.

Marie picked up the game, tapping Early and Isaac on their noses. "Forever you two can play Imperial Guard while the rest of us put this monstrosity to sea."

Early laughed at them. His curmudgeonly friend was now Deckmaster of the ship, his fractured arm still in its sling exempting him from labor. But Olan had refused to be inducted into the Blueguard. In the informal way the company now organized themselves, his dislike for protocol had won out.

Marie Gold had accepted the rank of First Mate, for though she was a ship captain in her own right, she'd been a pirate. "The captain lives or dies by the trust of her crew," she'd told Early, when he'd suggested she take command of the *Hope*. "And I don't have their trust, not really. Besides, having you as a captain of the Blueguard is a powerful symbol for the journey home.

"Just be sure to do what I tell you, and you'll be fine," she'd added with a merciless wink, before handing him over to Isaac and Taliss for their Imperial Guard induction ceremony.

Now, looking at his friends, Early found he could forget how inadequate he felt to his task. He drew himself up tall and straight, as he remembered Captain Mestrum carrying herself. Though he lacked her blue-and-white uniform, he touched her pendant, still worn close over his heart on its leather thong. He had sworn to return it to her family, and now he would.

"If you're in such a hurry to be underway, Deckmaster," Early said to Olan with a sly smile, "why aren't you ordering this rabble to weigh anchor? Go to it at once."

Olan rolled his eyes at his friend, realizing he was now getting what he deserved. "Aye, Guard-Captain! I live only to carry out your orders." He turned and stomped away, grumbling loud enough that he could be sure Early heard him.

"I'll see our departure goes smoothly," Marie said, and she gave Early a salute that was only half-mocking before turning on her heel and leaving the foredeck.

Early, Kori, and Isaac went to the very prow of the ship and turned, looking back along the deck as Olan and Marie's voices rang out with orders, and their friends set the sails for departure. The great red and green sheets bellied out as the wind caught them, and there was a loud snap overhead, at the very crown of the topsail. There, the Imperial pennant, red and white, flashed out like a serpentine tongue, as though the ship were tasting the weather for the voyage.

"How does it feel," Kori asked, "to just give a command and have a ship put to sea?"

Early leaned back, feeling the rail beneath his arms propping him up. "It's a far cry from running around mopping water from the planks and coiling rope, that's for sure. It's almost... relaxing. Strangely enough."

"That's a feeling that comes," Isaac said, "from knowing— even with all the weight of command on your shoulders—you have trusted friends at your back."

He pulled out his pipe, lit it, and hopped up to sit on the rail, heedless of the drop into the sea at his back. Kori and Early stared at him.

"Nothing to do now," the ranger said, punctuating his speech with a puff of fragrant smoke, "but try not to get seasick."

Early shook his head in disbelief and turned to look in the direction of their journey. The ship picked up speed and, for the first time in weeks, Early felt the clear salt wind in his face. He'd expected to be overcome by anxiety at the thought of commanding this alien ship with its small, untested crew, and at first he'd feared to take his eyes off the activity on deck for even a moment, trying to watch everything and everyone at once.

But just now, his ship stretching out behind him, with its full sails and its dreadful weapon; with its crew, their accidental hostages, and their uncertain, dangerous journey awaiting them... Early felt only the wind in his face and the song of adventure the sea had always sung to him.

Friends at his back, the future ahead.

ACKNOWLEDGMENTS

First, I want to acknowledge you, Dear Reader. You not only read my story all the way to the end, you're curious enough to want to read about people who matter a lot to me, the author, but who you don't even know. For giving me the gift of your time and attention to tell this little adventure yarn, sincerely, thank you.

I've been fantasizing about things like what I'd say on the *Acknowledgments* page of my very first novel since long before I ever started writing it, yet now that it's the only thing I have left to do before pressing the big red PUBLISH button I had installed on my desk, I find myself procrastinating.

Isn't that strange? By all rights I should be champing at the bit to get this thing out into the world, into your hands, but... It's a bit frightening to take the last step over the chasm from *guy who wants to write a novel* to *novelist*.

I've got to start with the person who led me as close to that final step as anyone could: my editor and coach for the last four years, the incomparable Joseph Nassise. You helped me find the holes in my story, sure, but way more than that, you helped me convince myself not to give up—that I have what it takes. Thanks, Joe.

To Brenda, for being my love and my partner in pancakes, but also for being the first person to read the book besides me and Joe, and for feedback that made the story better.

To Chris and Jacob, my other beta readers, big thanks—

though, Chris, you might find most of your feedback only makes it into Book Two.

Chris deserves an extra word of gratitude: he not only gives me painfully incisive feedback, he's been doing it for (glances at a calendar) 25 years. Thanks for being the other half of my creative brain, buddy.

Thanks to Ken, Kara, Flynn, Jordan, and the other friends who've cheered me on for years.

To my family, for withstanding decades of my lamentation about wanting to "be a writer"—and for a lifetime of love and support. Love you right back.

Thanks to the authors who don't even know me, but who have taught me so much about the craft and the business in their books and podcasts I owe them all a beverage: Joanna Penn, Lindsay Buroker, Jo Lallo, and Andrea Pearson of the Six-Figure Authors Show, Antony Johnston, Matt Legend Gemmell, Chris Fox, Nick Stephenson, David Gaughran, and so many more.

§.

Dear Reader, if you've made it this far... perhaps you'd like to go a little further. Be the first to find out about Book Two and join in the further adventures of the Decadin Empire by joining my newsletter.

Sign up here: djbooks.link/elderpb